Acclaim for Pepper Basham

"*Authentically, Izzy* is an absolutely adorable, charming, sweet romance that genuinely made me laugh out loud. A wonderful escape you're sure to fall in love with!"

—*New York Times* bestselling author Courtney Walsh

"*Authentically, Izzy* is witty, endearing, and full of literary charm. Grab your favorite blanket and get ready to snuggle into this sweet book that will make you believe your dreams will find you."

—Jennifer Peel, *USA TODAY* bestselling author

"I can't remember the last time I've read such a truly wonderful romance. Basham's *Authentically, Izzy* was smart, funny, and adorably bookish. I smiled all the way through and finished it with my cheeks hurting. All the Lord of the Rings references was the cherry on top for me. Izzy and Brodie have officially overtaken Jane Eyre and Mr. Rochester as my favorite literary couple. You have to read this book!"

—Colleen Coble, *USA TODAY* bestselling author

"Pepper Basham is at her witty and charming best throughout the pages of this bookish delight! Fans of Katherine Reay will feel right at home between the covers of this epistolary treasure. Featuring a perfectly sprinkled smattering of Tolkien, *Authentically, Izzy* proves that the best reality sometimes begins with a little bit of fantasy. I hope you have as much fun with this one as I did!"

—Bethany Turner, bestselling author of *The Do-Over*

"In *Authentically, Izzy* author Pepper Basham has created a delightful cast of characters who quickly become your friends. Izzy beautifully captures the nerd in all of us who adores books and stories—sometimes more than real life. When a family member decides Izzy needs to live her own story, it sends Izzy on a fun romp that leads to a sweet, sigh-worthy romance. Grab this one today!"

—Jenny B. Jones, bestselling author of *There You'll Find Me* and *Sweet Right Here*

"This book was so much fun! I was drawn into the story from the beginning and loved the emails and text messages between Izzy and her cousins. What was even more fun was seeing how Izzy and Brodie's relationship grew from a few funny messages to a sweet relationship. I loved how Izzy grew throughout the story and learned to love herself and find her own strength and love. And her cousins were a hoot! Luke was my favorite cousin. His emails and text messages kept me in stitches. I highly recommend this fun and romantic book!"

—Amy Clipston, bestselling author of *The View from Coral Cove*

"You don't see enough epistolary novels these days, so the format of this being told almost entirely through emails appealed to me straightaway, and I wasn't disappointed! We follow librarian Izzy as she meets perfect-sounding bookshop owner Brodie online and wonders if he's too good to be true. Filled with the wonderfully warm cast of Izzy's family, and the swoon-worthy email exchanges with Brodie, I absolutely loved reading this book and felt like Izzy was a real friend rather than a book character! A book written by a book lover, about a book lover, for book lovers everywhere! I loved it! In fact, the only issue with this book is that my to-read list has grown exponentially from Izzy and Brodie's recommendations! It's a book lover's dream read!"

—Jaimie Admans, author of romantic comedies

Authentically, Izzy

Other Books by Pepper Basham

CONTEMPORARY ROMANCE

Mitchell's Crossroads series

A Twist of Faith

Charming the Troublemaker

A Match for Emma

A Pleasant Gap Romance series

Just the Way You Are

When You Look at Me

Novellas

Second Impressions

Jane by the Book

Christmas in Mistletoe Square

HISTORICAL ROMANCE

Penned in Time series

The Thorn Bearer

The Thorn Keeper

The Thorn Healer

Novellas

Facade

Between Stairs and Stardust

Stand-Alone Novels

The Mistletoe Countess

Hope Between the Pages

The Red Ribbon

My Heart Belongs in the Blue Ridge: Laurel's Dream

Authentically, Izzy

a novel

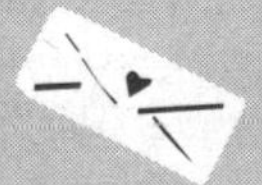

PEPPER BASHAM

THOMAS NELSON
Since 1798

Authentically, Izzy

Published in Nashville, Tennessee, by Thomas Nelson. Thomas Nelson is a registered trademark of HarperCollins Christian Publishing, Inc.

Published in association with William K. Jensen Literary Agency, 119 Bampton Court, Eugene, Oregon 97404.

Maps by Lydia Basham.

Thomas Nelson titles may be purchased in bulk for educational, business, fund-raising, or sales promotional use. For information, please email SpecialMarkets@ThomasNelson.com.

Library of Congress Cataloging-in-Publication Data

Names: Basham, Pepper, author.
Title: Authentically, Izzy : a novel / Pepper Basham.
Description: Nashville, Tennessee : Thomas Nelson, [2022] | Summary: "In this charming epistolary romance, a book-loving librarian is unwillingly enrolled in an online matchmaking service and embarks on a journey toward love that starts with emails to a quirky islander and ends in a choice that will change her future forever"-- Provided by publisher.
Identifiers: LCCN 2022015988 | ISBN 9780840714985 (paperback) | ISBN 9780840715036 (epub) | ISBN 9780840715173
Subjects: LCGFT: Romance fiction. | Christian fiction. | Novels.
Classification: LCC PS3602.A8459 A94 2022 | DDC 813/.6--dc23/eng/20220404
LC record available at https://lccn.loc.gov/2022015988

Printed in the United States of America

22 23 24 25 26 LSC 10 9 8 7 6 5 4 3 2 1

To Carrie, who has encouraged my book journey from the moment she read my debut and who is one of the most book-loving people I know.

ANSLING
ISLE of MÁRA
KERNVIK
OLD INSVYTHE
CARLSTERN
SKERN
PORT ALASTAIR
NEW INSVYTHE
TERFORD
WAITHE
PORT QUINNICK
MOUNTCASTER
S.I. AIRPORT
ISLE of SKREE
FIACLA

AÍSLING
WAITHCLIFF
EVENSCROFT
LOCH INNIS
MANOR
MARRA BRAE
HELMS FOREST
LIMMICK
TOFT VIK
SKERN
LOCH SELLA
LOCH KWEETH
CARLSTERN CASTLE
ELRI
LOCH BRISCOD
WICKTON FOREST
OLD INSWYTHE
QUINNICK CASTLE
HEBVERN VIK
PORT ALASTAIR
ROE
STERN
NEW INSWYTHE
PORT QUINNICK

PROLOGUE

Dear Reader,

This is a cautionary tale.

A tale of family, literary classics, podiatry, matchmaking, Shakespeare, and distance. Not exactly the sort of word grouping you may expect in a typical story, but some things aren't meant to be . . . typical. For example, shark hats. Or maybe heartbreak-induced introversion. (All right, the introversion was already there, but the heartbreak certainly didn't help.)

But there are pairs of things that do go together wonderfully well, like chocolate and peanut butter, mountains and seas, books and romance . . . unless, the date is allergic to peanuts, the mountains and seas are a world apart, and the only romance the heroine has had any luck with has been fictional. (See previous note about introversion.)

But two things that never go together well are family and . . . matchmaking, and that is the premise of this story.

Sort of.

And there are books.

Lots of books.

And a copious amount of talk about *The Lord of the Rings* with a swoony foreigner named Brodie. Who is almost perfect, until . . . he's not as perfect.

And a cliff house, but that's for later.

Anyway, I'll let you discover how all those fit together—or don't—for yourself.

And good luck.

Izzy

PS: And just because Luke is always right doesn't mean Luke is always right. I know of at least two times when he wasn't, and both were about women.

From: Taugen en Compt

In an attempt to bring more people to live among the beauties and vastness of The Skymar Islands, their majesties, King Aleksander and Queen Gabriella, along with the support of Taugen en Compt Houses of Parliament, are offering a substantial financial stipend for natives who encourage someone to relocate to any of the Skymarian Islands, whether by marriage, employment, adoption, or other means listed in the following attachment. Our islands are easily overlooked among the many larger countries surrounding us, but for those who wish to be a part of a vibrant community with varied landscapes, occupational diversity, and a quieter European life that combines our Scottish and Scandinavian cultures amicably, this is an excellent opportunity for resettling. Attached you will find a document outlining the financial remuneration, as well as an extensive list by which individuals may relocate under these specifications.

Taigh, Hlem, en Trolach
(Home, Faith, and Family)

PART 1

Of Matchmakers, Island Dwellers & Clark Gable

CHAPTER 1

From: Josephine Martin
To: Izzy Edgewood
Date: February 14
Subject: Heart-to-Heart

Izzy,

You know I love you. I want to begin with that.

Now, the only reason I'm emailing you instead of talking to you face-to-face is because I feel you won't hear me out. And you have no choice this way because your love for words and your natural curiosity will force you to read my message.

Since you do not seem to be as invested in your romantic future as you ought to be, I have decided, as your loving cousin, to help you pursue what we discussed last week at church. Before you gasp aloud, which I can practically hear all the way down Cherry Blossom Street, you need to understand that you have it all wrong. You think some Prince Charming is going to walk into your library and sweep you off your sneakered feet, but it doesn't work that way in real life. Not nowadays. And certainly not for someone who spends more time with fictional humans than real ones. You are missing out, Izzy, and I can't bear it. You are already thirty and not a date in sight.

I must rescue you from yourself.

I don't say these things to hurt you, but to spur you into action instead of allowing you to keep hiding in your books. Heart-to-

Heart is a wonderful online dating community recommended by several of the locals here, and I've taken the liberty of setting you up a profile. Currently your profile photo is Minnie Mouse, so unless you want the entire single dating world of Heart-to-Heart to think you're a Disney Princess–loving high school student, you'd better hop right online and fix it. I feel certain there's a book-loving man living relatively nearby waiting to speak bookish to you 'til death do you part. You just haven't met yet. Here is your chance.

Time is running out, dear Izzy.

Your loving cousin,
Josephine

PS: And yes, you still have to love me because that's what family does.

PPS: Heroines usually are swept off their feet while wearing something much more alluring than sneakers. I just thought you ought to know.

• •

From: Izzy Edgewood
To: Josephine Martin
Date: February 14
Subject: Betrayal

Josephine,

I have disowned you and will henceforth refer to you as Josie, both publicly and privately, until the day you die. And I promptly rewrote the horrid bio you set up for me. I am *not* a recluse. I take

Samwise for walks in the park downtown daily, and sometimes we go on hikes in the mountains. I get a cup of takeout tea from Beans & Things every morning before arriving at the library, plus I attend church on a regular basis. And I do have friends! My regular conversational partners at Beans & Things are excellent company and, while sharing charming and humorous stories as well as upcoming weather patterns, they keep me apprised of local news.

In addition to those facts of my habitual social interactions, I go to the movies with Penelope every time she's home from school, which is once a month, and have lunch or a bike ride with Luke when he visits or I drive the hour to see him. So, as you can see, I am not, nor have I ever been, a recluse—except for my senior year of high school, but after such an awful perm, who can blame me? I love your mother, but her experiments with color and perms should never befall a high school girl. Ever. Especially one who was still trying to outgrow her pimple apocalypse.

And, how could you even write in that horrid bio that I have a dozen gray hairs or more? Who does that? I haven't found any, let alone a dozen, nor do I while away my hours weeping over sappy movies. I weep over excellent writing and greeting card commercials. Do you know me at all?

I am perfectly satisfied with my quiet life, and though I won't deny I'd love to meet someone special with whom I can enjoy long conversations and walks, I seriously doubt my "Prince Charming," as you call him, will find his way onto an online dating community with a tacky caricature of Cupid as its logo. Once I figure out how to remove my profile from that embarrassing website, I plan to do so, but in the meantime, at least I've changed the profile picture and given a more accurate account of "the reclusive librarian" in your description. (I am inwardly cringing, I hope you know.)

And, Josie, leave my love life alone.

Sincerely,

Irritated Izzy

PS: Please thank your charming husband for sponsoring three tables at the annual library fundraiser. No one has ever purchased more than one, let alone three, and by our very first local podiatrist. He truly has a foothold in my heart (sneaker-fitted or not).

PPS: With my rather disastrous romantic history, it's no wonder I wear sneakers. Faster getaway.

From: Josephine Martin

To: Izzy Edgewood

Date: February 14

Subject: Reality check

Izzy,

If by "regular conversational partners" you mean the Farmer Four who get coffee every morning before going to their respective farms that they tend in their *retirement*, then it's beyond time to broaden your friend group. Avis Dalton turned a hundred at least fifty years ago and I don't think the other three are too far behind him.

You need even more help than I realized! Do you even hear yourself?

I will respond more later. Cleo just jumped across the kitchen and knocked over the cereal boxes again. Remind me why I'm the one who had to keep Penelope's cat? Are you really allergic to cats, Izzy? I have my doubts.

Josephine

PS: Patrick loves supporting the library and books, though he was a little surprised you did not have many in the category of footcare. I told him you'd make immediate additions upon his request.

• •

From: Penelope Edgewood
To: Izzy Edgewood
Date: February 15
Subject: Firstborn drama

Oh Izzy,

I just heard about what my sister did with the whole dating site and I'm so sorry. On Valentine's Day of all days in the world!! How could she! I'm sure you hoped you'd be able to get out of such sisterly bossiness since she's not your biological sister, but I just think Josephine can't help trying to fix everyone's lives, whether they need fixing or not. She's been trying to do it for years. Do you remember the parakeet we had growing up? He didn't listen to a thing Josephine said and it nearly caused her to have a breakdown at ten years old. It's a wonder she's survived being a big sister to Luke all these years. I think she could have gone into burglary with her particular gift for intrusion. We studied about firstborns in my psychology class at school and Josephine fits the profile to a T. Except the list didn't mention color-coordinating bedsheets and winter hats, but I took that to belong under the "structured" category.

She opened an account for me, too, and I don't have any trouble finding dates, so just imagine how bored she must be. If she sets an account up for Luke, too, can you imagine? He'll break her computer. The last thing my brother wants right now is another romance, you know. One solid disaster is enough for anyone, and he still hasn't gotten over it. (I considered sending him a link to the song "So Much Better" from *Legally Blonde: The Musical* as consolation, but I really don't think Luke would have appreciated it.)

I think men of true depth feel the sting of lost love the deepest of all. I read that once and felt the truth of it to the fiber of my soul. I really hope romantic catastrophes aren't hereditary. Between you and Luke, I'm doomed.

I suppose being happily married to a wonderfully indulgent man means Josephine must thrust her happiness on the rest of us. Once her babies are born, she'll have something else to take up her life instead of meddling in ours.

Twins! Can you imagine?!? That should keep her busy, if nothing will.

I'm off to practice projection with Olivia. I really don't know why I'm the one people are always asking to train them how to be loud on stage.

Love,
Penelope

PS: I noticed you changed your profile photo, but Izzy, I wonder if you should choose something different. If you want to catch the eye of some would-be Mr. Right, maybe you should post a photo of a more well-recognized actress or something. That would be more culturally eye-catching. I doubt most people even know who that Éowyn person is from those strange *Lord of the Rings* movies, so seeing a woman with a sword might give the wrong Impression. If you can't think of something better, you could always post your own photo. I posted a glamorous photo of the young Julie Andrews as my profile picture, because I really don't care about being culturally eye-catching if a Mr. Wonderful is classic enough to adore Julie Andrews. And you know how these dating sites work. It's not usually the best idea to put your real photo on display. Safety and all that. But if I was going to put my real photo, I'd add the one where I'm wearing the green sweater you bought me two Christmases ago. It brings out the color of my eyes and is one of my favorites, though Luke says the tree behind me in the photo looks like it's growing out of my head. He really doesn't understand style and artistry at all. Brothers!

• •

From: Josephine Martin
To: Izzy Edgewood
Date: February 15
Subject: JOSEPHINE!!

Izzy,

Do you hear yourself? You even type emails like an old person. "Henceforth"? "Perfectly satisfied"? "I weep over excellent writing"??? What are you doing with your life, my darling cousin? You should be thanking me for my attempt at an intervention.

And, you do *not* date. I'm not sure why, when there are plenty of nice men I've introduced to you. If you continue to compare every possible male specimen to one of your book heroes, you will become as single as the most fictional spinster you can imagine.

Spending time with my sister and brother does not count as a non-reclusive activity since they are your cousins. And the singles group at church has dwindled to such low numbers, they don't count either. Small-town, eligible bachelors are snatched up too quickly to take your time, Izzy. Heart-to-Heart is the only option for you.

And, for heaven's sake, take down that profile photo at once. Though the actress is lovely, no man wants to see a woman wielding a sword at him. It does not give off the best romantic impression.

And first impressions are vital. Especially online.

Lovingly,
Josephine . . . NOT Josie

PS: Patrick has a friend coming into town next week that I think you should meet. He's not a podiatrist, but he does have a promising profession: audiology. I've seen a photo of him and he has a lovely nose.

Heart-to-Heart

Date: February 17

Any woman who can carry a sword like that is the woman for me. Is that your most recent Halloween costume? I like cosplay too. I go extra on cosplay. I mean, if you're not going to go all the way with the costume, you shouldn't even try, right? But yours is epic. What a mood! I can create an awesome Aradon, if you want to be a pair. Where do you live? Is your sword real?

Tony

Heart-to-Heart

Date: February 18

Tony,

I had to look up what the word *cosplay* means. That alone should tell you something about our compatibility.

Izzy

PS: A real sword is the only kind worth having. And I have no idea who *Aradon* is.

Heart-to-Heart

Date: February 18

I like your bio but am concerned about your profile photo. Do you support the use of weapons to solve conflicts?

Paul

Heart-to-Heart

Date: February 18

Paul,

Do well-honed words and a solid arsenal of glares count?

Izzy

From: Izzy Edgewood
To: Josephine Martin
Date: February 19
Subject: I weep for your children

Josie,

What have you done to me?!? The only benefit of this online dating community is that I can think about my responses before I type them so I can say exactly what I want.

Otherwise, it's torture. What will your children think about this story when I tell it to them one day? They'll be horrified at the antics of their mother.

Izzy

PS: The peach cobbler you made for Sunday lunch was amazing. I'd love the recipe.

Text from Josephine to Izzy: I'll give you the recipe if you stop calling me Josie.

Izzy: Never mind. I'll consult the library or Google for a recipe. Thanks anyway, Josie.

Heart-to-Heart

Date: February 20

Good riddance to the Witch-king of Angmar, is all I have to say.

And I'm glad to see you're on the mend after helping to save Middle-earth, but joining Heart-to-Heart? I find it difficult to believe things didn't work out with Faramir, even though he had a tendency to look down on my countrymen at first, but that really couldn't be helped.

He was my favorite character, apart from Samwise Gamgee.

Brodie the Hobbit

From: Izzy Edgewood
To: Penelope Edgewood
Date: February 20
Subject: Hobbits and Heart-to-Heart

Penelope,

Someone messaged me on Heart-to-Heart, and he had no qualms about my sword.

And he knew who Faramir was. I'm intrigued. I might message him back, but I'm not certain yet. He knows about *The Lord of the Rings*. That's a definite plus in his favor. I wonder if he's short? Or has hairy feet?

Izzy

From: Penelope Edgewood
To: Izzy Edgewood
Date: February 20
Subject: Re: Hobbits and Heart-to-Heart

Izzy,

Who is Faramir? Is he the audiologist Josephine wants you to meet? What an unusual name. Is it Indian? And why in the world would you think he has hairy feet? That's just gross.

Oh dear, why are you always talking about that book series? Can't you become obsessed with another type of ring to change your *real* world instead of a fantasy one? (Though, I am a big proponent of imagination. And imaginary worlds, as you well know. Just recall my excellent part as Dorothy Gale in sixth grade. If I hadn't tripped over the cowardly lion's tail, it would have been a perfect performance.)

But I am proud of you for messaging the guy back. Maybe he'll be nice, at the very least. Maybe online is a perfect way for you to meet Mr. Right. You've always been excellent with writing and reading words, even if you don't necessarily like speaking them as often.

Penelope

PS: Make sure he's not married, but his height really shouldn't matter, Izzy.

Heart-to-Heart

Date: February 20

Brodie the Hobbit,

Faramir is still as valiant as ever, but we've decided to take a step back from our relationship to ensure our mutual affection isn't due to the natural camaraderie of suffering joint loss and trauma after the Battle of the Pelennor Fields.

Samwise is one of my favorite characters too. No greater friend, which is why my dog shares my favorite hobbit's name. There are definite perks to being a hobbit. No one judges you if you eat heartily, get lost in a good book, or enjoy solitude with an excellent cup of tea. There's a lot to be said for a hobbit's life.

Éowyn-for-now

PS: Though adventures are highly suspicious, I prefer the literary variety, so perhaps I won't be too suspicious a friend for a hobbit.

From: Izzy Edgewood
To: Penelope Edgewood
Date: February 21
Subject: Lord of the Rings clarification

Penelope,

Please tell me you're teasing about Faramir. I just can't believe you don't know who he is. I lived with you from the time I was twelve until I was nineteen and *still* you don't know who Faramir is? I'm going to choose to believe you're joking.

And I may not be an expert at romantic relationships, but I feel asking Brodie the Hobbit about his marital status on our very first communication might send the wrong message. Besides, I don't expect him to respond to me. Good men are usually snatched up too quickly, or that's what Josie says. And, as we all know, I've had my fair share of not-so-good men, so I'm not the best judge. Anyway, he likely found my profile picture intriguing and made a spontaneous comment. Either that, or he's Josie in disguise and I plan to make her reveal herself.

Speaking of Josie, the date she's set up for me is with an audiologist named Steve. I know nothing else about him, except that he's allergic to peanuts and prefers to meet at the restaurant instead of picking me up at my apartment.

When is the next time you'll be home from school? I'd like to pick your brain about the online classes program at your college. I've felt so unsettled for a while now, you know? Where do I fit? I'm not even sure. What does a woman who adores books, tolerates small groups of people, and has a magical love for bringing together the right people and the right books do with her life? There's not really a job description for "book pusher," and even if there was, it sounds like a profession where one might get arrested. If stepping through magical, fictional wardrobes was an occupation, I'd likely volunteer, just to have a chance to see the Professor's library. And then there's my recurring daydream of owning a manor house on a cliff by the sea, but since I don't fly and rarely travel, the ceramic replica of one I have sitting on my bookshelf will have to do. I've placed it right beside *Jane Eyre*, *The Secret Garden*, and *Dracula*, among a few others of my favorites that feature grand and mysterious houses.

Speaking of daydreams, I think it's past time for me to think about my future besides just working at the library—though it's still one of my favorite places because I can travel to hundreds of worlds without leaving my chair. Plus, Aunt Louisa makes the best coffee and it's served all day long.

What are men to coffee and books!

Love,
Izzy

PS: Do you remember who Samwise is?

PPS: I've researched opening a bookshop, but that requires math.

PPPS: Oh, and apparently Steve has a very fine nose.

Heart-to-Heart

Date: February 21

Éowyn-for-now,

I'm glad to hear you're taking things carefully with Faramir since, as you stated, you both have suffered such trauma. Fighting orcs and Nazgûl is one thing, but suffering under such a father as Faramir's is quite another, poor man. Perhaps it would be wise to test the waters with someone who's had a healthier family dynamic?

Samwise is a great example of friendship and the perfect name for a dog. My dog, Gandalf, passed away last year, and for a little while I had hopes he'd "rise from the dead" as his namesake had. I don't think I've ever had such an excellent dog. Perhaps my new puppy, Argos, will live up to his predecessor, but for now he seems more interested in destroying every pair of shoes I own and unrolling the toilet paper at the speed of light.

Yes, a hobbit's life is a superior one, made all the better by the camaraderie of a good friend, an excellent pipe, and an occasional adventure now and again, literary variety or not.

What do you and Samwise enjoy doing together?

Brodie the Hobbit

• •

From: Penelope Edgewood
To: Izzy Edgewood
Date: February 21
Subject: Re: Lord of the Rings clarification

Izzy,

Of COURSE I remember who Samwise is.

He's your dog.

Penelope

From: Izzy Edgewood
To: Penelope Edgewood
Date: February 21
Subject: Brodie the Hobbit

Penelope,

The Lord of the Rings movie series should arrive at your college address by tomorrow. Clearly, you've gone too long without seeing it. I am certain you can find almost any answer for life within the wonders of this story:

Should I stay home tonight and read a book? *"All's well that ends better."*

Why can't you look Great-grandmother Eloise in the eyes? *"The world is indeed full of peril, and in it there are many dark places."*

Should I climb to the summit of Sugarloaf Mountain? *"I'll get there, if I leave everything but my bones behind."*

If Beans & Things only has one chocolate croissant left and you're third in line? *"There's some good in this world, Mr. Frodo. And it's worth fighting for."*

How can I best prepare for Christmas at Grandma Edgewood's? *"We come to it at last, the great battle of our time."*

Should I read one more chapter, even though it's past midnight? *"A day may come when the courage of men fails . . . but it is not this day."*

You see how well they work?

AND . . . Samwise is only the very best hobbit in Middle-earth . . . or any other earth, if you ask me.

In other news Brodie the Hobbit seems to be a legit sort of fellow. Maybe. Who can really tell? We're online, so anyone could be anything. Just check your spam folder as a reminder of how many people with unpronounceable names have financially needy nieces that only you can save with your blind faith of offering money.

Anyway, Brodie named his new puppy Argos. Isn't that wonderful? I'm dying to know what his favorite books are, but I feel that may be a little too personal a question to ask this soon in our conversation. Books are intimate things.

However, if he's Josie in disguise, I'll catch his blunder fairly quickly. Her favorite books have recipes or cowboys in them.

I wonder what his profession is?

My date with Steve the Audiologist is tonight. Josie has warned me not to talk about books or sea urchins. She's afraid I'll bore him with my talk of books (of course) *and*, apparently, Steve had a fairly traumatic experience with a family of sea urchins at the beach last year and now walks with a limp as a result.

Did you know our library has an entire section on sea urchins? Fascinating creatures, really.

Love,
Izzy

PS: If Brodie the Hobbit isn't Josie in disguise, I think he must be a writer.

• •

From: Penelope Edgewood
To: Izzy Edgewood

Date: February 21
Subject: Sea monsters

Izzy,

Please don't talk about sea urchins. They always remind me of that creature I saw under the water when we went to the beach when I was six. I know you don't believe me, but I am sure it was a sea monster yet to be discovered. That's the real reason why I eat seafood with such ferocity.

Penelope

PS: Is *The Lord of the Rings* a musical? I think I would remember it better if it was.

PPS: Maybe meeting a man online or through Josie will turn out better than . . . previous relationships for you. One of my professors says, "Sometimes we can't see the cannoli for the cream." Wait, maybe he was talking about a marketing strategy, but you get the point.

Heart-to-Heart

Date: February 21

Brodie the Hobbit,

I am so sorry about Gandalf. Did you have him for a long time? If any animal should have the power to resurrect, I think it should be a faithful dog. They're such wonderful companions and the very best listeners in the world.

I've had Samwise for five years and despite having a propensity for pouting on occasion, he's the finest creature on earth.

And much like his namesake, he enjoys digging. Often. And with great zeal.

Training a puppy is definitely an adventure I don't care to repeat for a long time. If Argos is as fast and clever as his mythical namesake, he'll learn that shoes are meant for wearing and toilet paper, though a fun toy, is meant for human uses. Samwise treated the legs of tables and chairs as teethers and ended up wearing my curtains more times than I care to admit, though, I must say, with his golden fur he looked excellent in pale blue.

Curtains are superfluous though, I suppose. I prefer as much natural light as possible and the view from my front window is worth seeing, once you look beyond the dilapidated furniture shop across the street and the train tracks. Someday, I'll move just beyond town where the mountains show from every window. They're blue-tinted mountains here, not lush and green like the Shire, but still lovely in their own way. I think I'd find complete contentment in a world of mountains and seas and fresh air and books . . . oh, and coffee and tea, of course. Maybe it's just because of mainstream bookshops nowadays, but I think there's no smell quite so wonderful as the combination of books and coffee.

Or tea for afternoon and evening.

Izzy

PS: I have great aspirations of hiking to the very top of our largest mountain, but then I realize what sort of energy that entails and reach for a favorite book instead. I know it's a pitiful substitute, but my legs are never sore afterward, and it's much easier to drink a cup of tea while sitting.

• •

From: Izzy Edgewood
To: Penelope Edgewood

Date: February 21
Subject: Word-vomit shame

Penelope,

I'm an idiot. That is why I don't have a boyfriend. I just wrote a note to Brodie the Hobbit about dogs and toilet paper and the color blue looking excellent on Samwise. And I admitted that I would choose a book over hiking! Now I'm sure he thinks I'm a bookish simpleton. And probably lazy.

I need to stick to my books. They're much safer to my self-esteem. If I hear back from him, I'll know for certain he's too desperate to be reasonable or too mentally inconsistent to be trusted. Now I just need to figure out how to disable my profile from this blasted Heart-to-Heart, right after I go on this date with Steve the Audiologist.

Izzy

PS: Maybe I should message Luke to see if he thinks talking to a man online about toilet paper and curtains is an unforgivable offense in a budding friendship. Luke has to be honest with me, doesn't he? He's family, after all.

PPS: And please don't bring up he-who-left-me-at-the-altar (though typing his name would be much easier than using all the hyphens). Despite rumors, he did not end our engagement because of my disinterest in rock climbing or my inclination toward using book and movie quotes. If someone else has said something better, then why not use their words? It's simple logic.

From: Penelope Edgewood
To: Izzy Edgewood
Date: February 21
Subject: Re: Word-vomit shame

Izzy, you do like quotes a lot. Sometimes I can't tell when it's you talking and when it's some dead author whose name I can't pronounce, but I just have accepted it's how you like to communicate. You know? Like some weird literary code.

And once Chip broke up with you after Dad hired someone *else* as business manager, we all knew why he'd dated you for so long in the first place. Scoundrel. That's what he was. I'm glad he's gone, Izzy. For one thing, I was sure you were going to die on one of those rock climbing adventures, especially given your history with ropes, and two, he didn't know your favorite color or book. That should tell you something about a fiancé for certain. Especially a fiancé for you.

I'll write more later. Sandy needs me to help her get untangled from her twinkle lights again. I keep telling her to move them farther away from her bed, but she saw something on Pinterest she's determined to replicate.

Maybe Steve the Audiologist will be the one for you. I "hear" he's rich.

Penelope

PS: Luke says I'm not funny, but I can use puns just as well as he can.

From: Izzy Edgewood

To: Luke Edgewood

Date: February 21

Subject: Advice

Luke,

Do men find women who talk about toilet paper and curtains offensive or just ridiculous? And if they prefer books and tea over day-long hikes to the summits of mountains, is that an immediate turnoff?

Asking for a friend.

Izzy

CHAPTER 2

Heart-to-Heart

Date: February 22

Excellent choice of profile photo. I find that profile photos are a creative way to show personality. If you will notice, mine is of Sherlock Holmes, the renowned fictional detective. His precise extraction of information and unparalleled gifts of observation are two characteristics to which I can attest as personal proficiencies of my own. I feel certain you would find those talents attractive, as most women should, but I rarely have the opportunity of encountering like-minded partners. Most have limited knowledge of the more important things in life and others offer too simplistic conversations for my taste. If you wish for further knowledge about my many interests, I could send you several essays I wrote on the subject. One is entitled "Why Modern Women Are Intimidated by Intelligent Men" and another is "The Unfortunate Plight of the Great Romantic Men of the Contemporary Age." Both speak to the difficulties men, like myself, encounter while searching for mates who are not intimidated by their superiorities. I look forward to your ready response.

Doyle's protégé

Heart-to-Heart

Date: February 22

Doyle's protégé,

I believe you've hit upon the very reason why Sherlock Holmes remained single throughout the entire course of his fictional life. Have you happened to read *Pride and Prejudice*? There is a character in the novel named Mr. Collins of whom you may find some particular interest . . . and similarity of mind. Also, I feel quite certain I do not have the skill set I need to pursue a future with someone of your caliber. I hope you find the eighteenth-century female of your dreams.

Izzy

From: Josephine Martin
To: Izzy Edgewood
Date: February 22
Subject: Steve

Izzy,

How did the date with Steve go? I tried calling you last night but you never answered, so I had high hopes it was because you were still out enjoying your time with him. Patrick says he's an excellent golfer and enjoys collecting books. If you can find anything in common, Izzy, you should pursue him. He's financially stable, has never been married, isn't in debt, and goes to church. Men like him are in high demand and short supply.

And he doesn't like to fly either. He's perfect for you!

You need to consider the truth of the matter. Time is not on your side.

Love,
Josephine

PS: I feel certain you can overlook his overuse of the word *amplification*. Everyone has their unique peculiarities. You, of all people, should appreciate that.

From: Luke Edgewood
To: Izzy Edgewood
Date: February 22
Subject: Re: Advice

I feel you need to clarify the context for me to give an honest answer for "your friend." Is this the same friend who locked herself out of the library during circle time with the entire second grade class from Falls Springs Elementary?

Luke

From: Penelope Edgewood
To: Izzy Edgewood
Date: February 23
Subject: Re: Word-vomit shame

Izzy,

I just reread your last note.

What kind of name is Argos? Did you spell that correctly?

Why does it matter if you're ridiculous? It's an online relationship. This is one of those times where you can be authentically yourself and not worry about how it comes across. In fact, it sounds like the perfect way to start the possibility of a lifelong romance.

You don't have to worry about making a fool of yourself in front of him when you spill a milkshake down the front of your blouse just before going onstage for dress rehearsal for your debut part as Flower Girl #1 and then watch him cozy up next to the girl who beat you out of the lead role of Eliza Doolittle.

See? I bet you'll never have something like that happen with an online relationship. (I recognize my comment about authenticity may sound hypocritical since I still have my Julie Andrews profile photo up, but, as an actress of stage productions, I realize the crazies that are out there. In fact, I'm on stage with a few of them.)

Penelope

PS: He did trip over one of the flowerpots on set and got potting soil stuck on his perfectly straight teeth. (And before you ask, this time it was *not* my fault.)

* * *

From: Izzy Edgewood
To: Penelope Edgewood
Date: February 23
Subject: Steve the Audiologist

Penelope,

I'm so sorry about the play and the boy. It sounds as though he wasn't a good fit for you anyway. Your Flower Girl #1 outshines any Eliza Doolittle, I am certain. Men are so fickle; that is why I feel all the more resolute in my choosiness. Especially after he-who-left-me-at-the-altar (HWLMATA). And why not? If I'm almost perfectly content on my own, why would I long for halfway content with another person JUST to claim I have a boyfriend? No, singleness (with all of my fictional friends) is preferable over a poor choice.

As ridiculous as Josie thinks it is, I've always found a lot of truth in romantic fiction. What's wrong with expecting a man to treat a woman well? To share excellent conversations? To have similar likes—even unusual ones? To experience mutual respect and humor? Why do those kinds of things seem more frequent in popular novels and Hallmark movies than in real life? Is it wrong to wait for a relationship like that?

I know in-person relationships haven't been my forte, especially the ones Josie chooses, so maybe this online thing DOES have some perks. I think this is Josie's seventh blind date for me in three months. Seventh! I am NOT that desperate.

As far as Steve the Audiologist goes? Medical encyclopedias. Those are the books he collects. And though I find historical books, of any persuasion, valuable and worthy of protection, I never imagined I'd meet a man who enjoyed discussing the facts within a century-old medical book ad nauseam.

Tell me, Penelope, am I as overbearing as that when I discuss my fictional loves? Please say no. I don't think I've ever heard the suffix "itis" more times within a thirty-minute conversation in my whole life. This is not what I want for my future.

Josie has already messaged me and I can't bear to answer her. Do you think I should pretend to be sick to avoid seeing her at church? No, I suppose not. If I am to be anything like my sword-wielding Éowyn, I must act brave enough to meet my pregnant, misled, matchmaking cousin face-to-face. But Steve the Audiologist? Has my vibrant life of fictional wonders dissolved into the choice between spinsterhood and medical encyclopedias?

Izzy

PS: Sea urchins have no discernible face and can live up to two hundred years. I don't think there is a direct correlation between those two things. I just find them interesting.

From: Josephine Martin
To: Izzy Edgewood
Date: February 24
Subject: Stop ignoring me

Izzy,

I know you are ignoring me. Steve told Patrick that he enjoyed your dinner together, though you were a quiet date. Oh, why do you resort to your shy self with everyone except our family? You are much more interesting when you talk instead of sit there like a statue. No wonder strangers think you are aloof! Do you remember how long it took me to convince the youth pastor at church that you were not mute? You say it was because he wouldn't let you get a word in, but I don't believe you. I had no problem speaking to him at all. It just required a little extra volume.

It's one thing to be a good listener. It's quite another to not respond at all except with those large, unsettling eyes of yours. You must get over this shyness and force yourself to engage in others' lives for your future's sake, Izzy. Regular people tend to talk about more things than books, movies, and the pleasure of nature. Maybe you could find a book on audiology? Or golf?

Josephine

PS: I know I will see you at the library fundraiser. You can't ignore me there.

<u>Text from Izzy to Josephine:</u> Steve the Audiologist had a very fine nose.

Heart-to-Heart

Date: February 26

Izzy-for-now(?),

Blue mountains? Are they cold? Sad? (So sorry. Very bad pun.) I'm afraid my conversations improve with familiarity, though it takes some time to get beyond the notoriously imbecilic initiation or my unnerving silence (for fear of sounding imbecilic, I resort to speechlessness). My mother refers to my awkwardness as "lovely" and "an acquired taste," but mothers are required to say such things, I'm told.

I remember seeing sepia-colored, jagged mountains when I studied for a year in California, but blue ones? Now I'm intrigued.

We have beautiful mountains here. Most are eternally green. Very Shire-like. But I agree about natural light and a window view. I am currently renovating my own place and one of my goals is to ensure I wake to a view to help start my day with a proper perspective. As Keats said, "The poetry of earth is never dead," and there is something inspiring about seeing the world around us in all its beauty, isn't there?

As far as Argos, I feel he will live up to his mythical namesake in speed, if nothing else.

Do you have other favorite books besides Tolkien's classic?

Brodie

PS: Tolkien is enough to study for a lifetime, but there are so many great books to enjoy and I get the sense you're a kindred spirit in that way.

From: Izzy Edgewood
To: Luke Edgewood
Date: February 27
Subject: Josie at work

Never mind my previous question for "my friend." I've decided to end all communication. He quoted Keats and called me a kindred spirit.

It's a trap.

Izzy

PS: Josie is behind it all. I can smell her Rose d'Amour from here.

From: Izzy Edgewood
To: Penelope Edgewood
Date: February 27
Subject: It's all a trap

Penelope,

I've decided to end all of my communication on Heart-to-Heart. How silly I've been! I'd actually begun to look forward to Brodie's messages, checking as soon as I got home from work and smiling when his name popped up in my account, just like Meg Ryan in *You've Got Mail*.

And then Brodie quoted Keats. And referred to his own social awkwardness . . . and I knew it all had to be some horrible farce.

I can't do it anymore. It's too perfect. Good, single men don't join online dating communities, do they? And quote Keats and call me a kindred spirit?

So the only options are that he's a fraud OR Josie has played some horrible trick on me to get me to fall in love with medical encyclopedias and fine noses. Do pregnant women become more ruthless as their babies grow? And if she's having twins, does that mean she becomes doubly ruthless?

I suppose I should try another date with Steve. At least he reads. The three previous dates she set me up with hadn't picked up a book (other than comic books) in years. Besides, he's an audiologist. He ought to be a good listener, right?

Izzy

PS: Evergreen mountains? I looked up geography with evergreen mountains and there aren't any in the United States. Do you think he's lying? Josie has a lot of explaining to do when I see her at the library fundraiser tomorrow. How on earth could she pretend with such . . . believability? Do you remember when she was in the church Christmas play? She had trouble making the Innkeeper's wife sound remotely authentic!

PPS: Sea urchins do not have brains. I'm not sure what to think about that.

From: Josephine Martin
To: Izzy Edgewood
Date: February 28
Subject: What is wrong with you?

Izzy,

You did not act like yourself at the library fundraiser. I appreciate your special attention to me and Patrick (the cushion on my chair was a nice touch), although I can't help but think something is very wrong. I could tell you were trying hard to be talkative, even to Steve, but your heart wasn't in it. Was the turnout for the fundraiser not what you'd expected? Mother said it was the largest the library had in its history, which is in no small part due to you. You have so many wonderful talents that go unseen.

Are you in love? Are you a sulky sort of in-love person? It doesn't become you at all. Your smile takes on some sort of dangerous tenseness like a mad dog. Patrick did not seem to notice, but I did.

And I'm still not sure who you were talking about when you mentioned my friend Brodie? I have no friends named Brodie. Patrick has one named Bradley, if you'll remember. I tried to set him up with you two months ago, but you had an aversion to his cologne and his propensity for wearing waders.

Are you having second thoughts about him? I must say I prefer Steve to Bradley.

Love,
Josephine

PS: If you continue to look pale, I'm going to be forced to come visit you and personally make sure you're eating.

Heart-to-Heart

Date: March 1

I saw your profile picture on Heart-to-Heart. You are so cool. I've never seen anyone look so much like a real movie character before. You are awesome. I'd love to chat with you.

Marcus

Heart-to-Heart

Date: March 1

Marcus,

I think you may be too young for this web community.

Izzy

From: Luke Edgewood
To: Izzy Edgewood
Date: March 1
Subject: Re: Josie at work

Izzy,

What does Keats have to do with anything? This "friend" of yours would allow a dead writer to dictate her future? I think your friend is made of stronger and wiser stuff than that. If I recall correctly, kindred spirits are worth knowing.

Luke

From: Penelope Edgewood
To: Izzy Edgewood
Date: March 2
Subject: Puns & profile pics

Izzy,

I know you are depressed when you begin making horrible puns. I'm studying for an exam right now and will write more later.

I will say that the most ruthless acts I've noticed in Josephine lately have been about food, so I think you may be safe with Keats and Heart-to-Heart. What if Brodie is exactly who he seems to be? You once told me that authenticity is one of the most beautiful characteristics of a person. I've not seen a lot of it on the university scene, except when people are intoxicated or sleep-deprived. Oh, and also my drama professor, Dr. Lincoln—no one can wear that shade of pink without being completely authentic.

However, I don't want my only moments of authenticity to be while intoxicated (which has never happened, BTW) or when sleep-deprived. Now that I think about it, I don't want my most authentic self to be the one that comes out when I'm sleep deprived. I think I'm more like a Living Dead personality.

But anyway, isn't loving someone being comfortable with who they are by being exactly who you are? What a wonderful idea . . . and definitely not seen in the drama department often (Dr. Lincoln excluded).

Oh, I need to run!

Penelope

PS: I noticed you changed your profile picture to one of those old-fashioned authors. Why would you do that? Isn't that the author who cut off her ear and mailed it to someone? You are not being authentic, Izzy. Or at least I hope you're not. Your ears happen to be one of your best features. I hide mine with my hair.

• •

From: Izzy Edgewood
To: Luke Edgewood

Date: March 2
Subject: This day we fight

You are right, as usual.

This friend is made of stronger stuff.

Keats is no match for her.

I will come to the bottom of this like an impassioned and somewhat irrational Nancy Drew, or even better, Miss Marple.

Izzy

• •

From: Izzy Edgewood
To: Penelope Edgewood
Date: March 2
Subject: Glorious authenticity

Penelope,

I have decided to shower Brodie (or Josie, as the case may be) with the real Isabelle Edgewood. Why not? It will teach Josie a lesson and hopefully curtail any of her future matchmaking madness.

This day I fight!

Besides, the one sure way to run a fraud away is to beat him with . . . utter authenticity. Frightening authenticity.

Quote Keats?

Oh, I can do so much better than that.

Izzy the Valiant

PS: I have no knowledge of an author who cut off her ear and mailed it to someone. You are referring to an artist. The profile photo is of Charlotte Brontë. It's my attempt to garner my strength for the verbal tsunami to come.

CHAPTER 3

Heart-to-Heart

Date: March 3

Brodie,

Do I enjoy other books besides Tolkien? Does Charles Dickens love commas?

As Louisa May Alcott said, "She is too fond of books, and it has turned her brain." I'm afraid my cousin Josephine would agree. But I believe books have only served to turn my brain in a direction of constant wonder, appreciation, and imagination. You see, I've never traveled very far from home. The thought of flying terrifies me. But books have provided me continual journeys and adventures that my bank account could never finance. Besides my faith, stories became the catalyst to draw me out of the heartache and lostness I felt from my parents' deaths when I was twelve. They loved books, and somehow I felt them near me when I opened the cover to another new story, as if they journeyed alongside me. As false as the Mirror of Erised, I know, but the idea brought, and continues to bring, a special kind of comfort that nothing else has. I don't know if you can genetically acquire a love for books, but if so, I was doubly impacted. That should give you fair warning enough, but I have more.

Of course, I love nature too. I find in it (as so many authors describe much better than me) a remarkable and changing beauty, an ability to reset my perspective, and a reminder of a plan much bigger than my own. Though I tend to enjoy it more from a window, a car, or a front porch, at least once a week I venture out of my "reclusive" cave and breathe in the free air of a hike and the all-encompassing awareness of not being alone in the world.

Anne Frank, a very nonfiction person, captures it best, I think:

"The best remedy for those who are afraid, lonely or unhappy is to go outside, somewhere where they can be quite alone with the heavens, nature and God. Because only then does one feel that all is as it should be and that God wishes to see people happy, amidst the simple beauty of nature."

Doesn't she say it so well? I feel certain my dear cousin Josie could benefit from recognizing the grandness of God's plan in His children's lives, instead of feeling compelled to dramatically and too frequently intervene in the lives of others who are mostly content. How can I feel alone for too long when there is such a world!!

Stories have been powerful agents in my heart my whole life. Yes, I'm an introvert. My cousin might even refer to me as a recluse, but that's an exaggeration. I just find that the world and wonder of fiction provide ample imagination for a large portion of my life. Yes, I love being with my family (most of the time, but as with all family dynamics, some occasions and conversations are happier than others), but I am *not* a fan of my cousin's constant matchmaking schemes because, besides being an incredibly uncomfortable experience, they always seem to prove my cousin's thorough misunderstanding of who I am.

For example, she's not chosen one man, in all of her attempts, who is bookish in the least little bit. Not one can discuss the depths of human depravity shown in *Frankenstein*, or the excellence of Jane Eyre's upright and determined spirit, or the power of friendship on full display in The Lord of the Rings books.

I thought, perhaps, when she'd matched me with a youth pastor from a neighboring town, that I'd at least have someone with which to discuss thoughtful theology and the beautiful way in which God, creation, and love are displayed in fiction (both in written form and cinematically), but no, the poor man insisted on discussing politics, and not just *any* form of politics, but *church* politics. Clearly, there was some latent hostility rising from his previous church position, which made it perfectly clear this man was not for me.

I recognize my romantic history is a patchwork of mismatches and ill-fated decisions, which may lead my cousin to intervene, but I can assure you that if I'd known Dean only wanted help with passing his literature courses and he-who-left-me-at-the-altar only wanted a position with Uncle Herman's business instead of a lifelong commitment, I would have chosen differently.

Despite my family's usual disagreement (except for Luke and Penelope), I find, in fiction, remarkably accurate portrayals of the human heart, for good or ill. I learn and grow from what I read. I see in myself the pride of Lizzie Bennet, the misperceptions of Anne Shirley, the arrogance of Dorian Gray . . . and seek grace to become a better person without the same heartaches.

So, there you have it. If anyone in the grand, wide world is going to build a friendship with me, they must understand that they share my attention with hundreds of books, thousands of fictional people, a dog named Samwise (who is much more social than his owner), a love for nature, a devout faith, and a deep, though faltering, desire to become a better human in the small part of the world where I've been placed.

Oh, and I also speak in quotes much too often for anyone's benefit but my own.

So, quite appropriately, I end with a quote by the effervescent Mr. Disney: "There is more treasure in books than in all the pirates' loot on Treasure Island." And to this I add that I believe the best friendships hold as true a treasure as the greatest books—so only imagine how perfect the combination of both could be?

Authentically,

Izzy

PS: There you have it, Josie. Everything I've wanted to say to you for years in one rather succinct note. If you are going to continue with this matchmaking barrage, you might as well get a better understanding of whom you're matching.

PPS: And for the six-hundredth time, I do not like pistachios. The word is fabulous but not the taste.

PPPS: My Anne Frank quote was much better than your Keats.

From: Izzy Edgewood

To: Penelope Edgewood, Luke Edgewood

Date: March 3

Subject: Izzy the Valiant

Penelope & Luke,

There! I've done it. And, surprisingly, I'm not sorry in the least little bit. I feel justified and relieved and powerful in some kind of strange way.

I've poured out my soul in the most authentic fashion possible. I don't know that I've ever laid bare my heart like this, except for a sleepover at Lucy Lawrence's in eighth grade where I wept like a baby over watching *Bambi*. I don't think I'd really expressed my grief over Mom and Dad in such a real way. My tears ran like a hydrant. Needless to say, Lucy never invited me back again, but she did give me her copy of *Bambi*.

Expressing my effusive genuineness is a definite measure of Brodie's forbearance, Josie's level of commitment to this charade, and the entire usefulness (or lack thereof) of online dating communities.

Whatever the case may be, let the pages fall as they may, but I must say I feel incredibly happy at voicing my passion to another human being (even if that human being is merely my deceptive cousin). Josie deserves the verbal diatribe after all the false hopes and forbearance she's inspired.

And I sorted out a few things about my own heart in the process.

I love my life. I love the long walks and the mountain views. I love working with books and helping people find new stories to enjoy. I love our family, though I wish we were closer in proximity—especially you two—but your absence has spurred me into realizing I need at least one physical friend outside my family. That sounds pitiful, but I've been fairly satisfied with coworkers, fellow congregants, and my family in filling that social piece of my heart. However, with you both physically in two different states from me, I miss the physical connection I had with others. And Josie doesn't count, because her physical connections include more slaps to my arm or prods to my back than hugs (especially when the prodding is toward single men, regardless of age).

Books are excellent inspiration, but very poor conversationalists . . . and nonexistent huggers. I think I shall try to attend the next booksellers convention and, perhaps, take an in-person business class or maybe start with a seminar at the community college. The online bookshop community has been wonderful for gleaning all sorts of business knowledge, but no real friends. I still have the grand hope of owning my own bookshop someday. Maybe. If I can get past the idea of bookkeeping, math, and negotiating.

I think—as strange as it may sound at the age of thirty—I'm beginning to realize who I am and what I want. Or, at least the realization is beginning to emerge.

Penelope, I hope your performance as Flower Girl #1 was astounding. I have no doubt it was.

Luke, I just wanted you to witness my personal growth through words. I know how you love to talk about emotions.

With love,
Izzy

PS: Penelope, be wiser than your older cousin. Know your own heart as best you can before you attempt to discover whether another heart will match yours. It may take longer, but it keeps the scars and self-doubt to a greater minimum.

From: Luke Edgewood
To: Izzy Edgewood
Date: March 3
Subject: Emotions?

What are emotions?

Luke

PS: I cried during *Bambi* too. They used the word *twitterpated*.

Heart-to-Heart

Date: March 4

Izzy,

I've been called many names over the course of my life, some less flattering than others, but "Josie" has not been one of them.

Your matchmaking cousin sounds similar to my grandmother. Do you think there is a clinical diagnosis for obsessive matchmaking or do we chalk it up to overeager, loving family members with too much time on their hands? I think I prefer my grandmother making hand-knit sweaters in her spare time than attempting to knit up my future. Ah, that was an awful pun, but you get my point. Though I used to have a wealth of sweaters.

As far as books are concerned, I don't think I could have voiced my opinion as colorfully as you. Books have been a part of my life for as long as I can remember, and, yes, there is so much life in them that many times I have to remind myself that the characters on the page are not flesh and blood. I carried such agitation around inside me as I read *The Count of Monte Cristo* in my earlier days that my mother scolded me and threatened to take the book away before I could finish reading it. But I felt the injustice of Edmond's plight viscerally. Needless to say, her threat cut me to my core and I endeavored to guard my sarcasm, though I failed miserably at brightening my countenance. My wrinkled brow inspired the nickname the Blighty Mastiff, which was affectionately reduced to only Blighty and is a term my brother calls me to this day.

I am sorry to hear of your parents' passing but am glad to know you feel them near you when you read. It's no wonder you'd find such solace and enjoyment in books. In part, I feel your reasoning quite well, as I lost my dear father not too long ago and he loved the written word. Perhaps there is something to a genetic love of books. My family, particularly my grandparents and parents, provided continual inspiration on that score. I suppose one could say that I lived among books and lovers of books, which may be why I present as such a quiet sort when it comes to speaking words. I've been much more accustomed to seeing them.

And, yes, I find nature a sure connection to a heavenly realm. It's why I love my home so much. The air is clean, the breeze is constant, and the horizon never fails to remind me of my place in the world.

Would you mind giving me more details as to your blue mountains? My Google search has mostly landed me within the Blue Ridge Mountains of the eastern United States, though a few in Scotland arose as well.

Your comrade in bibliophilia,
Brodie (though if it makes you feel more comfortable, you can keep referring to me as Josie)

PS: Your Anne Frank quote was much better than my Keats. I raise you Lewis Carroll, since the mountains on my horizon are currently dusted with snow. "I wonder if the snow loves the trees and the fields, that it kisses them so gently? And then it covers them up snug, you know, with a white quilt; and perhaps it says, 'Go to sleep, darlings, till the summer comes again.'"

PPS: No job opportunity should ever cost a person's heart.

Text from Izzy to Penelope and Luke: I don't think Brodie is Josie. I'm going to go prick my finger on the needle of a spinning wheel and sleep through this disaster for a hundred years.

Izzy: Unless Josie has suddenly developed a wonderful sense of humor and a kindred understanding of a reader's heart, which she's never had before, this Heart-to-Heart

message cannot be from Josie. I'm forwarding Brodie's message to you both. Does this sound like your sister at all? Please say it does. Somewhere? Maybe the sweater-knitting part?

Izzy: Did I really pour my soul out to a complete stranger? From an online dating community? What do I do now?

Izzy: It is a very good letter.

Izzy: Off to find an evil fairy named Maleficent.

Luke: I felt the same way about *The Count of Monte Cristo*. I think you ought to give old Blighty a chance. And just think how many books you'll miss if you sleep for a hundred years.

Izzy: You are right. No amount of lifelong embarrassment is worth that sacrifice. Thank you for keeping me grounded.

From: Penelope Edgewood
To: Izzy Edgewood, Luke Edgewood
Date: March 5
Subject: Sweaters and Blighty

I love him!! I have no idea what *The Count of Monte Cristo* is, but his response to it and the nickname Blighty has me all aflutter. He's so eloquent and charming. I'm sorry to say this, but I bet he's old. Young, dashing men do not talk like that nowadays, unless they're a part of some costume drama production.

They certainly don't talk that way at the university.

Except my literature professor. But he's wonderful. And old.

Love,
Penelope

PS: Why would he need knit sweaters if he lives in California? Isn't it pretty temperate there?

PPS: I have decided to stop dating until someone in the possible relationship matures to the point of actually being able to date. I'm not that person, nor have I met that person yet. I actually think dates should involve conversations. Oh gracious, Izzy, I just sounded like you! I need to go buy some new shoes.

* *

From: Izzy Edgewood
To: Penelope Edgewood, Luke Edgewood
Date: March 6
Subject: Brodie the Mysterious?

Penelope and Luke,

If I can work up the nerve to respond to his very charming note (and I'm still trying to muster up that courage), I have no idea what to say. What could I possibly write after having smeared my heart across the page to the wrong person? And then, to have him answer as if I'm not some unstable, book-maniac recluse? I can't figure out if he's . . . real! And if he is, what's his angle? Why would such a man NEED an online dating service? Why would he want to continue corresponding with ME? Why would my attempt to call his bluff (or Josie's) have no negative impact on this correspondence at all?

Penelope is probably right. He's old. But how old is too old?

Why am I even asking that question? Clearly, Josie's desperation is beginning to rub off on me. I need ice cream.

Perhaps I should indulge in some movie talk? That would give him away at once, wouldn't it? As far as life-era?

Izzy

PS: He went to school in California. I don't think he lives there now.

PPS: Knit sweaters are very stylish, especially sweater-vests.

PPPS: I've researched evergreen mountains that are currently snow-capped with a constant breeze. I think he must live in New Zealand, Scotland, Ireland, Iceland, or Greenland. I've narrowed it down to those, unless he really is a hobbit . . . at which point in time, my dream of fiction blending into reality has finally come true. That would actually make a lot of sense.

Text from Penelope to Izzy and Luke: Gauging someone's age by movie choices isn't going to help you, Izzy. Just think of my favorites. People sing in them. And wear pinstripe suits and tap shoes. And have a tendency to croon and say things like "dahling."

Penelope: Wait, I wonder what that says about me?

Luke: Do you really want me to answer that?

Penelope: Shut up or I'll find that photo of you as a yodeler.

Luke: Don't start something you're not prepared to win.

• •

From: Luke Edgewood
To: Izzy Edgewood, Penelope Edgewood
Date: March 7
Subject: Re: Brodie the Mysterious?

Sweater-vests? Why does Mr. Rogers come to mind?

Which probably doesn't help with the age thing.

Luke

PS: What is it with all the PPSes?

From: Josephine Martin

To: Izzy Edgewood

Date: March 8

Subject: Pie

Izzy,

I dropped a pie off at your apartment just now. Thanks for leaving your back door unlocked so I wouldn't have to resort to edging on tiptoe to slide it through your window. However, I did notice what a disaster your kitchen was! Why on earth would you have a world map sprawled across your table with about fifteen thumbtacks holding it in place in one general area? Are you thinking of traveling? That would be wonderful. I think a change of scenery for you is exactly what you need! And think of all the new people you could meet!! I'm so proud of you for contemplating flying, Izzy. Despite your parents' unfortunate situation, flying is still one of the safest ways to travel. (Where have I heard that before?)

And are you having someone over for dinner? I noticed your Irish cookbook lying open by the sink. Please say you've invited Steve over for dinner. You are a very good cook when you set your mind to it, especially when you're trying out dishes from other countries.

Josephine

PS: My ultrasound is on the ninth. Then we will know whether to buy pink or blue! Patrick is excited to purchase tiny shoes.

From: Izzy Edgewood
To: Josephine Martin
Date: March 8
Subject: Re: Pie

Josephine (because of the pie),

Thank you. I accept your apology about the entire Heart-to-Heart initiation.

I'm not thinking of traveling any time in the near future, but I appreciate your concern for my kitchen's tidiness. However, before you hear about it from Penelope or Aunt Louisa, I have signed up for a seminar about the business program at the community college. I think it's time to start planning the future I want, instead of waiting for my future to happen to me.

And I am excited to discover whether nieces or nephews are in my future. Either way, you can be certain their first gift from their aunt Izzy will be a book. They make chewable ones for babies. I've already priced them.

Izzy

PS: How are you at knitting? Sweaters, in particular.

Text from Luke to Izzy: Stop procrastinating and write Blighty back.

Luke: I know you.

From: Izzy Edgewood
To: Luke Edgewood
Date: March 8
Subject: The Authentically Izzy Challenge

Luke,

I've decided to treat this entire "Hobbit Brodie, the Blighty Mastiff" situation as if it's as fictional as it feels and sounds, which means I am determined to be as much myself as I possibly can. If I am, it will prove one of two things: he is as much a fraud as I'm afraid he is, OR he is as perfectly wonderful as I'm afraid he is. I'm not sure which I prefer, but I am determined to be brave and figure it out . . . safely from behind my computer screen. Does that still count as authentically me?

Befuddled,
Izzy

PS: Mr. Rogers wears a cardigan. Not the same thing. Sweater-vests can have either a sexy, cerebral sort of appeal, an arrogant-prefect appearance, or . . . an elderly, pipe-smoking chap with a dour expression and a dog on his lap look. It's all about the wearer, of course. I think if you wore button-downs more often, it wouldn't hurt at all. Girls like that. Respectably buttoned.

From: Luke Edgewood
To: Izzy Edgewood
Date: March 9
Subject: Re: The Authentically Izzy Challenge

You already know the answer. Stop doubting yourself.

Luke

PS: Never talk to me about clothes again. You're terrifying. And confusing. "Respectably buttoned"?

Heart-to-Heart

Date: March 9

Brodie,

First of all, I need to apologize for thinking you were my cousin Josie (whose real name is Josephine, but I've been calling her Josie as punishment for the whole matchmaking fiasco).

As far as I can tell, you are not a married, pregnant, matchmaking woman with too much time on her hands, but since your profile picture only shows an adorable sheepdog pup (which I assume is Argos), then I have no way of being sure of this. Do hobbits have dogs?

My nickname isn't as delightful as yours. Blighty has so much more character than Izzy. I had to google photos of a mastiff since my canine history involves a blue heeler named Sparky, Darcy the border collie, and a schnauzer named Abraham Lincoln—we called him Al for short. He was my cousin Luke's dog. Now I have Samwise and he's a golden retriever. Dogs really are the most wonderful creatures, aren't they? I'm contemplating getting a friend for Samwise so that he'll have a companion while I'm at work. It only seems appropriate to name the friend Frodo, but I'm not sure what sort of dog will fit the name. I'm certain to spend too much time thinking about it. Names have power . . . or at least influence. As Anne of Green Gables said, "I don't believe a rose would be as nice if it was called a thistle or a skunk cabbage." I'm not sure what a skunk cabbage is, but it sounds awful, which adds more proof to my point.

Oh, there I go, speaking nonsense to a stranger. Again, I want to apologize for my verbal tirade. I would have never indulged my inner Lizzie Bennet if I'd known you weren't Josephine . . . or a complete fraud of some other sort. At this point I feel certain you aren't Josephine. Once we determine you are not a sheepdog, perhaps we can disprove the latter.

The very fact you messaged me back has me intrigued. Would you happen to have an extremely emotional sister (or girlfriend) who prepared you for such a rhetorical explosion, because your response has been much too laissez-faire for a novice.

I live in the Blue Ridge Mountains of Virginia in a small town near the North Carolina and Virginia line. Small towns are aplenty, but the closest city is about an hour away, which is fine with me because I prefer the serenity and quaintness of a slower pace of life.

What are your mountains like?

Izzy

PS: I raise your Lewis Carroll with Jack London's, "But especially he loved to run in the dim twilight of the summer midnights, listening to the subdued and sleepy murmurs of the forest, reading signs and sounds as a man may read a book, and seeking for the mysterious something that called . . . for him to come."

CHAPTER 4

<u>Text from Josephine to Izzy, Penelope, and Luke:</u> Get the blue AND pink ready! We're having both!!

<u>Izzy:</u> I am so excited to welcome a niece *and* nephew into the family! With over ten years of children's books experience, can you imagine how well-read they'll be by the time I finish with them?

<u>Izzy:</u> Just curious . . . have you ever read Keats?

From: Penelope Edgewood
To: Izzy Edgewood
Date: March 10
Subject: Sweaters

I had no idea how many university boys wear hand-knit sweaters until Blighty mentioned them in his note. I see them everywhere. Mostly from the English majors, but they do add a sense of prestige—except for the ones that have the furry look to them. My nose starts itching just thinking about them.

I wonder why I'd never noticed them before.

I adore sweaters on Ben, the guy who is playing Professor Higgins. He wears them well. But he's only interested in dating leading ladies, not flower girls. I feel certain he's meant for Hollywood.

Penelope

PS: Have you seen a photo of him yet? That would certainly help us with uncovering his age. Though Maria von Trapp and the Captain worked through their age difference well, age gaps seem to work better in a historical setting when war is involved.

• •

From: Izzy Edgewood
To: Penelope Edgewood
Date: March 10
Subject: Re: Sweaters

Dear Cousin,

The only photo I've seen is his profile photo on Heart-to-Heart, but it won't give you any real information. He's wearing a furry winter hat that covers his hair, dark sunglasses, and a coat that looks as though he's getting ready to go on an Alaskan adventure. His smile is nice, though. Happy. And he has light eyebrows, which makes me think his hair may be fair (or gray, but I refuse to let my imagination venture too far in the sweet, bookish elderly gentleman direction).

The photo he was referring to was of his puppy, Argos, who is quite adorable and looks like he needs to be wrestled into a cuddle about a hundred times a day.

I'm afraid to like his owner too much since I'm still not certain he's real. But he has an excellent sense of humor and I'm tempted to respond to his notes too quickly.

Izzy

PS: I am attending a seminar tonight at the community college for people interested in a business degree. I'm going to attempt to wear a welcoming smile, along with my fastest running shoes.

From: Penelope Edgewood
To: Izzy Edgewood
Date: March 10
Subject: Imaginary boyfriends

Being "unreal" has never stopped you from liking men before. Most of your boyfriends have been fictional, if I remember right. Or at least the ones you liked the best.

I had an unhealthy crush on Harry Potter when I was younger, to the point I even turned down a perfectly good date with a boy who resembled Ron more than Harry. It is a lifelong regret.

Penelope

Heart-to-Heart

Date: March 10

Izzy (If that is your nickname, what is your given name?),

I've adjusted my profile photo, but as you can see, the amount of fur I have on my winter hat makes me resemble Argos more than I thought. You may prefer the dog.

No apology is necessary. From the repeated mentions of Josie and matchmaking in your previous note, I deduced the problem and am happy to clarify your points. I am not Josie, have never been married or pregnant (though I am not averse to the first, I feel the second an impossible feat for me), *and* have rarely dabbled in the art of matchmaking, since I have such a difficult time finding a match myself. (Please note a previous message referring to my pun problem and/or chronic shyness.)

If I recall correctly, Farmer Maggot made quite a few threats of sending his dogs after garden poachers, so I do believe hobbits have dogs. Whether they are miniature dogs to fit the size of their owners or not I cannot say, but I feel certain Tolkien would oblige us, if he could.

Argos is indeed an English shepherd and despite his proclivity for destroying my footwear, he has the best personality, allowing my two-year-old nephew all sorts of liberties of ear-pulling and tail-catching Gandalf would never have permitted. Gandalf was an Irish wolfhound. In fact, his appearance reminded me a great deal of the wizard, though I never succeeded in getting him to wear a pointy hat. I am attaching a photo of Gandalf for your reference. If you find a friend for Samwise, you must name him Frodo. I don't see how you can do anything else. As for the breed, anything with hairy feet and a determined jaw should fit the mark, don't you think?

And, as to your comment regarding "speaking nonsense to a stranger," I've not felt as though you are a stranger since our first communication. There is something immediately comfortable in meeting another avid reader. A companionship of words and shared worlds that I find difficult to emulate with nonreaders. So let's say you were "speaking nonsense to a friend" and go on from there. In an effort to secure that friendship idea, I will clarify even more.

My name is Brodie Callum Sutherland, though in my part of the world the surname is sometimes spelled in its Gaelic form, Sutharian. I'm thirty-four and am a business owner on Skymar, an island country that has been a part of England, Scotland, and the Netherlands at one point in time or another. We are considered a constitutional monarchy now and are keen on celebrating and poking fun at our royal families as avidly as most places with royal families do.

The mountains near my home are called the Alnors and they resemble your round-topped Blue Ridge Mountains when not covered in snow. My family owns a growing business of which my eldest brother, Anders, and I are business partners, but our mother proves the *real* head of things, as mothers have a tendency to be.

I have two younger sisters. Isla, who is married and has two young children, and Fiona, who is only thirteen and would have put your "verbal tirade" to shame. I am not fond of coffee but am ridiculously attached to tea and Victorian sponge cake. I usually enjoy walks, but Argos is trying to turn me into a runner. I prefer the lifestyle of a hobbit in that regard. I live outside of one of the most popular cities on our island, but that is not an impressive size, and prefer the country space to a crowded town, though I enjoy visiting cities.

There you have it, a rather unimpressive overview, if I do say so myself, but my brain is of admirable soundness, the landscape out my windows is some of the best, and my family proves even better.

Your turn,
Brodie

PS: "It is no bad thing to celebrate a simple life." (I'll let you guess where this quote originates.)

• •

From: Izzy Edgewood
To: Penelope Edgewood, Luke Edgewood
Date: March 11
Subject: I know nothing

Maybe Josie IS as conniving as I previously thought.

I'm forwarding Brodie's newest message. He's too perfect. How can he be a real person?

A single, thirtysomething, book-loving, humorous, foreign man? I think he may have hit every check mark on my internal wish list that I've only ever mentioned to God! Not even Santa!

(Okay, I didn't have "pun problem" on the list, but that just makes him cuter!)

And . . . "speaking nonsense to a friend"? Lord, help me!

I'm terrified of what this means if I . . . really introduce myself? If I . . . care? And then it all turns out to be another instance of me falling head over sneakers, and instead of reciprocal twitterpation, I am being used for someone's personal gain that has nothing to do with happily ever after.

He lives an eight-hour flight away. On an island. Between Scotland and the Netherlands. They have almost five months of winter there! And from what Google says, 30 percent of the population speak some weird combination of Gaelic, English . . . Nordic something-or-other called Caedric. And, what else? In their northern mountains there are still isolated towns of folks from Scottish descent who only speak Gaelic. (I can't do languages!! You all remember tenth grade French class?)

And Brodie loves *The Lord of the Rings*. My favorite book and movie series of all time.

I feel as though someone in the universe is laughing at me right now.

Izzy

PS: Even with the Alaskan fur headgear and a rosy nose, he has a very nice smile. Smiles say a lot about a person.

From: Luke Edgewood
To: Izzy Edgewood, Penelope Edgewood
Date: March 11
Subject: I know everything

Clearly, he isn't perfect. He doesn't like coffee. I think you can do better.

Also, didn't you used to teach ESL classes at the library?

Luke

PS: Please never use the word *twitterpation* in a note to me again. My eye starts twitching.

PPS: The Joker's smile certainly tells a lot about him.

From: Izzy Edgewood
To: Penelope Edgewood, Luke Edgewood
Date: March 11
Subject: Re: I know nothing

Of course, anyone can *sound* perfect. Actually *being* perfect is another matter altogether, but he does sound too good to be true.

And I STILL teach ESL classes at the library! Twice a month! So . . . maybe languages aren't so scary, if they are visible. And not taught by a woman who tried to teach "southern fried French."

Maybe Brodie is a secret service person looking into my history and life!! Think about the coincidences in him listing out my hopes and dreams here, Luke! It's unnerving. I'm pretty sure God doesn't speak to a ton of people in the government. Especially about thirty-year-old single women's romantic aspirations.

It's terrifying to actually believe Brodie IS exactly who he seems to be. Trust is so hard.

Irrational Izzy

From: Izzy Edgewood
To: Penelope Edgewood, Luke Edgewood
Date: March 11
Subject: Re: I know everything

Luke,

I see. You wanted me to confess things on paper. Aren't you smart? I hate you.

Izzy

From: Penelope Edgewood
To: Izzy Edgewood, Luke Edgewood
Date: March 11
Subject: Re: I know everything

Why are we always so surprised when God gives us something we've been praying for? It's like we don't believe He's actually listening.

Penelope

From: Luke Edgewood
To: Izzy Edgewood, Penelope Edgewood
Date: March 12
Subject: Re: I know everything

I think that's the wisest thing Penelope has ever said. I'm glad we have it in writing.

Luke

From: Penelope Edgewood
To: Izzy Edgewood, Luke Edgewood
Date: March 12
Subject: Re: I know everything

Luke,

I say a great deal of wise things, but you are not at my college to hear them.

PS: I would like to take issue with the subject line that "Luke knows everything." For one, he was no good at choosing Christmas presents for his youngest sister. That color of yellow looks atrocious on redheads. And I'd never wear a feathered stole, except that one time when I had to stand in for Miss Hannigan in *Annie*.

From: Luke Edgewood
To: Izzy Edgewood, Penelope Edgewood

Date: March 12
Subject: It's a hard-knock life for you

Luke

From: Josephine Martin
To: Izzy Edgewood
Date: March 12
Subject: Changes?

Izzy,

Have you been exercising? I think those hikes are benefiting you. Your eyes beamed in church this morning while you were singing. And were you wearing a new dress? Green, even? Izzy, what is going on with you? Steve hasn't mentioned any more dates, and believe me, I've asked Patrick about it on a regular basis.

Thank you for the little package of chewable books. I had no idea they made chewable classics! You had to have purchased the entire inventory, Izzy!

By the way, Donovan from church was asking about you today. I think he recently broke up with his girlfriend and is now officially free again. Didn't you date him once or twice? Maybe it's time for a second chance? He likes movies. And church. And I've even seen him at the library a time or two.

Josephine

PS: Keats? I've heard of the name. Is he one of the children's book authors you love? You keep recommending books for me to purchase for the babies, but I can't remember them all.

From: Izzy Edgewood
To: Josephine Martin
Date: March 12
Subject: Re: Changes?

Josie,

I looked for a chewable Bible but couldn't find one. It seemed appropriate to purchase since somewhere, if I recall, we are supposed to be chewing on the Word of God. I thought the babies could start early.

They had chewable pizzas for babies as well, but I figured that would be too cruel.

Izzy

PS: Donovan is not for me. If you recall, he has difficulty with the word *monogamous*.

PPS: Never mind about Keats. He's a poet. I forgot that you are allergic to poets.

Heart-to-Heart

Date: March 12

Brodie,

Thank you for clarifying so much about yourself while also inspiring many more questions. An unimpressive introduction? How can you even think it? A loving family, a beautiful view, and a plethora of books! You are rich with treasures, and to have all three at once? Impressive isn't a strong enough word. Fortunate? Blessed?

I am glad to learn that you are not my cousin Josie, though I only have your word and a rather unidentifiable photo to go on. Actually, you are much wittier and well-read than Josie, so that does help your argument. Plus, the simple fact you not only get my *Lord of the Rings* references but make your own, is another factor against you being Josie. She still confuses hobbits and dwarves and thinks *The Lord of the Rings* are Christmas movies because they feature elves and a man with a white beard and pointy hat.

Matchmaking has never been my forte either. As a child, I couldn't even get a pair of pet rabbits to like one another, so why would I ever attempt humans? And matching socks? It's a lost cause.

I love the notion of finding comfort and immediate kinship in another reader. It's so true. But not just any reader will do. Readers with a certain measure of appreciation and respect create a stronger kinship than your fair-weather readers. I can't say I've ever known such an immediate friendship on such short acquaintance as this one, but it may be in part due to the fact we met online and all of the awkward "in-person-ness" that accompanies so many of my disastrous blind dates is conveniently absent. For example, how often would you say you use the suffix "itis" in conversations?

My great-grandmother met her future husband through correspondence (not that we are on that trajectory, of course), but she said writing allowed them to get to know "one another as souls first." There's something both daunting and beautiful about that sentiment.

So in the spirit of our kinship, I'll share a little more about me, though my information truly will be unimpressive.

My name is Isabelle Louisa Edgewood, a name I've always felt

I could never live up to. Izzy fits much better. Isabelle Edgewood sounds as though I should be the lady of the manor or an author of some regency novel. Izzy Edgewood fits the quiet librarian that I am. I live in the small town of Mt. Airy, North Carolina, at the foot of the Blue Ridge Mountains. In fact, if I stand in a certain spot on the sidewalk in front of my house, I can place one foot in Virginia and one foot in North Carolina, effectively being two places at once.

My uncle Herman and my aunt Louisa (after whom I'm named) took me in when my parents died, so their three children are like siblings to me. My aunt is the lead librarian at our local library, a place I've worked for eight years after fumbling through college and finally ending with a double major in library science and British literature. My uncle is a semi–well-known owner of a massive furniture store company known as Amwurst's. Doesn't that name just flow off the tongue?

I am not ashamed to admit that I'm almost as avid a movie watcher as I am a reader . . . but remember, I said "almost." I'm thirty, love keeping my feet warm, and am horrible at small talk. I'm not unkind, I don't think, but I just don't say a lot unless I feel I have something to contribute, and even then I have to feel extremely compelled to speak my mind.

In fact, if Josie could see how much I've shared with you, she'd likely fall over in shock.

As you see, my adult life has been rather unimpressive and . . . predictable. Hmm . . . I don't think I've ever really thought about it that way before and I'm not certain how I feel about the revelation.

Sincerely,

Izzy

PS: Tolkien has the best quotes, doesn't he? Here is an excellent one for perusal. "Never laugh at live dragons."

From: Izzy Edgewood
To: Penelope Edgewood, Luke Edgewood
Date: March 12
Subject: I still know nothing

What am I doing? If Brodie the Hobbit lives on the other side of the world, why am I encouraging any sort of . . . anything with him? Whatever this anything may be? Why would I invest my emotions in a relationship in which one of the two of us would have to move away? He seems close to his family. I'm certainly and devotedly close to mine. It's ridiculous really.

Did I mention he lives on an island? On the other side of the world! That requires travel. Usually flying.

Why am I even concerned? I sound as if this is the right hobbit for me, when there's been NO talk of romance between the two of us. I should stop writing him.

But I can't wait for his responses—like Christmas morning every day.

Oh good grief, somebody slap me. I'm starting to sound like a Hallmark movie, and I only resort to those during certain times of the year . . . for sentimentality's sake, of course.

Izzy

PS: What do I want? (This is a rhetorical question so, Luke, you are free NOT to answer.)

From: Luke Edgewood
To: Izzy Edgewood, Penelope Edgewood

Date: March 12

Subject: I still know everything

Izzy,

Slapping you doesn't help. I've tried, but maybe I should have used something more attention-grabbing than a toy fish. What you need is a deep breath and the right perspective. Distance isn't the key to a good relationship, communication is. Communication leads to trust and then commitment, and then you have what you really need most for your future, regardless of how that looks or where it is, islands or not.

It's sad when there have been so many mean girls and heartless guys in the world that we forget the worthwhile ones are still out there, probably as hopeful in finding the "real thing" as we are.

Luke

PS: "No talk of romance"??? You do realize Heart-to-Heart is an online dating site, right?

PPS: I won't even attempt to answer THAT rhetorical question.

Text from Penelope to Luke and Izzy: Where is my brother and who have you replaced him with? Luke, the email you sent to Izzy was absolutely beautiful. Maybe we're both wiser in writing.

Izzy: Luke, I'm in tears. Where did you gain such wisdom?

Luke: Dr. Phil.

Luke: Penny-girl, you've never taken advantage of the depths of my personality. Now I'm off to field dress a deer while I watch the Bass Pro fishing show.

Penelope: You're gross, Luke.

Penelope: BTW, which one do we talk about to distract Izzy from hyperventilating? Brontë, sea urchins, or Chris Pine? I can't remember, but I know that one of those would cause *me* to hyperventilate, and it's not the artist or the fish.

Luke: Penny-girl, you're gross. Don't mention Brontë, particularly *Wuthering Heights*. We know how that impacts Izzy.

Heart-to-Heart

Date: March 13

Izzy,

Some would say that speaking only when one has something to contribute is a sign of wisdom, which, to my mind, says a lot about you. Though the pressure of speaking in social settings can lead to the greatest of blunders from which no pun can save someone. Not that I speak from personal experience, of course. However, I will conclude that silence is only golden for so long within social settings before it descends into the depths of humiliation. Getting through those first few conversations, especially with a woman of interest, has always been my downfall, and I'm not certain why. I have an admirable command of the English language (or Caedric), but the world of small talk baffles me into a stupid state of near-muteness.

For some reason I believe your full name suits you much better than you realize. Or at least the you I'm coming to know through this online medium. Perhaps you haven't grown into it yet, but I've always found the name Isabelle pleasant, especially when spoken aloud. It has a lyrical quality to it. And the way you write, the wit and charm, fits well the name of Isabelle Louisa Edgewood, I think.

We have very few Isabelles here. There are Fionas and Bridgets,

Elaines and Brennas, Erikas and Ionas aplenty, but I don't know a single Isabelle except you. And, you are right, I am rich in treasures of the measureless sort. *Blessed* is the perfect word, though I shouldn't mind a bit more marketing knowledge to help with the family business.

I am captivated by your great-grandmother's sentiment about knowing someone's soul first. I should think it would certainly help with small talk. In the same spirit in which you shared it, I feel this unique way of "meeting" provides a glimpse into the heart of someone without the distraction of "in-person-ness," as you called it. Of course, we could be pretending. I'm not very good at pretending, though, and I would wager neither are you. But this is all conjecture from what I've learned about you through these notes thus far. I see no point in pretending, especially in this mode in which we communicate. To me, it lends itself to authenticity, if one wishes it.

I've researched your Blue Ridge Mountains and they are lovely. I can't imagine seeing such layers of mountains. The Alnors are vast, but since the island is rather small, the mountains usually spill into the sea at some point. It appears that your weather is rather temperate than more northerly or Midwest locations in the US. Is that so?

In reference to "predictable" lives, I would say that we are both stepping out into a very unpredictable adventure by corresponding, wouldn't you? And I'm quite pleased with this adventure thus far, even though my hobbit-ish nature raised a wary eye at first. Bookish friends are always worth an adventure, I think.

What do you enjoy doing most in your occupation as a librarian?

Brodie

PS: I never laugh at dragons, living or dead.

PPS: May I call you Isabelle?

CHAPTER 5

• •

From: Izzy Edgewood
To: Penelope Edgewood, Luke Edgewood
Date: March 13
Subject: Hobbit? Or not?

His mountains "spill into the sea at some point." Who is this man?! He can't be real, can he?

And he writes with such eloquence and feeling! I don't know anyone within our age group who would EVER write messages like this. EVER! Most of them wouldn't even know what the words *admirable* or *temperate* mean, let alone use them in deliciously beautiful sentences!

I am so afraid that this is one giant hoax and when it all surfaces, he'll be some eighty-year-old professor of ancient literature that smells of mothballs, lives in a hovel, and writes maudlin poetry under a female pseudonym.

I feel like I'm teetering on the brink of something terrifying.

Can it be true?

Izzy

PS: He asked to call me Isabelle! Who does that?

PPS: I wonder what his voice sounds like.

From: Luke Edgewood
To: Izzy Edgewood, Penelope Edgewood
Date: March 13
Subject: Definitely a hobbit

Izzy,

Read my last message to you again.

Luke

PS: His smile is too young for an eighty year old. I can't vouch for the mothballs or the female pseudonym.

PPS: You really need to expand your friend group. Or buy them dictionaries.

From: Penelope Edgewood
To: Izzy Edgewood, Luke Edgewood
Date: March 13
Subject: Re: Definitely a hobbit

Is it time for Chris Pine yet?

Penelope

PS: When is it NOT the time for Chris Pine?

From: Josephine Martin
To: Izzy Edgewood
Date: March 13
Subject: Dinner

Izzy,

Someone will be joining us for dinner at our house tomorrow night. His name is Murphy. Please do not mention that we had a cat with that name when we were children. That never makes a good impression.

He was brought on as the newest podiatrist in Patrick's practice, though he's been in practice for a while. That doesn't mean he's old. He's not old. He's mature. And he likes to read fiction.

He's also stable, friendly, and looking for someone to settle down with him.

Josephine

PS: He has a grandchild. That doesn't mean Murphy is old.

* * *

From: Izzy Edgewood
To: Josephine Martin
Date: March 13
Subject: Dinner deception

I am resorting to calling you Josie again. I'd refuse to come if I hadn't promised your sweet husband that I'd bring my chocolate chip brownie cake.

Your beef stroganoff better be worth every minute.

How many *children* does Murphy have? And more importantly, what are their ages? For some reason the idea of dating a man whose children are my age doesn't sit too well with me. Imagine Aunt Louisa marrying someone your age. He'd be your stepfather! There is no amount of stroganoff or brownie cake to steady that thought.

And, there is no war.

Izzy

PS: If loving me means you will continue with the matchmaking, would you please love me less?

Text from Penelope to Izzy and Luke: I want a Brodie. I know two couples who met through online communities. One is happily married with three children. The other . . . well, I can't remember how long his prison sentence is.

Luke: Reread your last text and think about it.

Luke: Izzy, what did Grandma used to quote when we were afraid?

Izzy: "Eat your vegetables or your hair will fall out"?

Luke: Other grandmother.

Izzy: "Have courage, dear heart." Thank you, Luke.

Heart-to-Heart

Date: March 14

Brodie,

My grandfather used to call me Isabelle and, apart from the smell of tobacco, I have excellent memories of him. I'm not sure what you mean by my "growing into" my name, but it intrigues me, much like a clue to something I must figure out, and I adore mysteries. Agatha Christie is one of my favorite authors in the genre.

I'm not good at pretending either. The dozen children who hear me read during story time at the library will attest to it, especially when it's a book I don't like. The poor things have been lovely about pointing out my frowns . . . or growls, on occasion. And no wonder James Barrie created something as wonderful as children's laughter to be the origin of fairies. Ah, *Peter Pan*!

It's much easier to be authentic with children than adults, I think, because they seem to see through us anyway and get right to the heart of the matter. Adults rarely indulge in such honesty and directness, which makes this conversation so refreshing.

Maybe the combination of anonymity and kindred spirits loosens some sort of boundary most awkward first-encounters build? Does that make any sense? And, to my own surprise, I like it more than I thought I would. Perhaps it's the company.

The weather here is fairly temperate, if by temperate you mean our winters rarely become abominably cold or our summers ghastly hot. We have days of both each year, but they aren't common. Though it never snows enough for me. There's something about going for a walk in the snow, seeing all the crystallized beauty, and then returning home to snuggle up by a fire with a hot chocolate and a good book to read. It makes the snow all the more magical to end it with such a scene. I suppose you have a great deal of snow in Skymar?

I love my work at the library because I can help people discover new stories, and, as I said before, the children keep me honest. I daydream about something different that still involves books but on a more intimate scale, and someday I hope to put those dreams into practice. But for now the library is the perfect spot for me. Unfortunately, I'm not sure what that "something different" is quite yet.

As far as hobbit-ish adventures go, I'm afraid I feel much more like Frodo in the "adventuring" department than his uncle Bilbo, but this bookish adventure we have started has certainly been a wonderful surprise.

What sort of business does your family have? Do you love it or are you struck with wanderlust for something else?

Izzy

PS: I've attached a photo of Samwise. That blurry spot in the corner is likely my thumb. I'm notorious for ruining the best photos with my thumbs. Samwise looks wonderful, however, so that is enough.

PPS: You may call me Isabelle.

From: Izzy Edgewood
To: Penelope Edgewood, Luke Edgewood
Date: March 14
Subject: Josie strikes again

I sat through dinner with Josephine and Patrick tonight and thought, *This is not my life.*

And it made me realize I want different, and I want *better.*

No matter how pregnant or good-intentioned my cousin may be, this matchmaking business must stop! She's bordering on neurotic! Austen's Emma has nothing on Josephine Martin!

Dr. Murphy Lewis had to have been fifty-five years old if he was a day. Fifty-five! And he has a three-year-old granddaughter whom he loves tremendously because he spent most of dessert showing photos to us. She is very cute and has double-dimpled cheeks, but that's beside the point. Am I in such desperate shape to become someone's step-grandmother at thirty years old? For some reason I feel like that may break some biblical law or something.

Now in Dr. Murphy's defense, he was a very nice man. A very nice GRANDPA of a man. He does enjoy reading fiction. Louis L'Amour, the quintessential Western fiction author. I've read two of his books and they're well written, but . . . those are the *only* books he reads. It was *almost* as bad as the forty-five-year-old man Josie tried to set me up with last year. Do you remember? He had a penchant for reading gothic horror novels, only dressed in black, stayed out of the sun to keep his complexion pale, and occasionally used words like *forsooth* and *aghast*. I had nightmares about him for a week.

Where does she find these people? Though I think that's when she was going through her low-sugar diet phase. She did a lot of strange things then.

At any rate, I told her that I wasn't interested in any more blind dates. If I am to die an old maid, then I'll learn to be content with my books, my dog, and my favorite slippers.

Thank you for listening,
Izzy

PS: Distance and fabulous conversations trump in-person stiltedness any day.

PPS: And Murphy was a very nice man.

Text from Luke to Josephine: Josephine, stop with the matchmaking. You don't know how to do it. Buy a dog.

Heart-to-Heart

Date: March 15

Isabelle,

I read my first Agatha Christie mystery last year and have devoured as many of her books as I could find since. She was an ingenious author. Her character of Poirot reminds me of my grandfather. He is a twitchy sort with the best heart in the world, but you wouldn't know it upon first meeting. He also carried a miniature comb in his shirt pocket (for he always wore button-downs) so he could keep his mustache in excellent order. Once, I saw him with it mussed and hardly recognized him.

Children keep us truthful, don't they? What exactly is a reading group with children? How does it work? By themes or a schedule? Can any child attend?

If you like snow, our higher elevations receive a solid amount each winter and usually into the spring.

Has your cousin Josie relinquished her matchmaking obsession since you've maintained this account or is she continuing her intervention? From your passionate response to her, I can only assume she's made quite the endeavor to "assist" you in finding happiness. My grandmother assisted with a fervor. At one point I invented a girlfriend to deter her good intentions from driving me mad. Those were three of the happiest months of my life.

Of course, I write those words with love. My grandmother is an excellent woman and I'm sure if I lived closer to her again, she'd enlist her friends at the care home en masse to rectify my singleness problem.

Skymar is a group of five islands—the largest is Ansling, followed by Fiacla, then Inslay, Kernvik, and several smaller ones connected to the larger ones by bridges, or, what we call *brus*. (Can you hear the odd mix of Scandinavian and Celtic among the names?

It's a proper indicator of our unique culture here.) I live on Ansling, which is a central location from which to run the family business. Last year I began renovating a country house outside of the village of Elri. It's an old family home handed down to me by an uncle and places me at a nice distance from most of the larger cities here (but nothing is very far since the island is small). My brother, who manages many of the physical aspects of the business, lives about 140 kilometers south in New Inswythe, one of the largest cities on Ansling. My mother and youngest sister remain in Skern, which is about a half hour away by car. Their central location is a perfect "headquarters" for the business. My eldest sister, her husband, and my nephew live on the island of Waithe.

My family is actually in the book business, started by my grandfather and carried on by each generation. You see, books are a part of my heritage, which I think is why we get on so well. We speak in books. It's a unique and intimate language.

I hate to admit this, but I just finished reading *Frankenstein* for the first time. It was an excellent adventure. I've never been drawn to the science fiction genre, nor have I had much experience reading epistolary, but my sister informed me that gothic horror is not like the term *horror* used in popular culture, and recent events have caused me to become much fonder of letters.

(Being in the business of books does not mean one is familiar with *everything* about books, clearly.) I shall attempt *Dracula* next and then I feel I'll need to take on something lighter. What would you recommend?

As with Samwise and Frodo, I believe a good companion on an *unexpected* adventure makes for the best sort of adventure. I'm happy to be your Samwise, as long as your dog doesn't mind sharing the name.

Affectionately,
Brodie

PS: Samwise looks like a hearty, happy dog. At present he's nearly twice the size of Argos, but I feel Argos may catch up.

PPS: What is your town like? What do you love about it?

From: Josephine Martin
To: Izzy Edgewood, Luke Edgewood
Date: March 15
Subject: Matchmaking

Luke (and Izzy),

Patrick told me the same thing about matchmaking last night after Izzy quite forcefully (for her) asked me to stop trying to find her a husband. (As you well know, Izzy, I am only trying to help.)

Patrick actually got a little snippy in Izzy's defense, at which time I burst into tears and ran from the room. He's never gotten snippy. Ever. Perhaps he's been working too many long hours.

At any rate, I have decided to let Izzy's romantic future fall as it may. What do I know of romance? Am I happily matched with a wonderful man and expecting two beautiful children? Do I exude the joy of a wonderfully romanced woman?

But I do love you. And I know you are one of the dearest people in the world, which means I want you to experience all the best things dear people should experience.

Plus, Luke, I'm having TWINS in less than five months. I don't need a dog.

Josephine

PS: Well, at least there's still Penelope.

From: Izzy Edgewood
To: Luke Edgewood, Penelope Edgewood
Date: March 15
Subject: Celebrations galore

I'm not certain what makes me happier. The fact that Brodie's family is in the book business or that Josie has stopped trying to find me a match. This is a momentous day that we must celebrate next week when Penelope comes home for spring break. I'll take you both to pizza at Larenzo's and we can get dessert at the bookshop next door. My dessert will likely be a book on Skymar with large photographs. Yes, I'll splurge in purchasing one. Borrowing one from the library just won't do this time. (Besides, I had Susan special-order the book just for me.)

I researched bookshops in Skymar and there is a book company known as Sutherland's. Could that possibly be his family's?! To quote a vernacular expression: Shut the front door!

His family owns a chain of BOOKSHOPS!! I really do feel as though I'm part of a reality television show and at some point (probably around the halfway mark) an ex-girlfriend from Christmas past is going to show up and alert me to my delusion. Or . . . worse, instead of being the genuine, wonderful, bookish-loving man Brodie appears to be, he's . . . a middle-aged, married man who actually lives in Detroit and only reads the newspaper . . . and not even the interesting parts.

But that can't be so. Can it? Not from the way he exudes such bookish charm on the page. Right? Can someone fake it this well through words? I've always preferred fiction to nonfiction, but at the moment, I'm not too sure.

I'm sorry I keep asking the same question, but . . . nothing has ever come to me this easily. Nothing! You two know that. Dean broke my heart at twenty-one. HWLMATA trampled on what was left of it at twenty-five . . . and took some of my savings along with him. I always get into trouble because I'm too trusting. Too starry-eyed. Why can't I recognize when I'm the only one giving in a relationship? Why does it take me so long, and so much heart-exhaustion, to realize that everything is one-sided, even the conversations? Have I learned from my previous disasters enough to try? To believe? Can I be clear-sighted now? After five years and at least three dozen self-help books?

It hurts too much to let go.

Izzy

PS: Yes, I sound melodramatic. I will empty a half gallon of chocolate chip cookie dough ice cream and be sensible again. But allow me my moment.

From: Penelope Edgewood

To: Izzy Edgewood, Luke Edgewood

Date: March 15

Subject: Re: Celebrations galore

Izzy,

I think you should ask him to have a video call with you. At least then you can determine whether he's old or not. Or wearing a wedding band. OR has an indention on his finger from having worn a wedding band. And if he doesn't use a fake background that makes you believe he's in some tropical setting, then even better, because he's confident in his own surroundings.

Plus, it will allow you to look for clues in the background of the video. I always do that on video calls. It makes me feel like a spy. One time I learned that a guy actually owned a dog, even though he'd never come visit my house because he said he was allergic. Come to find out, he only spent time with me because I helped him with his calculus homework! Oh my goodness, Izzy, that sounds exactly like HWLMATA, except I hadn't talked about marriage with Dawson yet. Just calculus and model cars.

Plus, it's easier to tell if someone is lying by seeing their face. Lots of grooming gestures and lack of eye contact are sure signs . . . or that's what my psych professor says anyway. And nose twitching. No, wait. That's something else. Never mind.

If all of these things pan out, I think he's perfect for you. Absolutely perfect.

And I'll totally take you up on the pizza and bookstore when I get home. I haven't had Larenzo's pizza in two months!!

Penelope

PS: Do you think they wear wooden shoes where he lives?

Heart-to-Heart

Date: March 15

Brodie,

Your grandfather sounds delightful. I've always been fond of slow-to-warm-up people. It gives me the sense of overcoming an obstacle to get to the worthwhile parts.

When I was younger, we had a neighbor who could have portrayed Miss Havisham in any Dickens retelling. She lived in a narrow gray house that resembled something you'd see on the streets of Victorian London, so it fit perfectly into my recent literary discovery. One day when she walked out in a white dress, I crossed the grass to see if she only wore one shoe. Thankfully, after I stumbled right into her path, she helped me to a stand and quite begrudgingly asked me in for cookies . . . which became a regular Tuesday afternoon treat from then on.

There's such a poignant message about the devastation of bitterness in Dickens's stories, don't you think? I feel certain that is why they impacted me so deeply, especially when I was tempted to hold on to my anger about my parents' death. I think, as a child, God used the power of fiction to prick my heart to a healthier mindset, even though the ache remains. I guess that is always a fixture because the place where my parents lived within my heart is still being held for them, like a bookmark of sorts—waiting to see them again. I like to think of their deaths in that way because it doesn't feel like forever. Just a pause before the end of the story.

No matter what the "critics" say, there is so much truth housed within fiction.

Your islands look beautiful (if Google can be trusted). One particular photo filled my screen, and I could almost taste the salt-sea air rushing over the cliffs. If I was ever tempted to write a novel, this looks like the perfect place for inspiration. I've always had a fascination with cliffs and looming manor houses and a broody ocean. Not that I've ever seen any of those things in real life, but my imagination conjures up all sorts of ideas. (I have seen a brooding ocean. We live close enough to drive, even if it takes about six hours to get there. I just have not seen the combination of the three things together, IRL.)

I'm attaching the photo of the sea and sky of Skymar so you

can confirm it's an actual existence near you. Oh, I hope so. What a beautiful place to live! It really does remind me of some of the scenes in *The Lord of Rings*. And the names! Elri? Skern? I'm grinning as I think of them. So storybook-like!

Speaking of stories . . . Storybook reading at the library is a weekly and quite momentous occasion made up of various stories (usually related to the season or a theme) and celebrated by children in various ages (we have three different story times based on ages). My aunt began these about ten years ago, but I took them over about five years ago because (as my aunt tells it), I can make better voices than she can. I have to admit, as much as I enjoy my solitude, I have the best time bringing these books to life for children. Their eyes light up, they laugh or gasp at all the right places, and I fall in love with the stories all over again. The only problems I've noticed so far are the occasional child who screams out the ending too soon, a rabble-rouser, or . . . little fingers who want to steal my reading paraphernalia. I've lost one princess hat, a rubber frog, a golden pirate earring, a scarlet apple eraser, *and* an arm-size pencil. I'm still not sure how a child escaped unnoticed with that pencil.

Of all the things I do at the library, this is my favorite, even more than opening up a book for the first time and smelling its newness. I just have this overwhelming love for the creative wonder with books and people.

I loved learning that your family is in the book business. What sort? I suppose there are various types of book businesses, but the only ones I really know about are libraries and bookstores.

I adored *Frankenstein* and *Dracula*, much to my aunt's and Josie's dismay. I can't understand why! I only tried to resurrect one animal during a thunderstorm, because the little dwarf hamster had barely lived a month. It deserved more time. Needless to say, the only thing I succeeded in doing was short-circuiting the microwave.

As far as lighter book recommendations . . . Do you prefer

classics or modern suggestions? Oscar Wilde's more humorous tales are a quick and witty read for me when I need something lighter, and they have enough sarcasm and cleverness to brush off the chill of any gothic horror, in my opinion. (Assuming you like sarcasm.) I recently finished *The Truth According to Us* by Annie Barrows, and found it a poignant and fun book with wonderfully quirky characters. I just started *A Walk in the Woods* by Bill Bryson and nearly spit out my tea I laughed so hard at one point. (It's always a detriment to lose one's tea in any form, but laughter might be the most forgivable.) Bryson's book involves his journey hiking through the Appalachian Mountains, so I already feel at home (and don't even have to leave my reading chair to enjoy them).

Where I actually live (in a duplex owned by a cattle farmer who has enough acreage to create a resort) is picturesque for the most part. The mountains line the horizon on two sides of me and then a gravel road leads through a field toward the main highway to the town of Mt. Airy. It's actually a wonderful example of small-town charm, with "old" buildings running alongside the quintessential old-fashioned Main Street. There's even a vintage barbershop, ice-cream shop, and sandwich place. Plus, it's the birthplace (and celebrated home) of actor Andy Griffith. You may not have heard of him, but he's pretty popular in these parts.

I'm attaching a few photos . . . without thumbs.

Izzy

PS: I'm glad we speak the same bookish language.

PPS: Would you be open to a video chat?

PPPS: No is a perfectly acceptable answer. One I don't use as often as I should.

CHAPTER 6

From: Izzy Edgewood
To: Luke Edgewood, Penelope Edgewood
Date: March 16
Subject: Long-winded & shortsighted??

Penelope and Luke,

I take back all I've ever said about being unable to write a novel.

I just wrote one to Brodie. Actually, I think my last three messages have been some of the longest I've ever written, except two years ago when I got into a verbal war with Professor Lindon from church about the efficacy of fiction among Christians. What did he think parables were?! He still won't speak to me, except when forced by playing Joseph in the Christmas play. I can't imagine ever speaking to an angel with such a tone of voice! I feel very much like C. S. Lewis's professor in asking, "What do they teach them at these schools?"

BTW, how was the spring fling, Penelope? Didn't you have a date for it?

Luke, I'm sorry to ask you this, but I think there's a loose board or two on my back porch and the landlord isn't in a hurry to fix them. I tripped this morning and nearly catapulted off the back. Samwise thought I was running after a squirrel, to which he proceeded to take off in pursuit. Twenty minutes later, drenched, we returned to the house, sans squirrel.

Would you look at those boards when you're in next week? Pretty please.

Love you more than words! (And that's a lot.)

Izzy

PS: I asked Brodie about a video call. I may need some help figuring out how that works.

PPS: And I may need someone to bring me chocolate if he turns out to be . . . not who I think he is. I have Brontë at the ready.

PPPS: I think if I ever get a cat, I should name her Brontë.

From: Penelope Edgewood
To: Izzy Edgewood, Luke Edgewood
Date: March 16
Subject: Clovis Bastien

Spring fling was wonderful. I went with Clovis Bastien (what do you think of THAT name, Izzy? One to rival your fictional favorites!). And though Penelope Bastien sounds absolutely fabulous, he was too much of a gentleman for me. I'm perfectly fine with starting a conversation or taking a man's hand now and again, but there are times when a woman needs a man to take the lead, in dancing and in romance. I don't think he initiated one question. Not one. But I only noticed, of course, because you all know how excellent I am at carrying on a conversation with myself.

Oh, by the way, I was accepted into the study-abroad internship program for next fall! They'll announce my particular country when we get back from break. I have my toes, eyes, and fingers crossed for Europe! Anywhere in Europe! Mrs. Thompson said that my background with the theater paired with my marketing major is quite unique. It's a very select opportunity because . . . it's a PAID internship. You have no idea the wish list I've developed through college to abate my shoe fetish for that moment when I get my first paycheck. My toes are tingling at the very idea!

Penelope

PS: Don't ask Mama or Josie to help with video chats. I'm pretty sure they've figured out a way to spy on conversations. Mama always knows things I've never told her.

PPS: The Skymar Islands were not a choice for the study-abroad program, but I asked the counselor to consider adding it. She couldn't even find it on her map. It makes me want to visit even more. Maybe we have to walk through a wardrobe to find it? (You see? I can do literary references too.)

PPPS: **gasp** Unless Brodie is lying!!

From: Luke Edgewood
To: Penelope Edgewood, Izzy Edgewood
Date: March 16
Subject: Anything but Clovis Bastien

Penelope,

I think the T-shirt you used to have makes things clear: "Of course I talk to myself. Sometimes I need an expert opinion." Maybe you can buy a new one and wear it as a disclaimer.

Luke

PS: Izzy, a quote you once shared with me: "It takes courage to grow up and become who you really are." You have more courage than you think. Maybe it's time to use it in the real world.

From: Izzy Edgewood
To: Luke Edgewood, Penelope Edgewood
Date: March 16
Subject: The mysterious library man

There's been an unexpected development, and I don't think Josie's involved. A man came into the library today, took a stack of books from the Classics section, and began to read . . . for three hours. I'm not sure what conclusions we can draw from *Wuthering Heights*, *Moby Dick*, *Animal Farm*, and *Gulliver's Travels*, but when he checked out, he began a conversation about the pleasantness of the library and its decorations (which I'm quite proud of. You can never have too much Irish ambience). Before I knew it, he'd asked for my phone number. While I stumbled through an answer, Aunt Louisa came up from behind me and gave it to the man. I think I smiled when he said he'd call. I'm not sure. Because somewhere in the middle of him asking and me trying to formulate a response, I lost sensation in my face. Why do I always do that when a man asks for my number?

Here's the quandary: Is it possible to cheat on a man I'm writing to online when I've never even seen his face? Would it be wrong to go out for coffee with a real-life person while having conversations of the bookish sort with an online person? (Not that Brodie isn't alive, BTW.) And we've only "known" each other for a month, though that month has been such fun. But it's not as though Brodie and I have made any sort of commitment. Right?

Izzy

PS: The library man looked every bit the part of a dashing rogue. Perhaps I shouldn't trust him.

PPS: Penelope, I'm sending a valid link to Skymar to assure you that it's a real place. Brodie is real, too, but I still haven't ascertained if he's human or marriageable. Also, he lives on the largest island of Skymar called Ansling. Yeah, a little confusing, but I'm learning.

PPPS: Luke, why do you have to be so obnoxiously clever?

• •

From: Luke Edgewood
To: Izzy Edgewood, Penelope Edgewood
Date: March 17
Subject: Re: The mysterious library man

Okay, you just went above my pay grade. I think you just started living your best (or worst) fictional life now.

Do they have counselors for things like this?

Luke

• •

From: Penelope Edgewood
To: Izzy Edgewood, Luke Edgewood
Date: March 17
Subject: Re: The mysterious library man

Oh my goodness, Izzy!! It sounds like something from the musical *She Loves Me*. Could Brodie *be* the library guy? An undercover spy to see if YOU are exactly as you seem to be online? After all, the man did choose classics, as you said, though the only two I've heard about are *Moby Dick* and the one we're not supposed to mention to you when you're stressed.

But why would you be stressed?? Haven't you always said you hoped to meet your future husband in a library? This is kismet! I'm all aflutter. Izzy! You are currently living *You've Got Mail*!

Did the mysterious library man have a Scandinavian-Celtic accent? Or wooden shoes? Those would have been dead giveaways for sure.

Oh, Izzy, just imagine what this could mean for you! No flying involved!! You can finally face your future and fall in love at the same time. I'm almost shivering with excitement.

Penelope

PS: Does the library guy have a name? I feel strange referring to him so generically.

From: Izzy Edgewood
To: Luke Edgewood, Penelope Edgewood
Date: March 17
Subject: Re: The mysterious library man

His name is Professor Eli Montgomery. Oh heavens, he has the same surname as L. M. Montgomery!! I wonder if he's read *Anne of Green Gables*?

And no, his accent was more standard American.

And he wore an open-collared button-up with a suit jacket, which, I won't lie, was rather swoon-worthy.

But . . . but what am I saying?? I've gone two years without meeting a bookish man and within the span of a month, I've met two? I don't think I'm made for this kind of drama IRL. Bookish men are like eating Josie's peanut butter swirl cheesecake. One piece at a time or you can't move for two days.

Izzy

PS: No one has answered my cheating-on-Brodie question yet.

PPS: Was the quote about lifelong and debilitating insecurities referring to me?

PPPS: Brodie hasn't emailed me back. Maybe I shouldn't have mentioned video calls.

Text from Luke to Penelope and Izzy: I'm not an expert on romantic relationships, but from a guy's perspective I don't think cheating starts until two people have decided to be exclusive . . . AND MET IN PERSON. I'm guessing from your hysterical and emotional reaction there has been no such decision. By the way, no one has ever called me swoon-worthy when I wear button-downs.

Penelope: Camo button-downs don't count.

Izzy: **Thank you for answering, Luke. The ALL CAPS wasn't necessary. Flannel can be very nice on you, especially when there are no bloodstains.**

Penelope: Oh yes! Flannel is much better than camo, Luke. Very Hallmark.

Luke: I regret my decision to join this conversation.

From: Josephine Martin
To: Izzy Edgewood
Date: March 17
Subject: Clark Gable at the library??

Mother just told me you met someone. At the library. It's wonderfully providential and I didn't even have to resort to matchmaking.

Josephine

PS: Mother says he looks like Clark Gable. Think of children with those eyes!!

Heart-to-Heart

Date: March 17

Isabelle,

Forgive my delay in writing. I've been traveling for work in the more mountainous regions of the islands and reception is spotty at best. Though the delay gave me time to contemplate your most touching recent message. I just arrived home at one o'clock in the morning, and with the six-hour time difference, it is my hope you will still receive this note within your waking hours.

This may sound mawkish, but I cannot help myself. Your description of a bookmark in your heart over your parents' deaths nigh brought me to tears. I've never heard such a sentiment expressed so beautifully and simply. Yes, that is how I shall think of my father from this point on.

You are remarkable.

My grandfather would like you, even if he didn't show it at first, but you can always tell if he's pleased because he begins to rub his mustache repeatedly. Grandchildren need such clues sometimes when their grandfather has a tendency to growl more than smile.

I have found fiction to meet me at the most poignant of times in my life. I learned the power of imagination through Narnia and the intimacy of true friendship in *The Lord of the Rings*. I found courage from Atticus Finch and an unexpected camaraderie with *Emma*'s Knightley. Let the critics say what they will. We know the truth, don't we? Fiction, at its best, speaks to the heart.

These islands are beautiful. Photos fail to do them justice. Though I've traveled to many places, there truly is no place like home, even with the unusually named villages and, at times, the chilly winters. Look up the cliffs of Brete Tarn. They are near my home and have some excellent legends wrapped around them, including a mysterious manor house or two. And of course, there are stories of pirates' treasures, long-lost lovers, and ghosts. But there are always ghost stories in ancient places. We've learned to live with the boca without instigating their ire.

And as far as your reading groups go, what a wonderful way to inspire children to love books! If I come to your library, would I have the opportunity to sit with the children and hear you read a story or two? I promise not to pinch one of your props, though I think I could sport a Gandalf hat rather well. Who wouldn't want to wear a pointy gray hat?

My family owns a growing set of bookshops known as Sutherland's Books. Grandfather built his first shop in 1964 in Skern with barely a coin to his name. He loves telling the story of placing his first book on the shelf and wondering how he'd afford to fill all the secondhand shelves in the space. People in the community began to donate duplicate books in their possession, and as grandfather sold some, he bought more from outside the community, but the village of Skern has always held our family's hearts in a special way. It is our goal to cultivate the same sense of community in all of our bookshops, but each one provides a new challenge. Growing pains, I suppose. And over the past few years, I'm afraid Sutherland's has not handled those growing pains so well.

I understand, speak, and even think in fluent sarcasm. P. G. Wodehouse is one of my favorite authors. Have you read him? Bryson's book sounds like an excellent suggestion, as I've read most of Wilde's tales.

I've never heard of Andy Griffith, but I shall know more about him by the next email. It seems there are a plethora of his television shows to view. Will those give me some sense of your world in Mt. Airy? Your photos are lovely. There are so many trees!

I look forward to hearing from you soon.

Affectionately,

Brodie

PS: I'm glad you speak bookish as well.

PPS: I would love to engage in a video call.

<u>Text from Izzy to Luke:</u> I've never been called remarkable before and I'm not quite sure what to do with it.

<u>Izzy:</u> Is it weird that he's read Jane Austen? You're the only man I've known who has read Austen and can actually talk about those books with some level of understanding and . . . without sporting a sneer.

<u>Luke:</u> Is it weird that you're an Avengers fan? Or that you adore Patrick O'Brian? You really need to have a better view of yourself.

From: Izzy Edgewood
To: Josephine Martin
Date: March 18
Subject: Re: Clark Gable at the library??

Josephine,

I feel certain you got your matchmaking habit from your mother.

Yes, Eli Montgomery does resemble Clark Gable to a degree. His eyes are more brown than Gable's gray-green smolder, and he has a nice smile, but otherwise I know nothing about him. He hasn't called. I'm not expecting him to and I'm perfectly fine if he doesn't.

Let's focus on Penelope coming home tomorrow, what do you say? Perhaps we can have one of our infamous sleepovers. By summer you may not feel much like staying up all hours watching classic musicals.

Besides, there is this really nice guy I'm talking to on Heart-to-Heart. I'm not sure where it will go, but I'm content with this, my job, beginning business classes, Samwise, and the upcoming celebration of becoming an aunt (well, second cousin, but since you are more like my sister than cousin, I'm going to keep referring to myself as an aunt).

See you tomorrow!

Izzy

PS: Don't you just love the word *remarkable*?

From: Josephine Martin

To: Izzy Edgewood

Date: March 18

Subject: Re: Clark Gable at the library??

What guy? If he doesn't live nearby, then I really think there is a perfect local option who showed up quite providentially at the library! A Mr. Gable to sweep you off your feet! Did you get his number? Maybe you could call him first?

Josephine

PS: I would find it "remarkable" if you had a date to bring to the Spring Street Fair. Maybe one that looks like Clark Gable!

Text from Eli to Izzy: Izzy. This is Eli Montgomery. Would you have time to meet for coffee tomorrow? Where's a good spot?

Text from Izzy to Penelope and Luke: So . . . Eli texted me to ask me to meet him for coffee. Thus it begins . . . again. BTW, when did guys stop calling first?

Text from Izzy to Eli: Hi, Eli, good to hear from you. Would you like to meet at Pages Bookstore? They have great coffee and pastries. Plus, they have books!

Eli: Bookstores are some of my favorite places. Tomorrow? 10:00?

Izzy: See you then.

Heart-to-Heart

Date: March 18

Brodie,

How was your business trip? Where are some places you've traveled that you enjoyed most?

The cliffs are stunning! I'd love to hear their stories and search for treasure. And if the ghosts behave themselves, I wouldn't mind exploring their haunts either.

I've never traveled internationally (except through books), but there's a piece of me that wants to. I'm not sure why the prospect makes me nervous. Perhaps it's a mix between being afraid some of the places I've read about will prove less magical in reality, the idea of navigating all the newness of traveling in such a big way, and my debilitating fear of flying.

Your photos and descriptions have resurrected the internal battle though, in a good way. Someday. It's that constant dream that seems just out of reach . . . at least for my courage. That sounds ridiculous, doesn't it?

And though I've never used the word *mawkish* before, I was happy to know you understood. You may use or be mawkish whenever you like. I appreciate that you appreciated my sentiments. I'm sorry about your father. Time turns pain into memory, but I feel as if there is always this missing spot in my life.

I've never read P. G. Wodehouse. His books look ridiculously wonderful.

I'm not sure how exciting my book reading would be at the library, but story time is open to the public, so of course you'd be welcome. And I happen to own a Gandalf hat as well as a deerstalker hat (though Sir Arthur Conan Doyle never references one for his famous fictional detective). I still wear it when I read *The Hound of the Baskervilles* to the middle school story-time group every October. If you need a pipe, I have one of those too. Gandalf style.

What a wonderful job you have! To own not only one but several bookshops! What are they like? I searched online, but there are only descriptions and no real presence. Do you want to grow them?

I picture quaint spaces with reading nooks and towering shelves. If your marketing person can post some photos of people enjoying Sutherland's, it may increase interest (or at least do it for curious southern Americans who ache to peek into bookshops virtually).

I cannot wait to get your reaction to Andy Griffith. So many of the people in my town share his accent, including me. So at least you'll have fair warning when we have our video chat.

Izzy

PS: I'm sending a separate email with days and times to see if any of those will work for you to have a video call.

PPS: Do you enjoy in-person conversations typically? Or are you more comfortable behind the screen?

Heart-to-Heart

Date: March 19

Isabelle,

I feel certain I will enjoy a face-to-face conversation with you. I look forward to tomorrow.

Affectionately,
Brodie

CHAPTER 7

From: Izzy Edgewood
To: Luke Edgewood, Penelope Edgewood
Date: March 19
Subject: As Izzy's World Turns

Penelope and Luke,

My morning started with an email from Brodie and now I'm off to a coffee meeting with Eli and then my first video call with Brodie tomorrow morning. I feel like a rom-com movie with a foreboding disaster nipping at my heels.

I can't wait to see you both tomorrow night for pizza! Hopefully my impending romantic doom will not happen by then. Usually the doom waits until the heroine is sufficiently entrenched in relationships . . . or at least that's been the case with my dooms. There is some safety in distance.

Izzy

PS: For some reason I feel like I ought to watch the last twenty minutes of *Austenland* on replay.

PPS: There's something very pleasant about the word *affectionately* isn't there?

From: Izzy Edgewood
To: Luke Edgewood, Penelope Edgewood

Date: March 19

Subject: Move over Sandra Bullock

You know those movie scenes where a woman walks through the door of a place, her hair flying around her in dramatic perfection, and all eyes turn to notice her brilliance as the camera pans from her stylish heels upward? Well, that's never been me, made all the more certain by the way I entered Pages to meet Eli this morning. I came through the same door I've entered since the store opened four years ago. There sat Clark Gable at a table by the window looking like he just stepped out of a fashion magazine. (Penelope, I wore the red sweater you bought me for Christmas last year since you said red looks nice on me, but I fear it didn't help overshadow the next part of this story.) I smiled, pushed my hair back behind my ears, took a step, and then . . . couldn't go any farther. My purse strap was hung. Well, I gave it a little jerk and . . . the head of Pages' seasonal leprechaun on display went flying through the shop. Almost in slow motion, it hit a book display table in the middle of the room, knocking over the book featured on the top of a precarious stack. Just as my shoulders started to relax, the rest of the books spilled over onto the floor like a literary domino game.

I rushed to the display, apologizing profusely to the owner, who (quite wisely) removed my swinging purse from my shoulder and helped me retrieve all the books and the decapitated leprechaun head without saying one frustrated word. She really is a saint.

Poor Eli stared at me from the table as if he'd looked into the eyes of Medusa. Of course, after watching my blunder unfold before him, turning to stone might have been preferable. At any rate, after the color in his cheeks returned (and the heat in mine lowered to human levels again), we had a nice time. He teaches

English literature at the community college with a preference for ancient literature. In fact, his third novel set in ancient history came out two months ago, and he promptly took me to the shelf where his books were.

When Pages' owner learned he was a local author, she quickly offered to have a book signing for him, since the locals are extremely supportive of their hometown celebrities. He politely refused, but looked ever so pleased when the owner moved a few of his books from the shelf to the local-author table display. I've never enjoyed novels set in ancient times, but, as any good reader should be, I'm open to new adventures. So I purchased one of his books and look forward to delving into it later this evening.

He was a perfect gentleman. Even wore a scarf with his classy suit jacket. You know, like something from *Dead Poets Society*. And he complimented my hair.

I'll share more with you at dinner. He's a rather new transplant to the area. He lives closer to White Plains, which gives him ready access to Winston-Salem for a bit of the city life he left in Columbus, Georgia. Josephine would love his accent. A southern Clark Gable! I'm not sure why he relocated to the little town of Mt. Airy. He said he needed a change of pace. Well, I'm certain Mt. Airy provides that! I get my fill of city life when Penelope drags me to Winston-Salem or Charlotte a few times a year to shop.

Despite the debacle with the decapitated leprechaun, Eli invited me for dinner Friday night. I figured after embarrassing him to such tremendous heights, I ought to say yes.

Izzy

PS: I'll meet you at Larenzo's tomorrow at six. I'm changing purses so I won't decapitate anything else. I'm sure Larenzo will be appreciative.

PPS: Thank you both for always listening to me.

Text from Luke to Izzy: Thanks for sending the brownies by Lance. Do you keep breakup anniversaries on a calendar somewhere? Never mind, I don't want to know.

Izzy: It's important to know you're not alone and that someone remembers with you. Brownies don't fix things, but at least they make the moment sweeter. :)

Luke: Your brownies confirm two things: (1) You bake better than Josephine. (2) You've confirmed a decision I've made that I'll tell you about when I see you. Thanks, Izzy.

• •

From: Izzy Edgewood

To: Luke Edgewood, Penelope Edgewood

Date: March 20

Subject: Brodie

Penelope and Luke,

I couldn't wait for dinner to share this with you. I just got off the video call with Brodie. The reception wasn't ideal, but our call lasted for an hour before things became so bad we had to end it. He thinks the problem may have been on his side, but we all know it's my inability to master technology. I think I have some sort of magnetic destructive field in my fingertips. Thank heavens my e-reader hasn't borne the brunt of my unintentional electronic homicidal bent. Brodie did mention that his house (the one he's renovating) is due for new Wi-Fi within the next week, so . . . maybe my inadequacy with technology isn't at fault.

At any rate, the first part of the call was filled with those awkward silent moments that have punctuated the majority of my dating life. He made a few comments about how pleasant it was to finally see my face instead of Éowyn or Charlotte Brontë. I returned the favor and added that the rustic look of his living room reminded me of Christmas. More silence permeated a few bumbling exchanges and then he asked about the most recent book I was reading (I didn't mention Eli's) and then asked about my day and, well, I told the decapitated leprechaun story (leaving out the Eli parts). Everything changed. He laughed. I laughed. And suddenly the person from the emails emerged into the conversation and our dialogue turned into a pitifully hilarious one-up to who has had the most embarrassing moments. I must say, Brodie's were impressive. Especially the one about the horse and a vat of pudding.

And I wondered if we'd have difficulty understanding one another, but his accent is not as thick as I'd imagined. There's a bit of a James McAvoy feel to it. He seemed to understand my accent fine. Maybe he's been practicing by watching *The Andy Griffith Show* reruns.

He has kind eyes. You know what I mean? The sort that encourages you to keep talking because you actually believe he's listening? There's something very comforting about that.

I'll tell you more when I see you at Larenzo's.

Izzy

PS: Before you ask, Penelope, there was no hint of a wedding band on his finger.

PPS: Sweater-vests are very appealing on men. Why haven't I noticed them before?

* * *

From: Penelope Edgewood

To: Luke Edgewood, Izzy Edgewood

Date: March 20

Subject: Re: Brodie

Are you serious? You send an email about a video chat with your Scandinavian-Celtic pen pal and tell us everything except what he looks like? What is wrong with you? Izzy, really, you should know me better by now. "Kind eyes" but no color? I just don't understand you.

Penelope

PS: Was his accent divine? Did he call you something endearing like "poppet" or "rosebud" or "cabbage"?

* * *

From: Luke Edgewood

To: Penelope Edgewood, Izzy Edgewood

Date: March 20

Subject: Re: Brodie

If you can't see me right now, I'm slowly shaking my head in resigned acceptance that Penelope is my sister.

Luke

PS: Did you share your experience on the runaway donkey? I could never decide who looked more afraid. You or the donkey.

From: Izzy Edgewood
To: Luke Edgewood, Penelope Edgewood
Date: March 20
Subject: Re: Brodie

I'm not sure how to describe him. He has one of those stares that disarms you, like you're the only person in the world. He didn't use it at first, though, shifting his attention from the screen, much like me, I think. But when he did finally focus on me, and with such blue eyes, I stumbled over more words than usual trying to remember what I was talking about. I can't even imagine how distracting it might be in person. They're a deep, dark blue.

His hair is light-to-medium brown and . . . well, a little unruly looking. Not in a bad way, just as if he didn't care too much about taming it. Perhaps it can't be tamed.

He fidgeted a little in the beginning and wore a rather severe sort of expression. Nervous, maybe? I think that's where the "mastiff" joke must have come from because he has some pretty impressive wrinkles there. Hopefully he wasn't disappointed. The conversation seemed to end well with a confirmation of another call.

Izzy

PS: His smile was his best feature in my opinion.

PPS: But his eyes were very nice, too, once I learned how to find my words and look at him at the same time.

PPPS: Luke, I'll save the donkey story for our next awkward silence. It's a showstopper.

From: Josephine Martin
To: Izzy Edgewood
Date: March 20
Subject: Laughter is a doorway to romance

Izzy,

I dropped by your house midmorning to bring a newfound recipe I thought you could make for Easter dinner. I already have my meal choices planned, but this would be an excellent addition and . . . Eli would be more than welcome to join you.

Speaking of Eli . . . when I got to the door of your apartment I heard laughter! You, laughing. I can't remember the last time I heard you laugh like that. Was it last year when you watched *Bringing Up Baby* for the first time? You and Penelope were in stitches.

Were you with Eli? Mother said you were meeting with him today. I think he's a regular at Beans & Things (just a hint, in case you want to find your way in that direction more often).

A man you can laugh with is worth keeping.

Patrick is more of a dad joke sort of guy, but the way he waits for me to respond makes me laugh. His eyes light up at his own jokes. It's really sweet.

I can't wait to hear more.

Josephine

PS: Here is something you'd appreciate. It came inside my fortune cookie today and I think it's incredibly appropriate for your little afternoon . . . date? "There is nothing in the world so irresistibly contagious as laughter and good humor." Can you believe Charles Dickens wrote that? I always thought of him as a dreary sort of fellow since he seemed to spend so much time thinking about ghosts and orphans and women who wear wedding gowns for much too long.

From: Izzy Edgewood
To: Josephine Martin
Date: March 20
Subject: Re: Laughter is a doorway to romance

Josephine,

I had a good time meeting Eli, and just so you know, before you talk to the owner of Pages, Eli and I are having dinner on Friday AND I already covered the cost of the leprechaun's repairs.

The dessert recipe looks fabulous, as long as Steve isn't coming to dinner, because this one has peanuts.

Izzy

PS: The movie was *Some Like It Hot*.

From: Brodie Sutherland
To: Izzy Edgewood
Date: March 21
Subject: Our call

Isabelle,

I can't express to you what a delight it was to talk with you yesterday. All of the previous emails seemed to merge into a better understanding of who you are, though it took me a little while to remember that I already knew you, in part. After we ended our call I purchased the first two seasons of *The Andy Griffith Show* and plan to start them tonight. I've never heard such a charming accent.

I'd love to discuss some more about your suggestions for Sutherland's online presence. We have a marketing director on the team, but she's my cousin and hasn't a great deal of experience, though she has an uncanny ability to inspire people into communicating. I feel certain she'd appreciate any feedback and suggestions you could offer. You fairly glowed with ideas as we spoke. I'm rather useless with things like marketing as I'm more of a financial fellow who continues father's excellent bookish connections because Anders, my brother, has the tendency to offend everyone.

Would you mind if I shared your email address with my cousin? Her name is Brynna Lund and she's . . . What's the word in English? Sprightly? She is a wonderfully generous person in every way, but especially with her words and affections. Conversations may feel like an onslaught, but in all honesty, you aren't required to do much else except nod, smile, and answer her questions. (Anders says that she "forces" people into communicating due to her persistence, so I'll let you come to your own conclusions about that. Anders's opinions are habitually singular.)

I'm giving you fair warning regarding Brynna so you can refuse the request and I will understand. Some people can only be taken in gram sizes rather than litres. Which woman in Jane Austen's *Emma* has the best heart but talks incessantly? I can't remember, but think of her when you think of Brynna, only younger and with much brighter hair.

Affectionately,
Brodie

PS: I cannot help but think of this quote by Robert Frost: "Half the world is composed of people who have something to say and can't, and the other half who have nothing to say and keep on saying it."

PPS: Brynna is not representative of that quote. But she does have a great deal to say.

• •

From: Izzy Edgewood
To: Brodie Sutherland
Date: March 21
Subject: Re: Our call

Brodie,

I enjoyed our conversation too. I don't think I've laughed so hard in my life. I would love to have met your uncle Sven! I thought sleeping inside of an animal to stay warm was only something that happened on *Star Wars* movies. I think Boy Scouts in Skymar are on a totally different level than the ones around here.

There's a part of me that wishes I could be a fly on the wall as you watch those Andy Griffith shows for the first time. I've grown up with them and everyone I know has watched them over and over again, but to enjoy someone's first discovery of this culture through those episodes? Well, the very idea makes me grin. I can't wait until you hear how Andy tells the story of Romeo and Juliet!

I'm not a marketing expert, Brodie. My cousin Penelope is currently getting a degree in marketing so I've learned some things from her, but I've also taken a few classes, I follow some online bookshop groups, and I helped out when Josephine had a cosmetics and bridal-wear store (she's been in the matchmaking business for a long time). I'm not sure I'm someone who could give *real* advice. I had to force (or sneak) my suggestions onto Josephine. Are you sure you want to trust my opinion? (Do you think Josephine and Brynna might be related on a verbal level?) Aunt Louisa allows me to do things for the library because her idea of using technology is to turn on the television with a remote.

Your accent sounds mostly Scottish to me, though I'm no expert on accents. There are some unique differences in it also. Is that the Scandinavian heritage coming out? I can't believe the Scots influence remained that strong when Denmark ruled Skymar for so long afterward. Those Scots are hearty folk, aren't they? We have lots of the Scots-Irish influence here in Appalachia.

You spoke English so well that it made me wonder . . . If English is only spoken by about 70 percent of the population of the islands, how did you learn it so well? Does your family speak it?

I'm looking forward to our next video chat tomorrow evening.

Izzy

PS: Generous-hearted and talkative is a much better combination than self-sighted and talkative. I'll take a Brynna over Dolores Umbridge any day!

PPS: To quote Shakespeare: "The lady doth protest too much, methinks."

From: Penelope Edgewood
To: Izzy Edgewood, Luke Edgewood
Date: March 22
Subject: Babies

Izzy and Luke,

I don't know why the babies kicked for you and not me. Even Luke felt them kick, but every time I'd try, they'd stop. I think they're already playing favorites and they're not even born yet.

Next time I'll sing to them. That should do the trick.

Penelope

PS: Don't forget to send that screenshot from the video call! You promised! I want to see what Brodie the Islander looks like! (And check his ring finger myself.)

From: Izzy Edgewood
To: Penelope Edgewood, Luke Edgewood
Date: March 22
Subject: Re: Babies

Penelope,

Maybe you just have a wonderfully calming effect. You used to do that for the dog.

Izzy

PS: Photo attached. It's not the best one because he came close to spitting out a sip of tea he'd just taken when I told him about decapitating the leprechaun. I'm still grinning over all the stories he told. It was like hanging out with you two, only with a little zing thrown in.

From: Luke Edgewood
To: Penelope Edgewood, Izzy Edgewood
Date: March 22
Subject: Re: Babies

Penelope,

Don't feel too reassured over Izzy's comment. That dog was fourteen years old. Everyone had a calming effect.

Luke

PS: Blighty had the whole set of *Indiana Jones* movies on his bookshelf. (I don't count number four.)

PPS: Should I be offended that I have no zing?

From: Izzy Edgewood
To: Penelope Edgewood, Luke Edgewood
Date: March 22
Subject: Re: Babies

Luke,

No one counts movie four.

Izzy

PS: Did you notice that the extended edition of *The Lord of the Rings* stood right beside them? Smart man.

PPS: You'll zing for someone special someday. I know it.

From: Penelope Edgewood
To: Izzy Edgewood, Luke Edgewood
Date: March 22
Subject: Re: Babies

I loved that dog. He never minded a good snuggle.

Penelope

PS: Luke, the zing is like the Christmas magic chime from Hallmark movies. It only pertains to romance.

From: Luke Edgewood
To: Penelope Edgewood, Izzy Edgewood
Date: March 22
Subject: Re: Babies

Maybe I don't want the zing after all.

From: Izzy Edgewood
To: Josephine Martin
Date: March 23
Subject: Asking for help is not a sign of weakness

Josephine,

Thank you for setting up a meeting with Mr. Fisher next week. You really didn't have to. The poor man is still trying to sort out his exit plan for a business he's owned for thirty years. Are you sure he's ready to talk about leasing the building this soon? And I'm not even sure I'm ready to take the plunge of opening my own bookshop. I love the concept of decorating that place and bringing people in to show them the joys of stories, but the actual business of it? That's a little terrifying. I'm still trying to garner the courage to open a spreadsheet.

I'm coming to clean your house Saturday. No arguments. Patrick is on my side in this. The doctors said to start taking it easy and you need to listen to them. I'd hate to find my way down to Dr. Turner's office and inform him of the way you're ignoring his specific orders. (I tutored Chuck Turner's daughter in reading so he'll pretty much do whatever I ask . . . so you'd better be a good patient.) No one would enjoy you being on bedrest. Least of all, you.

Why didn't you tell me you weren't feeling well instead of cooking the entire supper last night? Just because you *can* do everything doesn't mean you have to!

Izzy

PS: Please stop texting me Clark Gable pictures!

CHAPTER 8

From: Izzy Edgewood
To: Luke Edgewood
Date: March 23
Subject: One more time?

Luke,

Do you think it's weird to enjoy the company of someone I've never met in person more than about 90 percent of the people I know in person? Brodie and I talked via video chat for two hours tonight. He's so kind and funny. Sometimes, with his humor, he reminds me of you. Sarcastic and subtle, only he's a bit gentler. He's a big fan of P. G. Wodehouse. Have you read him before? We only have three of his books in the library and they were checked out, so I'll have to wait until they're returned to find out for myself. I refuse to e-read them if I can hold them in print form, you know?

Brodie's favorite *Indiana Jones* movie is number three, like you.

I've been thinking of you since you and I talked at Josephine's. I'm glad you broke up with Clare, but I know it hurts still. Two years is a long time to be with someone. But you'd stopped doing many of the things you loved most because she demanded all of your time. If someone loves you, she should encourage you to become the best "you" you can be and *share* in your dreams instead of rearranging them to her own designs. I never realized how much I need that in someone until HWLMATA nearly stripped me of dreaming altogether.

Clare never liked the idea of you quitting accounting to go back into construction, but I can't imagine you doing anything else. You love it so much and it shows. Always has. And though the idea of stonemasonry makes my shoulders hurt, it's a lucrative skill, especially for someone who likes it as much as you.

You know I understand how it feels to look back on a relationship and see all the broken parts . . . and wonder why you allowed yourself to keep living in it. But loneliness can be a scary place until we stop being afraid to be alone with ourselves. I didn't know that about myself, but I'm learning it.

It may sound weird, but now I know that love looks a whole lot like hours of comfortable silence on the couch together, or snort-laughing over inside jokes, or gentle words and tender compliments that warm the heart more than speed up the pulse (though those are nice too). I think if love is anything like what we've come to believe in our faith, we are left better and more secure than we were before. That's what I'm looking for. And you know, I don't think I would have appreciated it or even recognized it before now.

Maya Angelou said, "Have enough courage to trust love one more time and always one more time."

That's what I keep trying to believe, Luke. After everything. One more time.

You have one of the biggest hearts and most generous natures of anyone I know, even though you try to hide it. Someday you'll be someone's zing.

I'm really glad to hear you're moving back to Mt. Airy. I think we should pick up on our drive-in movie routine.

Izzy

PS: What is it that William Blake says? "Love seeketh not itself to please, Nor for itself hath any care, But for another gives its ease, And builds a Heaven in Hell's despair." In other words, "Love seeks not its own."

PPS: The boards on the back porch may not have been the reason I tripped, but I'm glad they're fixed now, nonetheless.

From: Luke Edgewood
To: Izzy Edgewood
Date: March 23
Subject: Re: One more time?

Instead of creating all the postscripts, why not just put the information into the body of the message? I'm still trying to understand if there's any rhyme or reason to postscripts at this point.

You're right about Clare. I just wish I'd seen it before I spent so much of my life with her.

I'm glad to come back home too. Already have three jobs lined up. One is building a rock fireplace for Grace Mitchell up in Ransom, which means a free meal every night.

I think you and Brodie have met through less conventional means, but the same truths still apply: two people building a relationship and trying to figure out if they are better together than apart. Despite all your teasing and self-deprecation, you have an immensely generous heart. It's why you truly believe in that "one more time" quote.

Someday a man will see behind your veil of introversion and catch a glimpse. Then he'll stop at nothing to show you how *he* sees you—and you won't be able to go back to anything less. You're worth that, Izzy.

Since I'm not against e-readers, I've downloaded one of P. G. Wodehouse's books and am already enjoying the humor. How's that for teasing you?

Please never type "someday you'll be someone's zing" ever again. You may want to stitch it on a pillow, but all I can think about is a really bad line in a rom-com.

Luke

PS: I can't fix your feet. Only your boards.

From: Josephine Martin
To: Izzy Edgewood
Date: March 24
Subject: Your bookish Rhett Butler & fashion choices

Izzy,

I can't help but feel that Patrick and I intruded on your dinner with Eli, but you appeared so genuine when you asked us to join you. And Eli was positively adamant! It would have been rude to refuse. Isn't he charming? How providential that he had a copy of his books on hand for us to purchase. I'm not much of a reader, but Patrick may like them.

Wouldn't it be a perfect match for you to marry an author? A bookworm like yourself paired with a man who creates books! And what wonderful work experience he has! To have worked in three different college settings over the past six years. Can you imagine the knowledge and talent he brings to teach at *our* community college! I imagine not many places can boast a PhD and author in their community college programs. It says a lot about his personality that he'd want to bring his expertise to our little town when he could find a job in so many other places.

I don't know why Patrick stayed so quiet all evening. The two of you barely spoke. It's a good thing that Eli and I have no trouble keeping a conversation going. Izzy, you must force yourself to talk to Eli if you want to snag him. You can't rely on me showing up every time. Surely you can find something related to books to talk about, though I do wish he hadn't discussed torture techniques in early Rome. I couldn't finish my chicken after that.

Josephine

PS: I left a box of clothes in the back of your car. Things I don't wear anymore. Please try some variety in your wardrobe. Black and brown are not the only colors in the world.

• •

From: Izzy Edgewood
To: Brodie Sutherland
Date: March 24
Subject: Brynna

Brodie,

I'm still chuckling at Brynna's first message. I suddenly feel that my emails to you weren't so long after all. Brynna's energy bubbles off the page so much that I actually laughed out loud. How do you manage such "sprightliness" on a daily basis? Do you have a sensory room to escape to after a conversation? But you were right, she does have a great deal of kindness in all of those words and loves you so much. In fact, she had so many good things to say about your entire family, it made me want to know more about them too. I guess the fact that your mom is English really answers the question about why you speak it so well.

I suggested a few simple changes to the website (photos of the inside of the shop as well as photos with PEOPLE in them inside the shop . . . We want the world to know that people like to be there). Featuring a book of the week on your blog or social media outlets may be a good idea, too, though Brynna alluded to the fact that there wasn't a blog and the website is fairly . . . archaic? I encouraged her to start simple but be consistent. All the information I've learned from classes list consistency as a key component in growing online engagement. Maybe she could try something with broad appeal to begin with and then as she becomes more comfortable, perhaps choose a different genre per day of the week to share a new release or enduring classic. I also included some social-media tips and tricks I've used for the library. I've been doing some extra research because I'm helping my cousin Luke build an online presence for the construction business he's starting here in town. He's allergic to social media.

BTW, as soon as the P. G. Wodehouse books were returned to the library, they were snatched up again before I could catch them. I settled on Sir Arthur Conan Doyle for now. However, to my surprise, Luke shows up at my apartment and reveals that *he's* the one who checked out the P. G. Wodehouse books from the library!! I saw him carrying one around yesterday. He even had the nerve to read a few funny quotes to me and then stop in the middle of an excellent scene and LEAVE THE ROOM! (I was ALMOST forced to purchase sight unseen, which I RARELY do when I can preview a book risk-free from the library.) However, there is no torture like an unfinished story! I'm trying to figure out how to get back at Luke. One time I left a copy of a bodice-ripping novel in the front seat of his truck for one of his work buddies to see . . . and then positioned myself across the street to watch the whole thing play out. I don't think I'd ever seen a human's face turn so red. He is definitely not the bodice-ripper sort of reader.

I look forward to our video chat tomorrow. I already know which tea I'm brewing for the occasion. And I'm making homemade shortbread in your honor.

Izzy

PS: I'm only ruthless to those I love. I don't try to embarrass the children at the library and, rarely, my coworkers. (If you met Luke, you'd understand why he's an exception.)

PPS: Do you read historical adventures set in ancient times? I'm currently reading a novel and I can't tell whether I'm having a difficult time getting through it because of the time period or the inflated characters.

From: Penelope Edgewood
To: Izzy Edgewood
Date: March 24
Subject: SCOTLAND

Izzy,

I had to message you as soon as I found out! My study abroad program next semester is in SCOTLAND!! Maybe I could take a little trip over to the Skymarian Islands and scout out Brodie and the Sutherlands. I'm very good at spying, you know. When we were in middle school, I unwrapped and rewrapped all of my Christmas presents four years straight without anyone ever knowing. And if you'll remember, I'm the one who knew Patrick was going to ask Josephine to marry him before anyone else did . . . and that was before he left the engagement ring out on the kitchen counter by mistake. I have a sixth sense about these things. I suppose being in theater for most of my life helps me read people.

I did send the link about Skymar to my professor, just so he'd know of it for future internships, and mentioned I'd be interested in switching if they found a place for me there. Though there aren't any musicals set in Skymar. At least with Scotland, I can put the soundtrack from *Brigadoon* on repeat.

By the way, a guy in my literature class is studying in Scotland too. He wears sweater-vests. Do you think he smokes a pipe? I've always envisioned sweater-vests and pipes together. I'm fine with the vest but I'd rather not date someone who smokes pipes. The tobacco smell sticks to your hair and clothes. Remember Grandfather! I'm going to see if I can get close enough to sniff him before I decide whether I'll flirt or not. You'd like him though, Izzy. He reads big books and has excellent posture.

Penelope

PS: Thank you for the care package. You know my love language is chocolate and Hallmark movies! And how on earth were you able to find an umbrella just like Mary Poppins's? I love it so much!! I almost started singing "Jolly Holiday" on my way to Advanced Public Relations, but it wasn't a holiday. I sang "Supercalifragilisticexpialidocious" instead.

PPS: Josephine said she met Clark Gable. She liked him a lot. What do you think about him? She took a photo of the two of you together, but I don't think it was a planned photo. It looks like she was trying to hide her phone behind her water glass, which made Clark's eyebrows massive.

• •

From: Izzy Edgewood
To: Josephine Martin
Date: March 25
Subject: Clothes and Eli

Josephine,

Thank you for the clothes. This batch actually had a few things that fit. The green sweater was particularly nice and the boots too. When did you ever wear a plaid skirt? It matches the navy blouse well but doesn't seem like your style at all.

Now, as to the practicality of some of the offerings. I don't wear high heels, miniskirts, shades of neon, or clothing that resembles an abominable snowman. I'm saving those for Penelope. If she doesn't wear them she can donate them to the drama department.

Eli enjoyed meeting you and Patrick. Yes, he always has copies of his books on hand and never tires of talking about them. I suppose if someone has invested so much time in creating a novel, they're going to feel attached to them—kind of like those two little lives you're carrying around with you now (only, your investment is much more . . . MORE . . . than paper-and-ink people).

To be honest, he is a perfect gentleman. Opens doors, asks some interesting questions, and really enjoys the higher-end restaurants in town. I don't think I've ever eaten such an amazing steak!

We have plans to attend the next bluegrass jam session at the Earle Theater on Friday. He's never been before, but first he wants to take me on a drive up the Blue Ridge Parkway. How could I refuse such an offer? The mountains are barely waking with spring!

I'll see you Sunday if not before. If you need me, call.

Henceforth, I shall refer to myself as Aunt Izzy. It has a nice ring to it, doesn't it? And instead of being like Austen's ostentatious Lady Catherine de Bourgh or supine Lady Bertram, my goal is to emulate the eccentric and adoring Aunt Betsey from *David Copperfield*.

Aunt Izzy

PS: When did you ever wear a caftan or tie-dyed shirt? And what sort of hat is that thing with the peacock feathers? I think this "nesting" you're doing has unearthed rare and disturbing clothing choices from your plant-based diet phase. You did some weird things during that year. Ones you can't remove without a great deal of pain.

PPS: I don't think you realize this, but you called Eli "Clark" on several occasions last night. Just thought you'd want to know.

From: Izzy Edgewood
To: Penelope Edgewood
Date: March 25
Subject: Re: SCOTLAND

Penelope,

How exciting! Scotland! I've always dreamed of going to Scotland. Are you properly prepared? I have a list of reading materials should you need one. It's sure to prepare you for every possibility, including surviving kidnapping, how to stowaway, the art of becoming an excellent thief, and tips on how to meet your dream Highlander through time travel. (Why do I keep renewing my passport if I've never used it? I think something needs to change. After all, Josephine says flying is the safest way to travel, though I'd prefer a magical wardrobe or even a portkey.)

As far as Clark Gable is concerned . . . we're still in the beginning phases. Conversations have been much better than previous first dinners with other men. He has an excellent vocabulary and is an easy conversationalist, never without something to say. Truly, he barely gives any time for silence between questions and comments, which makes my anxiety about finding the right words nearly nonexistent.

His reading interests are narrower than mine, but I suppose no one would find that a surprise.

And he is an excellent dresser. You'd definitely call him swoon-worthy.

I'm looking forward to learning more about his previous teaching experiences and what brought him to Mt. Airy from all the many other places he's been. I learned he has a sister who lives in Missouri near his parents, but he didn't talk much about them. He did seem interested in my opinions about what makes a good story, so we had a stimulating exchange about that.

I can't wait to learn exactly where you'll be in Scotland!

By the way, I'm talking with Mr. Fisher next week about his rental space. I'm not sure what he has in mind for leasing or selling it, but Josephine encouraged me to meet with him (in other words she set up the meeting, placed the reminder on my phone, *and* told me which outfit to wear to present myself in the most businesslike manner). Clearly I'm not listening to her. I'm not even sure I'm ready to make such a leap.

I'm off to have another video call with Brodie.

Love you,
Izzy

PS: There's really nothing wrong with excellent posture and I'm developing a deeper appreciation for sweater-vests.

• •

From: Brodie Sutherland
To: Izzy Edgewood
Date: March 26
Subject: Brynna and Wodehouse

Isabelle,

I'm still smiling over the idea of you dressing up as Gandalf, complete with beard, to read *The Hobbit* to your middle school group. Won't you give a demonstration during our next video chat complete with your best British accent too? I shall offer you a deal. If you'll read the first page of *The Hobbit* to me in costume, I'll attempt my very best Andy Griffith impersonation. Come now, if you can perform in front of a group of ten, what is one more?

Brynna cannot stop singing your praises. Very long songs, as a rule. Tolkien-worthy, in fact. But she's already begun to incorporate your suggestions with surprisingly positive responses. Not a great number yet, but as you've said, it takes time for changes to make a difference. Thank you for your generous heart. No wonder your library is doing so well!

I think I should like to meet Luke. I'm glad to hear he is enjoying Wodehouse. Perhaps he'd enjoy Terry Pratchett as well. He's a recent discovery of mine and the wit is superb.

I've always found literature set in ancient eras quite interesting. Homer's *The Iliad* & *The Odyssey* are a couple of my favorites, though I've come to enjoy more contemporary additions to the fictional genre, particularly if they include excellent descriptions of warfare. My uncle Sven had replicas of all sorts of weaponry, but particularly the ancient sort. We used to warn everyone to knock very loudly before entering his house.

On another note, the town of Skern is preparing for its Blossom Festival (or that is the translation in English—we call it Ditheanfest), which is a celebration of spring. April ushers in warmer temperatures and longer days. The entire town fills the streets to share their crafts, enjoy local music, and taste some of the first fruits of the season. I always plan to spend most of my week at the Skern Sutherland's shop during the festival. I'll send photos, if you'd like. The very best of festivals is in July: the King and Queen Festival. We celebrate art in all its forms. And, of course, excellent local cuisine.

It appears we are developing a certain pattern of video calls. Do those days and times consistently work for you?

Affectionately,
Brodie

PS: I found this quote by Wodehouse to be particularly fitting for our correspondence: "There is no surer foundation for a beautiful friendship than a mutual taste in literature."

From: Izzy Edgewood
To: Luke Edgewood, Penelope Edgewood
Date: March 26
Subject: Fictional-romance guilt or insanity?

Luke and Penelope,

I don't know why, but after I finished reading Brodie's most recent message, I wanted to cry. I'm not sad. I'm not sure what is wrong with me. Maybe the whole Eli/Brodie guilt is impacting me. Or maybe Josie's unpredictable hormones are rubbing off on people. Stay away, Penelope.

Izzy

PS: Luke, may I share your email address with Brodie? He'd like to talk Wodehouse with you.

From: Luke Edgewood
To: Izzy Edgewood, Penelope Edgewood
Date: March 26
Subject: Re: Fictional-romance guilt or insanity?

Authenticity matters.

I'd be happy to talk Wodehouse with Blighty.

Luke

PS: Somebody needs to have access to Brodie besides you. I can think of at least a dozen childhood stories you would never share with him. (And a few funny ones from adulthood too.)

Text from Izzy to Luke: I'm not sure I want to share your email with Brodie now.

Luke: You've already offered. I guess you'll just have to trust me.

Izzy: I'm doomed.

Text from Eli to Izzy: Izzy, I'm sorry I'm running late for our date. I'm on deadline for the next book and the words are flowing so well. Could we just meet at the Earle and forgo the Parkway this time? I'll make it up to you with ice cream after.

Izzy: Ice cream sounds good. See you at the Earle.

Eli: You're the best. I look forward to bluegrass and great company.

From: Izzy Edgewood
To: Luke Edgewood, Penelope Edgewood
Date: March 27
Subject: Eli and the theater

The jam session at the Earle tonight was extra special. Blue Ridge Strings debuted and, of course, dancing ensued. Jacob Carson, my favorite eight-year-old, gave me another lesson on square dancing etiquette, so I feel as though I'm less likely to destroy all of Luke's toes should he attempt to dance with me again.

Eli showed up about an hour late. The demands of the creative mind have no time expectation, I guess. He was in such good spirits and insisted on attempting to dance, and I couldn't help but laugh at the sudden spontaneity of his character. There must be some sort of euphoria that hits authors who reach a certain writing goal, because the man complimented me nearly every ten minutes and, likely from conversations with Josephine, asked me about my idea of owning a bookshop. His exuberance must have been contagious, because as he walked me to my car, he leaned over and kissed me . . . and I let him. Right in the middle of Main Street. Thankfully it was a relatively short kiss. Not quite the "kick your leg back" sort of kiss, but a nice, brief reintroduction to the world of real-life kissing. Having not been kissed for a few years, I have to admit appreciating the special attention. Needless to say, it was . . . sweet. He smelled like lemongrass and the sea. Eli is at that perfect tilt-your-head-back kissing height that I imagined as a teenager. (Sorry for the details, Luke. I'm sure you're cringing right now.)

Anyway, we've made plans to take a drive on the Parkway Saturday morning and I have the Book Parade that afternoon. Both of you should stop by! The children have much better costumes for the parade than I do. In fact, Penelope, I have a perfect outfit your sister gave me that resembles one of the creatures from Dr. Seuss . . . a Drum-Tummied Snum, I think.

Luke, I'm attaching a copy of the business cards I designed for you. Once I have your approval, we can order them. Just let me know at church what you think! I will exchange my hard work for certain library books you have in your possession.

Izzy

PS: Luke would look fabulous dressed as a Drum-Tummied Snum. Maybe *that* should be payment for the business cards.

PPS: Did you know that *dithean* means "blossoms" in Scottish-Gaelic?

• •

From: Luke Edgewood
To: Izzy Edgewood, Penelope Edgewood
Date: March 27
Subject: Re: Eli and the theater

Izzy,

There are moments when you do not have to copy me on emails.

Luke

• •

From: Penelope Edgewood
To: Luke Edgewood, Izzy Edgewood
Date: March 27
Subject: Re: Eli and the theater

Izzy!! I know exactly what you mean about kissing height. I've only dated guys who were taller than me, at least by two inches. Wouldn't it be horrible to never be able to wear heels because you'd dwarf your date?

Did Eli like the Earle Theater? And the wonderful music? It's one of my favorite things to do when I'm in town, but I think it's an acquired taste.

What were you wearing? That may have impacted his euphoria. I read that certain colors are more enlivening to certain men than others.

Love,
Penelope

PS: I'll see you at the parade, but I'm going as Dorothy Gale. Who can turn down red, shiny slippers?

• •

From: Luke Edgewood
To: Izzy Edgewood, Penelope Edgewood
Date: March 27
Subject: Re: Eli and the theater

Penny-girl,

I will reiterate. There are moments when you do not have to copy me on emails.

Luke

PS: I'll show up at the Book Parade as Tom Sawyer wearing a flannel shirt, jeans, and boots.

• •

From: Izzy Edgewood
To: Luke Edgewood, Penelope Edgewood
Date: March 27
Subject: Re: Eli and the theater

Luke, how is that any different than what you usually wear?

Izzy

From: Luke Edgewood

To: Izzy Edgewood, Penelope Edgewood

Date: March 27

Subject: Re: Eli and the theater

I'll have a piece of straw between my teeth.

Luke

CHAPTER 9

From: Izzy Edgewood
To: Brodie Sutherland
Date: March 27
Subject: Brynna and costumes

Brodie,

Costumes have been the topic of many a conversation lately. I'm trying to encourage Luke to be more inventive in his costumes, especially for the Book Parade next week.

As for your request? I'll dress in costume if you will! Are you up for the challenge? We could have an entire video chat in character, which should be pretty entertaining if you pull out the Yoda mask again. How long can you keep up the grammar of Yoda-speak, I wonder? I don't know, though, hearing your Andy Griffith impersonation may be more entertaining. What a conflict!

Our conversation about *Jane Eyre* last night has me contemplating whether Jane struggles a little with self-righteous pride. I'd never considered it before, so now I must reread the book to sort it out. I suppose you have stimulating conversations like this all of the time, but they're relatively new to me. The last invigorating bookish conversation I had was with a six-year-old who actually took Goldilocks's side in the Three Bears story. What are parents teaching their children nowadays? So what if there are talking bears who built a house and cooked porridge! It's never a good idea to break into someone's house! (I take serious book talk when I can get it.) That is why our conversations have been so refreshing! (BTW, whose side do you take in the Goldilocks story? Think very carefully before answering.)

Luke can be an excellent book conversationalist, but he's not very talkative, so as good as the conversations are, they're usually short.

How do you manage such positivity in a single person? I can feel Brynna's joy glowing through my computer screen with each message! And oh, how she loves Skymar! You've certainly shared so much about it, but I think Brynna is trying to convince me to visit. LOL.

I'm so glad some of my ideas have been helpful. It really is all due to Brynna, though. Her incorporation is what makes the difference and she's such an eager learner. I sent her to a few online sites to help with creating social-media graphics and banners. With a few tweaks, her ideas shone! She's a wonderful person to have on your team, Brodie, and so easy to work with.

As far as the library goes . . . I love working there, especially with the children, but to be perfectly honest, I've always dreamed of something else. I'm not really sure exactly what, though. I've contemplated opening my own bookshop or . . . some place I could cultivate an atmosphere to bring people together through books and stories? Well, that sounds about as wonderful as finding Aladdin's lamp, and though the library has the books, there's something about it that lacks the . . . I'm not sure. Magic? Connectivity? Something that used to fit isn't fitting anymore, I guess.

So . . . I have a meeting with a man next week who plans to lease (or sell) his antique shop in a few months. It's a fairly good location, but the building needs some work. The idea is a little daunting, to say the least, and perhaps I have a rosy view of it in my mind, but I've been collecting ideas for over eight years and they're nearly bursting to get out. We have an excellent bookshop in town, but she's already encouraged me to open another, especially since I have a different spin on my shop idea than she does. And it doesn't hurt to just dip my toe into this idea and see if it's the right one.

Blossom Festival? Ditheanfest? What a wonderful idea! I can't wait to see the photos. We have a large festival that happens in Mt. Airy, but it takes place in the fall. The Autumn Leaves Festival. Just before it we have Mayberry Days—a celebration of all things Andy Griffith. What does your spring look like? I'm imagining fairies and pink blossoms floating on an ocean breeze.

Speaking of festivals, on a much smaller scale our library is having its third annual Book Parade this Saturday (thus the costume talk). We build up the excitement (through the winter) by discussing characters from books, and each child chooses the character they're going to dress up as. Then we march down Main Street in our fashionable best (according to characters, of course). The shops down Main Street all get involved by making special treats and crafts of a bookish nature. We have characters from Laura Ingalls Wilder to Hercules to Arthur Dent marching with literary pride down the sidewalks. I'll see if Luke is willing to video some of it. Maybe even video live? Do you think you would be available around six o'clock-ish your time? (We usually start it at noon.) It really is worth seeing in real time.

And the King and Queen Festival? Just the idea of it makes me smile. What an excellent combination! Royalty and the arts!

I have our video chat schedule marked in purple on my calendar three times a week. Same days and times as last week? If you need to change them, let me know. My evenings are fairly flexible, except for Thursday evenings. I'm helping Josephine with housekeeping on Thursdays.

Thank you for these bookish conversations and the buds of a beautiful friendship. You've saved me from a life comprised solely of deep conversations with elementary school children. Imagine that! I am an expert in *Minecraft* and *The Legend of Zelda*, without having ever played either one. (Though I'm excellent at *Mario Kart*.)

Gratefully,
Izzy

PS: Wodehouse sounds like a very clever man.

PPS: Do you know what bluegrass music is?

• •

From: Josephine Martin
To: Izzy Edgewood
Date: March 28
Subject: The Book Parade

Izzy,

Where did Eli go? I thought he was joining you in the Book Parade. He promised me he would dress up as Clark Gable. It wouldn't take much. I told him you already had a top hat he could borrow.

You really outdid yourself with the Book Parade, Izzy. I was so proud of you! And dark blue is a lovely color on you. Who were you supposed to be? I'm so glad you chose to go with your natural hair color rather than the ghastly blonde wig you wore last year to be . . . who was it? Some elvish princess who handed out flashlights to small people? I've always preferred your brunette hair color. It's so unique with those tiny hints of auburn. Now if you'll stop adding teal streaks every once in a while . . .

But speaking of the parade . . . I think it's the largest procession you've ever had! I can't wait to have my babies join the parade. Are there any twins in literature? And don't you dare remind me of the ones from *Alice in Wonderland*. It's bad enough you've already bought them the Tweedledee and Tweedledum hats.

I hope to see you and Eli at church tomorrow. Isn't it nice to have Luke back in town? I didn't have to wait three days for a repairman to finally respond to my phone calls. Luke came after the fourth one. Patrick is excellent at changing light bulbs and trash bags, but that's about as far as it goes.

Want to get coffee Monday morning before work?

Josephine

PS: And why don't you bring a list of questions you could ask Mr. Fisher. We can go over them together.

PPS: You promised you'd never mention my tattoo ever again.

Text from Penelope to Izzy: Wasn't Eli supposed to be at the Book Parade, Izzy? I didn't see him on the video you sent! Kissing-height or not, an interested suitor should show up for a girl's favorite event of the year, if he can! I'm sure he isn't Brodie now.

From: Brodie Sutherland
To: Izzy Edgewood
Date: March 28
Subject: The Book Parade

Isabelle,

The Book Parade was brilliant! You are alive with creativity. It's remarkable, truly. The parade was your idea, wasn't it? From the time I've corresponded with you, it's become increasingly evident you have this almost endless supply of inventiveness that is both inspiring and contagious. I've been more productive in the past month and a half since knowing you than I have the previous four. Did someone in your life inspire your creativity or is it simply a God-given talent?

My mother was over the moon about the book parade idea. She adores books as much as Da did and one of her passions has always been inspiring children to love stories too. My parents worked together to find new ways to bring books to people in our community first, and then beyond. It's been a lot for her to take over in his absence (Anders and I are helping, of course, but she is quite determined to manage as much as she can on her own).

My uncle's and then my little sister's blindness spurred my parents to invent ways to bring stories to them, which is why Skern became a starting point for creating books in Braille long before other countries initiated the practice. My father even narrated a few books that have become local favorites. There's a great deal of comfort in finding an audiobook, even now, narrated by my da and hearing his voice speak to me through stories, as he'd done my entire life.

Luke provided an excellent live-video commentary along with attempting to sort out some of the costumes. I feel as though I already know him in part, through our conversations. His sense of humor is quite similar to yours. It was obvious how much the children enjoyed the parade, and evident how much you loved spending time with them.

Own a bookshop? It's perfect for you. What sort of Isabelle-like uniqueness would you bring into your shop? I get the sense it will feel very much like stepping through a magical wardrobe. Speaking of magical, you looked absolutely lovely in your costume. I didn't realize how long your hair was. It's beautiful. I shall never see Susan Pevensie in the same light again.

I have started rereading some C. S. Lewis classics. Do you enjoy his works in both fiction and nonfiction?

I did *not* know what bluegrass music was, but when I saw your question, I immediately researched it. Yes, I do like it. It sounds similar to some of the music here that stemmed from our Scottish ancestry. The stringed instruments and ballad-like songs. There's something very earthy and genuine in them, but I've never danced to such music. Have you?

Two left feet,
Brodie

PS: I accept your challenge for our next video call. What if I attempt Yoda with an Andy Griffith accent? "Ready are you? What'd y'all know of ready? For eight hundred years have I trained Jedi, y'all."

PPS: Yes, that was pitiful. Isn't it a wonder I'm still single?

From: Izzy Edgewood
To: Penelope Edgewood, Luke Edgewood
Date: March 28
Subject: Dorky Prince Charming?

Brodie has talked about me to his mother.

And he's adorably dorky sometimes. What am I to do with this? He lives on the other side of the world! He hasn't mentioned anything about a romantic relationship, but I end up daydreaming about him much more than a simple correspondence should inspire. Maybe I should end things now before my heart becomes more involved than it already is. Don't you think? I mean what could come from this? He has a family, a life, and career in Skymar. I hyperventilate at the thought of flying, let alone moving. And I'm sure he has no plans to move!

But the very idea of ending these delightful dialogues nearly brings me to tears. Is it possible to enjoy this sweet friendship without giving my heart away (as tempting as Brodie makes it)?

That's it. I'm pulling out my copy of *Wuthering Heights*.

Izzy

PS: Brodie thinks I'm beautiful. "Be with me always—take any form—drive me mad."

Text from Luke to Izzy: Izzy, I'm bringing over the cookie dough ice cream. Put down the Brontë.

From: Izzy Edgewood
To: Penelope Edgewood, Luke Edgewood
Date: March 29
Subject: Paper flowers?

Two bouquets arrived at my apartment this morning. One was of pink roses. The other was a bouquet of paper flowers, of different shades with words on them. The pink roses were from Eli. An apology bouquet. Evidently Eli stayed up late writing and developed a debilitating migraine. By the time he woke up, the parade was over. I wish I'd known ahead of time so I could have given his Mad Hatter Dinner ticket to Mr. Pressley. All the tickets had sold out online before he could purchase his. Maybe next year we should save some paper-copy purchases for our older population of folks who don't pay online.

Luke, I can only imagine you sent the others, because you know me so well! Paper flowers? Made from Shakespeare's sonnets!! They're more perfect than I can say! Where on earth did you find them? Thank you!

Izzy

From: Luke Edgewood
To: Izzy Edgewood, Penelope Edgewood
Date: March 29
Subject: Re: Paper flowers?

You know I'm proud of your book parade, but I didn't send you a bouquet of paper flowers. I would have sent something more practical. Like potatoes.

Luke

PS: Is face paint permanent? Because soap and water aren't working.

Text from Izzy to Luke: You didn't send the bouquet? Then who did? Penelope? (That doesn't seem in character with her. She's more of a singing-telegram or dinner-theater-ticket type person.)

Izzy: Oh no, Luke, did you let Johnson Lawson paint your face? You know he uses sharpies as a joke, right? Never trust an elementary school kid with freckles! I'll be over in a few hours with my special removal kit. Please tell me you didn't let him give you the Spider-Man face.

Luke: Then I won't tell you. See you soon.

From: Brodie Sutherland
To: Isabelle Edgewood, Luke Edgewood
Date: March 30
Subject: Face paint removal

Isabelle and Luke,

The video you sent of trying to remove permanent paint from Luke's face started my day off in all the right ways. I showed Mum and Brynna, and they laughed so hard they cried, quite literally. Fiona kept grinning from the accents and banter between the two of you. I can only imagine what she was envisioning in that pixie head of hers.

We are all in agreement that Luke could take on the Spider-Man look permanently, but the flannel shirt would have to go.

Affectionately,
Brodie

PS: I don't know why you should be "horrified" by snorting when you laugh. Genuine laughter, with or without a snort, is the only kind to really practice.

PPS: I look forward to our video chat tonight, Isabelle.

Text from Eli to Izzy: I'm so sorry to have missed your parade. May I take you out to dinner to celebrate your success? The local news station sang your praises. What great exposure! Let me make things up to you! You have my undivided attention now that I've finished my novel. Steaks? Mexican? Or the new German restaurant? I'm all yours.

From: Izzy Edgewood
To: Luke Edgewood, Penelope Edgewood
Date: March 30
Subject: Dating Eli?

So . . . Eli texted me about going to dinner to celebrate the parade's success. I don't know if my heart is in it, though. However, Josephine gave all the very vocal nudges at church (in front of half the women's ministry), that I was "dating" a nice professor right now. I don't care so much about what the women's ministry ladies think (half of them don't speak to me right now anyway because I dressed up as McGonagall from *Harry Potter* last year for Halloween) as much as not wasting an opportunity, you know? He's here. Right now. And he wants to get to know me better. That's worth a try, right?

I mean, Brodie is an ocean away. He's LIKE a dream. And there are times when I still wonder if he's real or some forward-thinking scientist who is deceiving me through excellent holograms.

Uncertain,
Izzy

PS: Luke, the black lines on your face were much lighter today! I don't think you'll scare the kids at the park if you go for a jog.

From: Penelope Edgewood
To: Izzy Edgewood, Luke Edgewood
Date: March 30
Subject: Re: Dating Eli?

Izzy,

I don't see why you wouldn't say yes to Eli, the author. It's a free meal and you like talking to him, right? Unless . . . you feel like your heart is much more attached to a single, sweater-vest–wearing Scandinavian Celt who will come and sweep you off your feet with his brogue, good looks, and Yoda impersonation?? Wow! What a combination! BTW, "dating" someone isn't the same thing as being in a "relationship" with someone, despite what Daddy says. He grew up during the time where two people still used words like *courting* and *betrothed*.

Penelope

PS: Wait, if Brodie sweeps you off your feet, does that mean he'd sweep you all the way to Skern or something? Oh no!! Izzy, I hadn't thought about that! Say yes to Eli, the author. I need to think about something else besides your sudden disappearance.

From: Izzy Edgewood
To: Luke Edgewood, Penelope Edgewood
Date: March 30
Subject: Re: Dating Eli?

Penelope,

I have no plans to move anywhere, hence the ongoing dilemma about dating or not dating two men on opposite sides of the world. (Good grief, that sounds convoluted.) My future is here, and besides, Brodie hasn't made any romantic overtures, per se. Besides, how could I even consider myself "dating" someone who I've never even met in real life, even if he wanted to "date" me? Which he's made no mention of *and* this has helped me make up my mind about Eli. (Can one even call an online date "dating"?)

Now the only question is steak, Mexican, or German? (You know how food choices for dates used to make me anxious? Compared to making lifelong romantic decisions, choosing restaurants is a piece of cake. Pun intended.)

Izzy

PS: Your dad is NOT that old. Most of the musical artists he loves are still alive and singing.

PPS: I looked up the word *dating* and the gist of the definition is two people meeting "socially" to ascertain future and long-term romantic compatibility. Therefore, I feel less guilty. A little.

PPPS: The word *aye* has a certain lovely appeal doesn't it?

Text from Izzy to Eli: I'd love to have dinner. What is your preference? German sounds like a fun adventure.

Eli: German it is! Tomorrow night? Seven o'clock?

Izzy: Great.

From: Izzy Edgewood
To: Brodie Sutherland
Date: March 30
Subject: Portable magic

Brodie,

You are the best Yoda Griffith I have ever known! I'm still grinning at your valiant attempt to combine the two. I still can't understand how you made the word *y'all* sound so delightful. Are you certain there isn't a little southern gentlemen in your family history?

The pointy green ears that bounced when you laughed became so distracting I forgot to ask you how Brynna liked the graphics I sent. She told me she adored them, but I have a feeling she's generous in her praise, as a rule.

Though I'm not a fan of Stephen King's books—not because of the writing (for he's an excellent writer) but for the itchy uneasiness his stories leave behind in my mind—I AM a supporter of his literary thinking. Here is an excellent quote: "Books are a uniquely portable magic." And to think we saw the magic come alive all the way down Main Street! The Book Parade pulls in so much of the community. I can imagine your towns would love something like this. Especially with all of the readers you have.

And what a beautiful family legacy you possess!! To love stories so much that your parents initiated bringing books to life for your uncle and sister . . . and then to so many more. Did your father ever narrate them in English? It explains why so many of my online searches about Skymar lead me to the book industry in one way or the other, particularly related to the fact that your islands are one of the top manufacturers of books in Braille! I've never thought about how words build pictures for the mind. I know it's true, but I've never really thought about it. Does your sister Fiona enjoy reading?

You are very kind. I don't feel particularly creative, but I'm grateful I can channel my almost-obsessive love for books into such delightful directions. Those children's smiles? An adult who shows up as soon as the doors open at the library to ensure they are first in line for the newest release of their favorite author? A story binding two uniquely different people together? It's fascinating and wonderful to me! I may not enjoy Josephine's matchmaking, but to match the right person with the right story is one of the most delightful things! It *is* kind of like magic happening right before my eyes.

What do you enjoy most about your job? Since you're a bookstore owner, I feel I could glean so much wisdom from you if I venture forward into my own little bookshop adventure. Maybe we could discuss it during our next video call?

I just finished reading George Orwell's novel *1984* for the first time. I don't care to read it ever again. It's brilliant and terrifying all at the same time. Please recommend something senseless, happy, and completely out of touch with reality so I can forget the possibility of the world turning into a totalitarian, repressive regime set to eradicate independent thought! I'm turning on the Hallmark channel right now for my own mental health. (Do you know what the Hallmark channel is?) Perhaps I should pick up *Catch-22*? Or Fielding's *Bridget Jones's Diary*? Or *Don Quixote*? What do you think?

Isabelle

PS: I've enjoyed *all* of C. S. Lewis's books. *Till We Have Faces* is one of my favorites, but I fell in love with Peter Pevensie when I was ten.

From: Izzy Edgewood
To: Penelope Edgewood, Luke Edgewood
Date: March 31
Subject: My life is a movie . . . but I'm not sure which genre

So I had a video call with Brodie before leaving for my dinner with Eli. (I'm squeezing my eyes closed at the very idea of . . . well, whatever it is right now.)

Eli and I had a good dinner. We talked books, and you know how much I love to talk books, but he did open up a little about his educational background and growing up near the coast. He doesn't seem to be very close to his family and isn't interested in getting a pet right now. He said "his stories are enough company and distraction for now." Being a person who has loads of imaginary friends, I could somewhat understand his statement—though I can't imagine life without Samwise. Also, he mentioned having some conflict with the university he was at before coming here and was "glad to move to a slower pace of life with folks who are generous-hearted." I've never been in academia, but the conflict among the staff of Hogwarts was constant, if not life-threatening, on a regular basis.

BTW, his ancient-historical adventure book was good. Not my favorite and a bit heavy on details at times, but interesting enough for me to finish it. Eli talked a lot about the writing process, so I know it must take up a great deal of space in his mind.

The new German restaurant in town is fabulous, BTW. We should go there together when Penelope is in from school next time. I couldn't pronounce half the dish names, but the waitress couldn't either so I didn't feel so bad about it, and when Eli tried, he ended up sounding like Arnold Schwarzenegger. Imagine that! A Clark Gable Terminator! LOL.

Anyway, Eli wants to try his hand at a contemporary romance novel. I always think it's interesting to get a guy's view on romance, so of course when he asked if I'd be willing to read a few chapters, I agreed. What an honor! I think it must be such a vulnerable thing to have someone read your infant words of a story! He's sending me the first three chapters. How exciting!

When he let me out at my house, he went in for another kiss (or at least that's what it looked like he was doing) and, for some reason, sweater-vests and Yoda masks popped to mind and I just couldn't kiss him. I'm likely never to even MEET Brodie!! How can he control my kissing future in this way?

What's worse: kissing a kind man just because he's physically present and nice enough, or daydreaming about a kiss to a possible Mr. Right that may never happen? What does Dr. Phil say about that, Luke?!

Brontë may be calling again.

Izzy

PS: Why does thinking about kissing have to be so preoccupying?

PPS: I think Yoda is my favorite *Star Wars* character.

CHAPTER 10

From: Luke Edgewood
To: Izzy Edgewood, Penelope Edgewood
Date: March 31
Subject: Re: My life is a movie . . . but I'm not sure which genre

Izzy,

I'm curious, and not about your kissing thoughts. If Eli did so much talking, what did he learn about you? Did he ask questions?

Yoda should be at the top of everyone's favorites list for *Star Wars* characters, but I feel your sudden interest in him runs in a more "islander" direction.

I don't think Dr. Phil would want to answer this one.

Luke

PS: Do you need me to bring ice cream?

PPS: I think your life is sci-fi and Eli is the hologram. Let's mix things up a bit.

From: Izzy Edgewood
To: Luke Edgewood, Penelope Edgewood
Date: March 31
Subject: Re: My life is a movie . . . but I'm not sure which genre

What do you mean? Of course he asked questions. Things like, "What do you like to do in your spare time?" Or "How do you respond when you're sad about something?" Though I'm not sure why he asked that. It was weird.

And I can be the heroine of this moment instead of hiding away. I'll purchase my own ice cream.

Sigh.

Izzy

PS: But I wouldn't mind the company. Brodie should be calling tonight because he can't tomorrow. You can join the discussion.

PPS: He didn't kiss like a hologram.

• •

From: Luke Edgewood
To: Izzy Edgewood, Penelope Edgewood
Date: March 31
Subject: Re: My life is a movie . . . but I'm not sure which genre

If he says something like, "Help me, Obi-Wan. You're my only hope," then we'll know something's wrong.

Luke

PS: Oh wait, never mind. He speaks fiction like you. That *Star Wars* quote is definitely a possibility in regular conversation.

• •

From: Penelope Edgewood
To: Izzy Edgewood

Date: March 31
Subject: Kissing talk

I want to be in a Brodie discussion. If he's going to sweep you away, I should at least get in on a discussion or two. He is not allowed to engage in any feet-sweeping without my approval, Izzy.

And I'm very happy you had a nice dinner with Eli. (Oh dear, your romantic life is becoming even more complicated than mine. Mean leading-man has suddenly become interested in Flower Girl #1 and I'm not sure why. I think it's because he heard how much my roommates enjoyed my cooking *and* I can waltz. For some reason he's attracted to waltzing.)

Eli must be terribly romantic if he wants to write romance books. What if he writes about you as his muse? Oh! I've always dreamed of being someone's muse. It sounds exotic . . . and possibly life-threatening.

Penelope

PS: In reference to kissing: Though my experience is limited in regards to this topic, I think the most important thing about a kiss is that you mean it. If you're not ready to mean it, then you're probably not ready to kiss. Did I get that thought from a classic movie? It sounds very classic, doesn't it?

PPS: I didn't include Luke on this email because he doesn't like kissing talk. Or classic movies.

• •

From: Izzy Edgewood
To: Penelope Edgewood

Date: March 31
Subject: Re: Kissing talk

Penelope,

I know your letter meant to help me, but . . . the idea of being someone's muse makes me feel . . . exposed. I can only envision Renaissance painters for some reason.

And there has been no talk whatsoever of feet sweeping. At all.

I love you anyway.

Izzy

PS: But I do like your thoughts about kissing. Even though I don't like your thoughts about kissing. You'll understand some day.

Text from Luke to Izzy: I don't think Clark Gable knows how to enter a church. Few people "saunter" down the center aisle to the second row when they're thirty minutes late to the service.

Izzy: He must have gotten the times mixed up. He doesn't appear to be one of those people who live by the rules of time, but there was certainly nothing wrong with his swagger.

Luke: I just got sick. Is it possible to use the word "sanctuary" to be protected from gross talk? Especially about a church service. Seems appropriate.

From: Josephine Martin
To: Izzy Edgewood

Date: April 1
Subject: Suits and swooning

Izzy!

Clark Gable looks excellent in a suit, doesn't he? I don't think half of the women in the church heard one word of the sermon from the time he made his way to your side on the second row. You're the envy of the entire single-women's section. Ah, I remember those days.

And I must say you made a fine showing in my old brown wrap dress. Much more stylish than what you usually wear, but I'd recommend a scarf with it the next time. You really need to wear more color. Beside Eli, you were like a wilted daisy next to a gallant ranunculus.

Josephine

PS: Next Sunday you should wear the little blue floral dress I sent. It would brighten up your pale face. I'm sure Eli would appreciate it.

From: Izzy Edgewood
To: Josephine Martin
Date: April 1
Subject: Re: Suits and swooning

Josephine,

Eli does wear a suit well. Much better than I could ever wear a suit. But comparing him to a ranunculus seems a little . . . I'm not even sure how to describe it. I'm going to ignore the wilted daisy comment. I do appreciate your fashion sense and I will even admit to liking several of the outfits you sent, but I am capable of dressing myself and have been for a few decades now. However, I do think it's time I got a haircut. Nothing drastic, but maybe some highlights and a few layers. If I'm going to start taking charge of my own story, it's time to make some changes.

Izzy

PS: Next week. I just called the hairstylist and I can't start changing my life until next week.

PPS: You're speaking in flowers. I feel like that should be a warning about something or other.

Text from Josephine to Izzy: What is going on with you? Are you sick? Is this what being in love does to you? Have things progressed that much with Eli? Highlights? Maybe we should call Mother.

Izzy: **I'm fine. Just realizing a lot of things. Good things. Highlights are definitely a part of it all.**

Josephine: Not teal! Please! Anything but teal!

Izzy: **I'm not in a teal mood. Maybe purple? To combat the wilted daisy look?**

Josephine: Isabelle Louisa Edgewood! I feel certain you are contributing to a few of MY highlights.

Izzy: **Josie, it's time to let go of this baby so you will be sufficiently prepared for your REAL babies when they arrive. I'll be okay. I promise. Even the wilted parts.**

Josephine: Stop with the flower references. You win.

From: Brodie Sutherland
To: Izzy Edgewood
Date: April 1
Subject: Revisiting bookish friends

Isabelle,

Your cousin's Yoda impersonation is better than mine. I'm not certain whether to feel disappointment or impressed. At any rate, I'm delighted you brought him on the video call. I must say I look forward to our video calls without exception but Luke certainly brought a hilarious addition. It is obvious how the two of you care for each other. Anders and I are close, but he is a bit more . . . stiff-shirted than Luke and therefore less likely to engage in Yoda impersonations or any other type of impersonations, unless he's occasionally and unintentionally going for Ebenezer Scrooge.

The photos of your mountains in spring are tremendous. The colors. The mountains. The vibrancy. I can only imagine that seeing them in person would be spectacular. I'm attaching a few photos of the islands in spring for your viewing pleasure. The cottage on the right of the cliffs in the photo is my grandfather's house (the one who carries a mustache comb). His view is beyond compare, in my opinion, and I'm biased in every way, though I have endeavored to re-create the view in my own way with my home.

I just finished reading Patrick O'Brian's series again. Those casts of characters are brilliantly portrayed. I read it once a year. That series and The Lord of the Rings, of course. Do you have a series that you must revisit, like an old friend?

Now I'm curious. What is it about the eldest Pevensie that turned your head?

Curiously,
Brodie

PS: Luke's complexion had a red tint to it. Please tell me it was because he was flushed and not due to the lingering effects of the permanent paint?

From: Izzy Edgewood
To: Luke Edgewood, Penelope Edgewood
Date: April 1
Subject: A friend for my heart?

So . . . Eli sent another bouquet of roses as a thank-you for me reading his chapters *and* he took me on the sweetest little picnic after church yesterday. It really was a beautiful day to view the azaleas beginning to bloom and the redbud in full purple array. (Just a note: I didn't see even ONE wilted daisy.) And Eli and I had some nice conversations about living in the country. He prefers to live near town but still appreciates the beauty of this place. He asked me what makes me laugh, and I told him excellent quotes, Samwise, and a few comedies I've loved forever. I couldn't shake the feeling he was taking mental notes on my answers, so I chalked it up to his very distractible mind.

I couldn't get him to open up too much about his past. Maybe he'll open up eventually. I've never valued freedom in conversation so much in my life, especially after all of these conversations with Brodie. It's made me realize how wonderful conversations with a man can be (besides you, Luke, of course). And you know, maybe I've never felt confident enough to try to be completely me in conversations . . . until now. It is very much like the quote Lizzie Bennet doles out on Darcy in *Pride and Prejudice* about his conversing easily with others. "I have always supposed it to be my own fault—because I would not take the trouble of practicing." And practice I have . . . and shall! Now that I've experienced the wonderfulness of it, I can't go back to awkward silence or one-way discourse. I am ruined to generic dialogue from this day forth.

I love these mountains, but I'm sending the most recent photos Brodie shared so that you all can appreciate the amazing beauty of his home. It looks like a magical place, like something from a historical-fantasy movie or a children's fairy-tale book. Unreal and vibrant and . . . too good to be true. Kind of like how I feel about Brodie.

Oh, but he's such a sweet friend. And that's how I see him now, as someone who fits into my day as easily as the two of you. I wouldn't have believed it possible that an online relationship could become so . . . real, but it has. Surprisingly and wonderfully real. No hologram could equal this.

And before you correct me, Penelope, it is only a friendship. I have to think of it that way. Even though we came to know one another through a dating site, there's been no talk of more. I'm happy with what it all is right now, and friendship "matches" have the potential to be every bit as powerful as the romantic sort. Just think of Merry and Pippin, or Eugene and Mortimer, or Sherlock and Watson.

Brodie seems to be such a *good* man. I mean, genuinely good. Yes he's quiet and quirky, but his heart is so full and kind. I never realized how much something like our conversations could mean to me. Simple conversations, without a kiss or handhold in sight.

Oh, how well Regency novels prepared me for this moment. Whew . . . what would dancing with him be like? I'm all aflutter!

This relationship with him has helped me notice a few things about myself, things I'd always refused to see. That I am worth knowing and seeing. That my thoughts and feelings matter, and though I've made lots of mistakes in relationships, they've not all been my fault. How could I have believed those lies for so long? Does hurt paired with insecurity somehow weed out common sense and replace it with blindness? It's made me want to really search deep for whatever dreams I've hidden away under the guise that . . . well, that they can't come true.

I would never have believed it and I don't really understand it, but how can I feel more connected to someone who lives on the other side of the world than to someone across the restaurant table? Does that make any sense at all?

What do I do with all these thoughts right now? I'm not quite sure. But there they are.

Wistfully,
Izzy

PS: It's strange to feel sort of peaceful about my romantic future for the first time in my life.

PPS: Can hidden dreams include flying?

• •

From: Luke Edgewood
To: Izzy Edgewood, Penelope Edgewood
Date: April 1
Subject: Re: A friend for my heart?

I'm surprised it took you this long to realize the ultimate value of words. Genuine ones. You're the bookworm after all. Funny thing about seeing trees and forests, isn't it?

My favorite friendship match is Calvin and Hobbes.

Luke

PS: I like Blighty. He laughed like he meant it.

PPS: I think your dreams are long overdue, unless it's the one about the giant book that eats people. I think you can return that one to the library now.

From: Izzy Edgewood
To: Luke Edgewood, Penelope Edgewood
Date: April 1
Subject: Re: A friend for my heart?

Speaking of words!! (Yes, Luke, I'm ignoring your big brother tone of voice.)

I just finished reading Eli's chapters. Oh dear, he cannot write romance. I actually cringed when reading something like, "She looked into his eyes, every fiber of her being hoping he cared for her. She trembled with the need for his love. For his acceptance of her. Even if all he ended up doing was allowing her to be near him. He was her everything. What would she do if he rejected her?"

This woman has no self-worth at all. Perhaps I should send excerpts of Lizzie Bennet, Jo March, or Hester Prynne to encourage a more well-rounded idea of fictional-female strength. "What would she do if he rejected her?" Grow a spine and create her own path, if she's worth the word *heroine*. And she wrings her hands incessantly. Why? Oh, let me tell you. "She ached for him to touch her fingers again. It seemed as if she couldn't keep her hands still from the memory of his warmth, so she twisted her fingers together, waiting. Hoping. When would he relieve her suffering?"

Oh good grief!

Maybe I should encourage him to return to ancient Greece.

Izzy

PS: Before you say anything about my similarities to his heroine, I will remind you that I am a changed woman. Or will be after my hair appointment. That is all.

PPS: Of course you would pick a boy with an imaginary tiger as his best friend, writes the man who had an imaginary monkey until he was . . . ?? Is Leopold still around?

From: Luke Edgewood
To: Izzy Edgewood, Penelope Edgewood
Date: April 1
Subject: Re: A friend for my heart?

Izzy,

The Easter Bunny is one thing. Don't mess with my monkey.

Luke

From: Penelope Edgewood
To: Luke Edgewood, Izzy Edgewood
Date: April 2
Subject: Re: A friend for my heart?

Izzy,

In my psychology class we learned that the best way to deal with sensitive artistic personalities like Eli's is to ask questions to help them come to their own conclusions. Directness may lead to internal wounds. Or was that about counseling teenagers? Oh well, I'm sure it works for both. And don't most authors write much better when they're depressed or angry? I seem to remember something like that from American literature class. Maybe you can become his inspiration with a little well-placed truth sprinkled in, Izzy. If anyone can sprinkle in truth for hard-headed and soft-hearted people, it's you! You've learned to do it so well with Mama and Josephine.

Thank you for sending photos of the Book Parade. I'm so sorry I didn't get to come. I had no idea they would have my internship interviews last week! What a time! You know, they asked me about Skymar and I have a curious feeling that they are considering sending me there instead!! Can you imagine!! I'll try not to get too excited about the possibility, but I've already favorited at least thirty webpages in anticipation. There is a musical set in Skymar! Did you know that? It's called *Hope Away*. I'm trying to scour the Internet for a glimpse.

As far as the Book Parade: You look wonderful!! I love how you curled your hair at the ends. I think the color of your dress really must have brought out your eyes because they looked so vibrant from the photos . . . Either that or it was the glimmer of terror as you tried to keep King Arthur from knocking Anne Shirley over the head with his foam sword. Terror makes my eyes look brighter too.

I hope I can attend the parade next year. I've kept my Cinderella dress since high school for just an opportunity like this! I'm afraid the Dorothy Gale shoes have gone the way of my roommate's puppy. When I found out, I may have yelled something about houses dropping, to which I was immediately remorseful. I've seen *Wicked*. Even the greenest witch has a deeper story.

I have a date with sweater-vest boy. (Mean leading-man didn't like it at all, so I was quite happy.) His name is Andrew. He doesn't watch Hallmark movies, but he likes *Poldark*, so there's hope. And he doesn't smell like tobacco. He smells like coffee.

Love,
Penelope

PS: I totally understand about the hair appointment and change.

• •

From: Luke Edgewood
To: Izzy Edgewood, Penelope Edgewood
Date: April 2
Subject: Re: A friend for my heart?

Hair appointment? Change? I'm not even going to ask.

Luke

From: Izzy Edgewood
To: Luke Edgewood, Penelope Edgewood
Date: April 2
Subject: Re: A friend for my heart?

Penelope,

Poldark says a lot about Andrew, as does the sweater-vest. With only that to go on, I think you definitely have a good start. I can't wait to hear how the date goes. You must call me to fill me in. I love to hear the excitement in your voice as you describe the evening. I also can listen to you lambast him in the safe haven of our conversation should the date turn in a less satisfactory direction.

The Book Parade exceeded my expectations. I was afraid, with fewer children picking up books nowadays, my little plan to encourage reading would blow up in my face, but it's only grown! We had four more businesses participate and thirty more children. I must say, Penelope, I don't think I've been as proud of anything in my life as I am of our community coming out to support smiling children donning bookish costumes.

I have started reading the next three chapters in Eli's newest manuscript. The woman, a librarian, has long chestnut-colored hair and brown eyes which are "too big for her face." Evidently they're the kind "a man falls into." Why does that sound like a compliment and an insult at the same time? Also, why does it sound like *me*?

There may also have been a reference to *The Office*, which I had mentioned as a television show that made me laugh. Hmm . . .

Love,

Izzy

PS: I tend to agree with Lemony Snicket when he writes, "Never trust anyone who has not brought a book with them." Digital ones count in this day and age, but a page-and-spine book in a man's hands? Well, I'm not sure there's anything as initially attractive in the whole world!

PPS: Eli kissed me quite by surprise. I would have to possess a large emotion, indeed, to initiate a kiss, and I seriously doubt that will ever happen.

Text from Eli to Izzy: Izzy, would you have time for coffee tomorrow morning? I have questions about the comments you left on my manuscript. Why would you think my heroine needs to be stronger? "She needs more strength of character," you said. I don't understand. Is this one of those feminist comments?

Izzy: Yes, I can meet. No, it's not a feminist comment; it's an editorial/reader one. In romantic comedies it's fine if the heroine is going to "grow" into more strength of character as the story progresses, but to be a "heroine" she really needs a few defining qualities as to why the hero would be attracted to her in the first place. There's nothing heroic about a weak character who doesn't make any decisions for herself, especially in a contemporary romance. Women have to like her.

Eli: Weak? She's not weak. She's just in love.

Izzy: Love does lots of things, I'm sure, but having a woman weep over a man giving her a brownie is usually not

one of them (with one caveat that only women truly understand). What can you give her that shows why the hero is attracted to her? That would help. Plus making her less weepy.

Eli: That's a little harsh, Izzy. When a woman is smitten, she'll act in many different ways. I'm surprised you'd call her weak to be in love.

Izzy: When you become a woman who is smitten, then you can argue with me. And, yes, women have a tendency to respond irrationally sometimes, but no woman wants to appear empty-headed or weak willed. Your female readers (who are the majority of romance readers) will not appreciate her.

From: Josephine Martin
To: Izzy Edgewood
Date: April 2
Subject: Mother

Izzy,

Have you spoken to Mother in the last few days? I know you've been busy with the Book Parade and the fundraiser, so you may not have had a chance, but you're going to love the news she has for you. Act surprised when she tells you, all right? In preparation for becoming a grandmother, she's retiring from the library! She's thought about it for a while, but with twins and the needs I'm sure to have, she's decided to go ahead and do it. You know what that means. You can become the head librarian! With the small raise and the natural prestige, you'll be set for the rest of your life. You won't have to go through the horrid chore of opening your own bookshop. Do you remember when I started my own small business? It was exhausting. If I hadn't had you helping me with the business side of things, it would never have done so well. This will solve all of your problems (except the boyfriend one . . . but you're working on that with Mr. Gable).

It really is a perfect solution for everyone. Mother has a successor she can trust to maintain her excellent vision for the library and you can continue with your lifelong obsession of books. No one could be better to carry on Mother's legacy than you, of course. It's all so wonderfully settled.

Perhaps you can use all the money you've been saving for the business (which isn't likely to succeed in town since there is already one successful bookshop) to travel like you've always wanted to do. What a wonderful opportunity all around! I'm so excited for you. I'm certain Mother will speak with you about it soon. She hopes to retire by September, but doesn't feel there is a need to hurry since she has you.

Oh, Izzy, don't you just love it when all of these points converge to reveal a perfect happily ever after?

Josephine

PS: What a perfect match for a librarian and an author to become a pair! And think how much his contacts could help support the library. It's almost too perfect!!

From: Izzy Edgewood
To: Josephine Martin
Date: April 2
Subject: Re: Mother

Is this a belated April Fools' joke, Josie? You don't seem the sort, but I'm just checking before I respond.

Izzy

PS: When all the points converge, it can also reveal a Bermuda Triangle.

From: Izzy Edgewood
To: Luke Edgewood, Penelope Edgewood
Date: April 2
Subject: Aunt Louisa and my future

I just got off of an excellent video call with Brodie where we spent half of the time sharing our favorite Calvin and Hobbes stories, when an email from Josie deflated my happiness like nothing else. Did either of you know Aunt Louisa planned to retire from the library in September? Josie says she wants to have freedom to help with the twins when they arrive, which I cannot fault her for at all, but retire?

And of course that means she's looking to me to take over the library, which vanquishes the bookshop idea or any other future dream-job ideas. I know Aunt Louisa and Josie have the best intentions, but I'd appreciate a say in the workings of my own future. I know you both understand. Luke, Josie had you enrolled in three different schools with your career all planned out as a veterinarian. And Penelope, she nearly forced you to become a contestant on some spinoff of *The Voice*.

True, Josie isn't as bad as Miss Havisham, but she's certainly on the same page as Austen's Mrs. Bennet with a little Catherine de

Bourgh stubbornness sprinkled in for good measure. Whatever hormone power those twins are giving her right now is only fueling the emotional madness!

I love the library. I've grown so much as a person and a part of our community since taking the job. It's allowed me the freedom to research marketing, small business tips, and creative ideas to enhance such a historical place, but become head librarian? Is that what I want?

My heart squeezes against the thought. I'm thirty. I've lived in this community my whole life. My best friends are my cousins. My favorite conversations are online with a man who lives in a foreign country. My dog has a healthier social life than I do.

Some days I feel as though I'm stuck on a conveyor belt with no ability to alter the course of my future. I don't expect starting my own bookshop to be an easy task, but succeed or fail, it would be *my* plan. Is it crazy to want to run away from home at thirty years old? To drop everything and redirect your life? To grasp the "what-ifs"?

I don't expect an answer. I think I just needed to voice my thoughts. Seeing them in print helps me process, as you know.

I love you both,
Izzy

PS: I've always liked the name The Prints & the BookWyrm. Isn't that a cute name?

From: Luke Edgewood
To: Izzy Edgewood, Penelope Edgewood
Date: April 2
Subject: Re: Aunt Louisa and my future

What do you want, Izzy? Once you know the answer, you'll become the heroine of your own story.

Luke

PS: The Prints & the BookWyrm is a fun name. Sounds like a book that needs to be written.

• •

From: Penelope Edgewood
To: Izzy Edgewood, Luke Edgewood
Date: April 2
Subject: Re: Aunt Louisa and my future

Izzy,

I think you're right about Josephine and the hormone hurricane. I've not been around a great many pregnant women, but I've seen all the *Father of the Bride* movies! Patrick is a prince, and he doesn't even wear sweater-vests.

Penelope

PS: I know you love the library, but I've always wondered if you'd fit there forever. Your imagination always seemed too . . . extraordinary for ordinary things, but what do I know? Luke still makes fun of me for pretending Santa Claus is real. How can I not? If I don't believe in Santa Claus, I'll never find my Hallmark hero, will I?

• •

From: Luke Edgewood
To: Izzy Edgewood, Penelope Edgewood

Date: April 2
Subject: Re: Aunt Louisa and my future

Penelope,

Hallmark heroes aren't real either.

Love,
Your brother, the Grinch

Text from Izzy to Luke: You are right, Luke. How pitiful that I don't know what I want, but Aunt Louisa's decision has spurred me into really contemplating this more than ever. Something MUST change and that something is me. BTW, a children's book with a title like *The Prints & the BookWyrm* sounds great. A book-reading dragon.
Luke: Or a book-loving woman and her own book-loving prince?
Izzy: Luke? Is that you? You almost sound . . . romantic?
Luke: Sorry, my dog got ahold of my phone.

From: Izzy Edgewood
To: Luke Edgewood, Penelope Edgewood
Date: April 3
Subject: The strange case of Eli and romance

Eli Montgomery is a curious sort of person. We just finished a short meeting for coffee at Pages Bookstore to discuss his current manuscript. He listened to my suggestions, asked questions, made notes, and then handed me three more chapters. Sometimes he is delightful company instead of distracted, a little moody, and ready to talk rather than listen. And he was so grateful to me for reading his manuscript and providing detailed notes in the margins that he complimented my purple blouse, my hairstyle (which consisted of a messy bun held in place by two pencils), and my complexion.

Oh, and he apologized for the whole "women in love have no spine" conversation. I think he really is clueless about the whole romance thing.

Speaking of romance, how was your date with Andrew, Penelope?

Izzy

PS: Guess what Eli's book "heroine's" name is? Bella. Hmm . . .

PPS: You don't think Eli would only be seeing me because I'm helping him with his book, do you? I have a tendency to find men who want me for the ways I can enhance their futures instead of wanting me for . . . me.

* * *

From: Luke Edgewood
To: Izzy Edgewood, Penelope Edgewood
Date: April 3
Subject: Re: The strange case of Eli and romance

Clearly you're the woman of his fictional dreams, Izzy. Pencil in your hair, great complexion, and an excellent editor. A romance built through Track Changes.

Luke

PS: If you have doubts, tread carefully with your heart.

From: Izzy Edgewood

To: Luke Edgewood, Penelope Edgewood

Date: April 3

Subject: Re: The strange case of Eli and romance

You've been reading too much Wodehouse. Or Shakespeare. I can't figure out which one?

Izzy

PS: The only hearts involved with Eli and me are of the fictional variety.

From: Luke Edgewood

To: Izzy Edgewood, Penelope Edgewood

Date: April 3

Subject: Re: The strange case of Eli and romance

I don't read Shakespeare. I watch it.

Luke

From: Penelope Edgewood

To: Izzy Edgewood, Luke Edgewood

Date: April 3

Subject: News

I've decided to quit school and marry Andrew.

We're an excellent match. He watched a Hallmark movie with me yesterday and didn't laugh when I got all emotional. Will you be my maid of honor? Josephine would never approve.

Penelope

PS: April Fools'!

PPS: Except the Hallmark part. And Josie part.

PPPS: Aren't most men clueless about romance?

• •

From: Izzy Edgewood
To: Penelope Edgewood, Luke Edgewood
Date: April 3
Subject: Re: News

Penelope,

Thank you. You just clarified so much for me. I love you.

Izzy

• •

From: Luke Edgewood
To: Izzy Edgewood, Penelope Edgewood
Date: April 3
Subject: Re: News

Penny-girl,

Check your calendar.

Luke

PS: I'm assuming you were not talking about me in reference to "clueless"? I'm the very model of a romantic. It's the flannel.

From: Brodie Sutherland
To: Izzy Edgewood
Date: April 4
Subject: Special delivery

Isabelle,

You should receive a digital gift within the next few days. Since you are so fond of Peter Pevensie, I've sent you a copy of my father reading *The Lion, The Witch and the Wardrobe.* His accent is thick, but I thought you'd appreciate it all the more. I don't know how I can compete with a king of Narnia, but I felt certain the Yoda ears left a lasting impression.

I answered a few of your questions in our last video call, but when I checked your last email, there is one to which I forgot to respond.

Fiona loves to read. Though she's excellent with Braille, she enjoys being read to most of all. I suppose it's from a habit our family began when she was a young child, well before she began losing her sight. I've always enjoyed hearing books read aloud, if done with expression. How about you?

By the way, have you ever considered writing? Your wit and charm in our emails lend themselves to an almost lyrical quality. Add to that your imagination, creativity, and love of books, and it seems the perfect recipe for an author. I realize you may not care at all about authoring, but learning you, as I am, I couldn't help but wonder.

I know I gave you a few lighthearted recommendations during our video call last night, but I thought of another one this morning. *Cold Comfort Farm* by Stella Gibbons. I think you'd enjoy the humor and the bossy heroine that sounds (at times) like your cousin Josie.

I enjoy my job for many of the same reasons you mentioned enjoying yours. Bringing stories to people. Helping them discover new adventures. When I opened the Brynnwick shop (the first one I started on my own), the wonder and excitement of the townspeople to have easy access to books humbled and energized me. I feel as though *this* is what God has created me to do and I'm gladly walking in it. Some of the intricacies of the business aspects are not my favorite, but the positives always outweigh the negatives, to my mind. I also enjoy getting to travel, now that Sutherland's is beginning to spread its wings across the Channel, perhaps. We are still trying to sort out the particulars of that decision. I have misgivings due to the costs, but Mum is determined.

Have you obtained Wodehouse from Luke yet? We've had a few humorous emails over the books.

Affectionately,
Brodie

PS: I have a booksellers convention in New York at the end of May. If you're amenable to it, I'd like to fly in a couple of weeks early and visit you while I'm relatively nearby. How would you feel about that possibility?

CHAPTER 11

From: Izzy Edgewood
To: Luke Edgewood, Penelope Edgewood
Date: April 4
Subject: Breakdown in progress

Luke and Penelope,

I no longer celebrate April Fools' Day. And the previous sense of peace and enlightenment is gone.

Do not message me unless you have absolutely nothing to say, no news, and no requests.

I don't think I can handle more this week. Between Josie and the library, Eli and his ill-interpreted romance, and Brodie and his news . . . I can't.

Izzy

PS: Is God laughing?

From: Luke Edgewood
To: Izzy Edgewood, Penelope Edgewood
Date: April 4
Subject: Re: Breakdown in progress

Does Brodie even celebrate April Fools' Day? Besides, Penelope must be rubbing off on you because today is the fourth. You can't NOT respond to him. He's a good guy. Get over your shock and email him back. I won't say God isn't laughing because, well, you're funny, especially when you don't mean to be, but I'm pretty sure He has something to do with this. You know, since He's an omnipresent, omniscient, all-powerful being.

You ordered espresso instead of tea for breakfast this morning when we met. It's obvious Brodie's request knocked you for a loop, but you love plot twists. You can handle it. Maybe it's the plot twist you've been waiting for your whole life.

Luke

PS: Never get espresso again. At one point you started speaking so fast I couldn't understand you—and your eye started twitching. It almost encouraged me to usher up a prayer or two for you.

From: Izzy Edgewood
To: Luke Edgewood
Date: April 4
Subject: Re: Breakdown in progress

Why am I so afraid of him coming, Luke? I've been asking myself this question all morning. I'm a changed woman after all (or will be in two days after my minimal hairstyle adjustment). The idea of meeting him in person carries with it a paralyzing mixture of fear and excitement. Is it because his visit takes him from being an almost fictional person and brings him to real life? Am I concerned once he meets me, our wonderful conversations will end because I'm not what he expected? Am I terrified he'll be everything he seems to be and my heart will never recover? And if he is . . . what happens next? We live thousands of miles apart. We have two very set, separate lives. I can't ask him to leave his family and community and I don't want to leave mine. Having in person conversations with him would add spikes to that impasse, that decision.

I've been okay with fictionally wonderful people. I can close the book after the last page and daydream about their perfect lives. If Brodie comes to Mt. Airy, he will most certainly step from a fictional, framed-by-a-computer-screen person into the real world.

I don't know any brand of cookie dough ice cream with the potency to comfort me in this situation, Luke. It's truly a moment for melodrama like Brontë. Or *Lord of the Flies*. Or a Shakespeare tragedy.

Izzy

PS: I don't think a haircut can prepare me for this kind of change. Maybe I need to do something really life altering in preparation . . . like kickboxing.

Text from Luke to Izzy: Didn't you just say something recently about being brave?

Izzy: I'm groaning at your reminder. Yes, I did! I just wanted more time to build my courage. Ack! Blast those fairy tales. I love them and hate them all at once right now.

• •

From: Izzy Edgewood

To: Luke Edgewood, Penelope Edgewood

Date: April 4
Subject: And the Eli mystery continues

Here's the most recent Eli manuscript information. Are you ready for this? His heroine (the LIBRARIAN named BELLA, just in case you didn't remember the strange and rather disturbing similarities) wears a lot of brown and struggles with making decisions, which is why she's so enamored with the hero, Ross, who gives her "timid heart an anchor on which to steady her fragile worth."

No. Just no. Want to see me make a few decisions? Here we go. I'm going shopping tomorrow and updating my wardrobe. I'm emailing Brodie and welcoming him to the Blue Ridge. I'm going to give in to the tug and read a Debbie Macomber book. And then . . . I'm going to tell Aunt Louisa that I'm not ready to become the head librarian. Okay, maybe I'm not brave enough to do the latter yet, but once I decide, I'll make the decision with great certainty.

Izzy

PS: To get really crazy, I'm going to eat mint chocolate chip ice cream instead of cookie dough. Ha! See there? Decision-making aplenty!

Text from Luke to Izzy: Is this an April Fools' joke? Mint chocolate chip? *gasp* You wild woman, you. Oh wait! It's April FOURTH. All of the other things are believable.

Izzy: You're not funny.

Luke: I'm hilarious. Write to Brodie.

From: Izzy Edgewood
To: Brodie Sutherland
Date: April 5
Subject: Peter Pevensie and Wodehouse

Brodie,

I wanted to go ahead and respond to your last email before our video call tonight to let you know the audiobook arrived in my in-box this morning. I'm looking forward to hearing your father read Narnia. I can only imagine what he sounds like as Aslan, if his accent and voice are anything like yours, so warm and soothing. The anticipation is thrilling. Thank you very much. Peter Pevensie could never compete with your Yoda ears and overuse of the word *y'all*. And, yes, I adore hearing books read aloud. There's something magical about closing one's eyes and just "feeling" the book wrap around you. Or at least that's what it's like for me.

I will tell you something that only Luke knows. I used to write children's books, but I feel I'm more of a concept story person than an actual nuts-and-bolts writer. (Though Luke has a great gift for rhyme and should attempt his own children's book with Dr. Seuss flare, but I can't convince him.) I love creating fairy tales of my own, but Luke is the only one who's ever read any of my ideas because I can't imagine them measuring up to the classics I hold so dear to my heart. Usually I come up with them in response to reading a poorly written children's book. Then I feel compelled to set things right, at least in my own mind, by creating one that's better. Some of my ideas revolved around Appalachian culture and I added a bit of Celtic "magic" from our ancestry to create more homespun fairy tales, but to be perfectly honest, my real love is creating an atmosphere for others to fall in love with stories. I don't know if there is a profession for "book atmosphere creator."

I love the sentiment that you're doing what God created you to do! I am still sorting out where I'm supposed to be and what I'm intending to do, but I know it involves books and children and . . . possibly dressing in a story costume on occasion. Dreams are tricky things, aren't they? Sometimes they feel as elusive as fog, other times as blinding, and sometimes . . . perfectly clear. I'm in the "foggy" spot right now.

I don't think anyone has ever referred to me as witty or charming. I'm glad you think so. I may be tempted to use your opinion as a defense when Josie calls me dull and uninteresting. Evidently, if I brighten my wardrobe, I automatically brighten my prospects. Very Cinderella-ish of her, isn't it?

Luke has relinquished one Wodehouse book. He's keeping the others to reread . . . and likely taunt me. He enjoys dangling words over my head at any opportunity. It really is one of the worst punishments known to booklovers.

I look forward to talking with you this afternoon.

Izzy

PS: I'm amenable (as well as pleasantly surprised and a bit nervous) to have you visit. Would you like me to send a list of hotels or . . . if you're brave enough, you could stay with Luke. He's offered, so that says something. I can't vouch for his cooking, but he'll provide a great deal of comic relief and, unfortunately for me, plenty of embarrassing stories from days long ago (or . . . not so long ago).

From: Dr. Eli Montgomery
To: Izzy Edgewood
Date: April 5
Subject: Edits

Izzy,

Your notes regarding my heroine are fabulous! You truly seem to *get* the heart of my story. I'm so glad we met. I feel as though we're a perfect pair—you with your eye for detail and me with my story creating.

How about dinner Friday night? The Italian restaurant on Main Street has a great reputation. I'll bring more chapters. You bring your beautiful smile and conversation. I don't think I've ever had as much fun talking books with anyone before.

Eli

From: Izzy Edgewood
To: Dr. Eli Montgomery
Date: April 5
Subject: Re: Edits

You're welcome. Yes, I can meet you on Friday. I think it would be good to talk over what makes a good hero in romantic books too. Readers will find him much more appealing if he talked less about his accolades, adventures, and pursuits and tried to show more care for others. Most heroes are that way, if you read more eclectically. It's a great character trait in both fictional and nonfictional people.

Izzy

PS: Good conversations are wonderful things, aren't they?

• •

From: Brodie Sutherland
To: Izzy Edgewood
Date: April 5
Subject: Books, atmosphere, and hobbies

Isabelle,

I knew it! I knew you had to have some sort of writing outlet for all the passion you have in your words. It seemed impossible not to reconcile the two. Are you an artist as well? Singer? Do you play any instruments? I attempted the trumpet, but my brother said I didn't have enough . . . what would you call it? "Hot air" to keep the notes solid. However, he took up the trumpet without any trouble. What does that say of my brother . . . and hot air?

I hope at some point, when you feel ready, I can convince you to share your story ideas. Then I can encourage you to do something more than hide them with Luke as your only audience. I have a keen eye for good stories and have tried my hand at a few nonsensical ones here and there (perhaps Luke and I should coauthor something Seussian and ridiculous). It's one of the reasons my father put me in charge of book ordering when I first started with the business. Some of the reason had to do with my natural love of reading, of course, as well as the speed at which I read, but Da used to say I had a nose for a solid story. I can only imagine what your stories must be like. And perhaps it has something to do with this foggy dream of yours?

And as far as creating an atmosphere for books as an employment—that is brilliant! A good story is one thing, an atmosphere that encourages marination in the story is icing on the proverbial cake. It is my opinion that good editors and storytellers do just that. When someone loves a story, that love casts some sort of spell to draw others into the magic. Excellent idea! I can only imagine how you make this sort of magic happen at the library after seeing your book parade.

I wish Sutherland's could find a way to differentiate our brand so we could have a unique yet broader appeal. That is one of my plans for the future, but if your story-atmospheric brain thinks of any ideas, I'll be happy to hear them. To be honest, the longer I work in this profession, the more I realize how very far behind the times our shops are. Mum and Anders are reluctant to change them, and I'm afraid neither Brynna nor I have found a way (or an idea) to inspire change.

You asked during our call last night about my hobbies, as if there are some other than reading. Since our call was cut short due to connectivity issues, I thought I could share a few through this means. As we've discussed before, I enjoy nature and walks. There are excellent places to explore near Skern but also all over the islands. Since taking on a co-owner role of Sutherland's, I've found such pleasure in traveling. Visiting new places in books will always be a joy, but adding the other senses to the experience really brings those books to life like nothing else. Otherwise I live a fairly quiet existence, except for trying to find a pair of shoes each morning that don't have teeth marks on them. I can become quite vocal at those times. Argos doesn't seem to be impressed whether my tirade is in Caedric or English. I'm also growing, very slowly, mind you, in my house repair skills. I've finally restored enough rooms in Waithcliff to reside here, but there are still so many things to do. However, I will content myself with my privacy, books, a fantastic view, and your virtual company.

In other news Fiona is attempting to convince me to sign up as her dance partner for lessons. My elder brother, Anders, will have nothing to do with it, so the task is left to me to look into her pleading face and say no. What a struggle between pride and the powerful force of a little sister. I have a feeling my pride will go before I fall . . . learning the quickstep.

There's a lovely forest near here that I think you'd enjoy. You can see mountains, trees, a lake that spills into a river, and then the sea. To my mind it's the best of every world rolled up into a two-mile walk. It's an excellent place to conjure up fairy stories, if one had a gift for it.

How is your cousin doing with her pregnancy? I think you mentioned the doctor was threatening confinement? From the impression you've given of her, I feel her confinement may bring the house down. Would that be a proper inference?

I see you've already made Luke aware of my travel plans. He's sent an email confirming your suggestion of a place to stay. He seems like a good chap, but is, as you've put it, very much like your older brother. This wouldn't be a case of "keeping your friends close but your enemies closer," would it? He'd find no enemy here. Only allies who want to become friends.

Affectionately,
Brodie

PS. I'm glad my visit is a pleasant surprise. I hope you'll continue to think so. I'm a bit nervous myself. I'm much more interesting on paper than in real life, but hopefully you'll overlook the blemishes and awkwardness. Just remember hobbits and Wodehouse and Yoda ears. If that's not a remedy for awkwardness, I have no idea what is.

PPS: At the risk of sounding more awkward than usual, your new hairstyle is lovely.

From: Izzy Edgewood
To: Brodie Sutherland
Date: April 6
Subject: Waithcliff?

You have a house called Waithcliff? If you tell me it is set on a cliff, I may think our entire relationship is one long daydream. Waithcliff? Brodie! That is a very bookish sounding name. Is it an old house? Damaged by war or age? Are there ghosts in the shadows? Or wives in the attic?

You must tell more on our next video call, because I have a girlish addiction to manor houses. Don't ask Luke about it! He may share too much information, especially in regard to my junior year of high school, a beach trip, and an unfortunate accident of breaking and entering.

Izzy

PS: I like to sing, but that doesn't mean I'm good at it.

PPS: And let's not discuss my drawing abilities.

From: Penelope Edgewood
To: Izzy Edgewood
Date: April 6
Subject: Brodie is CoMiNg!!!

Brodie is coming to visit!!! Sorry, I just saw your email. I've been in the throes of helping the community-theater kids perform *Mary Poppins* and even let them use my very own carpetbag purse as a prop. That should tell you how much I love them.

Oh my heart! Izzy, do you realize how much your life is like a movie? And all this time I thought you were more of a secondary character in a Hallmark show, when really . . . you're the heroine! I can practically hear the perfectly placed "Christmas magic" chime in the background. You must take Brodie on the Parkway and to a Friday night bluegrass jam session. Can he dance? If you bring him to church, maybe you should choose the early service instead of the regular service in case Eli shows up. Plus the nosy church-lady group comes to the late service, so you can sneak out without an assault.

I feel certain all this is due in part to the new shade of lipstick I gave you for Christmas, your decision to update your wardrobe, and your new hairstyle. The photo you sent is fabulous. The new cut frames your face so wonderfully, yet still keeps its length. Men respond to those sorts of little things, you know? If you start using perfume, just think how many men you'll have dueling over you.

Penelope

PS: In preparation for Brodie's visit we're going shopping when I come in two weeks. All I'm going to say is . . . ankles are everything.

From: Izzy Edgewood
To: Josephine Martin
Date: April 7
Subject: Decisions

Josephine,

I talked to Aunt Louisa today and told her how much I appreciate her faith in me, but I'm not certain I want my future to be at the library. You know I love it, but recently I've felt the need to expand upon a dream. I know the bookshop isn't your favorite idea, and it might not end up being mine, but I need to try something new. And if it turns out to be a failure, then it's mine to mourn and grow from on my own. I can't really explain it, but I feel as though I need to escape my own life. Or . . . start living it, maybe? Whatever that means, it begins with investigating and maybe trying to see beyond my current horizons. I don't know that I've ever really been brave enough to step outside of what was expected of me.

I know as the eldest in our family you feel responsible for the hearts of so many, and despite my exhaustion at your attempts to manufacture my happiness, I know the sentiment comes from a loving desire. But Josephine, it's okay for me not to know exactly what my plan is. And it's okay for my not-knowing to be different than YOUR plans for my life.

It's okay for me to find happiness in simple things like books and tea and children's laughter. I don't have to have all the answers right now, but for the first time I have this wonderful hope of a dream coming true. Whether that ends up being the bookshop or the library or something I can't even fathom, it's mine to decide. I want you to always be on my journey with me, just as I want to be on yours, but I'm still the one who has to live with the choices . . . so I need to be the one who makes them.

I love you bigger than the sky.

Izzy

PS: I have a friend coming to visit in a few weeks. I met him on Heart-to-Heart and he's . . . well, not from our country. I thought I ought to prepare you.

PPS: He doesn't look like Clark Gable, but he has a fantastic accent.

• •

From: Izzy Edgewood
To: Luke Edgewood, Penelope Edgewood
Date: April 7
Subject: The transformation of Eli Montgomery

Interesting Eli development. I'm not sure what's caused such a transformation, but the guy was . . . different today. He showed up to the library with a little bouquet of flowers, thanked me for being so generous with my time in helping with his book, took me to lunch . . . and didn't talk about the book one time. Instead he asked me questions about ME. (Can a new hairstyle evoke that sort of change?) I didn't realize how little he had gotten to know me until he started this new turn of questions. He wanted to know about my college experience. Asked about why I love the Book Parade so much. Wanted to know what some of my favorite stories were. Said my eyes looked like amber.

I'm sitting here at my computer a little shocked by his behavior. Sure, that sounds like a good conversation by anyone's standards, but it's just so . . . so . . . different.

What could have caused the sudden shift?

Izzy

PS: Blame my paranoia, but a sudden and unexpected change in behavior usually isn't a good clue to me. I'm trying to figure it out. Time to pull out Agatha Christie.

PPS: Editing has never caused such a transformation before, unless you count the love letter I edited for Anne Logger. I feel certain it's how Clint became her high school sweetheart and subsequent husband of a decade now. Oh good grief! They've been married for a decade? Why am I so old?!!

From: Penelope Edgewood
To: Izzy Edgewood, Luke Edgewood
Date: April 8
Subject: Re: The transformation of Eli Montgomery

Izzy,

Oh my word! What will you do? Two men vying for your heart. Are you writing these things down in a journal for your children to uncover in thirty years or so? Maybe you've wooed Eli's heart so much it's completely changed him into the hero he needed to be all along. (Possibly the best editing you could have ever accomplished!) What a thought! Of course, men could already come perfect, like Andrew is so far, but if they don't first arrive that way, it's nice to know a little inspiration can do the trick. Some men just need a nudge in the right direction. Maybe it's the sweater-vests.

Penelope

PS: Hairstyles are powerful things. Just think about Kate Middleton or Miley Cyrus.

PPS: Maybe Eli's sudden change in behavior is because he's in LOVE with you!! (Can you hear my squeal from here?) Love can be quite sudden, I hear. I've never felt it, but I know my movies.

• •

From: Izzy Edgewood
To: Luke Edgewood, Penelope Edgewood
Date: April 8
Subject: Re: The transformation of Eli Montgomery

Penelope, please never put the names Kate Middleton and Miley Cyrus in the same sentence again. There's no comparison.

Izzy

• •

From: Luke Edgewood
To: Izzy Edgewood, Penelope Edgewood

Date: April 8

Subject: Re: The transformation of Eli Montgomery

He said your eyes look like amber? Sudden change in behavior? I'd tread carefully. No perfume is that potent.

Luke

PS: I blame aliens.

CHAPTER 12

From: Josephine Martin
To: Izzy Edgewood
Date: April 9
Subject: Do you need help?

Izzy,

Are you going through some early midlife crisis? For heaven's sake, did you really want the purple highlights that badly? Well I'd prefer purple highlights to whatever this dreaminess is. I don't even know what to call it! How can you make a plan if you do not have a plan? That's why I am a part of your life! It's all very concerning.

And what on EARTH are you talking about? A man is coming to visit you who lives OUT OF THE COUNTRY?? Why are you pursuing *him* when you have a perfectly fine in-person specimen who already likes you? You can't be serious about this *stranger* coming? And which country? The Internet can tell you many things about many places, so I hope you've completed a thorough search as you prepare for this madness.

You'd better make sure Luke or Patrick is with you at all times. Can you imagine? I've read about online relationships being a cover for more notorious behavior, and you know that those fraudulent emails are usually from foreigners. I'm sweating at the very thought. (And no, it has nothing to do with my hormones!) How much do you know about this "friend," as you say? From a foreign country? Has he asked for money?

Is this why you're making such a ridiculous decision not to take the lead librarian position? Izzy, it's not like you to argue. I feel certain this "friend" is influencing you already.

I don't like this at all. Where is he staying?

Josephine

PS: I am not going to tell Mother about this whole online situation. With the amount of mismanaged packages she receives from foreign places, just imagine what she'd think of a mail-ordered man! Oh no, it's too much for her.

From: Izzy Edgewood
To: Josephine Edgewood
Date: April 9
Subject: Re: Do you need help?

Josie,

What did you think an *online* dating service was?

And he's not being shipped to me. He's coming by his own accord from a legitimate country. Don't worry, you'll like him.

Izzy

PS: Sometimes you're really strange.

From: Izzy Edgewood
To: Penelope Edgewood, Luke Edgewood
Date: April 9
Subject: Re: The transformation of Eli Montgomery

Penelope,

Neither man is vying for my heart, or at least I wouldn't consider a writer who needs to learn how to write real people and a bookshop owner who lives halfway around the world *vying*. Interested? Maybe. That's still up in the air too. No one's mentioned hearts or vying.

Your email made me think of something concerning Eli. I won't share it right now. I need more time to work it out and have a few experiments. Then I'll let you know for sure, but it had something to do with your statement about my wooing Eli's heart so much it turned him into the hero he ought to be. I've tried to be the "savior" of too many men. I'm not sure I want to try that again. It's never turned out well for me. It's no wonder all the "saving" needs to be left to a much higher and better power than mine.

Besides, it might be nice to just *be* for a change instead of trying to rescue someone.

Izzy

PS: I'm glad Andrew is proving practically perfect in every way. You deserve to have all your Hallmark-ish dreams come true.

PPS: I'm not sure that love is ever "sudden." It seems much too big to happen so fast.

• •

From: Brodie Sutherland
To: Izzy Edgewood
Date: April 9
Subject: Clarification

Isabelle,

I wanted to send a brief note to clarify times for my visit. I'll follow up with Luke as well. Please do not feel obligated to adjust your schedule. I'll be happy to explore on my own when you are otherwise engaged. However, I want to be clear from the outset that I'm coming with the sole purpose of meeting you. Everything else will only serve as an additional pleasure.

To be perfectly candid, I am not someone who trifles with others' emotions, nor do I make decisions rashly, so if this interest between us—this connection—is merely one-sided, I would beg you to tell me now and I will adjust my plans and correspondence accordingly. For my part I have hopes for something much more.

I have no set expectations, except to uncover how I can hold such a kinship with someone I've never met in person . . . and how that may strengthen when we are face-to-face. If you are willing to explore that possibility with me, I hope to arrive on May 2 in Mt. Airy, North Carolina. My flight-schedule options are attached.

Hopefully,
Brodie

PS: "You have been my friend," replied Charlotte. "That in itself is a tremendous thing." *Charlotte's Web* (one of Fiona's favorites).

• •

From: Izzy Edgewood
To: Penelope Edgewood, Luke Edgewood
Date: April 9
Subject: Um . . . remember that vying talk?

I take back my last email. One of them may have a certain interest in my heart. The other appears to enjoy my editing services with a little more enthusiasm than my conversation skills, but depending on the reason behind his sudden interest, we'll see what that means.

I'm forwarding Brodie's email because I feel certain it will make you all starry-eyed and smiley. (Not you, Luke. You'll probably feel nauseous and irritable.) I'll admit to feeling a little giddy with it myself. And then . . . a little nervous. Okay, in all honesty, a lot nervous.

Penelope, you know that scene in *You've Got Mail* when Joe Fox is outside the restaurant getting ready to meet the lady he's been corresponding with for a while (aka Kathleen Kelly)? Of course you remember it, because you breathe and eat these movies!

Anyway, I feel like Joe when he looks at his friend and says, "Kevin, this woman is the most adorable creature I've ever been in contact with." If he turns out to be exactly what he seems, I'd be crazy not to turn *my* life around and fall head over heels in love with him. I mean what guy says stuff like he does? Not referencing the accent, of course, but HIM.

But there is the crazy part. How can two people with totally different lives make something like this work for real? I have a life here. He has a life there. I have family here. He has family there. Creating a future seems perfectly impossible! But . . . I *want* him to come. I want to spend time walking with him and discovering bookshops together. I want to know if our conversations will flow as easily and sweetly in person as they do online. I want to believe after all the frustrations and heartache and false love I've experienced, that this . . . this is something *real* and *lasting*. That I'm worth *real* and *lasting* to someone. To him.

Dean and HWLMATA left me second-guessing myself and bitter against the idea that real-life romance still existed. In fact, this thing with Eli has been fine, but when I look back on my two previous major relationships, they fit the same description too. Fine. (At least at first, before I realized they were USING me.) I don't want to settle for fine when there can be such a man as Brodie! Have I been blinded by fiction? Am I naive to hope? Is it ridiculous to not take what's in front of me and close at hand while I can?

So sorry to wax dramatic. But there it is. My choice.

And my next email could change everything from this point on.

Izzy

PS: Perhaps I should try to write women's fiction. I suddenly feel inspired toward melodrama.

PPS: I want to meet him, guys. I want it more than I have words to say. And that's a lot.

PPPS: And I'm going to be brave.

From: Penelope Edgewood
To: Izzy Edgewood, Luke Edgewood
Date: April 9
Subject: Re: Um . . . remember that vying talk?

Izzy,

I think you were made for dreaming and if you ever really stopped, you wouldn't be the Izzy we know and love. Besides, it's never a waste of time to meet a foreign man with a lovely accent, as long as you're in a safe, well-lit place and your money is secure. Or at least that seems to be the best scenario for it in real life. In fiction the handsome, foreign men are either the heroes or gangsters. Or maybe vampires. You really can't tell for sure yet about Brodie, but since he wears sweater-vests, I'd bet he leans much more toward hero than gangster or vampire. Isn't that encouraging?

Penelope

PS: I think you are very brave. You've worked with Mama for five whole years AND have never let headbands go out of style.

From: Luke Edgewood
To: Penelope Edgewood, Izzy Edgewood
Date: April 9
Subject: Re: Um . . . remember that vying talk?

Izzy,

Why did you send that email to Penelope when you wanted a sensical answer?

The only sensical thing she said was the first sentence . . . and maybe the part about working with Mom, otherwise it's all nonsense.

Brodie is not a gangster or a vampire. He's also authentic. How do I know this?

He has a pair of Yoda ears.

Luke

PS: I'm rarely friends with gangsters.

From: Josephine Martin
To: Izzy Edgewood
Date: April 10
Subject: Re: Do you need help?

Izzy,

I thought you'd meet a man from *town* online. Not someone from far away.

Besides, you and Eli made the cutest couple ever when Patrick and I saw you at Mi Casa last night. *And* you were smiling. I'm so glad you wore red. Red looks fabulous on you.

I think it's going to be particularly awkward when your online friend shows up and learns about the man you've been *dating* for three weeks. It certainly puts you in a precarious position. They both may drop you, and then you'd be back to where you were over two months ago.

Think about this, Izzy! Maybe you should let the relationship with this online person go. What could he really offer you that Eli can't? If you and Eli work at it, I'm sure you can grow into the romance you've always wanted. He's teachable. He just needs some coaching, and since you've worked with children for years, I'm certain you can direct your skills to helping Eli become the man of your dreams.

Is the whole bookshop dream wrapped around this mysterious man? I called Penelope last night and she gave me much more information about your "Brodie" than I cared to know. He's from some mysterious island country near Scotland!! Do you think he'd drop everything to move to North Carolina? Because that's what he'd have to do since you don't travel!

And I imagine he's using all of those pretty quotes as a cover for some great deficiency in character. Or appearance.

Don't risk a real-life boyfriend for one who is more make-believe than real! It's so much like this library position. You could have something solid, dependable, and easy instead of something uncertain, unpredictable, and impractical. You've always been so good at taking my advice and so now you have it.

I tell you these things because I love you and I don't want you to lose more time.

With love,
Josephine

PS: You are excellent at what you do, Izzy. You always have been. You should be proud of your gifts and the way you can bring people together for the love of stories. You've even gotten Patrick reading.

• •

From: Izzy Edgewood
To: Josephine Martin
Date: April 10
Subject: Re: Do you need help?

Josie,

1. YOU signed me up for Heart-to-Heart. I would hope you'd considered all of the possible consequences before entrusting me to the cyber dating world. (And I might add, Brodie has been the best "blind date" of your career.)

2. I am not exclusively seeing anyone. Eli and I are getting to know each other and *mostly* I'm giving him feedback on his writing. Only within the past week have I felt like we're actually becoming friends because we started talking about more than *his* books. I've never met Brodie in person, but if he's willing to come so far to see me, I'm not going to stop him. People have fallen in love through correspondence for centuries. And the very fact that you mention Eli needs "coaching" makes me wonder if you've not been doing a little coaching of your own.
3. I've learned a few things about what I want in a relationship from meeting both Eli and Brodie. They represent two parts of my life. One is familiar, similar, and safe. The other is new, comfortable, exciting, and very unsafe (in the "predictability" department, not in the "kidnap me" way). But that's caused me to also realize . . .
4. Love isn't safe. Dreams aren't safe. I've played it safe for a long time by allowing others to make choices for me or by following the easy path. Maybe it's time for me to risk my future on something as unpredictable, uncertain, and impractical as a dream and my own heart. Adventures happen in unexpected ways, and maybe it's time to take the adventures from the page to real life.

Josie, I can't be the little orphan girl who came to live in your house all those years ago. The one you'd read to at night to keep my nightmares of the plane crash at bay. The lonely child who was so afraid to make a decision in this uncertain world of loss she'd entered, you'd make them for her. (EVERYONE made them for me.) The quiet loner who found refuge in her family and books. It's taken me too long to realize that the only way to become brave is to face what we're afraid of . . . and step forward. I could never have learned to be brave without our family's love, but now it's time to love me enough to support the strength I've gained from your love.

And trust that I've become someone who can make the right choices for my own future.

I love you, Josephine.

Izzy

PS: Warning: I'm going to quote a poet. From E. E. Cummings, "It takes courage to grow up and become who you really are." Thank you for helping me grow into my wings. Now trust me to fly . . . and maybe even literally.

From: Izzy Edgewood
To: Penelope Edgewood, Luke Edgewood, Josephine Martin
Date: April 10
Subject: The Heart of the matter

Luke and Penelope (and Josephine),

Eli and I had a heart-to-heart today and it was shockingly enlightening. First of all he shared that he'd been fired from his first teaching job because of a relationship with the chair of his department that went sour. (I didn't ask for specifics. I didn't want to know.) His second job had been highly stressful, so he came to Mt. Airy because of two reasons: One, in search of something smaller with less professional pressure in hopes of making writing his eventual full-time job. And second, to flee heartbreak. His fiancée of three years had broken up with him three months ago (did everyone see that—only THREE MONTHS AGO) and he was completely devastated and stunned. To him the breakup had come out of nowhere, without a clue as to why. Evidently my editing notes about the characteristics of a hero and what a heroine truly needs from her guy shook him into introspection. He began to see all the "ways he'd failed" in his relationship with her. How he'd been self-focused and driven, instead of really listening and showing he cared in a way she understood. I never imagined something like my edits could cause anyone to have an epiphany of life-changing proportions, but there you have it.

I told him that what he needed most right now was a friend and a story brainstormer, not a girlfriend. (He didn't fully agree with me, but I made my point clear.) His heart really is still so full of her and he has a great deal to think about—the last thing he or I need is a rebound relationship. After a long and beautifully thoughtful conversation, he seemed to understand, but I'm not sure with the whole "acceptance" thing, because he asked me to dinner this Friday. I politely declined and suggested we meet at the library for future book talks so that nothing will seem date-ish at all. (Though I am CERTAIN libraries can be romantic places in both fictional and nonfictional ways.)

It's strange how relationships work. I had a very Austen's Emma moment. Talking with Eli through his misunderstandings helped clarify my own. Life is too precious to hesitate when God offers the opportunity for something even better than what we imagine. I don't know how things might ultimately work out with Brodie, and I'm prepared to have my heart shattered. My future is here. His is probably there. But if I don't muster up some courage and risk the hurt, I'll regret it for the rest of my life, because I'll never experience the possible joy.

Some people are worth the risk.

Contemplatively,
Izzy

From: Izzy Edgewood
To: Brodie Sutherland
Date: April 10
Subject: Re: Clarification

Brodie,

Thank you for clarifying your intentions. I appreciate your honesty, so I will return in kind.

I've never connected with anyone so quickly as I have with you. I don't know if it's because of the mode in which we're communicating and the protection of hiding behind a computer, but I don't think so. I believe there has to be more to it.

I consider you my friend and make a timid admission that I'm curious if there can be more and how on earth that "more" could work.

As you learned from the email where I thought you were Josie (and I lay my heart bare), my romantic history hasn't been a sweet one. I am cautious, but that doesn't mean I'm not hopeful. In fact, that hopefulness has a lot to do with you.

So can we plan to meet as the friends we've become with the openness of becoming something . . . more? I look forward to the possibilities.

Authentically,

Isabelle

PS: C. S. Lewis captures my thoughts rather perfectly in this quote: "Friendship is unnecessary, like philosophy, like art . . . It has no survival value; rather it is one of those things which give value to survival."

PART 2

Of Shakespeare, Kisses & Shark Hats

CHAPTER 13

From: Anders Sutherland
To: Brodie Sutherland
Date: May 1
Subject: What on earth are you thinking?!

I just returned from dinner with Mother and I see now why you left two weeks early for the convention in New York!

A woman! And one you met online?

I know that parliament encouraged islanders to bring people into the country by various means to restore some of our population losses, but a girlfriend!! Hire a foreign assistant! That should suffice! You have neither the disposition to engage strangers easily nor the lack of sense such an endeavor would inspire. And though the financial stipend from bringing a foreigner to our island would certainly benefit our bookshop and allow Fiona's surgery at an earlier date, you have no notion that this woman would quit her life to move to Skymar! This is madness, brother.

I would have stopped you at the airport if I'd known in time. I'm a single man, not a year older than you, and I have no plans to dabble in some online dating site for a *wife*. Oh no! I'll look closer at hand, like in England or Scotland, even Denmark would be a better option than America. Despite the extreme differences in cultures, the woman would be nearly five thousand miles away from her family. What do you expect her to do upon meeting you? Pack up her life and come across the ocean to be with you? Think, brother! Clearly you have been reading too many romances. It is time to turn your mind to the nonfiction section. Our father found it suitable to bring an English bride to the islands and she acclimated beautifully. But an *American*?

I still can't believe it, and wouldn't have, if Mother hadn't been the one telling me. Brodie, this is not like you at all.

I do hope you get whatever ridiculousness out of your head and return to Skern a wiser man. If you want to settle down, I'll help you on the hunt from somewhere within a more predictable realm than America.

Anders

PS: I know Sutherland's could use the extra money, but there's no reason for you to go on this wild-goose chase around the world. Really, Brodie. It's unfathomable.

* * *

From: Ellen Sutherland
To: Brodie Sutherland
Date: May 1
Subject: Anders

Dearest Brodie,

I must apologize, my boy. While Anders was having dinner with me and Fiona this evening, I informed him of the reason you left early for America. Needless to say, he was at first shocked and then terribly put out. I thought you'd already talked to him about your detour to North Carolina before the convention or I would have kept him happily (or as happily as he ever is) ignorant of your more personal adventures. The poor boy really doesn't appreciate the romance of it all, but you know Fiona and I will be waiting to hear every word. I'm always appreciative of a good romance, but having lived one of my own, the nonfiction sort are my favorite kinds.

In fact I expect finely tuned details, son. And, as you are so excellent at doing, paint pictures with your words for your little sister. She can barely make out images at this point, but she has a tremendous memory of the world around her when she still had her sight . . . and you know her love for words. And you. She'll be hanging on every one of your descriptions.

Just so you know, I've finished the illustrations for Erin Linderholt's book. Oh, what a delight to draw dragons again. It has been much too long. I'm sending you digital copies so that you can review them and see how they fit for the publication and if you have any suggestions.

Always,
Mother

PS: Fiona sends her love and asks for you to describe Isabelle's perfume, or shampoo, as the case may be.

• •

From: Brodie Sutherland
To: Anders Sutherland
Date: May 2
Subject: Re: What on earth are you thinking?!

Anders,

I've only now received your email, as I wait to disembark the plane in North Carolina. Isabelle is to meet me at the airport and take me to her brother's house. My true visit starts tomorrow.

I didn't tell you of my plans for the very reason of your response. I know this is difficult to understand and I have no way of knowing how it will all turn out. All I know is that if I don't take this opportunity, I'll regret it for the rest of my life. (Be assured that not every American is like your former assistant. Isabelle doesn't collect bug corpses, nor does she overindulge in makeup. She also speaks in full, delightful sentences with much more varied, and less vulgar, wording, so hopefully that will put you at ease.)

My decisions have nothing to do with the government's "Foreign Spouse Initiative." It may have been the catalyst of my joining the online dating community, out of curiosity at best, but it's not the force propelling my meeting with or interest in Isabelle.

Anders, she is the most authentic and charming woman I've ever met. If she proves to be half of who I've come to know over the past three months online, then I'm tempted to do whatever possible to spend the rest of my life with her. I know you'll find this all exaggerated, but there's no other way to put it.

I know it feels out of character for me, but the proper emotions encourage a proper perspective. I've never known any emotion like this, so therefore have no way of knowing what my "character" would be. I suppose then, if it is madness or courage or an unquenchable curiosity, then I'm determined to find out. No book has sufficiently prepared me for this. Books can only take one so far. The rest is up to flesh and blood and courage.

Call me mad, if you will, and I will happily accept the madness if it means this could be true.

Brodie

PS: You would like it here. There is no sea in sight.

From: Anders Sutherland
To: Brodie Sutherland
Date: May 2
Subject: Re: What on earth are you thinking?!

Brodie,

It's perfectly clear you've been reading too much fiction. A few good biographies should set you to rights in no time. Go ahead and have your little experiment, but I wager you a roast beef dinner it will end up as a great disappointment. Endeavors such as these are rarely worth the effort, I assure you.

I will give you your little adventure and see your sense return in a few weeks, if not a few days.

Anders

PS: Be careful around there. I just looked up the Blue Ridge Mountains and found a startling number of photos with somber-bearded men and bears. I'm not sure how those two are connected to the mountains where you are, but there you have it. Though, I must admit to admiring the idea of no sea. The mere mention of those waves brings on a bout of nausea.

From: Izzy Edgewood
To: Penelope Edgewood
Date: May 2
Subject: Brodie is here and Josie is insane

I can't believe he's here, but he is. I only just now got back to my apartment after leaving him with Luke. Oh, Penelope! He's . . . well, he's just as I imagined and even more. Once we worked through some of our initial awkwardness, everything clicked into place as it has done in our online conversations and video chats. Brodie Sutherland. My wonderful friend! And I'm trying very hard not to worry about all the what-ifs. You know? Like once he really gets to know me, he won't want a future with me. Or what if he DOES want me but a future is IMPOSSIBLE? I am opening myself up to heartbreak of the acutest kind, and yet, when we met, every worry and possible disaster feels worth it. He is exactly the friend he's been for three months, only now within touching and smelling distance. (I know you understand what I mean. Luke would be gagging right now.)

Okay, okay, I'm getting ahead of myself. I told you I'd give you an accounting, so here we go:

I waited in the arrivals area and tried really hard not to second-guess EVERYTHING. My hairstyle, my clothes, my perfume . . . the choice to bring an "almost" complete stranger into my life for two weeks of "life with Izzy." I mean, online relationships are totally different than in-person ones. Virtual friendships mean bringing out my best for limited and controlled moments in a day. Carefully planning my words in charming and witty emails. But . . . now Brodie was going to see the *real* Isabelle Edgewood, tennis shoes and all?

You know what it's been like for me. Most of my previous boyfriends left because they wanted something else besides me, because I wasn't enough. What if I wasn't enough for Brodie too? (So much for all that "brave" talk, right?)

And then I started reminding myself of what Grandma Edgewood used to say:

"The anxious heart is filled with thousands of what-ifs that never happen, but the peaceful soul whispers hope-filled truth."

So I started listing truths I knew in no particular order:

1. Brodie was traveling from across the ocean to meet *me*, an idea *he'd* initiated.
2. He knows how to engage in excellent conversation (or at least my kind of excellent conversations).
3. He adores books and his family, from all I can ascertain so far.
4. He has an excellent command of the English language. (I mean, truly, my heart flutters a little with the wonderful way he can weave words together.)
5. He is funny, kind, and part-owner of a franchise of bookstores. A trifecta of perfection for my introspective, book-loving heart.
6. And he really seems to care about ME. Knowing me. Encouraging me.

I was getting ready to add a few more "truths" to my list when I saw a light-brown swell of erratic curls emerge among the crowd. My throat squeezed my breath to a stop as his familiar face came into view. Oh, Penelope, he was more handsome in person, especially with the way his hair bounced in total confusion in time with his walk. It really was adorable in a nerdish sort of way, which . . . as you know . . . is my favorite sort of way.

He searched the crowd and I almost ducked behind the man to my right just to give myself a few more seconds to prepare, but then I shook off the idea. After all, if he'd been brave enough to come all this way, I would certainly try to be as brave as him. So I lifted my chin and hoped my smile looked more welcoming than slightly terrified. (You know the one I mean. Josephine calls it my Joker smile. If I show less teeth, I think it's less scary.)

And then his eyes finally met mine. His eyes look even more aqua in person! You know that quote from *The Princess Bride* when Buttercup says, "like the sea after a storm"? Well, all thoughts of not giving the Joker smile went right out of my mind when he looked at me. As recognition dawned his smile spread across his face, complete with the teeniest dimple in one cheek, and my knees nearly buckled from the instant connection a screen and words had only hinted at. His grin grew, disappearing into his close-trimmed beard. Oh heavens! He never broke eye contact as he drew closer to me and all of a sudden my vision started getting blurry . . . because I hadn't taken a breath yet. So I gulped in a breath as he stopped in front of me and dropped his bag to his side.

Penelope! I know we'd always talked about the perfect man-height being about six foot two, but Brodie is maybe an inch or two taller than me, and I didn't mind it at all. I barely have to tilt my head to stare into his eyes, so just imagine how easy a kiss might be! And then (you're going to love this part. I'm getting wonderful tingles down my neck at the memory) he settled his palm against my waist and slowly leaned forward to place a kiss against my cheek. I sucked in plenty of air at that moment. Enough to get a wonderful dose of his spruce and mint cologne, and then my mind went foggy for a whole new reason. Whew. I wanted to cry and laugh and hug him all at once. But I didn't. (Well, not at that moment. Though I did later when he gave me *The Blue Castle* AND he's an excellent hugger.) However, at the moment I maintained some semblance of composure . . . after I drew in a few more breaths of his cologne. Then he looked down into my face, and with that wonderfully warm and enchanting accent of his, he said, "Isabelle Louisa Edgewood. It's a sincere pleasure to finally meet you."

Let me just say that video calls are NO comparison to the real thing. At all. Oh. MY. WORD! His scent, his smile, his eyes, and the way his accent curls around those vowels and consonants. I'm a goner! If this flops, I may never recover.

It took me a good five minutes to remember how to talk and especially how to talk to this wonderful man I'd been communicating with for three months, but once I found my rhythm, the conversation moved as if we'd just had a video call the day before! Easy. Sweet.

Until . . . (Insert the Jaws theme here.)

Josie!

She had driven all the way to Charlotte Douglas International Airport and perched herself behind a pillar in the arrivals area in order to spy on me! She's a horrible spy. I recognized her protruding stomach long before I ever saw her face. I attempted to give her a little tongue lashing before pulling her from behind the pillar to meet Brodie. Oh my word! I almost expected him to turn around and go back to Skymar as quick as the plane would take him, but as Josie waddled off in a huff (it's an odd sort of waddle when she's mad), his grin twitched and then . . . he laughed! A wonderfully real, deep, sigh-inducing laugh, which gave me all sorts of hope that if he could handle Josie's insanity, then maybe he could handle mine too.

I'm so happy he's here! I hope you can come in on the weekend to meet him, but if not, we'll try to have a video call with you. Though he wears sweater-vests really well, he wears his smile even better.

Hope to talk to you soon, and wish me luck.

Izzy

PS: And pray. Pray with the same ferocity as Mother Superior sings "Climb Every Mountain"! (I knew you'd appreciate that reference.)

From: Brodie Sutherland
To: Ellen Sutherland
Date: May 2
Subject: Meeting Isabelle

Mum (and Fiona),

I have much to tell you about my first day with Isabelle, and I shall attempt to make it as descriptive and sentimental as possible.

It was late when I flew into the closest large airport to the tiny town of Mt. Airy. Surprisingly, at six in the evening there were quite a few travelers, but only a handful awaiting arrivals, so Isabelle was easy to locate. Of course I think I should have noticed her no matter the size of the crowd. She's made a remarkable impression upon my thoughts.

She wore a dark-red coat, the color red of Fiona's favorite crayon, and although I'm sure she's worn her hair down in some of our video calls, It was nothing like seeing it in person. It's a chestnut brown with shimmers of auburn when the light hits it, and it falls around her shoulders to the elbows.

We noticed one another at the same time, I think, because she squeezed her hands together in front of her and offered a beautiful smile. My feet faltered, so did her smile, a little. I hope she wasn't disappointed. I'm going to suppose not, because she kept smiling and staring, without one grimace in sight.

So I rallied my wits again and continued forward, confidence a bit bolstered, and for a chap who could count on one hand the number of women he'd dated, to have one I'd grown so fond of look at me with that smile . . . well, to be honest, Mum, I nearly melted to the floor.

Perhaps that's what inspired the uncertainty of the next few moments. I suppose we saved up all the awkwardness we had avoided by beginning our relationship online for this in-person meeting, because I feel certain each of us stumbled over every sentence for the first minute. And then I nearly thrust the book I'd brought as a welcome gift upon her (a hardbound first-edition copy of L. M. Montgomery's *The Blue Castle*). In all honesty I was hoping to celebrate the plight of a quieter hero with my offering.

Her face lit with such a glow, I can't really describe it, and then she burst forward and hugged me. *Ach*, Mum, she smelled like spring. And she hugged me with such enthusiasm I can't contain my grin even now as I type this note hours later.

Somehow the book seemed to establish what we'd developed over the past few months of conversations, because everything became more fluid then. I don't think she meant to hug me, because she stepped back rather quickly, her cheeks almost matching her coat, but she's adorable. Simply put.

Now you know the feeling when someone is watching you? That "gooseflesh rising on the back of one's neck" feeling? I felt it as I was walking through the airport. Of course Isabelle looked at me as we conversed, but the sensation kept gnawing at me the longer we walked. It just so happened that right before we reached the baggage-claim area, Isabelle increased her pace and disappeared behind a nearby pillar, without one word of excuse. Suddenly I hear this conversation from behind the pillar:

"I can't even believe you'd stoop to this level. Really, Josie!"

"Do you think I'd let you meet some stranger by yourself without keeping an eye on you? What sort of cousin do you think I am?"

"I thought you were an adult, but now I'm wondering."

"I'm glad I came. Did you see how he walked right up to you and kissed you on the cheek? You've never even met the man before and he does that? Izzy, I don't like this at—"

"Do you hear yourself? Stop being ridiculous. And while you're here you might as well meet him so you can allay these crazy fears of yours."

And then from behind the pillar came Isabelle and a very pregnant woman—her cousin Josephine Martin. The resemblance shone in their shared hair color, though Josephine's was cut to her shoulders and very straight. After the woman gave me such a severe look that would make Ebenezer Scrooge shudder, we were properly introduced, made a few turns of small talk, and then parted ways at the exit of the airport, but not before she sent some additional glares in my direction for good measure.

Isabelle apologized profusely, at which time the laughter I'd been attempting to quell burst out. And after a look of surprise, her laughter joined mine . . . Then everything clicked into place, or seemed to.

We talked in the car, through dinner, and for a half hour on Luke's front porch before she left me for the night.

My travels had finally begun to catch up with me, and Luke seemed to notice, so we kept our conversation short, and he escorted me to a loft room with a view of the mountains, dark in the distance, framed by starlight and moonglow. Not so bad a beginning, I think.

And I have finally found a reason to enjoy being the shortest man in our family. My height is only about an inch or two above Isabelle's, which places me at the perfect tallness to notice the way the light changed the shade of her eyes from a dark brown to a tea color. Ah, is that sentimental enough for you?

But more news will have to wait for later. I can barely keep my eyes open. I hope this note finds you all well. I look forward to tomorrow.

With love,
Brodie

PS: Fiona, my room has log beams above like Grandfather's cabin in the mountains, except Luke hangs strange objects from those beams, like hand-crafted woodland creatures, antlers, and a few accents of greenery. My room smells like pine and soap, with the faintest hint of leather. You would think of Christmas.

CHAPTER 14

From: Ellen Sutherland
To: Brodie Sutherland
Date: May 3
Subject: Re: Meeting Isabelle

My dear Brodie,

Fiona is fairly floating from your last email. Thank you for all the wonderful details. I know she appreciates them, but so do I. It sounds as though Josie will keep hawk-eyes on you, but I don't see that as a bad thing at all. It hints at Isabelle being loved well by her cousin. I should think having lost her parents at such an impressionable age, she likely harbors fear or insecurities about relationships, wouldn't you? And I sense her cousins work as gatekeepers of protection, which is an endearing thought—though it may lend itself to more perseverance on your part, perhaps.

But I imagine it will not take the visitation of three Christmas ghosts to have Josie warm up to you. Once she gets to know you, she'll realize her suspicions were for naught. I cannot wait to learn more about your visit, especially your first full day in North Carolina. Please send photos, but don't hesitate to describe as much as possible for Fiona (and for my benefit. I love to read your words).

I have been pondering this idea of a book parade and am rather enamored with it. As the two of you feel more comfortable with one another, do you think Isabelle would be open to emailing me more information about how she began the event?

I hope you have a wonderful day.

With love,
Mum

PS: Fiona wants to know what Luke looks like and whether he has any pets. Also, did he handcraft the animals in your room?

• •

From: Brynna Sutherland
To: Brodie Sutherland
Date: May 3
Subject: Your Isabelle adventure

Brodie,

Losh! I can hardly keep my excitement from spilling over! Have you met her yet? Is she as lovely in person as she's been through email? You won't forget to send photos like you promised, will you? I'm fairly dying to see what she looks like.

How does she dress? You can tell a lot about the way a woman dresses, you know. Does she wear bright colors that blind you? Muted ones? Is she a flowery dresser or does she wear long sleeves all the time? I've heard of women wearing long sleeves to hide tattoos from their beaus. Of course, if she does have any tattoos, I'd imagine they'd have to do with books, wouldn't you?

I'll help you sort out the type of person she is by her style, make no mistake. I'm very attuned to this sort of thing you know.

If this all works out as only the best stories do, Fiona can have her surgery early, the bookshop will get a financial boost, and you'll be the hero of the entire family! Woo her well, dear boy. So many things count on how well you woo her. Your "forever" romance could fix so many things!

Brynna

PS: Have you seen the website lately? I'm making modifications by slow degrees. Whether she has tattoos or not, she certainly knows a thing or two about marketing and design.

From: Brodie Sutherland
To: Ellen Sutherland
Date: May 3
Subject: Mt. Airy & reading aloud

Mum and Fiona,

The past twelve hours have been a delightful and somewhat dizzying foray into an introduction to Isabelle-in-real-life, her family, and the charming town of Mt. Airy.

Where to begin? I suppose, at the beginning.

I was awakened by the howling entry of a large dog who looked to be a mix between a shepherd and some sort of hound. Fiona, you would have loved him. He was a soft gray with white and tan spots, and a face that appeared to feature a permanent look of surprise. This look could have been due to the perfectly placed tufts of darker gray just above where eyebrows should sit. He welcomed me with a solid lick to my face and then left the room as if his job was done. I'm still not certain how he opened the bedroom door, but we know how very tricky dogs can be at times when they are determined, don't we? Shona had to have been magical from the way she could enter and exit rooms.

I pulled myself from the bed, feeling much more alert than the evening before, and crossed the room to the window. Luke's house is a distance from town and atop a hill, so the view from the window afforded me an excellent prospect of the Blue Ridge Mountains in daylight. And they were blue! A misty, soft sort of blue, and on this particular morning fog cloaked the bottom of them so that it looked as though they were floating islands in the clouds. I thought the photos I'd researched had been tinted to add color, but no. It was quite a remarkable sight.

Luke greeted me with pancakes and bacon (or rashers). Much like with Isabelle, meeting him came with this unusual sense of déjà vu. Since we've been corresponding now for a month or so, we joined into conversation as if it was just the extension of another email. It's a very odd feeling, but at the same time comfortable and pleasant.

Isabelle wore her hair pulled back on the sides today. She has a small speckling of freckles across her nose that I hadn't noticed through video chat. There's something about her having those (and me being close enough to appreciate them) that causes me to smile quite often in her company. Of course, there are other reasons I smile as well. She's funny, but I don't believe she knows it. And as the morning waned (it took a little while for us to find our rhythm in conversation because, to be quite honest, I'm rather flabbergasted at just being near her in flesh and blood), we took a walk down Main Street, and her witty personality blossomed. I don't think she is as talkative around most people as she is with me, because her aunt fairly gasped when we entered the library and Isabelle was sharing stories from her first week of work there.

Main Street in Mt. Airy is as quaint and charming as my tour guide. It's very different from our towns, as you can imagine. Buildings line the main road, much like most villages back home, but these buildings are an eclectic mesh of stone and brick rectangles of differing heights. Most of the roofs are of black shingles or tin. And the shops were as varied as one could imagine. A Christmas store, candy shops, old diners, new restaurants, human- and pet-clothing stores, a bakery for people . . . and a bakery for dogs, old fashioned ice cream shops, a bookstore, antique shops, an old theater, a trading post, and (you both will appreciate this due to our newfound television series) Floyd's Barbershop, The Bluebird Diner, and the Snappy Lunch (where Isabelle and I enjoyed a fine lunch surrounded by memorabilia celebrating *The Andy Griffith Show*). I've attached a few photos.

Main Street smelled of popcorn and chocolate, and on the hour a large clock from the historic bank building would chime loud enough to alert stragglers of their tardiness. It made the television shows come to life all the more and gave me a deeper understanding of Isabelle's world.

After lunch we went to Isabelle's apartment, which is a little white building nestled on vast farmland with the Blue Ridge Mountains rising in the north on the horizon. Samwise greeted me with the enthusiasm of a long-lost friend. He's a beautiful golden retriever with a delirious love for peanut butter, and not just the food. When he finishes with the container, he knocks it around like a toy for half an hour, as happy as a lark. My equally enthusiastic reception of Samwise appeared to please Isabelle, because she linked her arm through mine and asked if I'd enjoy sitting by the window and reading from my current book. At first I was a bit embarrassed to admit I was reading *Little Women* for the first time—at her suggestion—but she put my worries at ease with a ready smile and an exclamation of how fun it would be to hear my accent read over Louisa May Alcott's words. How could I refuse such a warm invitation?

I don't recall reading aloud to anyone for a long time, except to Fiona. A quote here or there. But not entire pages or chapters. Yet we ended up spending two hours taking turns reading from our select favorites. She was enjoying Wodehouse and I laughed a few times at her ridiculous attempts at an English accent. I recognize it may sound boring to a large portion of the world, but I'd never had such a wonderful time with a woman. There's a comfort in sharing the same sort of interests, or obsessions as some may say, but it doesn't matter when you match so well.

All around, she's exactly what I expected and so much more. We talked so long tonight that we both forgot supper and we pieced together a meal of sandwiches, some leftover soup, a few delicious bread rolls, and the everlasting southern tea. I think you'd both find my amount of conversations impressive *and* that surprisingly, I'm not exhausted by them.

She has the weekend planned for a hike, a drive on the Blue Ridge Parkway, and a *Lord of the Rings* marathon. I feel certain that if I was ever going to fall in love, this is the perfect woman for me. In fact, Isabelle Edgewood would make it incredibly easy.

I hope this note finds you both well and happy. I shall write more tomorrow.

With love,

Brodie

PS: Fiona, there's a sweet fragrance in the air outside Isabelle's house. It originates from a beautiful flowering tree of white or blushed-pink color, almost as if the hue was brushed on with a painter's stroke. Isabelle says it is a magnolia. Your fairies would find lovely homes there.

Text from Izzy to Penelope: Accents and smiles are powerful things. I knew you would understand.

Penelope: Of course. It's perfectly natural with all the British cinema we've consumed. Has he kissed you yet?

Izzy: He just got here!

Penelope: That wasn't a no.

Izzy: No.

Text from Luke to Izzy: Brodie eats his french fries with a fork. If I didn't know he had Yoda ears and the *Indiana Jones* series, that would be a red flag for me.

Izzy: Maybe he thinks it's weird that we DON'T eat fries with a fork.

Luke: I can speak Klingon and quote *Return of the Jedi*. He will overlook it.

From: Brodie Sutherland

To: Brynna Sutherland

Date: May 3
Subject: Re: Your Isabelle adventure

Good morning Brynna,

Isabelle is as charming as you can imagine. I'm attaching a photo of us together in front of the Andy Griffith Playhouse. I find her clothing perfect for her, but I feel certain you will know better than I. As far as tattoos, I haven't noticed any, but I've not been in search of them. They don't matter to me.

You've made some excellent changes to the website. Isabelle mentioned exchanging an email with you last night for some additions. Father had a keen vision and plan for Sutherland's all those years ago, but I don't think he planned for the changing landscape of the Internet, as it has shaken book sales and even reading. We are behind the times, but I don't believe we are too late to bring Sutherland's back to its former success.

Isabelle and I have discussed the business a little, but I imagine we'll have more opportunities to brainstorm. She seems to enjoy the stimulation of creativity. Her eyes fairly shine from reined-in enthusiasm. So far the only time she's been overtly emotional is when we've talked of books or . . . when I stumbled along the sidewalk and fell to my knees, at which time she ran to my side, wrapped her arm through mine, pulled me into the ice cream shop nearby, and wouldn't allow me to leave until she'd made certain I was fine. Her determination rivals Mum's. Imagine that!

Brynna, I came to visit Isabelle solely for the purpose of knowing her better. I have no ulterior motives and am a bit surprised that you would turn your mind in the direction of the stipend. Yes, the financial ramifications of bringing her to Skymar would be a boon to Sutherland's and help hasten Fiona's surgery (which is certainly something we all desire), but Isabelle is not (and has never been) a pawn in the story. I would protect her heart as voraciously as I would any of my family, which includes all matters related to the stipend. In all reality, if our relationship should turn in a "forever" direction, I have as much chance of moving to North Carolina as she to Skymar. So put the stipend from your mind altogether. This is a matter of hearts, not funds.

On a different note, would you mind going by to check on Mother and Fiona on your way to the Skern shop? Anders is traveling and I'd feel better knowing you'd checked in.

Affectionately,
Brodie

PS: Now I'm curious, what do my clothes say about me? I've never heard them talk.

• •

From: Brodie Sutherland
To: Ellen Sutherland
Date: May 4
Subject: Star Wars Day

Mother, an additional note to share with Fiona:

I've been reminded by three people today (complete with lightsabers) that today is *Star Wars* Day. Luke even cooked breakfast in a cloak with a saber attached to his hip. Isabelle showed up with Princess Leia buns for her hairstyle, her saber (and an extra one for me) waiting in the front seat of her car. Evidently it's a very important celebration at the library and

I'm to attend the Force Party this afternoon. The creativity is certainly strong with this woman.

May the Fourth Be with You,
Brodie

<u>Text from Izzy to Luke:</u> I thought you were coming to the Force Party at the library today?

<u>**Luke:**</u> You stole my lightsaber. I couldn't come unarmed.

<u>Izzy:</u> Didn't you once say your smile was your secret weapon? You could have brought that. And I did NOT steal your lightsaber. I stole the extra one from Jason Rush (the tenth grader who kept arguing with me about Star Wars canon. He definitely didn't come armed with knowledge . . . and library rule is if you try to hit the teacher with your lightsaber, the teacher gets to keep it).

<u>Izzy:</u> BTW, thanks for taking such good care of Brodie. He's enjoyed getting to know you better.

<u>**Luke:**</u> I don't know how all this is going to work out, but I don't think I've ever met anyone who fits your weirdness like him. Isn't there a quote about that somewhere? Dr. Seuss?

<u>Izzy:</u> Well, actually it was originally written by Robert Fulghum and later attributed to Seuss. But either way it's perfect. "When we find someone whose weirdness is compatible with ours, we join up with them and fall into mutually satisfying weirdness—and call it love—true love." I'm not saying I'm in love, but I'd definitely say we have compatible weirdness.

<u>**Luke:**</u> Your response just confirmed all the weirdness I think about you and Brodie. Seussian or not.

From: Anders Sutherland
To: Brodie Sutherland
Date: May 5
Subject: The fast decline of American influences

Brodie,

I had thought you'd come to your senses about this entire online relationship fiasco, but after our phone conversation last evening, I am even more concerned. Why would you ever have your photo taken inside a police car, no matter how vintage? And why are you eating bear paws? Is that some sort of mountain delicacy that I don't want to know about? And I'm not too keen on this Luke fellow. Anyone who thinks putting vinegar into someone's coffee is an idea of a good joke cannot be trusted. You know my thoughts about Americans and this just proves my point!

Truly, Brodie. I think you should take the first flight from that place and spend the remainder of your American trip touring New York. Any group of people who eat that much butter cannot be a good influence.

Anders

PS: What in the world is a fritter?

From: Ellen Sutherland
To: Brodie Sutherland

Date: May 5
Subject: Re: Star Wars Day

Dearest Brodie,

What a wonderful message you sent us last night and then the additional note this morning! Fiona was quite enraptured by Samwise and his antics. She's determined to uncover whether Vaskr's tongue can reach to the bottom of a peanut butter jar now.

And the whole idea of being greeted with lightsabers and cloaks? I do believe these people are our sorts, Brodie. Pay no mind to Anders. He's always been terribly short on imagination, but he's excellent at spreadsheets.

The photos you sent were wonderful. I don't recall seeing you smile so broadly in a long time. You two make a fine pair. Has she given you any indication of her feelings other than friendliness? I know you've just met, but in all actuality you've known each other for months to this point. I must say, her smile appears quite as enamored as yours, but my mother's heart would only wish for the very best for you. And there's still the distance to consider, of course, should her heart turn in the direction of yours.

Fiona laughed so much over my description of the photo in the vintage police car. I of course had to rewatch a few of the episodes of *The Andy Griffith Show* and Fiona listened to the accents. She loves the way they talk. Does Isabelle sound like the characters on the television show? Fiona has been attempting to replicate the accent and I must say she's rather fantastic at it.

And Isabelle. How would you have known that a simple "trial" on this dating site would end up changing your life forever? For it has. You are not the same as you were in February, Brodie dear.

I have seen you grow in your comfort around others and your overall joyfulness. It does a mother's heart good.

I know your initial choice to join Heart-to-Heart was at the encouragement of the government's stipend plan, but look how God did something even better than you could have thought. Whatever the future, and even if we have to wait another year or two for Fiona's surgery, Isabelle has been a beautiful byproduct of you taking this chance.

What is the temperature like there? I cannot wait to hear about your *Star Wars* party this afternoon.

Please ignore Anders as much as possible. He desperately needs a romance of his own to shock him out of his terrible stagnation.

We look forward to learning more about your trip.

Love,
Mum (and Fiona)

• •

From: Anders Sutherland
To: Brodie Sutherland
Date: May 5
Subject: Mother!

Brodie,

Do not listen to Mother when it comes to this entire ordeal with your American online-woman. I just got off the phone with her and she talked as if you were ready to settle down and marry this stranger.

Anders

PS: You know Mother is a romantic. She cannot be trusted.

From: Brynna Sutherland
To: Brodie Sutherland
Date: May 6
Subject: Isabelle

Brodie,

You know I meant no offense whatsoever, but the financial benefits have to play in the back of your mind a little, don't they? Truly, it's a win all around. A darling romance for you, a speedier surgery for Fiona, and a bit of additional support for the bookshops. I don't see how you cannot think about the possibilities. But I shall refrain from alluding to the Foreign Spouse Initiative any longer.

And thank you for the photos! Isabelle is absolutely lovely! And won't she stand out over here with all that dark hair and those eyes! I have to think very hard to recall any one of my acquaintances who has dark eyes. I cannot wait to meet her! It's no good taunting us from a distance if we won't get the chance to see for ourselves, is it?

Just this afternoon she emailed me with some examples of graphics and she offered to make some for Sutherland's to show how they could appeal to different populations. Her creativity never stops. I love her for it. Brodie, if you don't marry her, would you at least give her a job? Or both! What a wonderful pairing you two would make both privately and professionally. And as the stipend report suggests, marriage AND employment offer an extra financial benefit! (Excellent thoughts, if you ask me.)

I'm utterly amazed at Isabelle's ease in coming up with ideas that perfectly fit what we need. She reads voraciously. From website designs to social media graphics to even some fun in-store activities to engage the locals and tourists alike, her initiatives boil over. She's a whirlwind of creativity and so generous with her ideas. In fact, I believe she's energized by . . . what did she call it? *Brainstorming*. How delightful! I'm not certain how to enact all of these things, but I imagine you and your mother could help. I'm attempting to watch a few videos on building websites and graphic design for marketing. Whether I can make the computer program work for me or not may be the issue at hand.

Brynna

PS: I hope you can convince Isabelle to come to the islands! It's truly a perfect fit for everyone.

From: Ellen Sutherland
To: Brodie Sutherland
Date: May 8
Subject: What a match!

Brodie,

I spoke with Brynna at the office today and we were both fairly enraptured over your new friend. Brynna took me to Mt. Airy's library website and I couldn't help but see the creativity you boast of in Isabelle on every page. And the videos of the Book Parade? Oh my heart! I don't think she realizes what a natural gift she has for celebrating books. She seems to have no idea of the gifts and talents she possesses with all this self-effacing and second-guessing. She draws people to stories and fairly exudes a love for them, and people, if you will note. She's always reaching out to help others in those videos. How lovely! And the video of her promoting a new release? Despite her introversion, she fairly beams on the screen when she discusses those beloved stories! She is certainly a young woman after our hearts, isn't she?

There's something unique about her uncanny way to match books to people. Is she a book whisperer? Yes, I laugh at that notion as well, but I cannot shake the underlying reality. Could you be in her life for much more than only a possible romance, but within the growth of your relationship you help her realize her true talents? That is what your father did for me. I would never have ventured into illustrating children's books if he hadn't used his endearing machinations to orchestrate opportunities. Even as he helped your grandpapa operate the bookshops as I took care of you children at home, he'd reserve one day a week to relieve me so that I could pursue my art. Every week. He was the dearest man in all the world and saw something in me I hadn't even realized yet. Love is a beautiful sort of magic in that way, isn't it?

I don't know what may evolve between the two of you, but from all you've shared, I can see some of myself in her—the uncertainty, the wandering spirit—but also potential. Oh, my dear boy, when a man loves a woman well, and she is a woman of any worth at all, she not only blooms beneath his love but takes every opportunity to love him in return. She cannot help it. And what a story that is to watch bloom!

Fiona and I look forward to your next report.

With love,
Mum

PS: Fiona asks for you to ring her. She misses your voice.

CHAPTER 15

<u>Text from Izzy to Luke:</u> Eli sent me another bouquet of roses. How many of those mean that he hasn't quite understood the "friendship" thing yet?

<u>Luke:</u> The fact that you're asking is probably your answer.

<u>Izzy:</u> Time to reiterate the "just your friendly editor" conversation.

<u>Luke:</u> Be clear, Izzy. Men need clear. So . . . be less southern.

From: Izzy Edgewood
To: Penelope Edgewood
Date: May 10
Subject: Sonnets and romance

Brodie has completely redefined romance for me. How could I have settled for those other guys? Was I just so messed up in my head and heart that I took whatever I could get? If I'd known a relationship could be like what I'm beginning to understand with Brodie, I'd have saved myself a lot of undue hardship. Yes, he's dorky and incredibly quiet around strangers—and even around Luke at times—so I'm the one generating conversations (weird, right?), but when we're together it's a constant flow of either excellent conversation or contented silence. There's comfort and excitement and anticipation and sweetness all wrapped up into these interactions. And he wants to *hear* from me! My ideas, my thoughts, my voice. What is that!!!

AND (as juvenile as it sounds) we held hands yesterday. He took my hand to help me over a stream while we hiked up Sugarloaf and then . . . he didn't let go. If there had been any uncertainty about our compatibility, it began to dwindle when he took my hand and was completely decimated by lunch when we debated between Lord Peter Wimsey or Hercule Poirot as the better literary detective. (Of course I had to fight for Peter, especially since he's paired up with the marvelous Harriet Vane . . . and the two EVENTUALLY fall in love.) Brodie held to his adoration of Poirot, though he did admit to the fact that "the right woman makes all the difference in any man's story." ACK!! I think you could have cooked bacon on my cheeks for a solid five minutes after that! How wonderful is that?? My heart declared right then and there that Brodie Sutherland is all he appears to be and so much more. (He also smells delicious.)

Oh, Penelope! My parents would have loved him with his dorky humor and tender heart. In a weird way he reminds me of Dad, only without the constant derby and unsightly waders! You know Dad always wanted to be an American version of James Herriot.

Anyway, I just wanted to share in my excitement. And to thank you for letting me share. I think Luke can see how well the match is, but talking to him about things like hand-holding and romance and Brodie's delicious smell make him start to twitch.

Love you,
Izzy

PS: Open-collared button-down shirts are just as nice as sweater-vests. Maybe even nicer. Whew . . .

PPS: We're reading Shakespeare's sonnets tonight by the fire. Thankfully it's supposed to be cool enough to have a fire in the fireplace, so it will not only be romantic but functional. I didn't need it to be functional, but it makes for a much better excuse

"'Even so my sun one early morn did shine with all triumphant splendour on my brow.'"

Brodie Sutherland was in her *apartment*! Sitting not two feet away from her. Brodie Sutherland was reading Shakespeare's sonnets to her in *her* apartment! They'd created this little evening routine of reading to each other since the second day of his trip, mostly after dinner and before board games or movies. But something about Shakespeare's *love* sonnets upped the romantic currency of the moment.

Izzy had never met a man who enjoyed reading with as much passion as her, and though she'd stumbled through reading aloud to him at first, his encouraging smile and ready engagement eased her into the habit without another hitch.

Listening to him talk brought all sorts of lovely feelings, but hearing him read? Heaven and earth, the sound brewed over the air and offered an internal hug that lingered long enough to bring a sigh. Deep, warm, with just the right amount of curling vowels and dipping intonation. Audiobooks may never satisfy again.

His hands cradled the old collection of sonnets they'd found at a secondhand bookshop during a lazy day of exploring. She'd felt those hands against hers, even once when he'd brushed a smudge of caramel icing off her cheek, somehow turning a super embarrassing moment into a Hallmark-worthy scene she wanted to recount to the beautiful-yet-short children they were bound to have someday.

Oh, she liked him. A lot.

She tried not to think about what would happen in four days . . . or afterward. Thousands of miles apart was one thing when you'd never met in person, but now? After she'd smelled his cologne and heard his laughter in real time? She couldn't imagine going back to life without him. They fit so well together. Frighteningly well. It all seemed too good. Too beautiful. Like someone dipped their finger into her dreams and painted them into reality.

Her grin almost spread into a giddy laugh. She squeezed her eyes closed in a moment of thanksgiving. What had she ever done to deserve something like this?

"'Yet him for this my love no whit disdaineth; Suns of the world may stain when heaven's sun staineth.'"

Would she have appreciated such open and honest affection, such transparency five years ago, or had the broken relationships of her past tuned her heart more toward appreciation of Brodie's personality than she would have without them?

"You pronounced all those 'th' words like a pro." Izzy wiggled her brows as he turned his aqua gaze on her. "Is that part of the Caedric language?"

His smile quirked and he released a low sentence of Caedric, without breaking eye contact. She didn't understand Caedric, but from the look on his face whatever he spoke translated into something her pulse seemed to understand.

"That . . . that sounded nice."

He wrangled with his grin. "I said that I didn't understand one word I just read from this sonnet."

"You did not!" Izzy's laugh burst out.

"Aye, 'tis true." His gaze fixed on hers, sparkling and welcoming.

Her breath caught just a little. She would gladly listen to him talk every day of her life, nonsensically or not. "If an unimportant sentence in Caedric sounds that beautiful, I can't imagine what one with meaning sounds like."

He studied her for a second, almost as if he planned to say something else, and then his lips crooked. "It's your turn." He offered her the book. "I challenge you to find one with more comprehension, Karre."

"Karre?" The unfamiliar word pooled and rippled warmth through her chest. "Does that mean something like sassy pants?"

"Sassy pants?" His grin spread into a laugh. "Um . . . not quite." He gestured toward the book. "Your turn and I expect you to choose well, since you love these sonnets so much."

She raised a brow at his reticence to explain the term but didn't press the issue. Could it be an endearment? A *romantic* endearment? Just for her?

"Very well then." She snatched the book and he leaned his head back against the couch, closing his eyes, his body stretched out in a lean line with his feet propped on the ottoman.

Izzy's attention lingered on his profile, his lips eased into a gentle smile she'd come to expect over the past week. She'd read about soul mates and always categorized the notion with glass slippers and talking frogs, but something inextricably linked her to him. She'd felt hints of it during their online communication, but now, in the flesh, the awareness strengthened into an almost tangible connection. Oh, how she wanted this to be true. Authentic. Hers.

He'd pretty easily slipped right into life with her crazy cousins, joining Luke on a few hiking excursions while Izzy had worked, even helping him with a construction job or two. He'd spent an entire two hours on a video call listening to Penelope talk movies and musicals followed by a thorough and dramatic interrogation about Skymar. And then three evenings ago, they'd joined Josie and Patrick for dinner, incurring Josie's not-so-subtle dislike. Josephine had never been one to guard her feelings. She basically cross-examined Brodie—even asking him of a possible criminal background—to such a degree Patrick intervened. But by the end of the meal, Izzy could tell Josie was softening. All Brodie had had to do was help with the dishes, ask about the twins, and compliment Josie's snow globe collection. He'd been positively perfect.

Her gaze dropped to his smile.

His kiss would probably be perfect too.

"Anytime, Miss Edgewood."

The comment, tinged with humor, brewed in the air between them and sent heat stinging her cheeks. Her breath squeezed in her chest, holding to emotions so big she barely knew what to call them . . . or perhaps she was afraid to give them a name because she *did* know what to call them. One was gratitude. The other?

Even saying it in her mind seemed too much.

She pinched the book between her hands and drew in a quivering breath. Her gaze dropped to a page and an idea pearled into action. She opened the book to her favorite sonnet, the one she'd listened to Richard Armitage read about three hundred times. There would be no going back if she read this one to him. It was one of the most famous, and not confusing at all. Brodie would understand and she'd lay bare her heart in the most vulnerable of ways. *"It is my spirit that addresses your spirit,"* as Jane Eyre declared to Rochester.

Izzy swallowed through her dry throat and began. "'Let me not to the marriage of true minds admit impediment. Love is not love which alters when it alteration finds, or bends with the remover to remove.'" Heat invaded her vision, but she didn't really need to see the words. Brodie's eyes were still closed. His lips at a fascinating tilt, almost . . . almost beckoning her forward. "'O no! it is an ever-fixed mark that looks on tempests and is never shaken.'"

The paper bouquet on the shelf near them caught her attention and reality clicked into place. Brodie had sent her the bouquet. He'd *known* her, even then.

How?

Her nose tingled as she shifted a few inches closer to him, the words shivering from her. "'It is the star to every wand'ring bark, Whose worth's unknown, although his height be taken.'"

Her breath pulsed shallow. He was now so close she could almost touch him, continuing the next few lines. "'Love alters not with his brief hours and weeks, But bears it out even to the edge of doom.'"

Could this be love? Did she even know how to trust her heart anymore?

"'If this be error and upon me prov'd, I never writ, nor no man ever lov'd.'"

His eyes opened then, and he stared back at her, unmoving. She laid down the book, moving nearer still, and with a timid hand she cupped his cheek, inching closer, and then she did something she never thought her wounded heart would have the courage to do.

She initiated a first kiss.

Isabelle's voice had grown closer, her words softer. Brodie soaked in the sound, the feeling within each syllable. Her storybook reading to the children oozed with emotion and animation, but now a vibrato of tenderness swelled over each passage, almost as if she said them . . . to him.

He attempted to control his breaths. The couch shifted next to him, but her recitation continued. Should he move? Open his eyes? He'd never been a confident lover, not that he'd experienced a great many romantic relationships, but his past had been more fumbling and reluctant than bold and debonair. Traveling across the world to meet her had been the most courageous romantic gesture he'd ever initiated. And now? He'd called her the one endearment that meant more than love—acceptance and admiration and tenderness—and to which he'd not been able to find an accurate English translation.

Then she shifted again. Something brushed against his arm. The soft scent of her fragrance swept as close as the sound of her voice.

"'I never writ, nor no man ever lov'd.'"

He raised his head and opened his eyes at the sudden silence and found she'd closed the small distance between them. Those large, fathomless eyes of hers stared into his. Uncertainty and something much sweeter softened those brown hues to amber. Her hair spilled around her face, brushing against his shoulder. With the slightest hitch of a breath, she placed her palm against his cheek and in achingly slow motion brought her lips to his. Her mouth barely grazed his, the ridges of her lips sliding over his to fit into place. Her fingers caressed his cheek and his breath trembled release.

He knew the cost of her initiation. Felt it to his core, but even more than that he recognized what she was admitting in this kiss. What she was offering.

When she pulled back enough to open her eyes, he sat up, bringing her with him, and in a gentle motion he cradled her cheeks with his palms and continued, with much . . . much less trepidation. In fact, uncertainty became the very last thing on his mind. Her lips softened beneath his, her fingers fisting into his shirt. The last hint of a question about her feelings disappeared, and he promised himself he'd do whatever it took to create a future with Isabelle Edgewood.

Text from Izzy to Penelope: The right kiss with the right man is worth it all, Penelope. Oh my, is it worth it!

Penelope: SQUEE!!!!!! Oh, Izzy! How wonderful! Though I do wish I hadn't been in the middle of the movie theater when I read your text. I disrupted my entire section with my response. Oh well, it was a silly man-movie anyway. I don't understand why men like to watch movies that have very little talking in them. And NO singing. Where is their imagination?! Anyway, I'm so tickled for you. I should be home tomorrow evening for a quick visit so I can approve of your dashing islander and his sweater-vests . . . or open-collared shirts, as the case may be. In person!

Penelope: I do like open-collared shirts as long as they're not open down to a man's navel. There's something about that look that either makes me think "drunk pirate" or "loose Spaniard." I blame operas.

Izzy: Sorry for the interruption but not the remarks. I can't wait to introduce you to him. As far as operas? I have no comment.

Penelope: What did Brodie's kiss say to you?

Izzy: Just one kiss wouldn't do.

From: Brodie Sutherland
To: Ellen Sutherland
Date: May 11
Subject: An answer to the visit

Dear Mum,

This evening I met Penelope, Isabelle's youngest cousin, who has auburn hair a little lighter than Fiona's. I believe Isabelle referred to it as strawberry blonde. She appears to be the most different in appearance of the cousins, not in her hair color alone but also with her gray-green eyes. She stared at me so long at one point, it became a bit uncomfortable. Isabelle remarked on her "slack-jawed expression like Uncle Herman every Christmas dinner," to which Penelope quickly corrected her expression with a delightful laugh. She doesn't appear to be hindered by one emotion for too long before it complies to another.

It is evident how much the cousins love one another. Very much as siblings. Their affability is more demonstrative than our family's, but the camaraderie is just as obvious and sincere. I had the sudden awareness of what Isabelle would have to give up to join me in Skymar, should our relationship continue its present course. How could I ask her to do that? I certainly wouldn't wish to leave the life I've built in Skymar, but I can't imagine, now that I've spent this time with her, planning a future where she isn't a part.

I'm sure that sounds premature, but I recall you mentioning how you knew Father was "the one" for you within the first week of your acquaintance. I feel the same about Isabelle, and with such certainty it's shocking. Whether she returns my affections with the same intensity, I do not know, but I feel as though I would be willing to redirect many pieces of my life to keep her nearby.

In response to your question from last night's phone conversation, today Isabelle and I spoke about our previous relationships. At first she was reluctant to discuss them, but after a little prodding, she opened up to me. She's borne the brunt of some scoundrels, Mum. It explained why, even after we'd agreed to officially begin dating, she seems cautious. My situation with Skye was nothing compared to Isabelle's heartbreak and humiliation. She apologized for her suspicion, for her disbelief that my intentions were true, and gently asked me to be patient with her as she took careful steps toward truly believing that "someone like me" could care for "someone like her." I hate the way her past has misconstrued her view of herself, but it helped me understand more about what you'd mentioned in trusting that Father truly loved you. How your heart must have been wounded for you to live in such self-doubt. I am determined to show her the truth. Not all men are scoundrels.

I am grateful beyond words for the example you and Father displayed of what love truly looks like.

Affectionately,
Brodie

PS: Please let Fiona know that Samwise likes to sing to the sound of emergency-vehicle sirens. He's quite good at it. The first time I heard him, it shocked me to such an extent I shot up from the table where Isabelle and I had been playing chess. Needless to say, my fast movements sent the chessboard and all its pieces vaulting through the air, and, to my utter humiliation, the black knight hit Isabelle directly in the eye. However, everything turned out fine. I took your long-held motherly advice and kissed her wound. She seemed to heal rather quickly after that.

From: Anders Sutherland
To: Brodie Sutherland
Date: May 12
Subject: Preposterous!

How on earth have you managed to convince yourself of this attachment to a practical stranger! And one who lives across the globe in some rural township in America! I have always thought you to be sensible, but I see you've taken leave of your senses in this account. Her hesitation provokes all sorts of warning signs, if one would take the time to push aside the hazy bloom of "love" and see clearly. I would wonder if her heart isn't distant or even attached elsewhere. How do you know someone who lives thousands of miles away isn't carrying on some dalliances while you wait all dreamy-eyed and forlorn?

I feel as though I've entered a Dickens novel and there is no way of escape!

Wake up, Brodie. If the money is not your objective, then detach your heart. It shouldn't be difficult. You only truly met her two weeks ago. How entrenched can one's heart become over such a short space of time?

I only say these things because I am concerned for you. You cannot know someone so quickly. It takes years to truly understand how two people will sort out a happy life together, so imagine the added difficulty of two different cultures. If you need an example of a southern American woman, I performed a quick Google search and the top listing was Scarlett O'Hara. Now think of that, I tell you.

Anders

CHAPTER 16

Brodie took the now-familiar trek down the sidewalk of Main Street toward the library, enjoying the wide variety of scents, from cherry blossoms to fried apple pies and the faintest hint of freshly brewed coffee. The town held an element of charm different from those at home, but he couldn't quite put his finger on the exact quality of difference. He'd observed that small towns across the world seemed to have a certain connectedness to them, but sprinkled in with their own uniqueness. Mt. Airy reminisced to bygone days of Andy Griffith, if Brodie guessed rightly. A barber's pole swirled in red, white, and blue colors, a colorful invitation to step inside for a trim. The ice-cream parlor welcomed patrons onto their parquet floor, the servers donning white caps and matching bow ties as if from a classic movie. And the pace fit into what he enjoyed most about Skern. Pleasantly relaxed.

The library came into view, its simple white-columned entrance setting it apart from the brick buildings framing each side of the street. Brodie increased his step, the call of books and his favorite book-loving lady drawing him forward. He'd seen her read to the children via Luke's video chat during the Book Parade, and she'd completely and utterly enchanted him with her faux accents and expressive dialogue, but the idea of watching her in real life ushered up a grin. She fit him in an oddly perfect sort of way.

He'd spent so many years hoping, without much real belief, that someone as book-obsessed and at times awkward might actually exist, and after two rather hurtful relationships—where both ladies turned out to be false—and a trip around the world, he'd finally found her.

And he was certainly hanging on for the happily ever after.

The spacious entrance to the library boasted walls decorated on either side with beach-related kid art. Ah, Brodie recalled Izzy telling him the theme for the next two weeks was ocean creatures. Beyond the entrance, the room opened to reveal neat rows of books, plenty of natural light streaming in from floor-to-ceiling windows, and all framing a large desk centered directly in front of him, where a rather unwelcoming woman of middle-age stood. A few other people stood nearby, but Brodie kept his focus on the librarian and donned a friendly smile.

She did not reciprocate. His pace slowed. Was this Izzy's aunt? Hadn't Izzy mentioned something about Josephine's influence on her aunt's opinion and how the woman hated the idea of some man from another country sweeping in and stealing Izzy away forever?

"Good morning." She didn't so much as flinch, but stared at him with such intensity he wondered if she read his thoughts. "I'm Brodie Sutherland. I think perhaps Izzy—"

"I know who you are." Her frown deepened as she examined him with narrowing eyes, but gave no further exposition.

"Ah, well, I was hoping to join Izzy's story time this morning." He checked his watch, just to give his eyes something to focus on besides her face. "Ten o'clock, isn't it?"

The older woman did not immediately answer, but her careful perusal started at the top of Brodie's head and traveled down to the notebook in his hands and back. If possible, the creases in her brow deepened into shadowy caverns enough to steal his Blighty Mastiff moniker without contest.

A young woman cleared her throat nearby, obviously waiting for the librarian to finish helping her.

"Wait here and I'll show you the way." Her gaze moved to a man Brodie hadn't noticed, who was standing to his left. In complete contrast to the scowl she'd offered Brodie, she bathed the stranger with a dazzling smile. "You too, honey."

The older woman disappeared down the library aisle and left Brodie standing in the residual silence with the stranger. He was a swarthy-looking fellow, dark hair waved back away from his face, and Brodie had caught a quick glance of uncommonly blue eyes, eyes now used to burn a stare into Brodie's profile.

A swell of undetermined uneasiness rivered up through his stomach as the silence continued, so Brodie finally turned.

The man's smile flashed wide. "You here for Izzy too?"

Brodie followed the man's gaze down to the notebook he held and back, an uncomfortable foreboding tightening every muscle in his body. *Too?* "Yes."

The man nodded and sent a grin to a young woman walking by before turning his attention back to Brodie. "Do you know how long her little story thing is supposed to last?" He glanced down at his phone, then looked toward the window as if gauging the accuracy of the time on his phone. "I thought I'd wait around to get a chance to see her, but it all depends on how long she's going to be with those kids."

Perhaps Brodie wasn't being charitable to this man, with his swath of black hair and two-inch height advantage. True, the very idea that he wanted to see Izzy pinched a frown into place on Brodie's face. But . . . wouldn't he expect people to come to the library to ask Izzy questions? He couldn't expect all of her visitors to be freckle-faced children.

"I believe story time is an hour."

The man's head came up from his phone, his gaze taking Brodie in as if for the first time. "You're not a local."

Clearly. "No, I'm visiting Izzy from abroad."

One of his brows tipped up. "Abroad?"

The question didn't need a response really, so Brodie merely nodded, the discomfort in his chest tightening with each passing second. Who was this chap?

"Well, Izzy's one of a kind, that's for sure. She just gets people. Understands characters and books." He leaned back against the counter and lowered his voice in a conspiratorial tone. "And she's great with romance too."

Brodie was incapable of responding, which didn't seem to impact the man at all.

"She's completely changed my life. Her creativity and ability to get to the heart of the problem? To read deeper?" His bright-blue eyes flashed to Brodie's face. "And her passion."

"Passion?" The word croaked from Brodie's throat.

"Of course, passion. Wow! She just keeps it bottled up until the right time and then . . ." He shook his head, his dastardly grin growing. "I'm just saying that, if you're going to make an impression on Izzy, you'll need to be an avid reader." The man continued, his chin taking on an arrogant tilt with a smile that seemed much too large for his face. He even seemed to lord his extra inches over Brodie, bending a little at the waist to accommodate the quiet a library required. "For example"—the man waved toward the books on the counter in front of him—"I've read at least five of these right here in front of me. Popular-fiction titles. These three in particular are very popular. You'll probably want to read them." He pointed to three covers with various aspects of Rome highlighted on the front. "Just a little advice." He took up the books he referenced and created a little stack in front of him on the counter like a little trophy.

An avid reader? Brodie surveyed the paltry stack of books the man referenced. Surely this stranger didn't dare lecture *him* on reading? Brodie's gaze fell to the piles of books on a cart nearby, taking inventory of the array of paperbacks and hardcovers, his attention pulled to a set of familiar loves. Without hesitation and a growing smile, he snagged the massive volume of Dickens's *Bleak House,* then a copy of *Harry Potter and the Order of the Phoenix*, which just so happened to have the largest page count of the series, and he topped his little book stack off with Melville's *Moby Dick*, leaving Brodie's book tower two inches taller—and much more prestigious-looking—than his competitor's. "I happen to be an extremely avid reader."

The man's eyes widened, and with only a hint of hesitation he stepped around the edge of the closest bookshelf and reemerged with four more books in hand. Without breaking eye contact, he added them to his growing tower, a look of unadulterated arrogance on his face.

Brodie almost chuckled. The loon had no idea with whom he was dealing. Casting a glance up at the category signs above the shelves, Brodie dashed off to the Classics section and returned with *Don Quixote, War and Peace*—both around a thousand pages—*The Hunchback of Notre Dame* at nearly two thousand, and grabbed The Lord of the Rings trilogy on his way back to the desk, carefully adding his finds to his growing set, which dwarfed the stranger's miniature list of modern paperbacks.

"You have not read all of those." The man's eyes narrowed into blue slits.

"I can give you a summary of each and every one if you want, and I keep a reading log." Brodie reached for his satchel at his hip. "With dates and—"

Without another hesitation, the man disappeared down the aisle again, this time returning with at least ten new books to add to his somewhat lopsided tower.

It was ridiculous. Brodie knew it. Most likely the stranger did too. And if Brodie had kept his good sense, he'd have stopped right there. But some primal urge spurred him back toward another bookshelf with the unstoppable quench for literary domination. In twenty seconds or less he returned with three undeniable winners: *Middlemarch, The Count of Monte Cristo*, and . . . the Bible, but he'd have won with just two of the three. The latter he brought along as a shameless boast.

Just as he was about to place the three-inch holy book on the tip-top of his book pile, the older librarian rounded the corner and came to a full stop. Her eyes bulged rather unbecomingly and then her entire expression firmed into a line of fury so fierce, Brodie lost every bit of his focus. His hand shook. From his periphery a movement of blue drew his attention and Isabelle emerged from a nearby doorway wearing a hat that looked like the massive head of a shark, her lovely bottom lip dropping.

And as the old adage proved, that was the final straw. The quivering book bumped Alexandre Dumas and in a slow, horrific motion, Brodie's tower of literary classics plunged toward the stranger's wobbly contemporaries, and both bastions plummeted to the floor in a massive crash.

Brodie's breath halted into the deafening silence that followed the catastrophe and then a quiet whimper rang out from the direction of the doorway. Pale faced and beautiful in her old-fashioned, belted dress, Isabelle rushed forward, followed by a collection of about fifteen children, all wearing some strange form of hat or other as if they were little Disney dwarves following their beloved princess.

At first he almost grinned as she hurried directly toward him like some melodramatic movie ending. "Oh, oh, are you all right?" He opened his mouth to respond, but just as she reached him, she dropped to the floor and swept her arms around the nearest book. "The bindings! The covers!" Her voice raised in pitch as she lifted the hardbound editions of The Lord of the Rings to her chest, her shark-hat bobbing as if to attack. "My precious."

"I really couldn't do much about it, Izzy, truly." The stranger waved toward Brodie, who'd dropped to his knees among the hatted children to collect the sprawling books. "He kept egging me on."

Isabelle's dark gaze came to Brodie's, a look of horror creasing her brow. "What were you doing?"

Brodie shot the stranger a glare and then placed his books on the counter, carefully taking a few the children offered. "Behaving as an imbecile." He retrieved a few more of the books, his face growing warmer as the implication of the last five minutes bled clear in his mind. Isabelle clearly had some romantic attachment with this stranger. After all that had happened between them over the past week, had he really been so blind or naive to think he had truly won her heart?

"I found one too, Miss Izzy," came a child's voice.

"Me too."

"I told you that you shouldn't have brought this foreigner here, Izzy." The librarian's harsh whisper carried enough volume to make her point quite clear. "Not when you already have a perfect catch." The woman's face wrinkled into smiles as she looked over at the stranger.

"Aunt Louisa, that really isn't—"

"You've always been my favorite librarian, Mrs. Edgewood," came the stranger's warm response. "The best I've ever met, actually. A perfect match, if you know what I mean."

"Miss Izzy, here's another one," a child interrupted.

But Brodie had already heard and seen enough. He needed air, distance. In usual style he'd jumped into a situation with full heart and found his expectations and reality stood chasms apart. He took the distraction as an opportunity to slide from the crowd and escape out of the library. His chest burned but he increased his pace down the walkway. Why had he opened up so much, so quickly? Had Anders been right? What an utter idiot he'd been!

Brodie knew it was possible she'd take a while to warm up to the idea of being with him, but . . . well . . . His feet faltered and he squeezed his stinging eyes closed. No wonder he'd taken so long to risk his heart again, but this time . . . he'd begun to truly believe in all the magic.

Not again.

Izzy had taken the hardback The Lord of the Rings into her arms and swept up the *Illustrated King James Bible* before standing from her place on the floor among the literary disaster.

"He wouldn't stop challenging me on the books I've read." Eli shrugged a shoulder and finally lowered himself to pick up one of the books from the floor. *Ebony's Fire*, if Izzy guessed by the color scheme. One of his own. She replayed his explanation in her mind.

"Why would Brodie challenge you about books?"

"Because Eli made it clear that he was interested in you, is what I caught from the conversation." Aunt Louisa raised a brow and sniffed the air, as if she cared very little for the whole thing. "Not that I could hear everything through the bookshelves, but I'd say Eli was making great strides in showing his reading abilities over that *foreigner*."

Another look at the books now stacked neatly back on the counter gave a clear distinction about who chose which books. Three books Eli had chosen were the ones he'd authored. Cheater.

And then there were the classics and beloved ones. All hardbound. All Brodie.

"Your interest in me?" She studied Eli, shaking her head. "We're not dating."

"I didn't say we were dating, though I have high hopes of winning you back." He shrugged a shoulder.

"Winning me back?" She shook her head, her voice rising well above story-time volume. "Eli, you never really *had* me. I was your editor. We were working on friendship, not romance. Is that what you said to him?"

"Whoa!" He raised his palms in defense. "I only talked about your passion for books and how great you are with romance."

"How great I am with . . ." Her mind clicked through the conversation.

She spun around to look for Brodie, but he was nowhere to be seen.

Air left her lungs in a burst, as she replayed the previous conversation and her subsequent reaction. *Brodie!*

Without another word she rushed to the door and out onto the sidewalk. Both directions gave no clue of his whereabouts, until she caught sight of him crossing onto Main Street, his stride long and fast.

She planted her foot to run, but as she tried to raise it, her foot caught. She looked down and lost her balance. The heel of her shoe wedged into the sidewalk crack. With a twist of her body and a hand to her skirt to keep it from flaring high enough to scar young children for years to come, something cracked and she hit the grass to the left of the sidewalk.

With a moan, she pushed up from the ground to find her heel broken from her shoe and a nice little slash down her right leg, as well as a throb in her ankle. Not exactly the classy, rom-com chase she'd been concocting as she shoved open the library doors in search of Brodie, but it seemed fairly appropriate for her real life. She gathered what was left of her shoe and her pride, and hobbled off on a painful run down the street.

What did he think? That she hadn't cared about him as much as the books? Her stomach tensed. Or that she was dating Eli while also stringing Brodie along?

Dear Lord, help me. My life has become a Bridget Jones rerun.

She increased her pace.

"Brodie!"

Her voice barely made a dent in the space between them, but she tried again. He didn't so much as turn around, but a few curious onlookers stared at her as if she'd lost her mind. She smiled but knew her behavior only confirmed the thoughts half the town had about her already . . . book spouting, exuberant storytelling, odd hats, and all.

She ran harder. He'd just crossed the street near the bank.

"Brodie," she called again, and this time his feet faltered. "Brodie, please."

At this, he stopped completely and made a slow turn in her direction. His expression slowed Izzy's approach and almost brought her to tears. Gone was his welcome smile and the ready glint in his eyes. The tender expression she'd grown to expect when he looked at her. Instead, a wariness pulled his lips into a frown and dulled his gaze. Oh, what had she done!

"I'm . . . I'm sorry," she rasped out as she attempted to catch her breath.

His attention dropped to her uneven steps and he rushed forward. "What happened to you? Are you all right?"

The tears won, then. Blurring his face from her view. "I . . . I fell trying to catch you." She waved toward her foot. "Broke my heel . . . I'm not sure what else." She reached for his arms, holding him in place. "There's nothing between Eli and me. Nothing."

He shrugged off her hold and stepped back, remaining quiet.

"You have to believe me. We barely even dated at all. And I ended everything once I realized how much . . . how much it meant for me to meet you." Oh, none of this was coming out the right way. "I was his rebound girl, I think. He'd convinced himself he cared about me more than I ever cared about him."

"I know the feeling."

The low response stole Izzy's breath and she whimpered, catching his arm as he turned to resume his walk. "No, Brodie, please. Eli may *think* he wants to be with me, but I've made it clear we are only friends. That's it!"

"Then what is this Eli said about knowing how much you love romance and are creative with him and—"

"I'm his editor."

"What?"

"In fact, the only reason I think Eli ever started dating me in the first place was because he knew I'd help him with his books. The veritable story of my dating life! Pretend romance for services rendered."

She drew in another breath, trying to ease the thrumming of her pulse in her ears. "He never really cared romantically about me and I never cared about him anywhere close to the way I—" Her breath caught.

He raised his brow as if challenging her to finish, but the words wouldn't come. What if she spoke them to him? What if she gave her heart and then . . . then everything fell apart? Dating was one thing, but expressing her heart? Being brave behind a screen and face-to-face weren't the same.

"What do you want, Isabelle?"

It was such a simple sentence offered from his soft, smooth, baritone voice, and the answer emerged so quickly in her mind, it shocked her. *You.* Could it really be that simple?

"What do *you* want?" *Perfect, Izzy. Very brave of you!* She inwardly groaned.

He studied her for a long moment, as if garnering his own courage or reading her mind. Maybe. In that case she wouldn't have to voice her thoughts after all.

"I want to be with you. That's what I want."

The declaration reverberated through her, shaking free a few tears. So simple. No games.

"You say that with such certainty."

And then his lips twitched ever so slightly, a tiny glint resurfacing in those familiar eyes. "Ever since *you* realized I wasn't your cousin, I've become more and more certain that I'd never meet anyone like you again . . . and I don't want to. To my mind, you're more than enough for me. Fairly perfect, actually."

"But . . . but how can you be sure of that already? We've only known each other a few months and just met in person." Even as she asked, her heart pinched against the doubt. Just looking into his face, realizing his care, well, maybe she knew the answer too.

"We're not teenagers who are still trying to sort out what we want from a life partner." He offered a gentle shrug, his grin peeking through just a little more. "Except for your current doubt, you've been everything I've wanted. How could I have known you'd not only be smart and kind and ridiculously creative, but also beautiful and funny and as much in love with stories as I am. Maybe even more so."

His words pieced together like the ending of a romantic comedy. She did love him. He was real and authentic and simply wonderful in all the ways she didn't know she wanted so badly. And the very idea of starting a day without knowing he thought about her somewhere in the world nearly brought her to tears . . . and she was already crying.

She didn't know how everything would work out between them living on two separate continents, but at the moment she was certain of one thing. It was time to step into the heroine role. Seize the day. Claim her future and her Brodie. And take up her courage.

"I want to be with you too." She sniffled, wiping at an errant tear. "I never imagined someone like you existed anywhere else but in a book, and then you showed up and I've had this fight-or-flight doubt that any of this was really happening. And if it *was* really happening, I'd envisioned all the ways I'd mess it up, because you're so much *better* than any book."

And then his smile flared wide as he breached the distance between them. "The highest of praise."

"I mean it in a very nonfiction sort of way."

"Aye, I believe you do." Without another hesitation, he slipped his arm around her waist and pulled her to him. As he closed the distance, her breath caught in anticipation, and then . . . his forehead hit the front of her hat.

Her eyes flew wide. Her *shark* hat! Had she hobbled down Main Street with a broken heel wearing a shark hat? Heat flooded her face and she opened her mouth to explain, but his knee-weakening grin stole her words.

Without so much as a glance around, Brodie nudged the shark-face, cloth teeth and all, up to perch higher on her head, and with a touch to her chin, he took her lips with his, regardless of the street, the passersby, or even a honking horn here and there.

Every doubt dissipated with his tenderness. Every fear dissolved with his gentle touch. This was what she'd been waiting for her whole life. And in one fluid motion, her foot, the heel-less one, tipped back and then popped up in instant synchrony with the perfection of this man and her heart.

Bring on tomorrow. She was ready for happily ever after.

From: Izzy Edgewood
To: Luke Edgewood, Penelope Edgewood
Date: May 12
Subject: An unexpected-yet-expected journey

Luke and Penelope,

I just saw Brodie off at the airport and I'm sitting in my car crying like a baby. This is ridiculous. How can I miss someone I've just met? And his flight hasn't even left yet! I'm losing my mind. He's wonderful. Too wonderful. Ridiculously wonderful. And now he's gone and I have to figure out what to do with that.

Plus, to add to the dilemma, he asked if I had any "holiday time" coming up in June. When I questioned why, he wondered if I'd be willing to fly to the Skymar Islands so I can MEET HIS FAMILY!!! (Yes, the capitalizations were necessary.) In fact, his exact words were, "I know it's a great deal to ask, but if I help purchase your ticket, would you come to Skymar for a week or two . . . or, perhaps, forever?" Moments like this are when I wonder if I read too much fiction. Men don't speak like that in real life, do they? I mean, isn't that one of the reasons I read fiction?

Do you think Bilbo felt this way when Gandalf showed up at his door and bullied him into an adventure? I mean, Brodie Isn't bullying me, of course. He's wonderful. But . . . well, I've never even been on a plane before. I don't even know if I can. I mean, I CAN, but . . . can I? And a part of the population of Skymar don't even speak English. And it's an island! You all know how I feel about boats, and islands are kind of like land-boats.

But how can I NOT go? I'm bound to him through books and laughter and heart-stories and words I've never spoken to anyone. And though I'm not a particular fan of self-absorbed and prickly Edward Rochester, his quote to Jane Eyre about ribs and strings and bleeding inwardly has become painfully poignant at this very moment as I contemplate the thousands of miles between me and Brodie. So I *must* go! But how can I go?

Besides, I've always wanted to travel to some of the places I've read about. Always. And people survive flying every day, even if my parents didn't.

Help!

Irrational Izzy

PS: I really am a grown-up. I promise. And I know exactly what I'm supposed to do. I just need to melt down first.

PPS: He's real, right? You guys saw him too?

From: Penelope Edgewood
To: Izzy Edgewood, Luke Edgewood
Date: May 12
Subject: Re: An unexpected-yet-expected journey

Izzy,

I really don't understand your analogy at all. Bilbo is still alive?!? I thought that cat died years ago.

Oh my goodness, Izzy! But what a quote! "Or perhaps forever"???!!! He already wants to marry you! Of course he does. I adore Brodie. He complimented me on my freckles. Any man who can appreciate freckles is worth talking to, you know? And I'm so glad Josephine didn't scare him away when she started lecturing him on the value of country life. I'd never seen her wield a spatula like that before. I've heard that pregnant women can be unpredictable, so just imagine how a pregnant woman with twins could be! It's a good thing Brodie has fantastic reflexes. Another attribute to add to your list for him. And you didn't *just* meet him. You've known him since February. I think that meeting him in person only secured your feelings—kind of like smelling the cookie before taking a bite.

As far as traveling? You must go! Then you can tell me all about it so I can prepare for my study abroad next semester. Plus it's the perfect opportunity for you to show him you care as much as he does. Though I think he cares more for you than you do him, but I'm fine if you want to prove me wrong.

Penelope

PS: From all I remember (and have heard) about your parents, Izzy, I think they would want you to travel because they loved traveling. Seems to be a great way to celebrate something they loved, kind of like you're taking them with you.

PPS: I refuse to debate you on the virtues of Edward Rochester. Suffice it to say, you are wrong. He may be misunderstood, but he's incredibly romantic and brooding and a little dangerous. Though he doesn't seem the sort to wear sweater-vests.

PPPS: Is there a *Jane Eyre* musical? I bet Rochester would be a bass.

From: Izzy Edgewood
To: Penelope Edgewood, Luke Edgewood
Date: May 12
Subject: Re: An unexpected-yet-expected journey

Penelope,

Clearly you have not watched the movies I sent to you. Please do so immediately. We cannot keep having these discussions if you have no idea who Bilbo, Gandalf, Samwise, Frodo, Aragorn, or any other *Lord of the Rings* characters are. We just can't.

Secondly, Brodie is adorable, and I am hopeful that by the end of the cookout, Josephine had warmed up to him. She stopped calling him Bradley, so that's definitely a move in the right direction. Patrick took the spatula away after the first two swipes in Brodie's direction, so I think that helped too. And . . . "smelling the cookie before taking a bite"??? I don't think I have a response for that.

Thirdly, traveling to Skymar is definitely a way to show Brodie I care about him. If only I can keep from hyperventilating on the plane to such an extent it drops cabin pressure to an all-time low and causes the plane to have to turn around in midflight . . . or crash. Of course, I would die with the memory of Brodie's kiss so that's not all bad.

Izzy

PS: You are right about my parents. I've never thought of it that way before.

PPS: I refuse to comment about your mild obsession with Rascally Rochester except to say HE WAS ALREADY MARRIED.

PPPS: And he was almost perpetually grumpy. Do you really want a man like that?

Text from Luke to Izzy: I can't believe I'm typing this, but Penelope does have a point about your parents. They would love seeing you fly. (As usual, the rest is nonsense.)

Luke: How much do you care about Brodie? Answer that, and you'll have what you need.

Izzy: Enough to take sedatives to fly to Skymar.

Luke: Call cousin Clark. With a pharmacy degree at his disposal, I'm sure he can fix you up the perfect courage cocktail. In the meantime here is a sentimental quote from Lao Tzu that is poignantly true and therefore I am forced beyond my usual texting repartee to share it with you. "Being deeply loved by someone gives you the strength. Loving deeply gives you the courage." Be brave, Izzy.

Izzy: Thanks, Luke.

Luke: I'm still trying to decide if I'm glad or not that I actually know who Edward Rochester is.

From: Izzy Edgewood
To: Penelope Edgewood, Luke Edgewood
Date: May 13
Subject: Re: An unexpected-yet-expected journey

Luke and Penelope,

I just sent Brodie an email after speaking to Aunt Louisa about time off. I've told him I'll come the third week of June as he'd suggested because it's some big festival they have in Skymar during that week, and he thought I'd enjoy seeing the culture.

I don't know what's going to happen next. I don't know how we're going to make this relationship work, but I do know that he's worth every fear and insecurity I have, because when I'm with him, somehow I feel like I'm a better version of me. There's something incredibly special about that kind of . . . love? Dare I even think it?

So I am going. And I am hoping. And whether all this turns out to be the perfect romance or not, somehow I know my heart needs to take this chance . . . to believe in my choices again. Brodie is worth it and so am I.

Izzy

PS: Luke, thank you for being brave enough to step into the world of repartee. Loving someone *does* give us courage. Sedatives may help a little too.

PART 3

Of Bookshops, Manor Houses & Being Brave

CHAPTER 17

From: Izzy Edgewood
To: Josephine Martin, Luke Edgewood, Penelope Edgewood
Date: June 21
Subject: Survived with everything but my pride

I've just landed and wanted to send you a quick email—while I have Wi-Fi access—to let you know that I survived the flight. I wasn't quite sure how my body (or my mind) would handle seven hours on a plane just to get to Dublin and then another two hours to Skymar International Airport, but I slept most of the way and only woke myself up once with my own snore. Now whether that's a testament to my lack of snoring or the potency of my cocktail, I can't say, but a few glares from my seatmate makes me wonder. (She had no right for glares . . . See my note below.)

Josephine, though I appreciate your intentions, drinking copious amounts of water while on a flight is not a good idea, despite the benefits of hydration. NO ONE wants to try to avoid doing the pee-pee dance while hundreds of people watch you wait for that teeny-tiny bathroom door to open . . . and *then* a sudden bout of turbulence hits. Can I just say I don't think I've prayed that hard since Penelope got her head stuck in that pipe under Grandpa Edgewood's house because she was pretending to be a rabbit. I had no idea firefighters answered calls like that. As a mom who has twins dancing on her bladder on a regular basis, I thought you might be a little more aware about these sorts of things.

Otherwise, besides my seatmate snoring like Luke's dog when I was actually coherent, the flight offered a beautiful view. I suppose there will be lots of views I've never seen before, since I've never traveled outside of the United States, but this flight, at night? Wow! The moon glowed down on the tops of the clouds like some magical world. I envisioned a dozen stories before sunrise. It was a great way to pass the time and I could pretend my seatmate was the disgruntled dragon in my make-believe story, until the cocktail took over and I lost consciousness for a while.

Unfortunately, as I wait to disembark my nerves have ramped back up to irrational.

Luke and Penelope, just so you know, if I die in some foreign country and Brodie's family turn out to be some mafia-like group that use their bookstores as a front, it was all because you forced me to go. Okay, *forced* might be a really strong description, but saying things like, "If you don't, you'll always wonder. You don't deserve that and neither does the man you choose." I think Penelope even hinted to me being a coward.

What's a girl supposed to do about something like that? My future at stake? My courage? How can a woman who is trying to be a heroine turn away from such a challenge? Well, I can assure you, if flying across an ocean with the threat of losing my "water" in front of a hundred strangers doesn't increase one's courage, I'm not sure what will! And as I wait to disembark, my courage is sufficiently stretched, despite the mafia possibilities.

Because (thank you, Luke) only my ENTIRE FUTURE hangs in the balance! No stress there!

Well, here I am. And so I will be brave and move forward into the great unknown of Brodie's family and Skymar—a country where a significant portion of the population do not speak English, so hopefully I'll never get lost on my own or else I may be putting those expert skills into practice I learned in playing Pictionary with you guys. (As I recall, I usually won, if I didn't have to draw animals . . . in which case we all know how that turned out. Yes, I do know that cows and monkeys look very different from one another.)

I kept reminding myself how Brodie and dreams were worth all of this and my parents would be smiling down from heaven. That helped. Especially when my thoughts turned to certain heartwarming memories of the lip-on-lip variety.

I'm not sure when I'll be able to send another email, but if you don't hear from me in a few days, just assume I've suffered the fate of Stevenson's David Balfour: been struck senseless, kidnapped, and am drifting on the high seas somewhere. (Is the guilt trip working?) Okay, okay, it's just my nerves, but the flight attendant has announced that it's time to disembark so . . . here I go.

I love you all.

Heroically,
Izzy

PS: I can't help but think of one of my favorite quotes at this moment: "It's a dangerous business, Frodo, going out your door. You step onto the road, and if you don't keep your feet, there's no knowing where you might be swept off to."

PPS: Let's hope the "sweeping" isn't by pirates.

Izzy hadn't been certain what it would feel like to see Brodie again. After all, it had only been a little over a month since he left Mt. Airy, but they'd continued their video chats and emails, except with a renewed sprinkle of something rather fairy tale-ish, if she thought about it. I suppose if you add some amazing kisses to any online conversation, the interactions shift into a new area, and boy oh boy, throwing a rockin' smooch—or dozens—into a budding relationship tipped the temperature into the cozy-sweater range of perfect.

She tugged her backpack onto her shoulder and followed the other passengers through the small airport, grin growing as she read passing signs, most bilingual. Of course she had no idea what the word *Karre* meant, but it looked lovely in written form—though Brodie speaking it was even lovelier. She'd attempted to google it, but even those answers gave vague definitions like "term of endearment" and "tender affection." Both of which were nice but ambiguous.

Overhearing his conversations with his mother on the phone when he visited nearly had her swooning from kneecaps to nose. He'd switch back and forth between Caedric and English without a glitch.

She straightened her spine and scanned the waiting area ahead.

Surviving the flight had definitely proven a great start to her very first international adventure. And after making it through customs without any major disasters (she didn't count the fact of having to ask the airline attendant to repeat herself for every sentence), she'd had time to tame her hair, change her coffee-stained T-shirt, and apply concealer to the moon craters beneath her eyes. All good. Even if jitters the size of drop-scare rides kept swooping inside her stomach, she'd arrived in Skymar . . . on the other side of the world. And Brodie would be here.

Hopefully.

She closed her mind to any more unrealistic imaginings that overreading tended to conjure up during high-stress, life-changing moments.

The crowd dispersed up ahead as various travelers found their waiting people and Izzy slowed her pace, attempting to keep her expression as placid as possible. "Terrified" probably wasn't the best first impression to make on someone's mind after not seeing him for a month. Though the fact that one of their last moments ended in her nursing a bleeding ankle while hopping along Main Street shoeless and wearing a shark hat had to help desensitize him to possible future scenes with her.

And then, among the strangers, a familiar pair of eyes met hers. Brodie's grin slipped from one corner to tip the other, and suddenly the flight, crime families, snoring dragons, and coffee stains didn't matter. She'd found him. Her whole body relaxed as tension slipped away with a sigh.

It was strange how connected to him she felt. All those emails and video calls, all those conversations blended together to create this inexplicable bond of friendship. Her gaze dropped to his lips again and heat rose into her cheeks. Well, a little more than friends.

Was this sweet, tender, and unexpected calm a hint to the truth she belonged with him?

The sweater-vests were absent in June, but she wasn't complaining. He walked toward her wearing a green polo, jeans, and a heart-stopping smile. Yep, that was worth any and every midflight terror or embarrassment from Mt. Airy to here.

They approached each other, pulled forward like magnets to metal, and without pausing, he slipped one palm to her waist, the other to her cheek, and touched his lips to hers. Since he only stood about an inch or two taller than her, it didn't take much shifting on her part, but the entire greeting took her by surprise. No "hello." No "I'm so glad to see you." Just a sweet, warm, delightful welcome of the nonverbal variety, which said all those things without using words. She admired his efficiency and slipped her hand to his shirt lapel to help him be efficient a little longer. Though she'd purchased about a dozen cedar-scented candles since Brodie left, none of them replicated the real thing. She breathed him in, his scent and his lips a perfectly delightful combination.

Her foot took a tilt up. Yep, just as good as the last time. *Fairy tales, here we come!*

"You look surprisingly rested for such a long trip." He searched her face, carefully slipping her backpack from her shoulder, as if he hadn't just kissed her into orbit in the middle of an airport.

Perhaps men of Skymar handled intoxicating kisses better than American women because it took a few seconds for her brain to absorb and then comprehend his statement. "Distance and makeup work miracles in a woman's appearance, I think."

His grin split wide and she stood in one of those dazed expressions like love-struck characters in animated movies when the hearts start ballooning from their heads. Yep, the flight and all the mafia paranoia were totally worth it.

"I'm so glad you're here."

"Me too," she whispered, falling in step beside him as they navigated the crowds toward the baggage area. "Oh, I brought you something!"

He paused and she reached into the front pocket of her bag, her teeth skimming over her bottom lip as she tried to tame her smile. *Calm down, Izzy.* She tugged the wrapped gift from its place and handed it to Brodie, nearly shaking from excitement.

His brows rose as he looked from her to the odd-shaped gift. She'd attempted to wrap the T-shirt around the book to disguise the contents, because, well, a book for a booklover was incredibly predictable. Though she never grew tired of them.

The book slipped from the T-shirt first and the glow in his eyes rewarded her careful perusal of every online Tolkien fan shop on the planet. "An illustrated hardback of *The Hobbit*?" He chuckled and leaned over to kiss her cheek.

"You were Brodie the Hobbit when we first met."

"Indeed." He examined the book and then looked back over at her. "I have the perfect spot for it on my shelf."

What self-respecting reader wouldn't?

He shook out the green T-shirt to view the front and his laugh reverberated against the sterile airport walls with such surprise, it ignited her own. The shirt had a silhouette of Yoda and in the center of the silhouette were the words "Yoda Best."

"I know it's corny, but it somehow seemed to fit."

"'Corny'?"

"Oh!" Language barrier. "It means quirky or silly."

"Then yes, it's corny." His grin stretched. "And brilliant. Thank you."

"It got Luke's approval."

"Of course it did." He graced her face with another tender look and they resumed their walk. "But I must admit, your presence is my favorite gift. I'm beyond excited to introduce you to Skymar, and we'll have a nice long drive to begin the introduction."

She released a long sigh, as if she'd been holding her breath all the way across the Atlantic. "I can't wait."

Within a half hour of their drive, Isabelle had fallen asleep. Of course Brodie imagined she'd wake up horrified at her unintentional blunder, but he rather liked the idea of her feeling comfortable enough to nod off in front of him. In fact, having her in his world inspired all sorts of future thoughts to make this relationship work.

Could he convince her to leave her life and family for his?

It all seemed rather impossible but as Lewis Carroll so famously wrote, "I've believed as many as six impossible things before breakfast." And he believed in this—whatever magic needed to take place to make it all a reality.

He had the entire two weeks planned to showcase every advantage Skymar could offer, and coming during the King and Queen Festival offered her the very best display of the islands in one place . . . with a few added benefits thrown in. He could already tell his mother had designs on Isabelle too.

Isabelle made the sweetest murmuring sound to his left, her head tilted toward him, her hair in wisps around her face. His chest expanded with a deep breath and a bigger hope. After two weeks getting to know her in person and months of online conversations, he couldn't imagine finding anyone else who fit into his book-loving nerd-world as well as her.

Enough—he drew in a breath—even enough for him to give up his world?

"Please," she whispered, her brow wrinkling, voice growing a little louder. "Open the door."

Brodie glanced her way before returning his attention to the road. Curious little dream there—of course jetlag can show itself in peculiar ways, he supposed.

"Open the door!" She sat up, eyes blinking wide, and then she looked around her, apparently orienting herself. Her gaze met his and she pressed a palm to her forehead with a groan back against the seat. "Good grief. Of all the times, why couldn't I have slowly opened my eyes like a sleeping princess instead of like some terrified cat?"

He burst out laughing. "What were you dreaming of?"

She grimaced up at him, her face half covered with her hand. "A snoring dragon that was blocking my way to the bathro—" She winced. "Never mind."

His chuckle reemerged. "I've not heard of those side effects from flying before."

"If you didn't learn from your visit to Mt. Airy, having typical expectations may not sufficiently prepare you for a relationship with me."

"Don't question my preparation, Karre, you haven't met my family yet."

"I like it when you call me Karre."

"I like calling you Karre."

Awkward silence following a subtle declaration of the heart rarely boded well for the giver. He sneaked a glance. She stared at him with a gentle smile curving her lips.

So maybe awkward wasn't so bad. "It sounds so much better than something like ducky."

"Ducky?"

"Yeah, I think I read it somewhere about an English grandma calling her grandkids that." She grinned, her cheeks brimming with color and his heart took a little faster rhythm. She seemed to catch the direction of his admiration because her face brightened even more and she turned toward the window. Then gasped.

His smile inched wide. "This is Inswythe Brus."

The ancient bridge extended from the island of Fiacla to Ansling, giving a rather breathtaking view of the harbor city of New Inswythe as they crossed the North Sea.

"Right. *Brus* means bridge."

"Yes, and this is by far the largest of our bridges and one of the oldest, and the main connector of the island of Fiacla to the largest island, Ansling."

"And that's New Inswythe, right?" She turned those shining eyes on him and nearly had him steering into the next lane.

"You've been studying your Skymar geography, have you?"

"I like maps." She shrugged a shoulder and wiggled her brows. "They're in books."

And snuggling up with her and a book sounded like a perfect idea. Forever. Heat climbed from his increased pulse to settle in his face. Yes. An excellent idea.

"But it looks more amazing in person." She pressed close to the window as the mainland of Ansling came into view to reveal the modern buildings and steel skyline of New Inswythe. The only hint of history from this distance came in the form of the Kirk ruins of Abbotskeld on a cliff above the cityscape in the distance.

"What's that place?"

Ah, of course Isabelle would notice it too. He had a certainty she'd enjoy the historical aspects of Ansling much more than the modern. Which suited him, since he lived near two of the oldest towns on the island.

"The church ruins from one of the first known settlements on the island of Ansling. Runaways, from all one can tell. Escaping religious persecution. They created that sight as a marker of their faith but also as a watchtower, since it leads into Port Alastair."

"One of the only places ships can come into port on the island," she stated as if from a book.

"Exactly, professor." He chuckled and she rewarded him with another beautiful grin. "On Ansling there are Port Quinnick—my personal favorite and a place we'll travel for some exploring—Port Kae in the northern section, and Port Ard Leathe—the main accessible points of the island, if one doesn't wish to climb a cliff."

"Unless one has a giant named Fezzik." One dark brow edged upward with her lips. "From my understanding he's pretty good at cliff scaling."

And with a simple reference to *The Princess Bride*, he fell a little deeper in love with her. Anders would likely ladle suspicion on her. Fiona would beg for Isabelle to read to her, and Mother would have designs to kidnap her for a shopping trip or two. But not if Brodie stole her first, because at the moment, he hoped at his core that Isabelle Edgewood fell in love with him and Skymar enough to change the course of her future several thousand miles in a north-easterly direction.

The landscape swelled before her like a strange mixture of the lushness of the Shire and the intimidating vastness of the Misty Mountains. Green hills interspersed with rocky ledges, all giving way to a view of endless sea on one side and quaint, idyllic villages on the other with a ragged row of barren-capped mountains looming in the distance. An occasional castle or ruin added to the wonder of Ansling. Izzy wasn't quite sure where to look next or how she'd remember it all, and taking a copious amount of photos from a moving car meant she'd have to delete more pictures than she'd keep, but . . . well . . . she wanted to remember it all. Share it all.

"There's a faster way to my mother's house, but"—he grinned at her from his periphery, inciting the tiniest flick of a dimple—"this way is more scenic and I wanted to impress you."

"You've succeeded. I don't think I've pressed my face all the way up against the window yet, but I've gotten pretty close." She inwardly cringed at the thought of leaving nose prints on his window. Good heavens she was the weirdest creature. Maybe the fact that he lived on such a small island meant his experiences with normal women were few, so perhaps she was unique enough to keep his attention, at least. Otherwise she couldn't quite figure out what he saw in her.

"Usually the drive from the airport to Skern is closer to two hours, but since you took a kip, I thought you could handle the four-hour scenic route, especially when we stop for dinner in Limmick. They have the best fish and chips on the entire island."

Her smile broke free for the millionth time. The view pulled her attention back to the fog-cloaked sea. "My world must have looked so bland to you."

"On the contrary, those mountains falling one over the other in a blue haze were magnificent, and the fact that you have roads on which you can drive to witness the views?" He shook his head. "In the northern edge of Ansling, some of the mountains are too high or dangerous for roads and many of the others are so remote, no one has taken the risk of creating a tourist opportunity."

A stone wall appeared to their right, blocking the view of the countryside, and in only a few minutes, two massive iron gates came into view, a golden seal embossed with the letter *R* on the front of them.

"One of the royal palaces—the main one, in fact."

Izzy flipped her attention from Brodie back to the passing gate as she attempted to peer down the long drive beyond the iron bars. "*R* stands for royals?"

"Yes, for the most part. It's from the Gaelic word for royal, which also starts with an *r*." He kept his gaze forward on the winding, narrow road ahead, but his grin resurfaced, as it had been doing the entire drive. Well, during the part when she wasn't unconscious and probably drooling while she talked in her sleep. Heat rushed into her face.

"We'll have the opportunity to tour Carlstern Castle"—he gestured behind them with his head—"near the end of the week in celebration of the King and Queen Festival. Once a year, during the festival, the royals open up their home for visitors." His brows gave a playful shake. "And you'll be here for a special offering this year. The book garden is being opened for tours for the first time in Skymar history."

"A book garden?"

"From what I understand the shrubs are shaped in such a way they resemble book characters. The rabbit from *Alice in Wonderland*, Wilde's *The Selfish Giant*, even a pumpkin carriage from *Cinderella*."

"I can't even imagine! What a wonderful idea!" A bubble, like drinking fizzy water, percolated from her middle up through her chest until it exploded in a giggle. "Brodie, this is amazing and I've only been here a few hours."

"Well, the simple plan is to get you to fall in love with everything about it so you'll have the overwhelming desire to return as often as possible. Just wait until you eat some of Mum's favorite dessert. It has the same addictive magic that the White Witch's delicious Turkish delight had on poor Edmund.

"Tricky, tricky." Izzy relaxed back in her seat. "Draw me in with a Brodie hors d'oeuvre, and snag me with fictional references and your mom's sweets?? Low blow, Mr. Sutherland."

"Whatever it takes, Ms. Edgewood." His gaze flashed to hers, tagging on a wink. "Whatever it takes."

CHAPTER 18

From: Luke Edgewood
To: Izzy Edgewood, Penelope Edgewood, Josephine Martin
Date: June 22
Subject: Re: Survived with everything but my pride

Izzy,

I thought you would have gotten used to snoring dogs after living in our house for so many years. You did share a room with Josephine for a while.

Luke

PS: Would you confirm whether you've been kidnapped or not? I have dibs on Samwise.

From: Josephine Martin
To: Izzy Edgewood, Penelope Edgewood, Luke Edgewood
Date: June 22
Subject: Re: Survived with everything but my pride

Luke,

I would remind you that I had a deviated septum in my younger years. It has since been corrected so I can assure you I do not sound anything remotely like your snoring dog.

And, Izzy, did you sign up for that phone-tracing site I sent to you? If you are kidnapped, we can find you and bring you back to Eli. I feel certain he would overlook your sudden wanderlust for a man who comes from an island that no one has ever heard of before. Of course you're nervous—just as I expected. The jacket I gave to you to pack? The rain jacket? Just remember, it can also be a floatation device.

Josephine

* * *

From: Luke Edgewood
To: Izzy Edgewood, Penelope Edgewood, Josephine Martin
Date: June 22
Subject: Re: Survived with everything but my pride

Josephine,

If she's kidnapped, I doubt she'll even see our emails, but good try on the floatation device.

Luke

* * *

From: Penelope Edgewood
To: Izzy Edgewood, Luke Edgewood, Josephine Martin
Date: June 22
Subject: Re: Survived with everything but my pride

Izzy!!!!

Why would you even bring up the pipe at Grandpa Edgewood's house?! Do you realize I had to sleep with a nightlight for three years after that incident and couldn't get in the bathtub without anxiety? The only reason I tried to fit into it is because Luke told me the pipe was the way to Wonderland. I've never listened to him about pipes since.

I can't wait to see your photos of Skymar and Brodie and cliffs. My internship professor said she should be able to give me an answer about transferring from Scotland to Skymar by next week! Just imagine if you end up marrying Brodie and I end up interning there! You'll have someone to help you pick out trendier clothes. I have a red cloche that would look fantastic with your dark hair. Think of all the cute boots we could wear in a place that stays mostly winter!

Can't wait to hear from you soon. With Josephine's plans in place, I imagine you'd probably have phone service if you were drifting in the middle of the ocean, so you could still send photos.:-)

Penelope

From: Izzy Edgewood
To: Luke Edgewood, Penelope Edgewood, Josephine Martin
Date: June 23
Subject: Re: Survived with everything but my pride

Cousins,

Clearly my imagination proved overactive, as usual. Instead of being hoisted onto a pirate ship, Brodie has swept me into a place that feels very much like another world. I pinched myself so many times I have bruises on my arm. I've attached photos, but they really don't do this place justice. I would have emailed you all last night, but by the time I made it to my room after the flight and meeting the family and talking with Brodie, I couldn't keep my eyes open. All I remember is sitting on the edge of the bed and slipping my shoes off, and then . . . I woke up nine hours later to the sound of something scratching at my bedroom door. I'll describe that later. But first I must tell you about Brodie's family.

Brodie's mom and little sister live in a cottage outside of the town of Skern. We're visiting Skern today AND the very first Sutherland's bookshop. I feel as though his mom might measure me in terms of my response to her dearly beloved shop. She's lovely, BTW—the very idea of a quintessential English lady. She reminds me of Julie Andrews (how about that, Penelope), even to the way she styles her soft-brown hair. What I didn't expect was for her to draw me into a hug at first meeting. I'd always expected English people to be sort of standoffish. I suppose that came from watching too much British television, but she was absolutely wonderful, though she had a bit of steel in her voice when she spoke of Sutherland's. Kind of like Granny Lucy when she referred to her favorite husband that nobody liked except her. I got the sense that any criticism—as if I'd have any—about the family bookshop should be voiced with extreme care or not at all. So even when she spoke of her excitement about starting a Sutherland's bookshop across the Channel in England—even though their sales are in decline across the board—I didn't say anything. Nope. But to keep from saying anything, I ate four scones and drank three cups of tea. It's a miracle I fell asleep at all. All the private bookshop groups I follow are quick to discourage starting a new shop to save an old one. I remember one lady using the quip "love the one you're with" and find out what's not working there before taking on a new and costly venture.

Ellen was wonderful otherwise. And kept calling me things like "dear" and "love" and talking about my hair. I almost thought she only hugged me so she could touch it. Evidently dark hair isn't super common in these parts.

I think if I steer clear of giving any advice on bookish things, I may not suffer the wrath of having a hairbrush thrown at me. Granny Lucy's aim was impeccable. Brodie's mom doesn't seem the hairbrush-throwing sort, but her near-obsessive love for teaspoons did make me a little nervous. I wonder what her aim would be like with those?

And his little sister, Fiona? Penelope, the two of you would have gotten along like long-lost sisters. She has a love for all things of the musical variety and adores dressing in vintage styles. I still haven't figured out how she knows what things look like, since she is legally blind, but Brodie said that the degenerative disease hasn't stolen her ability to see shapes or light yet. And if the color is vibrant, she is more likely to see it too. She wears lots of yellow and wears it well, as you would say, Penelope. The family is saving money to pay for a surgery that has the chance of restoring part of Fiona's eyesight, but since Sutherland's hasn't been doing well the past few years, they can't afford the surgery right away. And since the surgery isn't guaranteed to work, their insurance won't pay for it. It's a horrible catch-22. Despite the world moving forward into the cyber age, Skymar has not. Or so it seems in the parts I've seen so far. For the atmosphere and history and all-around beauty of it all, I'm glad they've not turned the island into a modern-era resort, but a few updates might help everyone overall—especially businesses like Sutherland's, you know?

Fiona has this wonderful strawberry-blonde hair and the cutest spray of freckles across her nose ever known to man!

She happens to be a Copper Westbrook fan, to which I quickly agreed to read one of his fantastical books along with her while I'm visiting.

The air here in the countryside has a wonderful scent of pine and sea and something else I can't quite define. Maybe one of the local flowers, but it's a sweet sort of smell, like freshly mown grass mixed with lavender or something similar. And there is—how to describe it?—a clarity to the air, like the feeling after a rain.

And the age of the buildings! Hundreds of years old and there are manor houses and castles! It really feels like I've stepped into a book with a charming, native Skymarian as my guide. Ooh, doesn't that sound magical? Lead on to the next adventure, dear Skymarian!

Luke, you would love this place. Mostly countryside with loads of vacant rock structures that used to be barns or houses. The people are trying to reuse the structures and renovate them for either single-family homes or vacation rentals. Brodie says that apart from fishing and agriculture, tourism is one of the largest industries here and the locals are trying to learn how to capitalize on that interest by recycling what they already have. I know you have a soft spot for stone masonry.

I've attached the address and phone number of Ellen's house at Josephine's request, so that if you can't reach me on my cell, you can leave a message there. I'm staying with Ellen and Fiona in their limestone cottage. My small attic room has a window seat pointed in the direction of the sunrise, or so I'm told. The rooftops of Skern are within view from my window—their slate, thatch, and tin roofs making a mismatched pattern in the distance. Two spires twist up into the sky above the rooflines noting two churches. Brodie says that his family attends one of them, but I can't remember which. I guess I'll find out! He says it's a five-hundred-year-old church! Five hundred years!!!! And that people are buried under the floor. (I'm going to try really hard not to think about that too much or else I'll look like I'm stepping through a cow field as I follow them to the nearest pew.)

Okay, I've probably bored you guys to tears. I can't imagine Luke actually reading to the end of this. Anyway, Ellen says breakfast is ready, so I'm going to run. Bookshop, here I come!

Love you all!

Izzy

PS: Scones here are NOTHING like the ones I make at home from a box. Nothing. They're so much better. I feel betrayed.

PPS: I can't even imagine why on earth Brodie likes me, but I'm happily basking in his nonsensical attraction.

CHAPTER 19

Skern fit every imaginable definition Izzy had ever heard of the word *idyllic*. An adorable combination of limestone buildings topped with gray slate, ivy-covered and whitewashed cottages with thatched roofs, and cobblestone streets leading by tearooms, pubs, bakeries, and antique shops. Spires of medieval-aged churches rose into the cerulean sky as a ruined abbey—perched on a hill overlooking the town—kept watch like an ancient sentry. Stone archways here and there connected buildings to create picturesque alleyways to back gardens, tiny houses, and more streets.

It was impossible to take it all in at one time.

A stone bridge crossed a river along one side of Skern that led to a park complete with a duck pond and playground. A striking cathedral was poised at the edge of town, its stained glass window glistening with rainbow light.

The pinnacle of her visit came when Brodie led her to the center of town. Nestled across from a thatch-roofed inn and a picturesque gazebo stood a three-story, ivy-covered stone building—Sutherland's.

Its wooden sign hung down from a black iron rod, like something from a Dickens novel. Izzy squeezed closer to Brodie, her arm nestled within his as they neared the bookshop. It seemed to her that he smiled all the time, especially in that adorably amused slant she found so appealing. Was he usually so happy? Or maybe it was just the place.

He loved this town, these people, and Sutherland's. His pleasure oozed from his conversations to the pleasant greetings passersby sent his way. He was living within his dream among these bookshops and this picturesque world of cathedrals and cobblestone streets and castles and cliffs by the sea. Had Izzy ever walked within a dream with such certainty? Did she even really know what her dream was? It was much easier to recognize when others found their "place" than finding it oneself, it seemed.

"Here we are." Brodie paused before a blue-painted door and tipped a brow. "I feel as though I'm readying for some exam or other."

She swung her attention to his face. "Because of me?"

He dipped his head before lifting his familiar gaze back to her. "I want you to fall in love with Skymar."

Her breath had paused on the "fall in love" part of his sentence as if baited to the happily ever after the word promised. *Love.* They'd tiptoed around the idea but neither voiced anything with certainty because, well, in Izzy's mind an entire ocean kept the idea of "till death do us part" in a precarious state of uncertainty.

"And especially Sutherland's," he finished, searching her face. "In fact there's a part of me that cannot wait for your assessment and another part that's rather fearful of it."

"Fearful?" A laugh burst from her. "I don't scare anybody, Brodie. Not even when I wear my shark hat."

"You underestimate yourself on quite a few levels, Karre." His focus grew in intensity as if he peered through her plethora of excuses, and somehow, instead of his X-ray vision stinging at the sight of all her insecurities, she wanted to step forward into whatever he saw that made him smile. "Just from the few conversations we've had about the business of independent bookstores and your vast knowledge on the subject, I have a strong feeling our untouched bookish world will fall terribly short of where it needs to be. And I value your opinion."

The sincerity in his words tried to find a place in her heart, but she wasn't quite sure what to do with them. It was so sweet! "Don't put too much stock in my knowledge." She shook her head and took his hand, giving it a squeeze. "You're pretty smart already, but you know that I'd love to help if I can."

"Yes." He squeezed her fingers back. "One of the many reasons I admire you. Your generosity."

She opened her mouth to negate another compliment, because since she'd been there he kept pelting her with them. And he seemed to really believe what he said about her. It was like walking into the warmest, safest hug over and over again. Why was she constantly surprised by his responses when she knew he was who he seemed to be? The way he was fully committed to their conversations. Or his seemingly genuine interest in her. And how he saw things in her she'd never recognized in herself, or if she had, she'd found a way to dismiss them.

His authenticity shook her. But why? She blinked. Wasn't this how a relationship was meant to be? Had she lived through so many broken relationships that when a good, interested man acts the way he's *supposed* to act when dating a woman, she is shocked? Or near tears?

How had she allowed all those wrong men to destroy her confidence? Steal her belief in her own knowledge and abilities? How had she pushed the real Izzy beneath a quiet, meek, compliant librarian, afraid to voice her deepest thoughts or be brave enough to be genuine?

Was that the reason she'd never really fit into her very own world?

"You really don't have to work so hard for me to like you. I think you're pretty great already."

"Being nice to you is never work." He tipped a brow and offered his arm. "Are you ready to meet Sutherland's?"

Her grin split wide, more at her charming escort than the idea of stepping into a seventy-five-year-old bookshop . . . and that was saying something. She slipped her hand into the warm crook of his elbow. "Lead the way."

She stepped through the door and was immediately encased in the entire spirit of the room. Her eyes fluttered closed, and she breathed it in. The bookshop might have been over fifty years old, but the building boasted centuries. There was something captivating about a sense of place that few people slowed down enough to feel anymore, but the aura of books and time and thousands of stories permeated the paper- and leather-soaked air.

Izzy had visited dozens of bookstores in her life, and every time she welcomed the invitation to join the story the bookshop told. She always felt as if she had been ushered into a place of old friends and familiar haunts. But she'd never crossed a threshold into a different time before—nonfictional, that is. Perhaps it was the fact that the buildings in Skern were several hundred years older than anything back home, or maybe it was because this bookshop had been around for decades. Or maybe the leathery spice of Brodie's cologne added an enticing swirl of fairy-tale-ish delight, but it all simply meant Sutherland's bones were meant for books.

And then her feet bumped into something, and her eyes flew open. A bookshelf stood only a few feet within the doorway. A used-book bookshelf. As her eyes adjusted to the dimly lit space, the immensity of bookshelves and books nearly pushed her back a step. Huge shelves, on every wall, filled with all sorts of stories. To her left, windows complete with window seats lined the wall, except that the window seats were covered with books instead of colorful pillows to invite curious folks to sit for a spell.

A black iron staircase spiraled to the far right of the front door, adding a unique bit of additional charm amidst the rows and rows of books. With used books at the front and new books at the back, the shop already set itself up as a deterrent for most tourists. Not book enthusiasts. Treasures were treasures to them, but your average tourist usually wanted straightforward, easy, and engaging. But if they could add in some modern ideas and create an atmosphere that caused folks to linger, Sutherland's had the potential for something special.

Sutherland's did not need to change its wonderfulness—it merely needed a little sprucing up to engage with the current century. Enhanced "magic," so to speak.

The lack of social media and online presence plus the layout and options of the store had to be two of the main contributing factors for Sutherland's drop in sales—Izzy's lips tipped and a twitter of excitement spun through her middle—which were things she knew how to improve. It was as if she'd been waiting for this opportunity her whole life, or at least since she'd started researching independent bookstores.

"How wonderful to see you here, Isabelle dear." Brodie's mother materialized from the back room, resplendent in a pale-blue summer suit of some sort of silky material. The Julie Andrews vibes swelled to full chorus. "Welcome to Sutherland's."

"Thank you." Izzy cast the room another appreciative look, only pausing her vision on a leaning bookshelf in the corner. "What a wonderful collection of books you have."

"Yes, books and memories." She nodded, sending the room a loving look. "And our dear bookshop may need the tiniest bit of updating here and there, perhaps new wallpaper upstairs, but otherwise it's as perfect as when Brodie's grandfather opened its doors."

Brodie swung his attention to Izzy but she avoided eye contact for fear he'd see every hesitation her body felt at his mother's adoration. Yes, the shop held a certain indescribable appeal intrinsic to its structure and history, but "perfect" wasn't a description Izzy would have used. "Classic" perhaps, but definitely in need of some tender loving care to raise its competition with current bookshops and online competitors.

"I didn't realize you'd be at the shop today." Izzy stepped forward attempting to redirect the conversation. "I thought we were going out for tea this afternoon?"

"We are, dear, but I'm seeing to the shop this morning while Brodie gives you a tour of Skern before his afternoon meeting."

Izzy raised a brow to her charming escort.

"Monday and Wednesday mornings are my workdays here."

At her continued stare he expounded. "One of grandfather's rules was that each family member who remained in the Sutherland's business had to work at least two half days in one of the bookshops each week to keep a "finger on the pulse of the people" as he'd say. So my usual days are Monday and Wednesday mornings, which leaves the weekends open for me to travel or to visit the other shops, as I'm the liaison."

"Your grandfather sounds as though he had a deep love for this community."

"Aye, he did." Brodie nodded and gestured toward the nearest bookshelves with his chin. "And books."

"It was a beautiful combination of personality traits that his son inherited as well." Ellen's smile softened as she ran a hand over a few books atop the nearest shelf, her love for her husband as palpable as the scent of books in the air. Ellen's gaze came up to rest on Brodie. "And his grandson."

"Now, Mum, you don't have to lather it on." He leaned over and kissed her cheek. "I've already promised to collect dinner from Farrow's this weekend."

She chuckled and shot a look over to Izzy. "It's only the best seafood you'll ever eat, Isabelle, but it is in Port Quinnick, a good hour drive from here."

"And since I have a meeting about our bookshop in Port Quinnick on Friday, I gave my word to bring back Farrow's in celebration of your visit, Isabelle." He leaned toward Izzy and said in a stage whisper, "And because Mum wouldn't forgive me if I'd traveled to Port Quinnick and failed to return with Farrow's."

Izzy's gaze switched between the two, her grin growing at their comfortable camaraderie. Mother and son. So many memories about her mother had faded with time, but one conversation stood out, especially now. After witnessing a young man tenderly caring for his elderly mother in the grocery store, Mom had nodded toward the pair and said, *"You can get a very good idea about a person when you see the way they treat their parents."*

"Well, you've definitely heightened my anticipation for this Farrow's feast." Izzy stepped closer to a few of the bookshelves, examining their contents. Excellent secondhand books. Definitely a venture worth promoting.

"Let me give you a proper tour of Sutherland's of Skern." Brodie moved to her side and held his hand out to her. "What do you say?"

She slipped her fingers into his and he tugged her through each row, giving snippets of tales from his childhood growing up among these storied walls. She caught glimpses of the sneaky ten-year-old hiding a plastic mouse on his father's stool or gluing pages of his math book together so he wouldn't have to do his homework. The love for the space oozed through him like the deep percolation of his voice, as story after story drew them up the winding stairs to a book-laden second floor with some children's books, and up to an arched third floor filled with antique furniture and taped-up boxes.

Brodie stopped talking midsentence, and with barely time for Izzy to prepare, he swept in and brushed his lips against hers, feather light. Skin barely touching skin. And then, as if that appetizer wasn't enough, he cupped her cheeks in his warm palms and took a deeper, longer taste. Sweet mercy! Warmth spilled from his touch, reverberating throughout her entire body and nearly puddling her to the dusty wooden floor. Her palms slid around his waist to smooth against his back. He'd kissed her when she arrived and once more as he said good night, but this kiss . . . This was a lover's kiss, a promise. He was playing for keeps.

Her breath hitched as she tightened her hold against his back, giving him full permission to keep ambushing her senses in such a knee-weakening way. Despite the uncertainties, she was playing for keeps too. That much she knew.

One of his hands slipped to cradle her neck and he brought the tantalizing kiss to a close, lowering his forehead to hers. His breath pulsed against her face as his fingers kneaded the base of her skull with some combination of soothing and need. Kind of like that kiss.

Only the sound of their breaths punctuated the quietness of the room. He remained so close. If she puckered just a little bit, her lips would find his again.

"How has something as simple as a month become much too long to be apart from you, Isabelle?"

Her eyes fluttered closed as the thrum of her name from his lips cascaded down her neck with pleasant tingles attached. Had any man ever wanted her like this? Not just the physical connection but . . . *her*? To have Brodie *miss* her and *want* her? Like this? Warmth pierced beneath her eyelids, threatening a teary release. It seemed too sweet, too good.

"After a kiss like that, a week will be too long." Her voice barely made it above a raw whisper.

She felt more than saw his grin. "Ah, I see my plan is working then."

"Capture me with an addiction to Brodie kisses, huh?" Actually the idea sounded rather intoxicating.

He tipped his head back to look into her eyes. "Well, I was hoping my charm and wit would suffice, but if you only want me for my kisses, I can make do with that."

"Actually, your *Lord of the Rings* references are really what swept me off my feet, but your kisses are a close second."

"And what would you do if I started speaking Elvish?"

"Good heavens!" Her eyes popped wide and her palms tightened against his back, drawing their bodies flush again. "I'd probably marry you on the spot."

His laugh rushed out, followed quickly by a lengthy silence as he brought his lips to hers again, thoroughly convincing her that she was an addict. Undeniably. One week? She was pretty sure she didn't want to go a day without being wrapped in his arms and encased by the scent of pine and mint.

"What brought on that rather wonderful display of affection?" Izzy asked, once she found her voice again.

He studied her with such tenderness, Izzy nearly rose up to let him know she'd never had a man touch her heart with a glance. "I'm glad to have you here." He gestured to the room. "In this bookshop. In my town." His grin crooked as he caressed her face with another look. "You can't really know me properly without being introduced to this place, these people. It's such a part of who I am. And"—he gave her fingers a squeeze—"with you here everything seems to fit rather beautifully together."

She averted her gaze from the intensity in his eyes, heat making a steady climb into her cheeks. All of that authentic admiration? For her? What was she supposed to do with that? She stifled a shudder. Wasn't this the part where the fairy tale started to unravel and all the lovely fantasy disappeared to reveal a pumpkin, some mice, a lost shoe, and a woman who'd gotten too caught up in the magic?

"Come, this way." He tugged her along to the corner of the room and then, after sending a rather dashing grin over his shoulder, opened a door that revealed a ladder. "Not quite a wardrobe, but an excellent view."

Her laugh burst out in surprise as she took Brodie's proffered hand, emerging into a sunny sky and warm breeze. A rooftop view? His warm, strong fingers wrapped around her cool ones as he drew her up and forward, steadying her against him as they reached the top. Izzy cataloged another "movie moment" next to all the ones she'd experienced since meeting Brodie Sutherland at the airport. Heaven help her! How could she go back to normal life after this?

He gave her hand a gentle squeeze, as if he felt the same zing as she had. He guided her to the corner of the roof where quaint town met green country and then blended into gray-blue sea before disappearing into a cerulean sky. Maybe she *had* stepped through a magical wardrobe, except into a world that was always gorgeous and never gloomy, with a little Mary Poppins chalk picture painting sprinkled in.

"It's . . . it's beautiful," she whispered.

"It is." And when she turned, he wasn't even looking at the town. He was staring at her and she'd never felt so beautiful in her whole life. All the shallowness, immaturity, and self-centeredness of the previous relationships bloomed clear. She'd never had a man look at her like Brodie did. See her like he did. This was the reason for the storybooks. This is what the warrior fought to protect or rescue. This beautiful and tender realization of being seen, loved, and loving in return. There was no going back to anything less. As Penelope would say, Brodie was designer while Izzy had been living on generic clearance items her whole adult life.

He cleared his throat and gestured ahead. "You can see all of Skern from here and miles beyond. That is Brawnlyn Castle, or what's left of it. It sits on the edge of Loch Sella." A stone ruin with an imposing tower perched like a lonely sentry overlooking the hillsides. And then there were the cobblestone streets of Skern, and the green rolling hills, and far in the distance the rolling sea. She almost laughed at the wonder of it all. She'd spent so much time reading stories, she never imagined actually living one, but here she was. Her fingers tightened around Brodie's. What had she missed all these years of being afraid? Of burying her heart, her life, beneath stories or duty or hurt? She loved serving her family, but how long ago had Josephine's or Aunt Louisa's or other people's requests to her become an expectation rather than an opportunity to truly choose? And would she have had the courage to choose her own dreams, even if she'd recognized them?

"We'll drive by those ruins this afternoon and through the Alnors, there." He leaned close and pointed out the sharp-edged mountains rising up from around the ruins and the loch. "My house is just beyond those mountains, by the sea."

"Of course it is." She released her held laugh, shaking her head. "You've been pretty secretive about this house of yours. Waithcliff, right?"

"Aye, though it was already given that name before I inherited it."

"You inherited it? It's a family home?"

"One of my uncles who never married. We were always close, and he asked if I'd want it. I'd fallen in love with the house when I was a child." He slid a hand around her waist. "But that is all I will say because, Karre, I want Waithcliff to be a surprise. I've worked on it for three years and am rather proud of what I've been able to renovate to this point."

"Everything has been a surprise." She sighed into him, assigning this moment a special place among the mental scrapbook she'd created called "Brodie." "It's hard to believe a place like this exists. You have it all. Oceans, mountains, lakes, castles, adorable villages." She waved toward him. "Inherited manor houses."

"Bookshops," he added.

She raised a brow. "Handsome and charming natives."

He shrugged a shoulder and tipped his chin in a dashing pose. "Our best feature."

"I'd agree with that." She showed her appreciation for their similar height by kissing his smile and then waved toward the quaint town stretching out before them to a green countryside. "But in all honesty every place we've visited so far has been remarkable! Like walking through a storybook!"

"Even the Inswythe Docks?" His brow rose in the playful way she was beginning to adore seeing in person more and more.

"Well, it gave off Dickens vibes, but still storybook worthy." She sighed and took in the view again. "No wonder you love it so much. I can't imagine people ever wanting to leave such a place."

"Right. One would think that, wouldn't they?" His whispered response pulled her attention back to him, his expression uncharacteristically solemn.

"Brodie?" She turned to face him. "I'm . . . I'm not asking you to leave, you know."

"I know." His lips softened back into a small smile, his gaze holding hers. "It's just that . . . well . . ."

Her stomach suddenly dropped, and the breeze took on an unexpected chill. Here it came! The moment when the romance took a dip into real life. The great reveal of some horrible reason why they could never be together, and all these lovely imaginings were nothing more than pen and ink.

"You know"—he drew in a breath—"you have to know that I care for you." He cleared his throat and ran his palms down her arms. "You . . . you have my heart, Isabelle. Almost from the start, you've had it."

She blinked. That didn't sound at all like a disaster.

"Brodie!" Ellen Sutherland's voice rose from below, echoing through the roof door. "Brodie dear, would you mind coming to take this call? Your brother is quite . . . flummoxed."

Brodie's shoulders bent with a sigh.

"He says it's something about gremlins and thievery again, I'm afraid."

Izzy felt her eyebrow raise.

"A few nasty business associates." Brodie shook his head and gave her shoulders a little squeeze. "Anders has a way of inciting conflict. It's a special gift of his. I'll be right back."

Izzy watched him disappear and then turned back to the view, allowing the fresh air to fill her lungs. She'd had Brodie's heart from the beginning? How? She braced her hands against the iron railing fence in the roofline. Of course an Éowyn profile picture would grab any true *Lord of the Rings* fan, but he wasn't talking about the photo. He was talking about *her*. And she understood, because something in her heart responded to him from the first email. A kinship.

She pulled out her phone to snap a few pictures of the view, when a message popped up on her screen. Josephine? Her breath stalled. Were the babies okay?

She pressed the message so that it opened into a very long text:

> Mother has decided not to retire after all. She took off the last four days to help me prepare for the twins and within that time we realized retirement wasn't for her and her constant presence in my home wasn't for me. I love her. She's a wonderful mother, but I cannot imagine listening to all of her "suggestions" about EVERYTHING all of the time. I've told Mother that I'd prefer for you to help me with the twins, so she's going to lighten your library schedule a bit when you return so you can have some flexibility. Won't that be fun? Besides, no one is as good at setting people at ease as you. How long are you in Skymark? Your little island friend will love Mt. Airy. It's a wonderful community and so accepting of foreigners.

CHAPTER 20

Brodie made quick work of the phone call, diffusing the confusion with the Gremton brothers and sending Anders a quick text of the results. Brodie still couldn't believe Isabelle Edgewood waited on the roof of Sutherland's of Skern on his little island just to be with him. His grin took another uptilt. He'd barely slept last night out of sheer delight in having her so near, meeting his family, seeing his world.

It had taken an entire day for the disbelief to finally melt into an eruption of gratitude. Gratitude that he'd meant enough to her that she'd brave a journey (with her history, not an easy one), taking her very first flight . . . to him.

Gratitude that she'd talk about young adult books with his little sister as if it were the most natural thing in the world. Gratitude that she'd held his hand and stared at him with those beautiful eyes as he pulled her through his family's legacy. And it seemed perfectly natural to show her exactly how grateful he was in an extremely tangible sort of way. From her exuberant reciprocation, she didn't seem to mind.

And it sealed his desire with even more certainty. He belonged with her. Plain and simple. Well, with an ocean separating them, perhaps not so simple, but certain. His smile slid off his face as he approached the ladder to the roof. But he had to tell her about the stipend and pray that she understood. That she recognized his heart over her fears.

He cleared his throat and topped the ladder. "All dastardliness of gremlins and thievery have been resolved."

"Only a true hero could use the word *dastardliness*." She looked up from her phone and grinned. "I always knew you were the heroic sort."

A sudden sting from her declaration dampened his levity. How could he tell her about the whole reason he'd joined Heart-to-Heart? "Careful, Karre, I am but flesh and bone as any other mortal, though I do feel as if my heart is a bit stronger and braver since meeting you."

"You really do say the sweetest things." She slid her phone back into her pocket, the slightest hint of a frown puckering her brow.

He took her hand. "What's wrong?"

"Wrong?" Her gaze flickered to his and then she sighed. "I just got a text from Josephine."

"Is she all right? The babies?"

She blinked a few times and nodded. "Yes, the babies are fine, it's just that . . . well, even here, thousands of miles away, I feel like I shouldn't be here."

His hope deflated. "'Shouldn't'?"

"It's not true. I know that in my head." She placed her hand over his. "I *want* to be here. I mean, after surviving my first flight, I'm definitely planning on staying awhile." Her smile almost resurrected. "It's just . . . I don't know. I feel stretched, I guess, like I'm supposed to be there, but . . . I *want* to be here."

And here was the unvoiced dilemma. A world apart with people, hearts, and obligations on opposite sides. He wouldn't broach that decision yet, but he'd known her long enough to speak to another.

"One of the things that drew me to you, besides your love of stories of course, was your intense loyalty to your family. It's quite admirable. We have a kinship in that as well as so many other things but, Isabelle, it's all right for you to step out into your dreams too." He squeezed her hand. "Perhaps your family may need you to do so in order to make *them* stronger."

Her brow crinkled with a frown, and she looked down at their braided hands, the happy street sounds from below filtering up to them in the silence.

"I know it isn't my place to say so, but sometimes loving people best means saying no, or taking your time to decide." He tugged her closer, examining her face. "You are generous with your time and help for others. It's a beautiful quality in you." He brushed a thumb along her cheek. "But I'm afraid you are not very generous with yourself."

She pressed her cheek into his palm, and he wanted to grab her and ask her to let him take care of her forever. To rest in just being who she was because that's exactly who he . . . loved. He breathed in the word and let it settle deep.

"I'm so glad you're here, Isabelle." He pressed a kiss against her soft hair, breathing in another dose of sweetness. "I don't take for granted what you overcame to be here. For me."

But I hope for you *as well*, he almost added, but the words didn't come. Perhaps it was better if she sorted out that part on her own?

She seemed to rally from her momentary melancholy and stepped back, donning an almost authentic smile. "And I plan to enjoy every minute." She looked around the roof and then her gaze settled on the rooftop door. "Thank you for introducing me to your world, your family, and to Sutherland's Books."

"And many more things, I hope." He gestured toward the rooftop door with his head. "But I'm afraid much of my life is taken up with these bookshops."

"Not a bad thing."

"No." He chuckled. "I'm assuming you approve of Sutherland's of Skern then?"

"It's a remarkable space." The faintest shift in her smile sent off a warning. "I can't imagine a better setting for a bookshop."

Ah, yes. A careful choice of words and a slight hesitation. He'd read her myriad expressions correctly as she toured the shop. With a slight turn, he studied her profile and she actively avoided meeting his gaze. He smothered a groan. Was it as bad as all that?

He shook off the worry before he narrowed his gaze at her with determination. Even if he didn't like it, he needed to hear her perspective. For Sutherland's . . . and maybe for Isabelle too.

"Let's sit." He gestured with his chin toward a set of chairs along the corner of one side of the roof where his mother had attempted some sort of failed flower garden. He took a seat beside her and folded his arms across his chest as he leaned back, examining her. "All right, share your thoughts freely, Karre."

Her forehead wrinkled and she stared back out over the view, her palm reaching up to rub at her neck again, a sure sign of nervousness. "Brodie, I know we've talked about ideas to improve Sutherland's, but it already has such great atmosphere and"—she waved a hand toward him—"all those books. How can that be wrong?"

"You're a horrible liar."

Her bottom lip dropped.

"You know it's true," he softened his lips into a smile. "I've watched your expression from across a screen or in person for almost five months. I've learned to read you."

She folded her arms across her chest and stared back at him—her battle stance. "Have you?"

"*Mm-hmm.*" He matched her pose, inciting the corner of her pinched lips to tip. "In the bookshop downstairs you wanted to say something, but you didn't. Your eyes did that thing."

"My eyes did that thing?"

"Yes, they grow wide and then your eyebrows ping and your lips tighten closed as if you're trying to stop whatever you're thinking from bursting out into words."

She stared at him in silence before her smile flared. "My eyebrows 'ping'?"

"They do." His grin spread into a chuckle. "Don't doubt me.

Video chatting is not a preferred substitute for in-person communication, but it does provide ample opportunity for close observation and your brows certainly . . . ping." He held her gaze, sobering. "And I'd wager that whatever you are keeping inside is worth hearing, Isabelle."

The smile faded from her lips. "Why are you so determined?"

"Because what you think, who you are, matters to me."

She shifted in her chair, bringing her hands to her lap. "But as far as this bookshop is concerned, this isn't my business. It's *your* family bookshop."

"How many conversations have we had where you've detailed what you'd do to make a bookshop thrive?"

Her teeth skimmed over her bottom lip as it puckered into a hesitant frown. "A few."

"Dozen." He bent forward, resting his elbows on his knees. "You have a gift. Something not everyone possesses. I don't. Mum doesn't. I can do the numbers and have the meetings and talk about why I love a certain story. Mum can convince anyone to buy a book, and usually two. But you see something I can't. You have an awareness of how stories fit within a bookshop in such a way to draw people in. I've watched you read to children and talk with people on the street back in North Carolina. I've seen how you decorated the library and engaged curious readers. Isabelle, why not spread your wings *here*? I want to see you fly."

She blinked over at him, those large eyes taking on a glossy hue before she blinked again and cleared her throat. "Brodie, sharing stories in a library with first graders is not the same thing as renovating a family legacy."

"Or a family antiquity, if we don't do something to save it. You were made to bring stories to life. And *this*"—he waved toward the door to the shop—"is a keeper of stories." He leaned closer to her. "We could share it all together. Life, books, *Lord of the Rings* references."

"Why is sharing this with me—hearing from me—so important to you?" The question quivered out of her, piercing him.

"It's what people do when they care about each other. I want to know everything about you, which includes your dreams and thoughts. I want you to trust me enough to be authentically you."

A breath puffed from her pout and she turned away. What was wrong with her? Why couldn't she see what he did? From all the stories she'd told of her love for books—for all her marketing ideas and creative structure. This opportunity was perfect for her. What was he doing wrong? Pushing too hard?

"Help me understand." He softened his voice, begging her to cross whatever rift separated him from reaching this spot of her life, her heart. "We've had thousands of conversations about all sorts of things, but any time I attempt to ask for your suggestions or critique, you change the subject or deflect. We've talked about controversial topics, so fear of some disagreement can't be the reason." He took her palm into his. "We've even discussed your very poor decision to love Mr. Darcy when he's clearly a serious and somewhat disgruntled sort of person without one hint of puns."

She shot him a mock glare. "On that one we'll have to agree to disagree for eternity."

He wrapped both his hands around her cool fingers. "I want this relationship to become permanent, which, if you agree, means you'd become a part of my life *and* my family." He punctuated his words with a press of his fingers against her knuckles. "We'd be partners, you and me. Your ideas, your silly fictional crushes, and even your criticism—I want you to be free to share all of them with me. It's how the best romances work."

"I . . . I know that."

"Then your ideas matter and you'd end up as an equal part of *this* family, which means your voice is as important as anyone else's."

"That's not true." She jerked her hand from his and stood. "You can't just step into a family like that!"

"Well, I'd expect it to take time with Mum and Anders, of course, but you and I already are at a place where we can share—"

"I can't just push my ideas on your family. I'm an outsider, Brodie."

"My entire family has heard a nauseating amount about you for the past four months. You're not an outsider any—"

"I am. No matter how long people have known each other." She began to pace as Brodie stood to his feet. What was she talking about? "A family already has particular expectations and roles. There are dynamics already set up." Her voice broke, raw. He shifted a step forward, but she continued pacing. "You can't just expect me to believe my opinion is going to make a difference when your family already has places I don't fit into."

"But those grow with time."

She turned to face him, her eyes red-rimmed. "You can't just walk into a family and expect it to be the same. To really belong. Even if you're blood-related to them. It's still *their* family."

She blinked as if her confession shocked her.

Brodie stared back, replaying her words, attempting to make sense of her response. *Their* family? Outsider? Air burst from him like a punch to the stomach. Had she felt like an outsider in her own family all this time? Unable to chart her own future because of the fear of being rejected or unheard? His mind reeled through what he knew about her. She'd taken a job with her cousin because her cousin needed help. She'd taken the job at the library because her aunt needed help. She'd gone to a community college so her uncle and aunt's finances would not be strapped with "another" kid in college. Could all those things be byproducts of a deeper uncertainty?

He shuffled a step forward. "Isabelle—"

"I can't." She shook her head and pressed her palm against her stomach. "I . . . I need to go for a walk or something. Sort this out."

"Of course." He ran a hand through his hair and glanced down Welcome Street in Skern. "Of course." He backed toward the ladder door, gesturing for her to follow. "Skern is a good place to walk. Think. And there's an excellent pastry shop at the end of Welcome Street, situated directly across from the park."

She nodded, her eyes glossy with unshed tears, and all he wanted to do was take her in his arms and fix everything. But it seemed he couldn't reach her pain. This time, only Isabelle could reach those hurting places. Brodie offered a little prayer—as he helped her down the ladder—and a heavenly touch.

Text from Izzy to Luke: Do you have time for a chat?

Luke: Hey, aren't you across the ocean?

Izzy: Yes

Luke: How much is this text costing me?

Izzy: You're hilarious. Not. I'm using Wi-Fi.

Luke: That island has Wi-Fi? That's good to know. I thought you were going to have to pull out the Morse code.

Izzy: Luke, really. I'm trying to have a serious conversation here.

Luke: Why?

Izzy: Luke!

Luke: Okay, but I can't get ice cream to you from here.

Izzy: Sometimes I hate you.

Luke: I know.

Izzy: Did you ever wonder why I was closer to you than either of your sisters? That I could talk to you about almost everything?

Luke: Have you been nipping at some of the native nectar on Brodie's island? Because I'm really not ready for a repeat of your conversation about Joe Kingsley from junior year. There are some things male cousins do NOT need to know. I'm actually getting nauseous right now.

Izzy: I'm not drunk, Luke. I was having a conversation with Brodie (after a text from Josie) and, well, Brodie was trying to get me to open up to him, to be . . . well, he called it "authentically" me, and I realized that I don't know if I've ever been truly authentic with anyone since I was twelve years old.

The phone suddenly buzzed in Izzy's hand and she brought it to her ear, turning her face away from the table of two under the open patio of the bakery only a few feet away.

"What's going on? Are you okay? What did Josie do?"

"No, it's not just Josie," she whispered, warmth pooling in her eyes at the sound of his voice. "And I'm not in any trouble. I just . . . I just—" Her voice caught and she swallowed.

"Do you need me to come and get you?"

She sniffled through a weak laugh and wiped at her eyes. "I love you, Luke."

Silence paused the conversation. Just the awareness that Luke was on the other side of the phone somehow drew her frayed emotions back together.

"You lost your parents, Izzy. That's traumatic."

"It was." She drew in a shivering breath. "It is."

"And it would be for anyone, but you are not hurting alone. You're a part of our family."

She smiled at his attempt to help. To fix things, as he always tried to do. "But, Luke, maybe I'd convinced myself that I wasn't really a part of your family. I was looking in, like through a window. There was already a big sister and a little sister, and . . . and I think I'd convinced myself that your family didn't *need* another sister. I was kind of thrust onto you guys."

"That's not true." Came his quick reply. "That's never been true."

"I think I had in my head that I would take away from *your* family, so I had to make sure I didn't overstep the bounds. Make sure I never got too comfortable, so I didn't crowd out the people who belonged in your family. I always needed to earn my place, like I didn't truly belong. That . . . I don't know."

"*Our* family," he corrected. "And earn your place? Izzy." And then he released a sigh she almost felt through the phone. "That's why you turned down going to Georgetown, isn't it? Because Josephine was going there, and you knew what kind of stress it was causing Mom and Dad."

She pinched her lips together, the truth piercing into her with sudden awareness. She had.

"And is that why you worked for Josephine instead of taking the store-clerk job at Ebony Books in Winston-Salem?"

She groaned and released a quiet sob. She *had*! Was that the reason?

"Izzy, you've been as much a sister to me as Josephine or Penelope. In fact, sometimes I like you better than either one of them because you talk more sense on a regular basis."

Her breath released in a half-chuckle, half-whimper.

"But I don't love you any differently or less, and I know that Mom and Dad and both of *our* crazy sisters would say the same thing. I mean, we're all screwed up in ways, and we don't love perfectly, but that has nothing to do with you. It's just us being humans."

"It's not about you guys." Her eyes fluttered closed. How could relief also feel so sad? How many years, opportunities, had she wasted because of this fear?

"Stop beating yourself up. I can practically hear it through the phone."

"You think you're so smart, don't you?"

"You texted me for a reason."

She rolled her eyes, but since she didn't benefit from him seeing her, or her grimace, she huffed instead. "My bad."

Silence paused the moment. Already, just at the admission, she felt something break inside her. An understanding? Freedom?

"Maybe Eli was good for you."

Had she heard him correctly? "Eli?"

"I think he got you mad enough about book heroines and romance that it forced you to voice your thoughts as well as that wasted sarcasm you keep in your head. It's been aching to get out for years, and the difference between him and Brodie just intersected at the right time to make everything explode."

"Explode seems like the appropriate word right now." She groaned into her hand as she reached for her cup of tea with the other.

"In a good way. Like confetti."

"You really can't pull off Penelope vibes, Luke."

"You're right." He sighed. "It sucks, Iz. All of it. And I'm sorry. But I'm glad too. Because if it took all of this for you to grab the reins of your own life, to really be you, then it's a good thing."

"Yeah." She nodded as the heat from the tea mingled with the tears in her eyes. "I am glad too. I think."

"You know, Izzy." His tone sobered, softened. "I wish you'd told me this before now so you didn't have to struggle through years of wondering."

"I didn't even know it until now. Not really."

Silence paused the conversation, but there was comfort in it. Understanding. And . . . joy? Bittersweet relief? She swiped a hand over her misty eyes.

"That would explain why you always had the jerk boyfriends."

She almost choked on the sip of tea she'd just taken. "What do you mean?"

"Well, if you didn't feel like we loved you enough to belong, why would you ever believe you were good enough for the right guy? I mean, it took being tricked into meeting Brodie for you to really act like you do with me. And he *sees* you. The simple fact he was able to get this conversation out of you says something."

She nearly buckled over from the impact of his words. Tears clogged her throat, stealing her response.

"So I guess that's something to thank meddling Josephine about after all, huh?" He groaned. "But let's just keep that between the two of us. The last thing Josephine needs is reinforcement that she's a matchmaker."

"Luke," his name scraped over her burning throat. She still had so much to sort through, but at least now she'd begun to understand. To see.

"Yeah, Izzy?"

"I love you."

"I love you too . . . sis."

CHAPTER 21

"Where did she go?"

Brodie looked up from his computer at the bookshop's counter to find his mother standing nearby with an armful of Agatha Christies.

"She took a walk, Mum."

"For two hours? When she's come to see *you*?"

The edge in his mother's voice didn't help the twinge in his chest or his forehead. Yes, it had been two hours, and he'd considered going in search of her at least a dozen times, but something stopped him. The sudden realization on her face? The hurt? Wounds he couldn't touch no matter how long he held her. And from his brief acquaintance with Isabelle, she struck him as the sort who needed space to sort through her feelings, much like his elder sister. But if he didn't hear from her soon, he would take to a full-on woman hunt.

Or at least text first. Then commence the hunt, if necessary.

"She uncovered some news she needed to sort through." He turned back to his laptop, unseeing. Perhaps he *should* go in search of her now.

"Well, I hope she's not lost, dear boy."

"It's Skern, Mum." He shot her a weak grin. "Not Inswythe or Port Quinnick."

She rolled her eyes for his benefit and placed the books down on the counter, her gaze searching the nearest window. "Yes, well. She liked the shop. I could see it in her eyes."

"Yes she did." He drew in a breath and turned completely toward her. "But she also sees more."

"More?"

"All those ideas in her head, ways to improve what we have. She has that vision, that information, that she's studied for years, waiting to use it."

"Yes, well, we shall see."

He groaned. "Mum, you remember the Book Parade? And the website ideas she sent to Brynna? And the marketing suggestions? Not only is she a wonderful person from head to toe, but she also carries a magic about bookish things."

She looked away, her gaze roaming over the room. "Your father loved this place."

"And so do I." He stood, bringing her attention back to him. "But Father also had to make adjustments from Grandfather's plan so that Sutherland's could grow and change with the world."

Mother gave her head a small shake. "Brodie, there's so much of him here." The unvoiced plea in her voice nearly wilted him to the chair. "If we change things . . ."

"Mum, he will always be a part of this place." He took her hands in his. "And Isabelle isn't going to turn the shop on its head, but I can assure you, her ideas will help. If I can convince her to share them."

"You don't think she will?"

"I'm not certain." He released her hands and stepped back. "She doesn't want to intrude on what we have here, but from what I've been able to glean from the information she's shared and my own research, opening a new shop isn't the right choice. In fact, it would likely only lead to worse financial strain."

She pressed a fist to her chest and scanned the bookshop, as if saying goodbye to it.

"But we're not a lost cause." He pressed a kiss to her cheek and she spared him a shadowed smile. "We're at a crossroads, but I believe we can make a fresh start."

"I'm not agreeing to change anything in this shop until I hear what exactly the two of you have in mind beyond website updates and social media exploits. Those don't impact the walls and bindings of this place." She shook her head again. "But if you plan to take away what we've done all these years, Brodie—"

"Mum, you know I don't take relationships lightly or carelessly."

She studied him a moment and gave a slight nod.

"Then trust me. I believe this opportunity may be the very thing Isabelle . . . and Sutherland's needs most."

Her lifted brow was her only response as she collected the Christie books. "If she ever finds her way back," she added, before disappearing into the back of the shop.

Well, it may take more than pretty talk and earnest pleas to reach beyond Mum's fear of losing Da's presence in this shop, but at least she hadn't refused outright. He cringed. Or burst into tears. He sighed down into the chair and looked up toward the window, only to meet Isabelle's eyes from outside as she came to a stop on the other side.

Her dark hair fell over her shoulders, a striking contrast to the yellow blouse she wore.

He slowly rose from his seat, keeping his gaze fastened on hers. Her eyes pleaded with him through the glass, and he moved a few steps closer. What did he need to do? Stay? Run outside the shop and embrace her? As if she recognized his indecision, her lips crooked and she disappeared from view only to emerge through the front door, the entry bell jingling her entrance.

"Hey," her voice rasped as she hesitantly stepped toward him, clutching a small takeaway box to her chest.

"Hello." He pushed his hands into his pockets, waiting for her cue on what to do next.

She offered him the box with the insignia of Antoinette's on top. "I brought you an apple danish."

His smile spread as he took the offering. "I love apple danish."

"I know," she whispered.

Silence breached the gap between them and filled with the same connection he'd come to recognize as uniquely theirs. Her round, red-rimmed eyes hinted at the struggle she'd experienced while away, but the trace of a smile encouraged him that she'd made it through the struggle on the right side. She rubbed the back of her neck and looked away, a tiny wrinkle puckering her brow.

"I have an idea." He cleared his throat. "Alice, one of the other store clerks, should arrive in half an hour." He shifted a step closer to her. "What do you say we go for a drive? I have a particular house to show you."

She stared at him for a moment, her dark eyes brimming with tears before her smile broke free. "I'd like that a lot."

The landscape spread before her in lush greens with dashes of white and lavender blossoms bringing the idyllic palette to full bloom. A mixture of round-topped and jagged mountains rose in the distance, in an unusual combination of shapes and sizes. Some looked like they'd been broken away from the other, with serrated edges, and others made smooth silhouettes against the azure sky. Mossy-green earth scaled up two-thirds of the mountainside until it met a stony cap of gray or brown for the final third. The road weaved between and around them, each bend revealing another little wonder such as a village or a valley view or a hidden manor house or a beautiful loch. Growing up in the mountains prepared her for the pretzel-like ride, but even her beloved Blue Ridges couldn't compare to the otherworldliness of Skymar. Did all the islands look like this one?

And the air? Clean with a tinge of sea and pine. A combination Izzy had never imagined working so well together. Back home there were the mountains and then there was the ocean, and never the twain shall meet, but here the sea wafted a few hours in every direction. It tinted the breeze in subtle touches while more inland, or with more robust scents as the ocean drew nearer.

Brodie didn't broach the subject of their previous conversation. He simply talked about the countryside and explained a few of the ruins or the Balleycraig Manor House or the village supposedly buried beneath the waters of Loch Kewilth. Everything emerged out the window in vibrant color as if they'd stepped into a chalk pavement picture from *Mary Poppins*, and all the while Brodie gave her permission to keep silent.

"I don't want you making up any wild ideas about my home so I ought to prepare you."

"Too late." She tossed him a grin. "The drive alone has me waiting for the characters of James Herriot's novels to show up from among the emerald hills and scattered forests."

"Ah, I half expected you to say *Cranford*."

She touched his arm. "Oh my goodness, how could I have forgotten *Cranford*!" She laughed. "And the fact *you're* the one to mention that series makes me all sorts of happy."

His grin crooked and her heart squeezed in response. "You keep underestimating my reading experience, Karre."

And the endearment! The vibrato of his deep voice smoothing over that sweet endearment settled within her, like a tender sort of anchor. She smiled. She trusted him. Deeply. Maybe all these wonderful ways he believed in her paired with this new revelation she'd uncovered with Luke changed things. Made sense of years and years of her life.

She relaxed back into the seat, soaking in the growing awareness. "You're definitely full of wonderful surprises, Mr. Sutherland."

He kept his gaze ahead on the narrow road but held his grin. "Well, I'm afraid I may disappoint you a little with the house. Since I'm in midrenovation, a large part of the house is still in disrepair, but I'm making progress."

She could practically feel the excitement oozing from his posture as he sped over the hills, closer to his "cliff house" as he called it. What was she supposed to think about a place like that? Agatha Christie?

Dracula? Brontë's Thrushcross Grange or . . . she shuddered . . . Lovecraft? She studied Brodie's profile and shook her head. Nope. Let's stick more with Herriot or . . . her lips tilted upward . . . Wodehouse. Yes, he was all things bright and beautiful and good.

And she gave her heart completely over. Come what may. She wanted to be with Brodie Sutherland.

He caught her staring and hung on for a second. "I really want to kiss you right now."

"It's definitely a benefit of in-person interaction."

"I'll make certain to take an extended time on that particular benefit once we arrive at the house, because"—he turned the car into a drive with two rock pillars on each side—"here we are."

A little bronze sign within each rock pillar showcased a faded name: Waithcliff Manor.

Her eyes widened, and she sucked in a breath.

"Ah, I see your mind spinning with Brontë and Dickens." He chuckled and started down the drive. "But I'm afraid you'll find more of a derelict manor house for now, though I'm quite proud of what I've accomplished thus far."

"Well, you have to at least have a kitchen, right?"

He nodded. "And a bit more than a kitchen. The government of Skymar is invested in restoring existing structures on the islands, so one can apply for special funds. But those additional funds arrive in trickles instead of gallons, so in between work and family, the renovation process has taken some time. And the larger and basic needs had to happen first. Windows. Stonework. Electrical and plumbing. So in order to stretch those funds, I've learned how to make certain repairs and restorations by watching copious amounts of YouTube videos."

"YouTube is powerful." Izzy turned back to the road ahead. "I fixed my sink because of a YouTube—" Her sentence cut off as a tower rose above the trees ahead. Izzy leaned forward, hands on the dashboard. The tree-lined drive opened to reveal a beautiful stone house of grayish tan. The "tower" Izzy had seen—a turret—rose up on the right and just beyond it . . .

"The ocean," she whispered, catching glimpses of the sea through the veil of trees as Brodie brought the car to a stop in front of the house. And this time she *did* press her face against the window. She *had* stepped into a dream or a former era or . . . whatever.

"I usually enter through the kitchen, but I wanted to give you the special tour."

Izzy barely had time to lift her mouth off the floor before he'd come around to her side of the car and opened her door. She took his outstretched hand and he pulled her forward, his attention shifting from her face to the house.

"It's slow going, you understand, but I want to do it right." He fingered through his keys as they neared the double dark-oak front doors with frosted glass embossed in the top third of the doors. "So I've only finished a few rooms thus far and only on the ground floor."

"It has a tower," Izzy rasped out as he placed the key in the lock. "Like . . . like a real tower."

He paused and turned toward her, his brows giving a shimmy. "I know, which I believe should become the perfect reading room, don't you?"

"Oh my goodness. That would be amazing."

"Exactly what I thought too." He began to push open the door and then stopped. "It's still a work in progress. Remember that as we tour."

"Stop stalling and let me see this castle of yours." She nudged him forward and with a renewed grin he leaned over and took her lips with his. A soft, swift touch, but enough to bring her pulse into a responsive gallop.

With a squeeze to her fingers, he pushed open one of the double doors to reveal a beautiful but simple foyer. The stone floor led forward through an arched opening where a stairway curled up and out of sight. A lovely teardrop chandelier hung from a white ceiling adorned with diamond-shaped designs.

She wasn't sure why she'd expected dark colors and leather, complete with dead animals on the walls. Maybe fictional daydreaming didn't always give a clear representation. This tasteful simplicity matched *her* hero, though.

A sudden movement slid into her vision. Fuzzy, grayish white, and at a full run, up bounded a beautiful dog with every bit of welcome dripping from his overly large tongue. Brodie intercepted the furry bundle just before he made contact with Izzy's jeans.

"Ah, I see the welcoming committee is in good form today."

Izzy laughed and dropped to her knees, rubbing a palm over the dog's soft head. Well, she tried. The puppy licked her hand well before her palm ever made it to his fur.

"Hello, Argos." At the sound of his name, the puppy wiggled free from Brodie's hold and squirmed right into Izzy's chest, licking her face with all his might. She giggled and pulled back, redirecting the puppy love to her hands again.

"*Ach!* He's trying to drown you." Brodie took the puppy by the collar and gave him a little tug. "But he'll calm down after a bit. He's as excited to meet you in person as I was."

"Samwise could keep up with him, I think." She pushed to a stand as Brodie smoothed his palms over each side of the dog's face in a calming fashion. He proceeded to give Brodie a sound lick on the nose, to which Brodie looked up at her with an apologetic shrug . . . and she pretty much decided she loved him. Bookshop or not. Cliff house or not.

Him.

"Now he's calming a bit so we'll let him join us on our tour until we head upstairs." He stood and shot Izzy a wink. "Too much trouble for a curious dog to cause in the unfinished upstairs."

"Well, this entry is absolutely lovely." Izzy waved toward the room and Argos took it as invitation to come back to her side for another pet.

"You like it? I just completed it last week in expectation of your arrival." He led the way forward, with Argos dashing off to sniff or chew on something or other before rejoining them. "Mum chose the wall color. I'm not exactly a decorator so every room that I've finished so far has been an exact re-creation of something I found online. But the chandelier is original to the house."

"I love the rich taupe color with these pale stone floors, and . . . the chandelier is stunning."

"Those are the original floors." His expression was bright with excitement, like a little boy with a new toy. "I've been able to restore all the floors so far except those in the garden room. I did these myself."

"You did an excellent job. Wow. I am beginning to wonder if there is anything you can't do."

"I'm not a visionary like you. And you have a much easier way with people than I do." He walked to another set of double doors to the right. "And truth be told, I'm a bit messy."

Which still seemed fairly small in comparison to all the things he did wonderfully well, like care, and tenderness, and a quirky sense of humor.

"Here is my next project. The sitting room." He opened the doors to reveal an empty room with white walls and floor-to-ceiling windows lining the front. The large-slabbed wooden floors lay scratched and aged, but Izzy could envision them restored. A honey color with sage-green walls, perhaps? And freshly painted crown molding. The barren room came to life in her imagination. A bay window at the far end showcased a glimpse of sea. What a wonderful place to sit and daydream!

"You're seeing the potential, aren't you?"

She sent him a grin. "So much potential."

"Do you know how to renovate?" He narrowed his eyes. "With all your creativity, I'm certain you'd be an excellent partner."

She raised a brow, wondering if he'd meant the double entendre or if her heart just seemed to read between every one of his lines like he was taking his quotes from a romance novel. "I can paint."

"Well, that's excellent, because I paint poorly."

As if he meant for her to be here . . . with him, painting his *cliffside manor house*!

They continued from the sitting room into another—a long, elegant space with an enormous marble fireplace. Brodie thought it had been a dining room.

"And now for the spaces that are actually complete. Here's the kitchen."

Immediately they entered a room almost large enough to fit Izzy's entire apartment. Light-oak floors complemented the white kitchen cabinets that wrapped around one-third of the room. The rest of the space encompassed a small table and chairs by a bay window and a sitting area in a cozy half-circle in front of a small fireplace, bookshelves on either side. She recognized the space from their video chats. Brodie's wall and throw-pillow color choices breathed of the sea—a soft blue-green—which could be seen in the distance through the kitchen windows.

Argos dashed across the floor to attack a mangled tennis shoe in the corner.

"Ah, another casualty to the puppy."

Izzy laughed and stepped farther into the cozy room. "You have everything you need in this one room. Kitchen, living, dining." Izzy stepped forward, entranced. "It's wonderful."

"I'm so glad you like it." He gestured toward the table. "And actually, I had hopes of making dinner for you, if you'd like?"

She laughed, wrapping her arm through his and leaning her head against his shoulder. "Is that a trick question?"

"Good." His grin crooked with an added twinkle in those eyes as he stared at her. Could this really be her future? With him? He was worth her future, but . . . how could she even imagine leaving home?

She pushed the thoughts away. She didn't have to make that decision today.

"I've renovated the room across the hall into a bedroom, but it would make an excellent study in the future, and it has an adjoining washroom." He pulled her through a different exit from the kitchen into a hallway. "But there's one unfinished room I *must* show you because I think it should be the library."

He closed the door behind them, trapping Argos in the kitchen, before slipping up a narrow stairway, likely used as servants' stairs in its historical life. They emerged into a hallway that spilled out onto a landing from the grand staircase she'd seen in the entryway, doors on all sides. The center boasted a skylight with unique stained glass designs that cast rainbow colors against the staircase below.

"I only had the skylight restored last month because it took a year to locate enough pieces to attempt a replica of the original." At her look, he continued. "My uncle had dozens of historical photos of the place left by his grandfather before him, and I wish to restore as much as I can." He tagged on a wink. "Except for things like updated kitchens, washrooms, and electricity. I'm quite fond of running water and working lights."

She chuckled and linked her arm back through his again. The barren, broken walls waited for careful hands to stitch them back to their former beauty. The stone floor, similar to the entry, awaited repairs and refinishing, but the potential was there. Everywhere. Like an unedited story. Or a blank canvas. Her imagination brought the space to life, like the bookshop. All it took was a little "seeing beyond" as her dad had called it, though Izzy's seeing beyond had been kept safely within the confines of her family's expectations.

She paused on the thought a moment as Brodie drew her around the grand staircase, where they passed a few closed doors before stopping in front of another set of double doors.

The twinkle in Brodie's eyes deepened and she couldn't help but smile back. He was genuinely excited to have her here, to see his home and his world.

"This is a seaside room, which is the only place for a proper library in this house, if you ask me."

He pushed open one of the doors and flipped a switch on the wall. Light illuminated the large room from a dazzling chandelier that looked like tree branches spreading soft light to all corners. The ceiling rose at least ten feet, framed on two sides by white, paneled walls, which only waited for repairs, followed by some elegant bookshelves.

Had this been a ballroom? She shifted a few steps into the room as her gaze fastened on the opposite wall, where a massive, arched floor-to-ceiling window gave a remarkable view of an endless blue horizon. The scene pulled her forward, her mind re-creating the space into a well-stocked library. Teals and rich browns to celebrate sea and earth. Paintings on the walls. A fire in the stone fireplace with two high-back chairs poised for a pair of readers. She could almost picture a cat sitting on the window seat, basking in the afternoon sun.

She breathed out a sigh. "You'd never want to leave."

"A perfect place for a respite from the world, isn't it?" He offered her his hand and led her toward a door situated by the window. "And with this view."

Izzy's breath caught as they stepped out onto a stone balcony. At this level they rose above the surrounding trees, and the sea spread before them in miles and waves of gray tide and azure sky. A few rocky islands dotted the coastline that stretched in a crescent shape to her left, begging for a quiet stroll.

"Brodie, I . . . I don't have words. It's amazing. All of it."

His smile spread and he leaned back against the stone railing, the wind tossing his hair in wild puffs. "I'm pleased you like it."

"Like it?" Izzy's gaze pulled back to the view. "It's perfect."

"Even all the broken and older parts?"

"The older parts create character." She shrugged, running her hand along the stone railing with its tiny scratches and bumps from years gone by. "And maybe the broken parts too."

"Indeed, and then there are the unexpected beauties, like the chandeliers that only wanted some polish and care to show their true character."

She looked over at him, his words holding an undercurrent of meaning. Maybe? But he didn't clarify, only propped his elbows against the railing and turned his face toward the sea. Gusts of wind tossed his golden hair in distracting disarray. Izzy breathed in the scent, the feel of this place and moment with Brodie. It didn't seem real. But none of it had. Except the embarrassing parts. The rest felt like God had reached into her imagination with all its fictional convolutions and pulled out things she hadn't even thought remotely possible. Why would He do that for her? Had she gotten Him wrong too? Had she failed to really believe His love and goodness included her too? That she . . . belonged?

She felt the continued rumbles of an epiphany, and she was in the best spot, wasn't she? With Brodie.

"Our family would often holiday there, at Elrith Waite." He pointed toward the beach line in the distance. "It's a . . . cove, I think is the American description. And we'd take a boat from Elrith Waite to Cairn Mara." He gestured toward one of the islands in the distance. "To explore and picnic. We'd stay here with my uncle, though he only lived in the lower part of the house, which is why the upper level requires more work. But I fell in love with the narrow halls and vast views. So when he asked if I would want it—"

"You had to say yes!" A lonely manor house perched away from the world? Of course!

"Exactly." He covered her hand on the railing next to his. "I knew you'd understand." He chuckled and dipped his chin, as if embarrassed. "I can't really explain it, but I knew I wanted to live here. That this is where I belonged."

The word reverberating through her. *Belong.*

"Just like that?"

"Just like that." His gaze locked with hers. "It was the same feeling I had when I saw you in the airport the first time. I just knew."

"You knew what?" The words barely made it out on a whisper.

He leaned close and tasted her lips again. Her eyes fluttered closed and she brushed a palm against his cheek.

"I wanted to be with you. That . . . well, we belonged together, wherever together might be."

She inched back, her cheeks warming beneath his stare. "How can you be so certain about so many things, and I can't even figure out what I want to do when I grow up?"

He chuckled and allowed her question to blend in with the sound of crashing surf and rustling trees, the moment suspended in time, soaking into Izzy's uncertainty with a gentle touch. She replayed her earlier interaction with Brodie and subsequent conversation with Luke, and after a moment she leaned her head on Brodie's shoulder. His arm slipped around her waist, turning the simple movement into a hug. She buried her face into his neck, breathing him in, clinging to the sweetness of his company, his care. He made it so easy to believe in fairy tales. To . . . place a toehold on the faith that he really cared about her . . . as her. Maybe she was a whole lot like this house, standing alone in disrepair, and just needing the right person to see her potential. To care enough.

The hush of the distant waves and the twitter of birdsong lulled across the silence like a gentle serenade. His nearness, his comfort, ushered a sweet calm through her and she drew in a deep breath. Trusting him with parts of her heart she was just beginning to understand.

"I never realized that after my parents' deaths, I doubted really belonging somewhere. Anywhere. Even with my cousins."

He lowered his head to hers, his only response.

"It doesn't make sense now, in hindsight. They loved me. I knew it, but I felt as if I'd stepped into *their* family. I never realized I'd spent my life trying to belong without really believing I did."

He moved, nodding. "Do you think that also impacted your choices?"

"Definitely." A sad little laugh puffed out. "And my relationships. I tried to force myself into fitting, to *being* what I thought they wanted. And I've loved working at the library, but it still was something my aunt encouraged me to do since I adored books, but it didn't quite fit either." She looked up at him. "Not like how I see things fit for you. You're doing exactly what you love, what you were meant for."

"But I didn't always know it." He pushed her hair back from her face, attempting to rein it in from the wind's hold. "Believe it or not, I started university with the intention of becoming a teacher."

"A teacher?" She laughed. "Did your parents support that with the family business expectations?"

"Of course, and a teacher is a noble profession, but after only a year away from the bookshop, I realized I truly loved working in the family business, so that's when I made up my mind to pursue a business degree, and the rest is history, I suppose." He grinned, studying her. "But I can see how the uncertainty of belonging would have a drastic impact on learning who *you* really are. That's the only reason why I suggested you work your magic on Sutherland's. I think, instead of stepping into something someone else has made for you, perhaps you could unleash it with your complete authenticity right here. No strings. No mold to fit. Just . . . you doing what you do best. Loving books and people in a creative way."

Loving books and people in a creative way?

She searched his face, a face that had become more and more dear with each passing conversation. Each additional touch or kiss. Did he truly see that in her? And was he offering her this unbelievable opportunity to see if what she loved could be formed into a real profession? A place to belong?

Could she be brave enough to try? She met the confidence in his gaze.

Maybe now.

"You think your mom would let me try?" She blinked away the tears forming in her eyes. "I have a lot of ideas."

"We might have to prod her a bit, offer a deal, but more than that, I think *you* need it. The freedom to create, to see your ideas enacted."

She pressed a kiss to his jaw. "How come you're so smart all of a sudden?"

"I'm not really all that smart or I'd have sorted out more of the problems of Sutherland's before now." He tugged her close, securing her against him. "But I've become a very avid study of a certain bookish American, and I would like to show her what I see she's capable of . . . and who I see her to be."

She sighed and stared back at the horizon, her mind swirling with possibilities. "Well, I might overwhelm your mom. I mean, my brain is already buzzing with easy fixes."

"Like?"

"Well, since the King and Queen Festival is happening Friday, I'd immediately feature a bookshelf with royal reads, and I'd create a display window with a mixture of new royal releases, old popular bestsellers of the same genre, as well as some local favorites." She turned to him, trying to help him envision the possibilities too. "And I'd truly create a children's section in Sutherland's. One that brings the innate magic of the bookshop to life, especially for such a magical week as the King and Queen Festival. There really should be children's prince and princess paraphernalia for sale, like swords and crowns and stuffed dragons."

"Stuffed dragons?" His brows rose.

"Of course! Stuffed dragons are all the rage." She began to pace across the balcony. "And one of the real selling features of new bookshops is merchandise. Bookish paraphernalia—like bookmarks and notebooks and coffee mugs with things like a typewriter on them and popular bookish quotes. And local gifts like the jewelry made from those scree stones you talked about only being in this part of the world, or local handcrafts. I mean, you've said Skymar is known for its woodcrafts and wool wear, so why not see how we can feature some of those in the shop. Nothing big, but maybe unique bookends or handmade jewelry or scarves and fuzzy socks. Fuzzy socks, mugs, and books go together in a very special way." She turned toward him, hands in motion as she talked. "And that would support local businesses so they'll refer people to Sutherland's too. When I walked through Skern yesterday, I saw all sorts of merchandise that Sutherland's could easily promote." She took another turn around the balcony, excitement building with the speed of her words. "And we'd need to reorganize the bookshop for the most effective way to bring people in, kind of like from the streets to the shelves." She laughed at her own comment.

"'From the streets to the shelves'?" Brodie joined in with a chuckle. "Brilliant."

She paused her steps and faced him, breathing in his compliment. "Thank you."

"Excellent way to accept a compliment, Karre."

Her smile brimmed. He was right. She usually deflected or redirected the conversation when compliments came. But . . . but she could be grateful for her God-given talents and passions, couldn't she? After all, God must have given them to her for a reason. "I'm trying."

His gaze searched hers. "I know."

With a reluctant pull from his gaze, she began pacing again. "This might be a big change for your mom, but . . . secondhand books shouldn't be in the front of the store, unless there's a very special secondhand we'd like to showcase. Featuring unique books and new releases in the front grab folks' attention, especially tourists. And children need a bookish spot that screams 'my place.'" She met Brodie's amused expression. "What?"

"I didn't realize what I unleashed with that simple request."

She folded her arms across her chest and stared at him, her stomach quivering a little with the fear she'd overstepped the offering. "You gave me free rein, right?"

"I did and I'm happy you believed me." With a flash of his smile and a grab of her hand, he pulled her back into the house.

"Where are we going?"

"To make a game plan." He tugged her toward the stairs. "We only have three days before the festival begins, so we need to decide which parts of this plan we can make happen and which we can't."

"Wait." She pulled him to a stop. "You want this to happen before the festival?"

"I'd love to show you what you are capable of and I'd love to show Mum what a little creative thinking can do. What better time than one of the largest festivals of the year?" He leaned close, teasing her grin. "Are you up for the challenge, Karre?"

This was her chance. Her opportunity. He was holding out a precious gift for her to take all these ideas and see them become a reality, without her having to keep the books or deal with meetings or anything like that.

"As long as you're with me, let's do it!"

He pressed his lips to hers in a quick kiss. "There's nowhere else I'd rather be."

CHAPTER 22

Text from Izzy to Josephine: Josephine, I love you, but I want you to reread your message to me and ask yourself one question: What if Izzy's future isn't in Mt. Airy? (I'm not saying it's not, but what if?) What if the love of Izzy's wonderful family, including her well-organized and generous-hearted eldest cousin, has prepared her to be brave and try something totally different than anything any of them had ever imagined? Izzy knows it's scary and possibly sad, but she's only able to take a chance because she's been loved so well by . . . her family. Izzy just wants you to think about that. (And Izzy will stop referring to herself in third person now.) I'm sending a longer email to all of you, so hopefully . . . well, hopefully it will explain a little more.

Izzy: I know you love me too.

From: Izzy Edgewood
To: Luke Edgewood, Josephine Martin, Penelope Edgewood
Date: June 24
Subject: Epiphany of all epiphanies

Dear Cousins,

I've had a breakthrough, I think. I won't go into all the details about it, but suffice it to say, I think I've pinpointed not only one of my deepest problems but also one of my greatest loves. (And no, Penelope, it isn't Brodie, though my heart is certainly moving in that direction.)

Yesterday Brodie and I developed a strategy to put into practice some of the things I've learned and love about books and book shopping. As you all know, I've been slightly obsessed with bookshops for years and have a great deal of information in my head that has been spending more time in daydreams than reality, but with Brodie's encouragement and some nudging from Luke, I've stepped out into that reality.

Taking a dream from its perfect place in your head and placing it into the precarious real world is a dangerous endeavor. Whether the dream is a romantic happily ever after, a practically perfect job, or an abject vulnerability of laying our own skills and talents bare for the world to see and judge, when the shine is placed in daylight, what does it really look like?

So with those foreboding thoughts in mind, I've taken a leap into bringing my dreams to life. Hopefully they'll emerge more like a waking princess than a Frankenstein's monster, but here we go. When Brodie and I presented my suggestions to his mother, I thought at first she might refuse, and who can blame her?! A young woman sweeps into her son's life and suggests upending her dear husband's life's work? Ugh. When I state it that way, I do sound like Frankenstein's monster. But as I explained that these little adjustments won't change the heart of her store at all, but are more like adding clothes and jewelry to a well-built (in fact, I think I used the word *classic*) model, she seemed to catch the vision, admittedly reluctantly.

So here's the plan: For the next three days we are going to put into place some of my suggestions and rearrange the shop. Brodie is going to contact local folks for merchandise we can introduce to Sutherland's and its shoppers. (He's asked for my help in doing this since, surprisingly enough, I'm the bigger talker of the two of us.) Ellen is going to help me restructure the store, as well as bring Brynna in for some social media/website suggestions. The King and Queen Festival is one of the largest events in Skymar, so if we're going to measure the impact of change, *this* is the time to do it. If I don't check in as frequently, just assume I'm buried beneath hundreds of classic hardcovers. Actually, I can think of worse ways to die.

I know Aunt Louisa allowed me to help decorate the library, but I've never been given the liberty of actually putting feet to all these imaginations in my head. We've worked the entire day and are taking a break for supper, but I'm sure we'll be up late tonight and tomorrow. Penelope, you would love this festival. It's all about royalty. I found this princess hat in one of the toy stores here that looked exactly like the pink one you used to have. The one you wore all. Of. The. Time. Was that the one that got stuck in a tree when Uncle Herman accidentally used it as a kite for Josephine's school project?

I think that if Ellen still likes me after all of this and if Brodie still wants to kiss me even when I'm a sweaty mess from shifting books around for four hours, then I could very well be living my own fairy tale right here in Skern.

I'm attaching photos of Brodie's house. Yes, those are REAL photos of Brodie's house. I'm still trying to wrap my mind around it. Luke, you'd love the woodwork inside this place. Two-hundred-year-old craftsmanship, from what Brodie says. I added a few of those pictures, too, just for your benefit.

I have a feeling the only sight I'll be seeing for the next two days is the inside of Sutherland's of Skern, so photos may be on the low side for the next email; however, since I'm in a bookshop and there's a Brodie around, my visual needs are happily satisfied. Speaking of vision, I've given Fiona the job of sorting the Braille books in a very specific order *and* in helping me update the children's book section. She reads even more voraciously than I do and she has a memory that's a little scary. I thought I was the only person who categorized favorite books in alphabetical order in my head by the author's name! She's helping with kid merchandise too. I want to adopt her, but she already has a wonderful family and I don't even know if I'll have a job when I get back to the States.

Anyway, I've gotta run! Lylla, one of the shop assistants, is trying to put Austen in the Fantasy section and someone needs to help her realize that Mr. Darcy, though swoony at times, is not in the fantasy genre . . . well, unless he's coming out of a pond in a white shirt. Then, maybe.

Love you all!

Izzy

PS: Ellen has the full set of Waverley Novels from 1857!!! She keeps them in a locked case, along with several first edition Austens and an embossed history of Skymar from 1812. She's promised to show me some of her other treasures too! I think my wild ideas are growing on her.

PPS: Having my boyfriend make a candlelit dinner for me in his cliffside manor house wasn't even on my bucket list! And I still got it!

From: Luke Edgewood
To: Izzy Edgewood, Josephine Martin, Penelope Edgewood
Date: June 24
Subject: Re: Epiphany of all epiphanies

Izzy,

You can't be Frankenstein's monster. You don't have the square-shaped head for it.

The craftsmanship is great. Some of those logs look hand-hewn.

You alphabetize books in your head? Not just on your shelves? And here I thought you were the semi-normal sister.

You promised on several occasions to refrain from mentioning he-who-shall-not-be-named in the white shirt. If I ever was tempted to be an Austen fan, which I've not been, the amount of times that guy is mentioned would kill any desire for it. He sets up unrealistic expectations for guys too. I've been grumpy for years and still haven't found the perfect woman.

Luke

PS: Penelope still wears that princess hat.

PPS: I've made dinner for women before, too, and it hasn't helped.

From: Penelope Edgewood
To: Izzy Edgewood, Josephine Martin, Luke Edgewood
Date: June 24
Subject: Re: Epiphany of all epiphanies

Oh, Izzy!!

That house is a fairy tale! I can't even believe those photos are real! And the sea is so magical—and a safe distance away. I know you all keep saying sea monsters are not real, but I am sure I saw one during our beach trip when I was seven. It was *not* a clump of coral, no matter what Luke says. It had eyes!!

And do be careful, Izzy. I see a strange white smudge in the corner of one of the photos of the empty sitting room. Do you think it's one of those ghost photos? What is the history of some lonely, cliffside manor house that has been left to deteriorate for years? Highly suspect for a possible haunting, you know? Even though I don't really believe in ghosts, of course, but still . . . I'd certainly want to know if there were any murders that took place there, especially if I was planning on my happily ever after and all. (Recall *Hamlet*.)

Oh! I still have my princess hat. It's in a keepsake box with my poster of Chris Pine, my favorite hair scrunchies, a gel pen given to me by Tommie Cauldwell, and the shoes I wore on my first trip to England. There's also an old pack of bubble gum, but I can't remember why it's there.

I order my books by color. They're much prettier on the shelves that way.

All these pictures just heighten my excitement about my internship. It's very strict, though. I think I'm going to be placed in some kind of governmental position because the amount of paperwork I have to complete for the intern position is enormous.

Anyway, I'm so excited for you and your dreams, Izzy. Maybe this one will come true!!

Love,

Penelope

PS: I already feel a kinship to Brodie's mother. It's the same feeling I have when I see anyone who remotely resembles Julie Andrews. Maybe I can meet Ellen when I come to Skymar!

PPS: Isn't there some Bible verse about God doing exceedingly and abundantly above what we even think? *Exceedingly* and *abundantly* are very optimistic words in the right context. For some reason it makes me think of *The Sound of Music*.

PPPS: Luke, Izzy's dinner probably didn't consist of french fries and freshly caught trout. Romantic food makes a difference.

• •

From: Luke Edgewood
To: Izzy Edgewood, Josephine Martin, Penelope Edgewood
Date: June 24
Subject: Re: Epiphany of all epiphanies

Penny-girl,

I think that once you take a photo of a ghost, they can't live in that place anymore. Maybe the same thing is true for sea monsters.

Luke

PS: Everything makes you think of *The Sound of Music*.

PPS: Trout is the most romantic food in the world.

<u>Text from Izzy to Luke and Penelope:</u> That was a mean thing to send to Penelope. You know she'll research photos and

ghosts now for a week and then end up terrifying herself into not sleeping!

Luke: When you become a big brother, you can tell me how to do it.

Penelope: Maybe wearing a button-down (white or not) that isn't flannel every once in a while might help you find your dream woman.

Luke: Says the woman who still wears a princess hat.

Penelope: I'm dressing for the job I want.

• •

From: Josephine Martin
To: Izzy Edgewood, Luke Edgewood, Penelope Edgewood
Date: June 25
Subject: Re: Epiphany of all epiphanies

Izzy,

Those photos truly are amazing. Are you certain that house is really Brodie's? You know, men will go to all sorts of lengths to impress the woman they like. Just be careful. You are very far away and there's not much we can do to save you from mishap, though I have contacted my great uncle who works in the government to let him know where you are in case we should be forced to find you. He's not known for being a very chatty person, but I was wholly surprised that he seemed nonplussed about my request to research Brodie's family. You would think government officials would take these types of things more seriously. At any rate, Maybelle, the secretary from the sheriff's office, has given me several websites to research that give detailed information about various countries of the world. Skymar's crime rate is surprisingly low and their main source of income is fishing, agriculture, and tourism. Really, Izzy? Fishing? What would you do in a fishing place?

And did you know that winter lasts almost half the year in Skymar? Almost HALF THE YEAR!! I can barely stand a month of solid cold. Can you imagine half a year of it? Except right now. Right now is the hottest summer we've ever had. And I think something is wrong with Patrick. He's taken to wearing his winter coat indoors in June!! Perhaps he's coming down with something. I've been sweating every day!

At any rate, I hear that men who are about to become fathers for the first time do strange things.

I'm so glad you're enjoying your time in that little bookshop. You are much too generous with your ideas, Izzy, and I've always thought so, but make sure they're not trying to steal them.

The babies are growing at preposterous rates, or so it seems. If they remain as active outside of my body as they are inside my body, I may have to hire Penelope as a live-in nanny. Oh, Izzy, you'd be the perfect live-in nanny . . . but only if that fits into YOUR plans. (See? I'm trying.)

I need to go. Babies on the bladder are not comfortable at all. And I'm starting to cry again. What is wrong with me?!?

Josephine

PS: Penelope, Tommie Cauldwell is still in prison. Please get rid of the pen.

Sutherland's looked like something out of an advertisement.

After spending one whole day moving shelves and a morning with Isabelle as he introduced her to local business owners (who loved the idea of Sutherland's showcasing some of their merchandise), Brodie had needed to complete a few business meetings in the afternoon, so he'd left Sutherland's only to return to Isabelle's handiwork on full display. Of course, watching her passion rub off on the locals only secured the many talents he already knew about her, but it was a delight to see how others recognized and responded to them too.

After hours away, he was a bit concerned when he couldn't find Isabelle anywhere on the first floor. In all honesty he'd been so distracted by the transformation of the shop, he may have detoured a few times before actually searching in earnest. The first window display beamed with lights and festive decorations, couching top-seller royal reads as well as a few favorites, with crowns, silk, and even several pieces of fine scree jewelry and a coffee cup or two to boast their new addition of merchandise. They'd even taken one of the old vanities from the attic and repurposed it as an almost "magical" mirror complete with modern-day fairy tales atop. In the other window Izzy had placed a massive stuffed dragon peering down from its perch on some shiny bluish material, which must have been used for sky or clouds, and this window was clearly meant to appeal more to the younger population with its foam swords, wooden shields, and handy display of children's royal headgear.

He entered, half in laughter and half in awe. He'd only been gone five hours, and he'd left Isabelle, Mum, Fiona, and Brynna busily restocking shelves they'd moved to various new places in the shop and unboxing merchandise he'd delivered earlier in the morning. How had they accomplished so much in such a short amount of time?

The front room still held its massive number of books, but instead of merely rows and rows of shelves, there were now little nooks for reading. Each window seat boasted pillows and soft lamps nearby for added light. A mismatch of antique furniture from the attic scattered throughout the shelves, each adorned with merchandise and softening the angles of the shelves with a cozy charm. Coffee cups, tea towels, plaques with book quotes, notebooks, and other book-related gifts begged for perusal from the tourist and local alike. Twinkle lights dotted various places and even twisted up the spiral staircase. Unbelievable!

"It's a marvel, isn't it, Mr. Sutherland?"

He turned to find Lylla carefully placing books on the shelf near the checkout counter. *Fairy Tales*, the embossed collection they'd ordered several months ago. The teenager's smile mirrored his own. "Isabelle's taken everything in hand and done this." She waved toward the room. "It's better than anything I've seen in New Inswythe or anywhere else on Ansling, if you ask me."

"I think you're right, Lylla." Another laugh burst from him as he pushed a hand through his hair. "I knew she had a gift, but I had no idea."

"We've had folks trying to get in the doors since nine this morning. I've had to keep telling them we'd open tomorrow, but they're nearly bursting to enter." Her ponytail swished with a shake of her head. "And she hasn't even started on the ideas she has for the website yet. Said she's going to work on that tonight with Brynna. Can you imagine?"

"No, truly. What she needs is a respite for a few hours." He stepped farther into the shop, searching for any sight of Isabelle. "She must be exhausted."

"You wouldn't know it to look at her." Lylla shrugged her shoulders. "She's been laughing and humming like the happiest person in the whole world. The rest of us might need a respite, but I'm not sure she does. If you ask me, she seems more energetic with each new project."

As if in response to Lylla's declaration, the sound of laughter reverberated from overhead.

"They've been up there the past two hours working on the children's place, as they've termed it."

"'Children's place'?"

Lylla nodded with an added shrug. "Your mum's over the moon. Fiona's positively wild about it. Said something about a 'touch box' for certain books." Lylla's pale eyes widened. "Don't ask me. I haven't the foggiest. And I've not seen so much cloth and puff animals inside a bookshop in all my life. If it's to come out anything like the ground level, it's bound to be smacking good."

"Aye, smacking good . . . " Brodie murmured, following the sound of the laughter. His mother's joined in with Isabelle's. He bypassed the spiral staircase for the larger stairs near the back of the room, following the sounds. At the top of the landing he froze. They'd transformed the entire space into some magical world for children. A few large throw pillows waited on the hardwood floor at one corner and the shelves had been rearranged into various categories to break up the enormous space. Shimmering teal cloth partially covered some of the exposed beams in the ceiling, giving the appearance of sky or clouds above to arch over the myriad displays of colorful children's books and miscellanea. He truly wished to linger and explore.

"Wonderful! You've returned." His mother walked toward him from a corner of the room where small bookshelves were framed by an assortment of puff animals. "Did you bring the puzzles?" She waved toward a few empty shelves by the window. "We have shelves awaiting them."

He shuffled another step forward. "They're in the boot."

"And did Marcus have any additional children's games to offer?"

He nodded, still taking in the room. He'd toured various bookshops around the world and this one measured up to them. Even if it wasn't complete and empty shelves awaited more books or merchandise, the vision shone delightfully clear. No magical wardrobe necessary.

"Brodie?"

He blinked out of his stupor to find his mother and Isabelle standing nearby, staring at him, the latter's forehead puckered as she searched his face.

"It's remarkable, Isabelle." His attention shifted to his mother, his response unexpectedly breathless. "Truly."

"Isn't it?" His mother wrapped an arm around Isabelle's shoulders. "I thought the loss of what your father had designed would wound me, but once we began shifting things here and decorating things there, I realized Isabelle still understood the heart of my husband's love for this place. She even made a very special section for our secondhand treasures, as she called the used books."

"Secondhand treasures," he whispered, all of it too much to take in at one time. "What a perfect name."

"And we've listed the section as such downstairs," Mum added.

His attention landed on Isabelle, air bursting from his nose in a strange sort of shocked laugh. "Isabelle, *this*." He gestured toward the room. "This is what you were made to do," he breathed out the sentence, pushing a hand through his hair as he turned to take in the room again. "I can't believe it's the same shop. You must be exhausted."

"I've loved every minute." She shot him a grin, the glimmer in her eyes failing to show any weariness at all. "I mean, you can only do so much with a library, and my aunt would only give a certain amount of freedom, but the two of you just let me create. I'm at my best when I'm creating bookish things, or talking of bookish things." She skimmed her teeth over the bottom lip with a shrug. "Or pushing books on people."

"A bookshop is the perfect place for a book pusher to work, my dear. In fact, I can't think of a single occupation more fitting."

Isabelle shook her head with her laugh, the dark hair of her ponytail swishing. "Well, I don't know that there are many jobs out there in the world for book pushers and bookshop decorators."

"It's more than that and you know it." Brodie approached, sighing again as he scanned the room. "You have this book knowledge that's remarkable, this unique passion for it, and a sense of how to remodel a bookshop, as well as a way of matching people with the proper books."

"Well, if I had more time, I could really get things set." She rubbed her palms together, an added glint in her dark eyes. "This place is filled with such natural character and charm, it breathes the invitation for creativity. And all that antique furniture upstairs? If we interspersed more of it throughout the shop, it would add a sense of homeyness to everything. Some of the high-backs upstairs would work wonderfully for reading spots."

"What a brilliant idea!" He stared at her, blinking. "We've always wondered what to do with those furnishings."

"I'm pleased beyond what I can say, my dear. You need to find a way to use these gifts as a part of your daily life. Such creativity and innovation! I can't believe you're not knackered."

"With the third floor free of some of the furniture, we could create office space, Mum." Brodie laughed. "Part storage and part offices. Skern has been our central location for years, but we've never had an actual place fit for an office."

"Look at the two of you." Mum clasped her hands together. "The perfect bookish duo." She laughed and then released a happy sigh before turning to touch Isabelle's cheek. Isabelle's eyes rounded and a sudden sheen glimmered to life in those dark eyes, but it wasn't from sadness. No. His lovely American smiled. A sweet, grateful smile.

His heart expanded to post-Grinchlike proportions at the sight.

"So, Brodie-dear," Mum turned her attention on him. "I believe your lovely friend is due a proper reward for all her hard work."

"I couldn't agree more." He exchanged a look with his mum and then reached for Isabelle's hand. "We have an evening appointment to tour Carlstern Castle and then we'll enjoy a nice dinner in the city before we return to Skern. With an imagination like yours, Karre, you simply must visit a *real* castle."

CHAPTER 23

From: Anders Sutherland
To: Brodie Sutherland
Date: June 27
Subject: Twinkle lights???

Brodie,

What have you done? I thought you said your little girlfriend was going to make a few adjustments to the bookshop, but I visited Skern today to find Sutherland's completely transformed. Pink parasols?? White twinkling lights? Puff dragons? Grandfather would be rolling in his grave! Who approved of placing a plastic crown on the statue of Lord Percival II? Plastic? Did you speak to Mother about these things? It's positively preposterous. And what happened to the History section? It's been replaced by plush pillows and picture books and a pair of fighter planes hanging from the ceiling. I have no words. How any of this will help sales is beyond me! People visit bookshops for books, not . . . theatrics and teacups. I expect things to return to their former structure and predictability once Isabella returns home. I just hope we haven't lost too much business by then.

Anders

PS: What do twinkling lights have to do with either books or royals? Clearly Isabella is American.

From: Brodie Sutherland
To: Anders Sutherland
Date: June 27
Subject: Re: Twinkle lights???

Anders,

I have attached ten links to various successful bookshops in countries neighboring ours. Twinkling lights are all the rage. And I think Lord Percival looks rather dashing with a crown. He always wanted to be king, as you recall from history, so we've just fulfilled his wish posthumously.

I look forward to allaying your fears about sales once the festival is over.

Brodie

PS: *Isabelle* is her name and I'm rather fond of her being an American.

From: Izzy Edgewood
To: Luke Edgewood, Penelope Edgewood, Josephine Martin
Date: June 28
Subject: The Book Matchmaker

Cousins,

I'm so sorry I've missed emailing you guys for the past few days, but the whole bookshop thing has taken up almost every waking moment. I can't tell you how much fun I've had.

I'm exhausted, overwhelmed, thrilled . . . and I've nearly cried three times. I love books! I know that's not a surprise, but more than that, I love helping people not only love books but experience them.

I know your mom loves me, but I've spent so many years keeping quiet about my ideas because I'd convinced myself that I shouldn't say anything, that I needed to keep quiet because she and Uncle Herman were so kind to take me into your family when I lost mine. I know it's crazy and untrue, but the idea kept me quiet when I should have spoken and still when I should have moved. But something happened when Brodie and his mom gave me freedom to renovate Sutherland's. Actually I think it all started with Josephine's matchmaking madness with Heart-to-Heart. The anonymity to be me and then the realization of me pretending to be someone else to help Eli and then how Brodie encouraged my authenticity when I didn't even realize I was opening up to him . . . Well, here I am. The Book Matchmaker.

What is that, you may ask?

It seems that after we restructured what we could over two days, the curious locals couldn't get enough and the tourist traffic from the incoming festival had an upswing. The place was so crowded, they even called in Anders, Brodie's brother, who appears to be less enthused with customer interaction. Needless to say, I took over his shift when he couldn't remember who wrote *Great Expectations* and then later made another child cry—those were unrelated events.

It was like I'd stepped directly into a lifelong dream that I didn't even know I longed to find. Listening to what people were looking for, helping them find the right book, sharing my love for the stories and even finding a few new reads for myself. So when Brodie brought a young woman to me, with an adorable glint in his eyes, he said, "She wanted to see the Book Matchmaker." As Brodie told me later, one person mentioned my "matching" them with a few books and from that point on the moniker stuck.

I found my perfect job description! If only it paid! LOL.

But seriously, if I could work with books and decorate a bookstore without having to worry about all the money business and meetings and presentations that Brodie talks about, I would be doing what I feel I was made to do. Like I have the past three days.

Can one of you guys find that perfect job for me?

Anyway, after a lovely day working with Ellen and Fiona at the bookshop, Brodie took me to tour Carlstern Castle, where the current king and queen of Skymar live. Oh my, it was amazing. It's only open for tours during this festival and people secure their tickets a year in advance, so Brodie's mom gave her ticket to me so I could go. A real king and queen. Can you imagine actually meeting one of them in person inside their own home? I'm sure it would be something to remember, even if it was accidental or something like that. Penelope, you would have LOVED it!!

Photos aren't allowed inside, so I attached the website so you can see a few of the rooms, but I just can't imagine living in a place like that every day. (And I would add, the photo of the library doesn't do it justice. Or the one of the dining room. WOW!)

Brodie and I enjoyed a quiet dinner together before ending the day by having a website/social media brainstorming session with

Brodie's cousin, Brynna. I can't tell you how much fun I'm having! And Brodie, well, he's just perfect.

Brodie has some meetings tomorrow in Port Quinnick, one of the oldest historic places on Ansling. While he's in meetings, I get to tour the place, and I'm so excited because I can tell from the way he talks about it that he loves the city. Lots of history and even some interesting legends. Plus I have a list of businesses I'd like to visit for possible bookshop merch. *Squee!!!*

I'll share more tomorrow with photos!

I think all of the excitement is starting to catch up with me, so I'm going to call it a night. I love you all and please let me know how everyone is doing. As you can tell, I'm having the best time of my life.

With a fairy-tale sigh,
Izzy

PS: People of Skymar believe there are tiny book fairies who tend to mistreated books while everyone's asleep at night. Brodie and I started brainstorming a children's book about it when I became fascinated and asked questions. It even rhymes! Once I finish, I'll share it with you.

PPS: Local author Evangeline Lawrence signed a copy of her book *Among the Tides* today! It's definitely been a day of amazing meetings!

• •

From: Luke Edgewood
To: Penelope Edgewood, Izzy Edgewood, Josephine Martin
Date: June 28
Subject: Re: The Book Matchmaker

Izzy,

You're not going to get by with that so easily. I believe Brodie mentioned something about a very interesting and "accidental" meeting you had at Carlstern. Interesting that you would leave out something so . . . royally memorable? That just isn't fair to your loving family.

Luke

PS: The Book Matchmaker? Really? It fits so well, yet I'm still rolling my eyes.

From: Izzy Edgewood
To: Penelope Edgewood, Luke Edgewood, Josephine Martin
Date: June 28
Subject: Re: The Book Matchmaker

Luke,

What exactly did Brodie tell you?

Curiously,
Izzy

PS: Just so you know, nothing necessarily *bad* happened.

From: Luke Edgewood
To: Penelope Edgewood, Izzy Edgewood, Josephine Martin
Date: June 28
Subject: Re: The Book Matchmaker

Brodie and I email on a regular basis, Iz. We talk books and brainstorm some renovation ideas he has for his house. He mentioned your tour and asked if you'd shared about meeting the queen. Something simple like that, but I've known him long enough to almost hear the story behind that question, so you better spill the beans or I'll ask Brodie.

Luke

PS: I know things about you and I'm not afraid to use them. Be nice to me.

• •

From: Izzy Edgewood
To: Luke Edgewood, Penelope Edgewood, Josephine Martin
Date: June 28
Subject: Re: The Book Matchmaker

Cousins,

Fine! Since Luke seems to know everything about everything, I will tell you the embarrassing moment I had today at Carlstern Castle, which hopefully will *never* happen again. The castle really is amazing. And I was overwhelmed by the tapestries and the craftsmanship and the art on the ceilings. So it was quite natural that when Brodie slipped away to return a phone call for the bookshop, I kept touring. When I saw what appeared to be an early edition of *Middlemarch* through a cracked door in a passing room—okay, it wasn't quite a passing room. It was across the hallway from the room I was in—but I saw bookshelves, so naturally I gravitated toward the room. In my defense the door was partially open.

It led into a breathtaking library. Two stories of books. So of course I scanned (okay, visually inventoried) some of the shelves, and that's when I saw a woman sitting in one of the nearby chairs, staring at me. She was lovely. Soft-blonde hair, pale eyes, and posture to impress the Dowager Countess of Grantham. So I did something brilliant like say, "Isn't this an amazing library?" to which she replied with, "Indeed." And then we exchanged some simple banter before I made a comment about how I would rearrange the shelves to make the more popular books more accessible. I cringe to think about it now. She smiled in a very generous way. Okay, so truly she looked like she wanted to laugh. Then I mentioned that for a royal castle, their History section looked pitifully small. (Envision me with my head in my hands right now as I relive this scene.) At which time, Brodie arrived in the doorway and looked from me to the woman standing nearby, and then he did the strangest thing. Or I thought it was strange at the moment. He bowed his head, made some greeting in Caedric, and then I very clearly heard the words "Your Majesty." Then everything clicked into place and my face grew hot enough to toast marshmallows. I'm serious. And then you all know what happened. My eyes started watering because I was so embarrassed, and Brodie thought I was going to cry. I didn't cry. I gave some sort of curtsy, which may have looked more like the failed flight of Penelope's rescued parakeet, Pebbles. And . . . nearly knocked over one of those stand-up globes that I found out later, thankfully, was a gift from some duke of something to the queen's grandfather sixty years ago. I'm going to boycott globes in bookshops in the future.

Anyway, we left before I could somehow destroy the royal line, though Brodie was quick to inform me, between chuckles, that the king and queen are incredibly generous and kindhearted people . . . and would likely retell this story to their posterity for generations to come. I'm going to keep using the "I'm an American" excuse for as long as I can (sorry US of A).

There you have it. Now I'm going to douse my retro-embarrassment with a hot chocolate and some pepperkake from Antoinette's. Unfortunately I've had the hardest time finding mint chocolate chip ice cream, but Sutherland's has three different editions of *Wuthering Heights* so I feel well prepared for the aftermath of my humiliation.

It's almost two in the morning here in Skern. I really need to go to sleep.

Mortified,
Izzy

PS: Brodie is better than mint chocolate chip and Brontë, just so you know. He hugs. I never even made it to the second page of Brontë.

PPS: The queen kind of looked like Julie Andrews, just so you know. And I told her so, before I knew she was the queen. I don't know if that won me brownie points or not, but it ought to have. Who doesn't love Julie Andrews? Between Ellen, the queen, and three other ladies I met today, there's a surprising influx of Julie Andrews look-alikes, but really . . . who can blame them? As Anne of Green Gables says, "Imitation is the sincerest form of flattery."

• •

From: Penelope Edgewood
To: Luke Edgewood, Izzy Edgewood, Josephine Martin

Date: June 28
Subject: Re: The Book Matchmaker

You MET. A. QUEEN!!!! I can't even imagine. What were you wearing? Please tell me you didn't have on one of those bookish T-shirts of yours. You know the ones I mean. "Go away! I'm reading" or "Bookmarks are for quitters" or, the worst one, "I stopped reading to be here! Not a fair trade." Even if you met her in a library, those do not set the best first impression for a queen. Not that I've ever met one, but I've seen *The King and I* and even performed in *Hamlet*. There is a certain protocol, Izzy. Maybe you'll get another chance to make a first impression. I'm sure if you meet her again, she probably won't remember you. Royals see so many people, they can't remember everybody.

The photos are fabulous!! The official website says that the library has over forty thousand books! I feel certain their History section is more than adequate. And did you know that Julie Andrews starred in the Broadway version of *My Fair Lady*? It's important. She really sang her songs, unlike Audrey Hepburn. I just thought you ought to know in case someone asks you about it.

Can't wait to see more photos!

Love,
Penelope

PS: I don't see why you wouldn't think you're a part of our family, Izzy! Clearly I fuss at you like I do Josephine or Luke. In fact, most days I like you much better than either of them.

PPS: I adore the title The Book Matchmaker. You could set it to music like the matchmaker song from *Fiddler on the Roof*.

From: Luke Edgewood
To: Penelope Edgewood, Izzy Edgewood, Josephine Martin
Date: June 28
Subject: Re: The Book Matchmaker

Izzy,

I'm glad to know that I can stop stockpiling ice cream to deter you from delving into an unhealthy dose of Brontë. I'll send my future donations to old Blighty.

Luke

PS: Penelope, you're underestimating the queen's sense of humor. She may own one of those T-shirts.

From: Izzy Edgewood
To: Luke Edgewood, Penelope Edgewood, Josephine Martin
Date: June 28
Subject: Re: The Book Matchmaker

Penelope,

It's good to know that if you meet the queen during your internship, your love for the stage has sufficiently prepared you. And no, I was not wearing one of my bookish T-shirts. I actually wore the red summer dress you bought me for the trip. I'll be okay if the queen doesn't remember me. I'd rather leave a better impression than "rebel, bossy, bookish American tourist." Well, I wouldn't mind the "bookish" part so much.

And of course Julie Andrews is practically perfect in every way.

Izzy

PS: Luke, maybe you should write a rhyming children's book with Brodie. I can only imagine how Seussian that could be.

From: Penelope Edgewood
To: Luke Edgewood, Izzy Edgewood, Josephine Martin
Date: June 28
Subject: Re: The Book Matchmaker

Izzy!!

You wore the dress I bought you to meet the queen!! That means I was practically there with you!! Wait until the girls at school hear about this!

Penelope

From: Luke Edgewood
To: Penelope Edgewood, Izzy Edgewood, Josephine Martin
Date: June 28
Subject: Re: The Book Matchmaker

Penny-girl,

I have no words.

Luke

From: Josephine Martin
To: Penelope Edgewood, Izzy Edgewood, Luke Edgewood
Date: June 29
Subject: Re: The Book Matchmaker

Izzy,

I'm sorry I haven't responded to your emails. I've been reorganizing Patrick's sock drawer, the kitchen pantry, and Grandmother's sewing room underneath the stairs. It really is amazing what you can find in a place no one's touched in nine years. I think I located someone's missing hot-pink scrunchies and Penelope's violin. Why the violin would be in that untouched place, I have no idea. Needless to say, I now have enough space to store Patrick's golf paraphernalia.

I'm so glad you are having such a nice time on your little vacation, and I'd like to reiterate one point about your self-reflection. You have always been a part of our family, Izzy. I've never thought of you as anything else. If I seemed to gravitate toward asking for your help or relying on you for important things, it's only because I always found you fully capable and willing. Maybe I tried to give my advice too much and guide you in certain directions, but I would never want to lead you somewhere you were not meant to go. I think I can say this for Luke and Penelope, too, that we've always believed in you. In fact, there are more days than not that I envied your creativity, passion, zeal, and love for what you do. There aren't many people who ever truly find their place or niche in the world. Most of us just do what needs to be done. But you're one of the unique few who *have* and we want to celebrate that with you.

Maybe that's why Mom encouraged you to take the library job, because she caught a glimpse of that passion inside you and wanted to see what you'd do.

I need to stop writing because I've started crying again. Just know I love you and whatever decision you make about books or romance or annoying bookish shirts, I will love you still.

Josephine

From: Izzy Edgewood
To: Penelope Edgewood, Luke Edgewood, Josephine Martin
Date: June 29
Subject: Re: The Book Matchmaker

Josephine,

Your note brought me to tears and I'm not even pregnant.

I'm so grateful that I'm learning that love comes in all different shapes, sizes, and personalities. I can't believe it's taken me this long to see that love gives me freedom, not chains me down. Even if you guys don't agree with me, you're going to love me, and I think that's the part I needed to really understand most of all.

And I hope you have the best time ever organizing the rest of the house, Josephine. I've never felt that type of passion for the organization of anything . . . Well, except maybe books.

Izzy

Text from Izzy to Luke: So that's where you put Penelope's violin!!! I always wondered.

Luke: Someone had to be man enough to protect the living.

"Thursday was our biggest sales day in ten years, Isabelle." Brodie's grin unhinged as he steered the car along the motorway, his hair fluttering in the sea-salted air blowing through the windows. "One day. And Mum said that today is already superseding yesterday. You're like a miracle worker."

Izzy smoothed her palms down her slacks, warmth branching through her chest. From her talk with Luke, to Josephine's email, to her absolute delight in spending time with Brodie and his bookshop, she couldn't seem to tame the dizzying excitement coursing through her. If life was going to wait until she was thirty to start happening, then it sure hit with an explosion of confetti.

"I can't thank you enough for trusting me with your family's legacy." She sighed and leaned back into the car seat. "I'm honored and overwhelmed."

"*You're* the one thanking *me*." He gave her fingers a quick squeeze before returning his hand to the steering wheel. "After all these months of growing to love you and learning about who you are, it was as much a pleasure to see you explore all of that magnificent imagination of yours as it was to watch the people swarm into the shop."

Had he said *love*? She pinched her hands together, determined to hold back a junior-high squeal. Of course he loved her. He'd shown her in his actions and words and gentleness—heat soared into her face—not to mention his kisses. She embraced the awareness and her heart's ready response. "I'm so glad," she whispered.

"And now you're the Book Matchmaker?" He laughed. "How perfect is that!"

She stared at his profile, the sharp angle of a chin framed with his closely shaved golden beard. His nose with a tiny bend in it, evidently from a "row with Anders" over *Robinson Crusoe*. The way his blond hair swept back from his forehead as if brushed back by the wind. And her smile softened. He loved her. "People like to give labels to things."

"In this respect the moniker fits like a glove." He shot her his charming smile. The sea behind him, the wind tousling his hair, those eyes staring at her as if she was Margaret Hale and he, John Thornton. Oh, she desperately needed to rewatch the last ten minutes of *North and South* when she got home. Her brow shot skyward. Or . . . better yet, an acting out of the kissing scene.

"It's crazy how that Book Matchmaker name has stuck."

"You've not only read so many books you can relate to innumerable readers, but you even set the stage for people to fall in love with books. The bookshop is transformed, and you haven't even done all you wanted. Don't you see how remarkable you and your gifts are, dear Isabelle?"

She hadn't. Not for so long. But now . . . now she was beginning to realize she deserved a chance to be loved by a good person. To find equal footing for the romantic road of life. To *be* loved, not just *to* love. And . . . well . . . she had worth all on her own. It truly was amazing how a shift in perspective, an understanding of her own identity in this world and the next, changed everything. She was loved. End of story.

Not only that, she had skills and talents worth using and giving. Thoughts worth sharing and challenging. A solid mind and heart worth trusting instead of hiding all of it behind the safety of silence.

"Thank you, Brodie." Her eyes stung so she looked away, toward the rolling green countryside that lay dotted with stone houses and white sheep and . . . her future? The heat slipped from her face. A world away from home?

"I don't believe in pretense and insinuations when it comes to matters of the heart, Karre. I want you to know up front and honestly exactly where I stand. What I think."

Her attention pulled back to his profile. He was just wonderful. Through and through. But home? Family? Her heart squeezed to the painful spot.

His lips quirked. "To quote a popular fiction that feels rather appropriate, 'I love you because the entire universe conspired to help me find you.'"

His quote from *The Alchemist* nearly pushed her struggle to the background, but it lingered between them, waiting for an answer . . . a choice. She smiled over at him and forced the darker thoughts away. "It required an entire universe to match up two people who live an ocean apart, I guess."

"That must be why it took so long, but it's been worth the wait."

She sighed away her worries and basked in the rightness of being . . . loved by him. Loved! *By him!* "It has certainly been worth the wait."

Every hurt. Every insecurity. Every question why. All of them led her to him. And now.

"What does Karre mean?" She breathed out the question, her throat on fire. "You use it a lot with me and I . . . I've been wondering."

He drew in a breath, his gaze catching in hers. "It has no proper English translation, but it captures a host of words, feelings really. My dear, my love, my admiration and hope. The word is meant to encapsulate them all."

"It's beautiful, particularly when you say it . . . to me."

His attention fastened on her. "I don't say it to anyone else."

Her breath squeezed and she let his declaration soak through the worries and tremulous hope like a promise. How could she return to life thousands of miles away from her heart? How could she step back into a life of the same when she wasn't the same anymore?

He turned back to the road and gestured ahead of them. "Port Quinnick."

The cliffside road wound ahead and disappeared into a conglomeration of buildings hugging the side of the coastline and trailing down to the sea, as if in a race to see who could reach the water's edge first. She leaned forward, taking in the view. Buildings of all sorts, mostly older-looking structures, jutted out of the hillside as boats of all shapes and sizes studded the gray-blue sea along the coastline. A haunting ruin towered over the port city on a nearby hillside, beautiful and eerie in its position with the swirl of dark clouds behind.

"What is that?"

He didn't even look in her direction, only continued his grin. "Ah, I knew you'd like Fearnrose Abbey. Are you envisioning the burned halls of fictional Thornfield in your mind?"

She rested her elbow against the car door and leaned toward the sight, the cool wind blowing against her cheeks. "Definitely, but even with all its brokenness, it's still such an intriguing site."

"Perhaps because of it." He nodded, slowing the car so she had time to take a few photos from their current vantage point. "And it has a story, should you wish to hear it."

"Seriously." She rolled her gaze to his. "Do you even need to ask?"

He looked at her with such unveiled affection, she nearly breached the distance and distracted him from driving with a kiss. "I hope you know how glad I am that you're here . . . with me, Isabelle."

To that she did lean over and kiss his cheek. "I'm glad to be here with you, too, Brodie."

"Well, then." He cleared his throat and drew in a breath. "Legend has it—"

"Legend has it? Are you kidding me?" She laughed. "I can already tell I'm going to love this story."

"I can practically see your mind conjuring up all sorts of imaginings." They began a descent toward the port. "Well, then, legend has it that there were three priests who were brothers, both in the biological sense and the spiritual sense, and all three had talents and interests in architecture. Each came to Skymar and wanted to make their mark on the people here, so the eldest two, who were considered the greater of the talents, built their own churches on separate points of the island of Ansling. Fearnrose was completed first by the eldest of the three. The second eldest built Kilnen Abbey just north near the town of Elri, a bit smaller than his elder brother's edifice."

"Why am I having *Goldilocks and the Three Bears* vibes?"

His laugh burst out. "Sorry to disappoint, but I'm not aware of a Goldilocks in this story; however, the youngest brother did assist both of his elder brothers in their endeavors, but they discouraged him from taking his somewhat unique views of architecture into developing his own place of worship."

"But of course he didn't adhere to their suggestions."

"Of course not." Brodie raised a brow. "Though he was the quietest of the three and spent many years supporting his brothers' endeavors, he had a burning desire to create something with his own skills. To give, as he saw it, of his own talents, so he chose an unlikely island for his plan."

Her expression must have shown her confusion, because he chuckled. "Yes, all of Skymar is made up of islands, but the youngest brother built on an islet known as Skree, which is just across a land bridge from Port Quinnick." He pointed out the window toward the ocean and in the distance Izzy could make out the faintest hint of a small land mass among the fog.

"There he built his own offering to God through architecture. An odd sort of creation, and somewhat ignored by his brothers, but beautiful in its own way and quite providential to the future of Port Quinnick."

Izzy squinted to make out the mass in the distance, but all she noticed were rocky mounds and a plethora of trees.

"When Vikings came to the island of Ansling a thousand years ago, they ransacked villages and cities and destroyed churches, but they didn't burn the Kirk of Skree because they didn't know it was there. Thousands of people crossed to the island and hid within the church, which was built of the very rocks on which it hid. And thanks to the forward-thinking of the youngest brother, Elerk, who had cultivated gardens and a self-sufficient water system, the people who fled to Skree survived in hiding without the persecution and devastation of those who remained inland."

"What a remarkable story."

"Indeed, and it so happened that Elerk the Younger met Katarine during his hiding, which led to a marriage and eventually, through that bloodline, the first king of Skymar, who led Skymar in its independence and to the prosperity you see today."

The ocean disappeared behind the city buildings of Port Quinnick and Izzy sighed, nestling farther into her seat. "So that's the ruin you've been hinting for me to investigate while you're in meetings this afternoon?"

He shrugged. "I imagine you will have plenty to investigate with the history of Port Quinnick and all of its marvelous shops, but I'd advise you not to miss Kirk of Skree while you're here."

"How can I not visit it! My curiosity is sufficiently piqued."

"My grandfather always loved the story of Elerk the Younger because Grandfather was the youngest of three boys, and when he'd tell the story, he'd always add at the end"—Brodie furrowed his brow and dipped his chin, lowering his voice into a gravely imitation—"Brodie, my boy, remember Elerk and his story. It's about taking what you have within you, what God-given gifts you already possess, and falling in love with them. Making them work for your future. Uniquely. That's how you make your life worth living, for yourself and others."

Sneaky man. "Did you make this story up?"

"Of course not!" His brows shot high. "You doubt me?"

"I doubt your very convenient moral of the story."

His eyes rounded in pure innocence. "It's true through and through. You can ask Mum, though I may have added a few convenient parallels for your benefit."

"So your next occupation is historical fiction, then?"

He chuckled. "Only if you'll help me write it."

She quieted a moment, allowing his words to take residence around her doubts. She'd felt it. The joy of using her gifts to create something beautiful and useful . . . and to touch other lives in the process. The past two days had proven it all the more. "That's what you've done, isn't it? With Sutherland's. You've found where you belong. Who you are."

He brought the car to a stop on the side of the street, trees and street lamps interspersed among stone, brick, and a very few glass-and-steel combinations of a newer business variety, but even those somehow were worked into the picturesque display of the rest of the city.

He turned to her. "In part, yes. I find great satisfaction in living in this book world and all it encompasses." He searched her face. "But I hadn't really felt complete in my story, if you will, until I traveled to a little town in North Carolina and met a certain bookish beauty."

"That line was wonderfully executed." She leaned forward, drawn by the tenderness in his expression.

"And genuinely felt," he whispered as he touched his lips to hers.

Aye, her heart sighed. She breathed in the pine and spice and everything nice that Brodie Sutherland offered her. The decision she'd have to make to pursue a future with him, a long-term future, quaked through her with torrential force. She'd never been the risky sort, except in reading choices. She'd never considered herself brave or adventurous or daring, but a life with Brodie required some entirely nonfictional courage. And she'd been practicing courage lately.

For the first time since giving her heart away in high school to a guy who only wanted her for her literature smarts, she completely and unreservedly released hold to Brodie Sutherland. In fact, she loved his world too. And it didn't take too much imagination to see herself living and working alongside him in his bookishness till death do they part. But even if it meant a life on the other side of the ocean from home?

She squeezed her eyes closed as his arm came up around her shoulder.

Yes. She could be brave enough for something like that.

From: Izzy Edgewood
To: Luke Edgewood, Penelope Edgewood
Date: June 30
Subject: Babies on the way!!!

I'm so glad I was near the bookshop watching the King and Queen Parade so that my phone picked up your texts! It took a little finagling, but I was able to get my flight changed to this evening. (Weekend flights are tough to find! I had no idea!) I know the babies will be born before I get there, but how could I wait three more days to see them?!? It's not every day you become an aunt-cousin for the first time.

I won't get to Mt. Airy until late tomorrow night, but if visitor hours are still open, I'm driving directly to the hospital. Please keep me in the know of how things are going. I should be hooked up to Wi-Fi until I leave for the airport around seven this evening, so if the newest members of the family make their debut before then, let me know.

Brodie and I are going to finish up a few things at the bookshop and then have a late lunch with his family before he drives me to catch my flight. I've loved every minute of being here with him. It's amazing what you can learn about yourself and the person you're dating when given the opportunity and the close proximity. He just keeps getting BETTER and BETTER.

And at the risk of sounding sentimental, he's making me better and better, too, just by being who he is.

I should probably tell you guys this before I get home . . .

Brodie proposed! We were having breakfast this morning at a little café in Skern overlooking Brendwater (a nearby lake) and he took my hand into his, gave me the sweetest smile on the planet, and said, "Isabelle," (in his lovely accented voice) "would you come work for Sutherland's?"

I can hear Penelope's disappointment from here, but I'm not disappointed at all! I'm ecstatic.

His proposal, such as it was, is actually a perfect match for me. He, his mother, and brother met last night and created a position catered specifically for my talents and interests as Creative Marketing Director of Sutherland's Books. They even want me to offer a link on the website called the Book Matchmaker—where readers can email in to ask for specific recommendations to which I'd then refer them to our "developing" online bookstore! Oh, OH! There's so much to do!!!! I've never been so sure about anything in my life, and you guys know what a big deal that is!

The plan would be to start the job virtually with a goal of moving to Ansling within a year.

I know this will cause a kink in so many plans for home and for the library, but I already have a few recommendations for my replacement.

Just so you know, Penelope, Brodie did hint around at the other type of proposal, but I have a feeling he's waiting for a special occasion . . . and probably a little more familiarity. I can only imagine after becoming better acquainted with my idiosyncrasies, oddities, and mountain-size insecurities he may want a little more time to consider a lifelong attachment. Besides, it's pretty quick for two people to email, meet, and marry within the first year of knowing each other, right?

Can you even believe it? Me, of all people? Leaving Mt. Airy for a transatlantic adventure? Who would have thought that after struggling through what I was meant to do for years and years, that my dream *found* me instead of me finding my dream?

Okay, I've gotta run. One of the kids in the children's section decided to stick a Mathlink cube up his nose and nobody seems to know what to do about it. Clearly they've not taught four-year-old Sunday school before.

Love you all and see you soon,
Izzy

PS: Did I mention that Brodie said he loved me?! It took me a few hours, but I worked up the courage to tell him too. Love!

PPS: I am *almost* tempted to sing.

• •

From: Luke Edgewood
To: Izzy Edgewood, Penelope Edgewood

Date: June 30
Subject: Re: Babies on the way!!!

Izzy,

You realize you just opened yourself up to having Penelope list EVERY happy couple she knows (and even those she doesn't) who have married after knowing each other less than a year. Maybe even less than a week. I know some of her friends. It's terrifying. I'm just warning you so you'll be ready for the verbal onslaught when she sees you next.

I'm really happy for your new job. The commute is gonna be a bear, though. Maybe old Blighty can invest in a private jet or boat for you. Or Floo powder.

Are there book perks for family members? Can't wait to hear more about it when you get home.

Also, how'd the kid make out? Sounds like a booger of a time.

Safe travels,
Luke

PS: No babies yet, but I don't think Patrick's podiatry experiences sufficiently prepared him for Josephine giving birth.

From: Penelope Edgewood
To: Izzy Edgewood, Luke Edgewood
Date: June 30
Subject: Re: Babies on the way!!!

IZZY!!!!!!

Luke just told me to check my email (I was messaging my internship coordinator about flight details for Skymar! *Squee*!). Anyway, how could you lead me on like that? A job offer is NOT the same as a proposal! Though I'm beyond happy for you to find something bookish. You're so much better with stories and spines than, you know, other things. And to get to travel? Experience the world? Oh my goodness, I'm thrilled for you, except I'm not, because then I'll miss you terribly! Who will go Christmas shopping with me for all those hard-to-choose gifts, like . . . for Uncle Lawrence? Izzy, you have to promise to visit once a year, if for no other reason than to help me with Christmas shopping.

Luke is no help at all in the hospital. He just sits there like a stump watching me pace back and forth and occasionally humming the Wicked Witch of the West's theme in time with the clip of my heels. He really is the most annoying brother! But he did show up with iced tea and muffins from Loralee's, so at least he's good for something besides exasperated-glare practice. And he's a good hugger.

Patrick is a dream! He's only raised his voice once and that was to call a nurse to stop his nosebleed. Evidently, Josephine, in her current mental distress, hit him in the nose. He's still smiling, though. I overheard him encouraging one of the nurses to offer something to calm Josephine down and the nurse responded with a chuckle, adding something about nitrous. Maybe the nitrous is for him? I feel like I've heard the word before, but Luke is laughing so hard he won't explain it to me.

He really is the sweetest sort of man, though. Not Luke. Patrick. I think Patrick is one of those quiet, gentle types that emotional women need to survive. I just hope that he doesn't have a swollen purple nose in their first family photos. Though purple would likely brighten those hazel eyes of his.

Luke is still laughing, BTW. I hate him. Okay, I don't hate him, but, well, you know . . .

I can't wait to see you! I'm so excited for you to share all you've seen and learned in Skymar so I'll be armed for the internship! They really aren't giving us very much information to go on.

I've attached a list of very happily married couples I know who met online and married (not online) within a year. Luke told me to delete five of them because of several unmentionable details about their current not-so-happily-ever-afters, but I left the rest, even though the last couple no longer live in the same state as each other. Evidently long-distance works for their marriage too.

Love,
Penelope

PS: I really can't imagine a Mathlink cube fitting inside of any child's nose. I think you're making that up, Izzy.

PPS: Floo powder? Commuting? Luke is such a dork!

Now Izzy knew what a tug-of-war rope felt like.

As she sat around the table with the Sutherlands, and Ellen shared funny stories about Brodie, Izzy wrapped the sound of Brodie's laugh around her. He had an arm draped casually over the back of her chair, giving full access to his scent of spice and pine. They'd discussed her new position over the first part of lunch, each additional idea sprinkling excitement like fairy dust over the future. Brynna had joined them. Though her marketing skills weren't stellar, her artistic abilities proved fantastic, and with only a few conversations over the past several days, she'd succeeded in creating an updated logo for the bookshop. Simple. Classic. And perfect for the new look Izzy and Brynna had discussed creating for their brand.

"Their" brand! As if Izzy was a part of the family. In all honesty, apart from Anders, she'd been encapsulated into their world as if she'd always belonged, and *this* time she recognized the acceptance a lot better than her twelve-year-old self had.

Brodie's fingers slipped into her hair as he rested his arm behind her, and she nestled a little closer into this family moment. Maybe fitting into this world wouldn't be so painful. It definitely had its Brodie-size perks, as well as a few Sutherland's book-type ones too. They'd never replace her beloved cousins, but wasn't growing up and flying all about finding where *you* belonged?

"The turnaround for the Skern shop has been remarkable." Ellen took her fork and brought a fry to her mouth. Izzy was still trying to sort out eating fries with one's fork. Brodie seemed to read her mind because he reached onto her plate and snatched one of her fries with his fingers, then popped it into his mouth, adding a wink for good measure.

"And you haven't even put any of your ideas to work in the other shops, Isabelle-dear."

"Now, now, we always have a good turn during the festival, you know." Anders poked at his fish with his fork, before raising his gaze to Izzy. His eyes were more of a gray-green beneath a set of rather impressive sandy brows. "Time will be the real test for whether Isabelle's creative ideas are making improvements."

"Codswallop, Anders." Ellen's exclamation drew all eyes. "Have you ever known Sutherland's, in all the years you've worked with it, to have a weekend like we've just experienced? The numbers were outrageous and the only difference we can account for is Isabelle."

He made a grumbly sound and poked his fish with renewed zeal.

"As I told you all from the beginning, she's exactly what we've needed all along." Brodie lowered his arm to Izzy's shoulder and tugged her nearer.

"A new perspective from a creative mind who adores books as much as the rest of us," Ellen added. "Yes, she belongs so nicely. A remarkable addition."

Ellen's compliment warmed Izzy's face but also settled deep. She glanced around the table. Except for Anders, she really did seem to fit among this bookish bunch.

"Remarkable." Brodie's whispered reply, so close to her ear, nearly melted her into the floor. Books, creativity, and that man?! Moving closer certainly brought wonderfully tactile benefits of being near Brodie that none of her cousins could replicate. And the job? Down deep, she knew it was exactly what she was meant to do.

"I can't even imagine what you'll do when you actually have some time, Izzy-dear." This from Brynna, the only one in the family who referred to her as Izzy. Her bright-blue eyes shimmered beneath equally blue, glittering eyeshadow. Paired with her strawberry-blonde hair, it made quite the first impression. "Likely get us started up with ten new shops by Christmas?"

Her light laugh echoed through the room, joined in by others.

"She hasn't made any plans to move here that soon, Brynna." Brodie's voice brewed into the conversation. "Though I wouldn't complain at all if she wanted to find her way to Skern sooner rather than later."

Izzy's gaze caught in his.

"Perhaps by the time you move back, Isabelle, I'll have had my surgery and will *see* all the changes you've made myself," Fiona added, her searching eyes scanning Izzy's direction.

Izzy's heart double-squeezed at the thought. "That would be

wonderful, Fiona. Then *you* can give the display tables your special charm."

The girl's smile grew wide.

"Well, once Brodie gets the stipend for hiring you, they'll almost have enough saved for the surgery, so it may very well be before Christmas." Brynna added another laugh. "And what a gift that would be to the entire family!"

Brynna's words hung in the air.

"'Stipend'?" Izzy repeated. "For hiring me? What do you mean?"

Brynna's eyes widened and she looked to Brodie before turning her attention back to Izzy. "It's nothing, really." Brynna rushed to add, her cheeks darkening. "Don't pay me any mind."

"You didn't tell her?" This from Ellen.

"No." Brodie shook his head, his gaze never leaving Izzy's face. "I tried at one point and then we were interrupted. It never seemed to be the right time."

"The right time?" A sudden chill branched from her chest up into her cheeks as she turned to Brodie. "What are you talking about?"

The longer he stared at her, the colder she became. Stipend to hire her?

"The government offers substantial financial incentives to anyone who can bring new people to Skymar. It began two years ago with the hopes of repopulating since many of the younger generation are moving elsewhere."

"Liona came all the way from Indonesia to marry Cousin Kurt," Fiona's happy voice broke into the stillness.

Izzy blinked, comprehension making a slow and painful appearance.

So Brodie joined Heart-to-Heart in order to find a woman to bring to Skymar so he could get money to save either Sutherland's or his sister's eyesight? Her hand flew to her stomach as the realization ignited a physical punch. But that couldn't be right. She looked back at Brodie, searching his face. Not Brodie too.

"So you're given a financial stipend if you hire someone or marry them?"

"What do you say to some dessert?" Ellen stood, her smile tight. "Brynna, Fiona, Anders. Help me get it from the kitchen, won't you?"

The last sentence brooked no refusal, even from Anders. The rest scattered from the room with Brynna and a bewildered Fiona bringing up the rear.

"Isabelle, I can assure you that this is not what you think." He rubbed his fingers over her knuckles. "Not at all."

The voice she'd grown to adore sounded far off, strained . . . very un–Brodie-like.

"You don't get a financial stipend for hiring someone from out of the country?"

"Yes." His other palm lowered to her shoulder. "But that's not why we offered you the job."

She pushed away from the table, breaking her contact with him. Her gaze never left his, her mind clicking through nearly five months of conversations. "Is . . . is that why you joined Heart-to-Heart? Because of the stipend?"

"Isabelle."

She stood, backing away from him. "Did you?"

"No." He came to his feet, holding her gaze. "I mean, at first I joined because I thought 'why not' since I had no romantic prospects at the time, but then you showed up and I . . . all I wanted was a chance to know you better, and then it didn't matter about stipends or governments. All that mattered was you and me."

She drew another step back, shaking her head, her chest aching from the effort to keep her tears at bay. This couldn't be happening. Not Brodie. He'd been everything good and right and wonderful. "How . . . how can I believe you? You started dating me to earn money?"

"No. That's not the way of it. You *must* know it's not, Isabelle."

The gentle curl of his voice over every syllable in her name nearly softened her to weeping. But she stiffened against the desire. She'd learned how to wrap her emotions in coldness to make it through the remnants of a devastated relationship. She could do it now. Even with Brodie.

She would not change her whole life for a voice. Or an accent. Or sweater-vests. Not when all she'd been from the beginning was a check. The job instead of a marriage proposal? Had that been some sort of way to hold off a more permanent relationship and still gain financially? All the times she'd played the fool in the past stabbed into her paranoia. Had . . . had she gotten it all wrong again?

"Is that why you offered me the job? To get the stipend? To . . . to get me to stay?"

"No, please don't take this any further in the wrong direction. I can see now how it may seem misconstrued, especially with your past relationships, but I offered you this job because it is what you were meant to do. You thrive in it."

"It just so happens to also help your business." The accusation slipped out and she cringed from the sound of it. She'd given him a lot of her ideas, a great deal of her energy, and all of her heart . . . for another charade?

He tilted his head, studying her. "From all you said, you seemed to want to help and I wanted to show you what I'd learned about you over the past months. I wanted you to see what you were capable of." He sighed and ran a hand through his hair. "Perhaps I should have told you about the stipend from the beginning."

"'Perhaps'?"

"Would you have even gotten to know me if I had told you?" His jaw tightened. "Would you have taken a risk on seeing how well we are together?"

She looked away, twisting her fingers together in front of her. "Probably not."

"I tried to explain on the rooftop but was interrupted." He shifted another step closer. "And considered telling you while we were at Waithcliff, but I didn't want you to feel I'd trapped you all the way out there without an escape. Though, I'd hoped you wouldn't need an escape."

"I . . . I gave my heart to you. I believed you, not just about romance but about me."

"And those things are still true. All of them." His voice gentled, pleading. "Don't throw everything away because of this. We are well-suited for one another. I *know* you feel that. It has nothing to do with money or anything else. It's about two hearts. Isabelle?"

She stared up at him, half of her aching to believe him and the other half terrified of making the biggest mistake of her life. If Brodie proved as false as Dean or HWLMATA, she'd be left with a much more devastating recovery than wounded pride, a broken heart, and an unpaid wedding bill. She'd have moved countries, quit her job, and started over far away from her most ardent supporters.

"Why am I always a means to an end?" She spoke the whisper more to herself than Brodie as she backed toward the hallway. "I've . . . I've just wanted to be enough." Her voice broke and she growled against the weakness. "But . . . but every time I find out it's all pretend." She searched his face. He was supposed to be different. He'd carved a way deeper into her heart, her life, than any of the others. "Oh, how I wanted you to be different."

"I am." He waved a hand between them. "This is. Think about all our conversations. All we've been through. Who could pretend for so long?"

"I dated Chip for a year and was engaged to him for another one."

"I'm not Chip." His words ground low. "When will you just trust what's happening here? Trust it to be good and right and very real?"

"You're not the one risking everything. My family. My job. My life. I want to believe you're the type of guy who would still care about me once I've uprooted and you get your money, but . . ."

"The fact that you even question that . . . ?" The gaze that met hers held a steely look. "Surely you don't take me as the sort of person who'd play sport with your heart."

"It certainly looks as if you're the sort."

His chest deflated as if her words stabbed him.

"I'm . . . I'm sorry, Brodie." She'd hurt him, and instead of feeling better, her stomach churned. "Maybe I'm not what you thought, and maybe I'm . . . I'm not brave enough to risk everything for a hope that might be a sham. My heart isn't strong enough for that."

A sob shook through her as she turned from the room, her last view of Brodie's pained expression branded into her mind. Her heart pulsed an agonizing rhythm as she ran up the stairs to her room, but her mind sifted through memories, moments—hundreds of them that beat against her doubts.

No. Wasn't he like all the others? She shook her head. She needed to leave Skymar before her wounded heart turned right back around and stepped into a possible lie from which she may never recover.

CHAPTER 24

"Wow," was Penelope's only response as she sat across from Izzy in the waiting room of the hospital.

Luke only stared, dark brows high and arms folded across his chest.

"Yeah." Izzy sighed and leaned back into the waiting-room chair, rubbing her tired eyes. She'd spent the past fifteen minutes apprising her cousins of her horrible last scene at the Sutherlands' before heading to the airport. The flight home had been miserable. She'd practically curled up in the fetal position in her seat and wept until she'd fallen asleep. When she'd finally arrived home, it was too late to visit Josephine, so here she sat, first thing in the morning in the waiting room with her cousins, trying to hold herself together to see those twins and the new parents.

"Just . . . wow," Penelope repeated, tugging at a strand of her strawberry-blonde hair, her bottom lip puckering into a pout.

"Places really offer money to have people move to their country?" This from Luke, who'd remained quieter than usual during the entire recap, while Penelope gasped, sighed, and commented on random aspects of the story such as, *"Oh, what a sweet thing for Brodie to say."*

Which didn't help Izzy's much-needed feelings of self-justification.

"I've been researching it during layovers. The government is trying to find an incentive to increase the population since younger people seem to be moving away from Skymar for more corporate jobs in bigger cities."

"So the incentive is for a good reason," Penelope stated, and somehow the sentence made Izzy feel even worse. Everything seemed wrong. Off. Broken. Izzy's tired eyes fluttered closed.

"Not good enough to use an innocent person to gain it, unknowingly."

Luke's statement sank through her, resurrecting a little of her ire. But not enough. She felt sick.

Silence fell upon the conversation again. Izzy pressed her palm into her stomach. She wanted to go home, curl up with Samwise in her bed, and cry for another hour . . . or twenty.

"So you just left the house without telling anyone?"

She opened her eyes at Luke's question. "I left a note and got a taxi to the airport."

"Well, if you feel that Brodie is the sort of guy who would do something like this, then I think you're completely right in the way you responded." Penelope leaned forward, her hazel eyes rounded, sad. "He just seemed so nice and real. I mean he did have a book war with Eli over you, and he fought for your ideas with his family."

Izzy groaned and sent a glance to Luke, but he didn't say anything, just sat there like a frowning, bearded gnome, giving her no indication about what was going on inside his head. Maybe she didn't want to know.

"And he wore Yoda ears and made horrible puns," Penelope added. "That isn't the usual way people try to trick women into romance."

"Hey, guys."

They all looked up to find Patrick standing nearby, his hands in his pockets, and though his dusty-blond hair stood in all directions, his broad smile stretched wide. He looked a whole lot better than Izzy did after not having slept in the last twenty-four hours. "Come meet the kids."

The trio followed Patrick down the hallway and entered a room bright with morning light and dozens of flowers, no doubt due to Patrick's ready indulgence of his wife. On the bed sat Josephine, her dark hair perfectly arranged, her makeup almost hiding the purple smudges under her eyes, and a little bundle in each arm. One blue. One pink.

"Oh my goodness! Oh my goodness!" Penelope ran forward, her smile so big Izzy wondered if it would outsize her face. "Oh, oh, may I?"

Josephine offered a tired smile and nodded toward the bundle nearest Penelope. Blue. "Meet Noah Riley Martin."

Penelope brought the wiggling bundle into her arms. "Look, he's so round." She rushed over to Luke. "And he has Josephine's dark hair too."

The cherub face scrunched and he puckered his lips, before releasing a massive yawn that had everyone in the room . . . well, every woman in the room . . . oohing over him.

"And here is Ember Greer Martin." Patrick took the pink bundle and placed it into Izzy's open arms.

Luke edged close, peering over her shoulder, his lips gentled into a smile.

"You're an uncle," Izzy whispered, as the round blue eyes looked from Izzy to Luke.

"Yeah," he murmured, touching Ember's little hand until the tiny fingers wrapped around his large one. "I am."

No one else was close enough to hear it, but Luke's rasped reply crumbled with emotion. Izzy looked over at him and smiled. "Want to hold her?"

His eyes widened and he stepped back, rubbing his palms against his jeans. That was a yes, maybe.

Izzy didn't wait for a reply before placing the bundle into his arms. As soon as the blankets settled, Luke's expression melted into one of wonder. Ember looked more curious than anything else, and Izzy nearly burst into tears all over again.

So tender. So gentle.

Such love.

Brodie would be that way with kids.

The sudden thought nearly undid her careful control. How could she even think that about him after what she'd learned? But . . . but the man she thought she'd known wouldn't have used her for money. Never. He'd have been affronted at the very idea.

Just as Brodie had been.

She turned toward Josephine and took the empty seat at her side. "How are you doing?"

She rested her head back against the pillow and sighed. "I'm tired but so happy. They're beautiful." Josephine looked up at Patrick, her eyes glowing. "And they have a wonderful father."

Patrick leaned down and kissed Josephine's head, then groaned and stumbled back, pressing his fingers to his nose. His bruised nose.

Izzy winced, but Patrick only grinned. "Josephine was amazing, Izzy. What she had to do to bring our babies into the world? It's"—his eyes brightened—"it's a miracle."

Izzy looked back at her cousins and their corresponding niece and nephew, and a sweet tenderness swelled through her. Family. Belonging. Love.

All of them took risks. Faith in those people loving you even when you're not very loveable. Belief that they'll speak truth into your life when you need to hear it . . . and give you a good nudge too. Yeah, she knew what authenticity looked like because she'd seen it her whole life, even if it came in imperfect ways.

And, her breath wobbled, she'd seen it in Brodie too.

Maybe she *was* strong enough now to trust her own heart.

"They're beautiful. Both of them." Izzy covered Josephine's hand with her own. "I'm so happy for you and Patrick."

Patrick chuckled and walked back over to Penelope and Luke, peering down at the newest little members of his family like the happiest man alive.

"I really don't deserve him, Izzy." Josephine shook her head and smoothed out the blanket covering her from waist to toes. "He's the best man in all the world and I don't know how he can put up with me, but I'm so glad he does."

Izzy squeezed Josephine's fingers. "He needed your liveliness, Josephine. Your passionate love for your family. You brought brightness to his quiet life, you know."

Josephine's dark gaze shifted from Izzy's to fasten on Patrick, her smile wobbly. "I'm sure I got the better end of that decision, but thank you for saying so." Her attention came back to Izzy. "Luke came and talked with me about . . . about what you'd struggled with and how Brodie"—her bottom lip wobbled a little—"about how he heard and saw all of your talents. About how he encouraged you to show them." She cleared her throat. "I'm sorry I'm not the one who did that for you. I've only ever wanted you to be happy."

The bridge of Izzy's nose began to tingle with the warning of coming tears. Good grief. How did she have any more left to cry? "I know, Josie."

Josephine offered a quick chuckle and nodded. "I'm so glad you've found that in Brodie. Every email or phone call just confirmed how good he is for you. For *you*." She shook her head when Izzy attempted to interrupt. "I've thought about seeing you two together and then I reread your emails several times, especially the last few, and I could hear it through your words. You belong with him. I've never seen you as animated or excited or . . . *you* as when you're with him."

Izzy cleared her throat and drew in a deep breath. Now wasn't the time to divulge all that had happened over the past two days. Her heart convulsed against the thought. Not even two days. And the pain she'd seen on Brodie's face when she left?

The man who'd book bantered with her, encouraged her weirdness with his own, gave horrible Appalachian-Yoda impersonations. Her smile spread. Won a book battle over her, believed in her dreams . . . Her throat tightened. He believed in *her*. No, it couldn't have all been make-believe. And she needed to see him face-to-face to have him prove her fears wrong.

She reached over and pressed a kiss to Josephine's head. "Thank you, Josephine."

"For what?"

"For reminding me what is really important."

Ember had just started fussing and poor Luke had her held away from him as if he didn't know what he was supposed to do next, so Patrick swept the little, wriggling bundle from her uncle's arms.

"She's probably hungry."

To which Luke bolted for the door, but oblivious Penelope just kept cooing over Noah as if they were the only people in the room.

Izzy met Luke at the door and walked out with him. "If I can get a flight for tonight, would you drive me to the airport?"

His sneakers screeched to a halt in the hallway. "What?"

"I've been wrong, Luke. I was scared and paranoid and—"

"Stupid?"

She shot him a glare.

"Irrational?" He added.

"Yes, but after all I'd been through, I was just afraid—"

"Pigheaded?"

"Okay, now." She caught his arm so he turned to face her. "You can stop being so nice about it."

"Izzy, I consider Brodie my friend, and I've never been able to consider any of the men you've dated a friend before." He settled his gaze on hers. "He's a good guy. He really cares about you in all the right ways. And you're a whole lot smarter than you used to be."

"Thanks." She exaggerated her eye roll and her shoulders slumped. "He may not want to have anything to do with me after the way I left things."

"True." Luke nodded and drew in a breath before refocusing on her. "But you get to decide if he's worth that risk or not." He cleared his throat and leaned close, looking around as if to check if someone was listening. "You know that quote I sent you before, 'Being deeply loved by someone gives you strength. Loving someone deeply gives you courage'?"

"Yes, Lao Tzu?"

He shoved his hands in his pockets and shrugged. "Fortune cookie."

"I thought you said it was your dog texting."

"*He* got it from a fortune cookie."

Her tears burst free with her laugh and she wrapped her arms around Luke's neck. "I love you so much, Luke."

He stepped back, shaking his head, but his smile squeezed out beneath his attempt at a frown. "I really need at least one level-headed relation, Izzy, and I'm holding out hope it's you."

"Then you'd better help me get to the airport." She slipped her arm through his and pulled him toward the elevator. "And I wouldn't mind a few prayers that Brodie Sutherland has as forgiving a nature as I hope he does."

CHAPTER 25

Sutherland's Books brimmed with people. Izzy barely made it through the front door after bumping into several small groups either entering or exiting, arms filled with shopping bags complete with the old Sutherland's logo, but by next week they should have a few with the new logo in place.

She paused to peer at the window display, a wonderful mixture of modern and classic, heart and head. A piece of her had already become a part of this place—not just her heart, but her creativity and this internal epiphany of who she was and what she wanted. For her life and her heart.

Inside, happy shoppers scurried in all directions, and Izzy followed the tide, staying among the crowd so that as she crossed the threshold into the shop, Lylla or Alice wouldn't immediately notice her entrance. Izzy wanted to get her bearings before she met whatever fate Brodie doled out. She deserved his ire, maybe even his rejection. But she hoped, oh how she hoped, he recognized a soul who loved him and was willing to hang on tight, now that she'd gotten brave and smart enough to know what "real" looked like.

She slipped down aisles and around corners of the magical place of which she'd become particularly fond. Enchantment and anticipation swirled among the bindings and the decorations and the general love of all things story. She couldn't help but smile at the bustling areas of laughing children and excited conversations. *Home?* Her pulse settled into the thought. Yes, she wanted to be here . . . in the middle of this bookishly wonderful family with an extra-wonderful bookish islander.

If he'd still have her. Her throat constricted. A careful shuffle placed her safely behind a solid row of classic fiction and she rested her head against the shelf of Dickens, slowing her breathing so her pulse dimmed in her ears.

Would Brodie hear her? Would he give her a second chance? She doubted a dramatic Anne of Green Gables apology would work in her favor. No, he'd always been direct with her, and she'd return in kind, even if it ended with a deeper heartache than she'd imagined only days earlier. If she didn't try, she'd never know, and Brodie was worth the risk.

She shook her head to clear it of all the horrible scenarios of his rejection floating through her mind and caught sight of two little girls occupying one of the window seats, their heads almost touching as they looked at a book together. Another smile waited on her lips. Stories inspired hope. Dreams. Romance.

And courage.

She'd learned more about those things while knowing Brodie and visiting Skymar than in the five years leading up to this day. Her heart settled into the welcome sensation of belonging to this magical place, in the joy of discovery and imagination. In the adventure of new journeys and pleasant warmth—of comfortable familiarity. If given one more chance, she'd hold to it all and never let go. Her gaze shot heavenward. *Just one more chance. Please?*

For better or worse she'd spent the majority of her flight rereading all the correspondence between her and Brodie. Unfortunately she cried about as much on the flight back to Skymar as she had leaving it. How could she have been so blind? Allowed her insecurities such a hold on her heart? She loved him. Something had come to life inside of her when he'd started their correspondence. She wouldn't lose a future with Brodie without a fight—even if that meant she had to fight him to do it.

She slipped through the rows and people, sliding her hands over a few familiar book bindings to help garner her strength. It was Monday morning. He worked on Monday mornings, didn't he? Would he be here?

Then she stopped. Above the sound of two women debating over which Debbie Macomber book to purchase, a familiar voice brewed in deep baritone. Brodie! She straightened, trying to locate the direction.

"I've heard of epistolary novels before, but not that particular one." His answer came from the other side of a bookshelf in the Historical Romance section. "Could you tell me more about it?"

Izzy drew in a breath and peered around the side of the shelf. Brodie's back was to her as he bent near to an older woman who leaned close in intense discussion.

"Have you never heard of it? I read it years ago. It's all written through letters around the World War II era, I believe. You should know it. *Especially* you." She shook her head of blonde color that looked a little too blonde to be natural. "It takes place on an island and it's a story where two people fall in love through letters before they even meet in person. Well, the blooms of love start then, but the actual love comes when they meet in person, of course."

"Yes." He cleared his throat. "It does sound like a rather fascinating work of *fiction*."

Her heart squeezed. Sadness curbed his tone with a little hint of bitterness thrown in on that last word. She pressed her fist to her chest. She'd caused that. *Oh, Brodie, please forgive me.*

"Fiction starts from somewhere," came her quick retort. "But there was some tragedy that happened during the war, and it's about the folks on this island who start a book club, and the main lady in the story is an author, I think."

Izzy nodded as she recognized the description of the book, and the woman must have caught sight of her movements, because her gaze caught in Izzy's. Izzy attempted a weak smile and a strange glimmer twinkled in the woman's pale eyes.

"I don't know that I've ever read that one," Brodie answered. "If we had our new database working, I could—"

"Perhaps we should ask one of the other workers about it." The woman motioned toward me. "Young lady, could you give us a bit of help here? We seem to be at a loss and you appear to understand."

Izzy's chest seized. No use hiding now. She drew in a deep breath and forced a smile as she stepped forward.

"I think the book you're after is *The Guernsey Literary and Potato Peel Pie Society*." She flashed a glance at Brodie as she neared.

He stared, his lips parting in surprise. She pushed an apology into her expression as much as she could, hoping her eyes spoke for her in the interval. His lips pinched into a frown. Oh no, old Blighty showed up instead of Prince Charming. Her palm pressed into her stomach. She deserved it, though. She'd thrown his trustworthiness back in his face.

"Yes, that sounds familiar," the woman responded, drawing Izzy's gaze back to her.

"Um . . . it should be here." Her words quivered out on a breath as she passed between the two with her head down and her focus on the nearby bookshelf. The Romance section. Ironic.

She swallowed around the lump in her throat, every ounce of self-control attempting to keep the tears at bay. He'd offered her so much: her dreams, his heart, a place to . . . fly, and she'd run away from it all.

With careful fingers, she drew the book from its place and then trained her attention on the woman. "It's a sweet story with a tender romance that started as an unlikely friendship over books." Izzy's voice caught on the admission. Like her and Brodie.

"What a marvelous beginning for a romance, don't you think?"

Could this woman unintentionally make things any more awkward? "Um . . . it does sound rather fairy-tale–like. Though of course there's a part where the heroine gets a little messed up with knowing what she wants, but"—Izzy swallowed through her dry throat—"but . . . but don't worry. She figures it out in time for a happily ever after."

"I read for the happily ever afters." The woman searched Izzy's face in some strange way.

"I'm fond of those too. My favorites, in fact." Izzy handed the book to the woman and blinked back the tears while stepping past her back to the bookshelf. "And if you're interested in another of the same style, you might enjoy *Daddy-Long-Legs*. Earlier time period but still epistolary. And such a light-hearted read. Good for cheering the heart."

"'Cheering the heart'?" She held Izzy's gaze, her smile growing, and then she took the proffered book. "Well thank you, dear. I've always had a soft spot for these types of stories. You see, I fell in love with my husband through letters before we ever met in person. People don't seem to do much of that nowadays."

"I think that's what makes it so special." Her throat squeezed as she felt Brodie step closer behind her. "You have these wonderful conversations, opportunities to be intimate with someone in such a unique way, so when you finally meet him for the first time, it's like you're looking into the eyes of someone who knows you already, maybe even better than you know yourself."

"Aye." Her expression softened and she studied Izzy with a knowing look. "It sounds as though you've experienced corresponding with a sweetheart of your own?"

"Yes, I have . . . um . . . I did." A sigh pressed her shoulders downward and she refused to look in Brodie's direction. Her eyes began to sting. "But much like Juliet in this story"—she tapped the book in the woman's hand—"I'm afraid I . . . I lost my way and may be too late to make things right."

"Do you love him?"

"Yes," the word burst out like something between a sob and a laugh. "I do love him. He's one of the best people I've ever known."

One of her pale brows took an upswing. "And does he love you?"

Clearly this woman was placed in this moment to incur complete agony upon Izzy's already throbbing heart. "I think he did before . . . before I hurt him."

"I suppose the only way to know for certain is to travel to wherever he lives and find out, isn't it? A very brave thing to do, if you ask me." The sparkle in the woman's eyes flared and she raised a brow to a point just over Isabelle's shoulder. "Well, Brodie my boy, it seems the next move is up to you."

What? Izzy blinked and looked from the woman to Brodie, who stood much closer to her than he'd been a few minutes ago, his mastiff brow still intact.

He studied her with those brilliant-blue eyes of his as if weighing every intention running through her brain, before he turned his attention back to the woman. "Thank you, Aunt Karina. You've made a sufficient scene to share later with all of your lady friends down at the tea room."

Every ounce of heat left Izzy's face. Her voice refused to work. *Aunt Karina?*

"Isabelle, this is my aunt Karina." Brodie gestured toward the woman, his eyes searching Isabelle's as he continued, a forced smile on his lips. "Aunt Karina, this is Isabelle Edgewood."

"You look exactly like your photos, my dear. All that glorious hair." She raised the book in her hand. "And thank you for this as well as the other suggestion. As I said, I have a certain fondness for stories that turn out well."

With another pixie grin and a pat to Brodie's cheek, the fair-haired woman walked away, leaving a series of chuckles in her wake.

Izzy's brain began to piece the little scenario together. She lowered her gaze to the floor, shaking her head. "Your aunt."

"Brynna's mum." Brodie's response held no emotion, his voice so near and yet . . . far. "But everyone in my entire family—in fact, the entire town—knows who you are, Isabelle, the Book Matchmaker from America."

"Oh." And the woman who broke their boy's heart. She kept her gaze fastened on the Austen shelf nearby, a taunting punishment of happily ever afters that nearly ushered up a groan and then a retreat toward the door. *"Loving someone deeply gives you courage."* She raised her eyes to his. She loved him. So much. And she belonged wherever he was.

He continued to study her, arms folded across his chest. "You flew all the way back to Skern?"

"I hurt you face-to-face, so I . . . I wanted to make amends face-to-face." She released a slow breath to keep her tears in check. "If I can."

His jaw twitched and his gaze roamed over her, taking in her hair, her eyes, his expression unreadable. "Fiona went to bed in tears and Brynna hasn't slept well since you left because she's blamed herself for the whole fiasco."

"I'm so sorry, Brodie. I never meant to hurt them. I was wrong. So wrong. I should have known that you were different than anyone else I'd ever met." Her gaze came back to his. "So much better, but I'd been hurt so many times, the whole stipend thing seemed to follow the MO of my romantic history. But then I reread our correspondences and thought about all the things I love most about you."

"You love me, do you?" His voice had lost its edge.

"Aye." The word he used so often quivered out of her with a sniffle. "Even though I've done a poor job of showing it lately." Her vision blurred but she refused to lower her gaze. "I want you, to be with you, if . . . if you can forgive me. And if you think you can want the same thing."

His gaze bore into hers, searching, extracting whatever information he could, and then he gently tucked a loose strand of her hair behind her ear. "Aye, I can."

Her breath hitched. "What?"

His lips caught her word and she melted into him, her hands trembling up to wrap into his hair. Part-sob, part-laugh slipped between their kisses until she pulled back to cradle his face with her palms. "Are you serious?"

"Was the kiss not answer enough?" He winked and squeezed her closer, giving her another lengthy kiss that stole her breath. "And you want me, do you?"

"*Mm-hmm*," she murmured, pressing her forehead against his, holding him close.

"You can have me, Karre." His lips quirked into an unruly grin. "And I'll throw the job in too."

She laughed out a sob. "A bonus already?"

"What can I say? I'm a fool for a beautiful, bookish woman and an excellent apology." And with that, he brought his lips back to hers with such thoroughness, her doubts about finding a shelf-space in his heart dissolved to dust. In fact, she was pretty sure she'd made it to his Favorites shelf. He'd certainly made it onto hers. Featured book, even.

"Actually, I think I'm the benefactor of this particular bonus, Isabelle Edgewood. And I'm a fan of happily-ever-after stories, too, particularly the real kind," he murmured against her lips before sneaking another kiss and reminding her what a difference being loved made to dreams and futures and learning to be authentically you.

So their story may have started out between a human and a hobbit, but it ended rather deliciously like a Tolkien-ish happily ever after. *"And he took her in his arms and kissed her under the sunlit sky, and he cared not that they stood high upon the walls in the sight of many."*

And Brodie didn't seem to care either (not that they were on top of a wall or anything), but standing in the middle of a crowded bookshop fit their story a little better. He proved he was quite adept at not only caring and forgiving, but kissing a woman exactly like he knew how. And Izzy wasn't complaining one bit. In fact, she encouraged his practice with great zeal. How perfect to confirm a bookishly wonderful, long-distance true love in front of the epistolary Romance section of a bookshop! If that isn't the setup for a happily ever after, Izzy didn't know what was.

From: Izzy Sutherland

To: Luke Edgewood, Josephine Martin, Penelope Edgewood

Date: August 3

Subject: Once upon a time

Dear Cousins,

I just wanted to let you know that I'm going to remain in Skern for another week before I return to the States. Brodie and I are working out the logistics of my new position with Sutherland's Books and I'm just enjoying all the extra in-person time with him before we're separated again.

It hasn't been hard to find my place back in the family here, because the Sutherland ladies were all a little put out with Brodie for not mentioning the stipend from the start, so it seems Brodie was suffering from a broken heart from my leaving and a few tongue lashings to boot. (Anders remains the same, so . . . I'm still on the bottom shelf of his interest.)

But I'm grateful that it's all in the past now, and I can make plans!

Josephine, please keep sending those adorable photos of my niece and nephew. I can't wait to cuddle up to them again when I get home.

Penelope, you are going to love it here. Brodie's family have offered to help you with life here as much as you'd like . . . and there's a theatrical troupe in Skern, which might pique your interest.

Luke, if you take care of Samwise as well as you take care of me, then Samwise may not want to come back to live with me at all. However, I know his favorite treat, so maybe I still have a chance.

I created the Book Matchmaker link on Sutherland's Books website today. We've already gotten a hundred hits or so and a dozen messages for me to help readers find their perfect literary fit. How ironic that after all my complaining about matchmaking, I'm now in the business of it myself—though I prefer my sort with fictional matches than with real hearts.

I am glad for it, though. It took being forced into unwanted matchmaking for me to discover who I was, what I wanted, and my own perfect match. Isn't that what we all want down deep? To be seen for who we are, even with all our flaws, and be loved anyway. Completely.

Thank you all for being that to me. I can't wait to share the rest of this life adventure with you.

Love,
Izzy

PS: Now all we need to do is find the right match for Penelope and Luke, Josephine. But I'll leave that in your very capable hands. Luke, you can thank me later.

From: Penelope Edgewood
To: Luke Edgewood, Josephine Martin, Izzy Edgewood
Date: August 3
Subject: Re: Once upon a time

Izzy,

Oh my goodness! You gave Josephine PERMISSION to match us? I'm so glad I'm leaving the country. Thankfully there won't be any crazy matchmakers over there.

Penelope

PS: I love the photo you have on the Book Matchmaker link. SOOOO much better than the earless author one from your Heart-to-Heart profile.

PPS: There's a fun theater group on Heart-to-Heart with a subgroup from Skymar! I've already joined (as Julie Andrews, of course)!

• •

From: Luke Edgewood
To: Izzy Edgewood, Josephine Martin, Penelope Edgewood
Date: August 3
Subject: Re: Once upon a time

Izzy,

I hate you.

Luke

• •

From: Izzy Edgewood
To: Luke Edgewood, Josephine Martin, Penelope Edgewood
Date: August 3
Subject: Re: Once upon a time

Luke,

There's just something about being blissfully happy, you know? I suddenly feel compelled to sprinkle joy into the lives of others.

Izzy

PS: You're welcome.

"It is delightful when your
imaginations come true, isn't it?"
Anne of Green Gables

THE END

Acknowledgments

This book was one of the funnest books I've ever written, and it is in no small part due to the people who became a background part of its creation. There is no way I will remember everyone who encouraged me in this process, but here are a few:

Carrie, Joy, and Beth, thank you for always coming alongside me in every book journey, especially this one. We encouraged each other through Covid, and I think Izzy certainly helped. Thank you for always being on "my team" and helping me believe more in myself with each new story. I am so grateful for you all!!

I can never thank my street team, The Pepper Shakers, enough for their continual encouragement in every story and how they spread the word with such excitement. You guys touch every story before the rest of the world, and I'm so grateful for you.

Susanne Blumer, thank you for letting me pick your brain about owning a bookshop and all the intricacies of the process. I hope *Authentically, Izzy* sprinkles as much "magic" on readers as you and your team display in Sassafras on Sutton.

Rachel McMillan, thank you for championing this story and me. I'm grateful we talk the same bookish language and can bring our imaginations to the pages in so many ways (though you are MUCH more like Izzy in your massive reading than I am). I'm grateful you are my agent and friend.

It has been an absolute blast to work with Becky Monds on this story. Becky, thank you for believing in this story and in me. Thanks for taking a chance on it and for overflowing with constant encouragement, fantastic direction, and . . . a great sense of humor. Luke loves you.

Books don't just magically appear, no matter what fantasy stories say, but . . . every book I've ever written has a team of personal elves who keep my private life moving forward so that my fictional life can make it to the page. My five "not so little" elves (my kids) never fail to celebrate each book with me, even by listening to me complain or laud all of my imaginary friends. (I'm refraining from referring to my husband as an elf, though he is equally supportive). Thank you all for loving me so much. I am grateful beyond words that God allowed me to spend this nonfictional life with you. I'd also like to give a shoutout to my daughter Lydia, in particular, whose lovely artwork is on display FOR THE FIRST TIME EVER in a book! Her maps of Skymar and Ansling were specially crafted from her love for me and this story. (She is also one of my BEST book pushers out there).

And to the Author of my faith, I am so grateful for your love and for the gift of imagination. And thank you for loving stories so well that you wrote yourself into ours so we could have an eternal happily-ever-after.

"Now there are also many other things that Jesus did. Were every one of them to be written, I suppose that the world itself could not contain the books that would be written" (John 21:25).

Discussion Questions

1. What are some characteristics about Izzy that you notice in the beginning of the story?
2. How do you know that Izzy's family are emotionally close to each other? In what ways do they show they love each other?
3. What are some things about Brodie that cause Izzy to keep writing to him?
4. When someone doesn't feel like they belong somewhere, how can it manifest itself in their lives? Characteristics? Choices?
5. How does being truly "seen" and loved change Izzy from the beginning of the book to the end?
6. Do you think the epistolary style offers any unique perspectives for the reader that the third-person style does not? If so, what are they?
7. If we compare Eli and Brodie, how do we, as readers, know that Izzy should choose Brodie over Eli? What characteristics does Brodie show that reflects a better match for Izzy?
8. From a Christian's perspective, how does recognizing your life has a greater purpose not only change the way you face hardships and hurts but also how you live your life?

About the Author

Photo by Michael Kaal

Pepper Basham is an award-winning author who writes romance "peppered" with grace and humor. Writing both historical and contemporary novels, she loves to incorporate her native Appalachian culture and/or her unabashed adoration of the UK into her stories. She currently resides in the lovely mountains of Asheville, NC, where she is the wife of a fantastic pastor, mom of five great kids, a speech-language pathologist, and a lover of chocolate, jazz, hats, and Jesus. You can learn more about Pepper and her books on her website at www.pepperdbasham.com.

Facebook: @pepperbasham
Instagram: @pepperbasham
Twitter: @pepperbasham
BookBub: @pepperbasham

From the Publisher

THEY'RE SHARED!

Help other readers find this one:

- Post a review at your favorite online bookseller
- Post a picture on a social media account and share why you enjoyed it
- Send a note to a friend who would also love it—or better yet, give them a copy

Thanks for reading!